INTENSIVE CARE

RICHARD REINKING

ISBN: 0692862730
ISBN 13: 9780692862735

For my children, with love, Amy, Rachael, and Daniel.

Prologue

Sam Harper pushed open the double doors of the one-room country church to stand on the wooden porch and see if his visitor was coming. The parking lot was empty. Harper pulled out a handkerchief from his back pocket and wiped the July sweat off his bald head. He checked his watch. It was almost time.

The church building behind Harper, its white clapboard topped by a traditional steeple and cross, was ninety years old. After faithfully serving three generations of Muskogee County Baptists, Harper had purchased it, paying $30,000 in cash and renaming it the Church of the Redeemed Believers. The gravel parking lot in front exited through a narrow gate and onto an asphalt two-lane county road. The road cut through a natural woodlands of oak and cottonwoods and eventually led to the state highway about a mile away. As Harper waited, not a single car or farm vehicle passed by. People seldom traveled in the remote location of their property, and most every one of those who did, Harper knew.

Harper wore a white shirt with a thin black tie, the same he wore every Sunday when he preached. Wrinkled black slacks fit snug over his stocky frame. His shoulders and arms were massive, a result of toiling as a manual laborer many long days in dusty fields. He looked more like the common farmer he had been his whole life than a simple rural preacher. Three years earlier, when he reluctantly attended a local tent revival at his wife's urging, Harper had seen "the light" and was baptized in the muddy Arkansas River. Now he pastored a flock of forty or fifty souls, most every one a farmer like Harper, and all living within a few miles of his small church.

Harper seldom complained about the Oklahoma summer heat, born and raised a stone's throw away, but even for him the temperature, approaching 105 degrees, was becoming almost unbearable. He loosened his tie and pulled at the wet shirt clinging to his chest. From the dense scrub oaks nearby, a chorus of cicadas interrupted the Sunday peace with a high-pitched, piercing sound. Harper took a few steps off the porch and looked up and down the road in both directions, but there was no sign of him. After waiting a few minutes, his impatience growing, he returned indoors to busy himself collecting the discarded bulletins from the morning worship service and replacing the hymnals in the pew racks. Humidity from a brief early morning shower steamed the windows along both sides of the sanctuary, the condensation obscuring the view of the forest that surrounded the property. He rose up as he heard a truck enter the parking lot, throwing gravel as it skidded to a stop. A door outside slammed shut, and seconds later the front doors to the church were flung open. A teenager walked in.

"Hi, Jimmy," Harper said, glancing at his watch.

"Hi, Pastor Harper," Jimmy said, raising his hand in greeting.

Jimmy was barely seventeen, lanky, with cropped hair and a severe case of acne. He was dressed in a dirty white T-shirt, mud-caked sneakers, and faded blue overalls. He looked around the church nervously.

"No one's here," Harper said.

"Just like you wanted. I was hoping I was on time."

"You are. Do you have it?"

"It's in the truck."

Harper followed the teenager onto the porch. Once outside, Harper fished in his pocket for his keys, locked the church, and set the alarm. After briefly examining the contents in the back of the truck, Harper climbed into the driver's seat and started the engine. Jimmy opened the door on the passenger side and slid in.

The church property, called the parsonage by Harper and most of the members, totaled 120 acres and was located near Taft, a rural town of four hundred, roughly ten miles due west of Muskogee. The area was heavily wooded and surrounded by a barbed-wire fence, with only the church and its parking lot visible from the county road. Harper drove the truck around to the back of the church to the gated entry of a narrow private lane gouged out of the trees.

Harper stopped, unlocked the padlock, and removed the bulky chain before swinging the gate open. He drove the truck through and locked the gate behind them. When they had traveled about two hundred feet, the road opened into a clearing. In the center stood a single-story house, box-shaped, painted white, with a screened-in front porch and a one-car detached garage, typical of the farmhouses in the area. Nearby, extending fifty yards to the left, was a pistol range with six targets opposite a covered firing line. Behind the house were four dilapidated outbuildings of various sizes. The largest was a weathered-wood barn, leaning precariously to one side.

The preacher guided the truck down a narrow path beside the barn and stopped. Tucked tightly to the rear of the structure was a metal shed, approximately ten feet square, sitting on a cement base and padlocked with a heavy-duty combination lock. The shed, unseen from any of the open areas of the property, sat only a few feet from the edge of the forest thick with underbrush and fallen debris.

"Unload the bags there by the shed," Harper said, pointing to the ground as he climbed out of the truck. "I'll take care of them later."

"Yes, sir," Jimmy said. "I don't mind putting them inside the—"

"No," Harper interrupted sternly, still pointing. "On the ground there is fine."

Jimmy opened the tailgate and lifted a blue plastic tarp off the truck's contents.

"The poor women of your church will appreciate these bags of fertilizer, Pastor Harper," Jimmy said, picking up the first forty-pound bag.

"It's a small gesture," Harper said flatly, "for those who grow their own food."

Jimmy began unloading the dozen bags, 480 pounds of nitrate fertilizer, placing them in a neat stack near the shed.

"You weren't seen, right, Jimmy?"

"Oh no, sir. I snuck them out of old man Jefferson's barn about three o'clock in the morning, just like you suggested. He ain't got no dog or nothing. Not a sound."

"Good job, Jimmy."

"He won't miss them. Don't look like they've been touched in twenty years, covered by an inch of dust. Nothing in that barn's been touched in a long time."

When Jimmy had finished, Harper pulled out two twenty-dollar bills and offered them to him.

"No, sir," Jimmy said, raising his hands to refuse the money. "I feel good about doing this."

"Son, I insist."

"No, sir. I don't want the money."

"Okay, then," Harper said, slipping the twenties back into his pocket. "Let's get you home."

"Pastor, are you sure you don't need help delivering these?"

"No," he answered. "I'll do it later."

"I told my mom what a great thing you were doing."

The words had barely left the teenager's mouth before Harper was in his face.

"I told you to tell no one," Harper snarled. "No one!"

Harper's anger caught Jimmy off guard, and he stepped backward, nearly stumbling. Harper moved forward, his face red with anger. Jimmy backed away until he felt the hot metal of the truck against his back.

"It was...just my mom," Jimmy stammered. "I...I didn't think you'd mind."

"You said you understood."

"I know, but—"

"God hates liars," Harper hissed. "The Bible says, 'He that speaketh lies shall not escape.'"

"I'm...I'm sorry," Jimmy said. "Gosh, Pastor Harper, why would you keep this a secret?"

Jimmy felt Harper's strong calloused hands encircle his neck, the force of Harper's arms pinning him against the truck. Jimmy's eyes betrayed his sudden fear.

"Hell's eternal fire is for those who disobey God," Harper said coldly, tightening his grip.

Jimmy's feeble attempt to scream was prevented by the pressure on his throat. His stomach welled up into his chest.

"God smites the disobedient. He destroys the wicked."

The preacher's hot breath stung Jimmy's face. The teenager closed his eyes, and the blood rushed from his body. Jimmy's heart pounded, his anxiety consuming him. His lungs begged for air.

"The angel of God is merciful. His justice measured."

Jimmy heard the voice as though at a distance, fading from his consciousness. He felt his legs wobbling, his muscles growing weaker, giving way. His head began swimming, his thoughts disjointed. He couldn't feel his hands—they had seemed to go numb—but he hoped they were pushing this man away, hoping they were pushing, fighting for his life.

Finally, his knees buckled, his body collapsed, and all went black.

CHAPTER 1

Dr. Paula Barrett tried her best to ignore the commotion in the intensive care unit around her so she could finish her progress note and enter the lab and medication orders. Paula's patient, a retired Presbyterian minister, had arrived at the emergency room the evening before with pneumonia. The seventy-year-old had always enjoyed good health, working full time, playing tennis three times a week, and traveling to mission sites around the world. A visit to a sick child in his congregation had given him the infection, but he had delayed seeking medical care for several days, and the illness had become overwhelming. He was now on a ventilator in critical condition, avoiding death, but just barely.

Paula sat at the doctors' desk, clicking medical entries on a computer screen. She was the only female pulmonary doctor on staff at Saint Luke's Hospital, and despite women having long claimed their place in medicine, a woman physician in the ICU was not a particularly common sight. Paula was petite, five feet two inches tall, with olive-tan complexion, brown eyes, and brown hair tied into a single long braid, traditional Cherokee style. She wore a white jacket over a dark-blue dress, modest and conservative. Most people thought she was a nurse. She hated that.

Fatigued from a weekend on call, Paula was anxious to complete her Sunday evening rounds in the hospital and go home. The minister was her last patient. She had examined him, reviewed his lab results, and adjusted the ventilator. Her final task was documenting findings in the electronic medical record. When she finished, she could leave. Hopefully, she'd have a quiet evening, go to bed early, and start the week rested. It wasn't likely.

Paula was so tired that the screen was getting blurry. Computer monitors, typing orders, digital medical records—all were relatively new. It wasn't that long ago when charting on a patient was much easier. Even just a few years earlier, when she was in training, she'd jot down a brief note of her findings on a piece of paper in a plastic folder and then pick up a phone to dictate her complete report. The dictation would be typed and show up the next morning. Quick and efficient. Now she entered the entire patient's information by clicks on a computer. It took longer, and at times she felt like a data entry clerk instead of a doctor. Progress!

The most critical and challenging patients at Saint Luke's Hospital were treated in the intensive care unit, and this was Paula's favorite area of the hospital. Remodeled three months earlier, it was designed with ten patient rooms on the perimeter of a large open area. A sliding glass door and blue curtain for each room provided privacy for the patients, though for practical reasons they were seldom closed. In the center of the unit was the nurses' station, surrounded by a desk for the doctors' and nurses' charting and phone calls. Paula noticed the unit was crowded with people, not at all unusual for seven in the evening on a Sunday night, made up of mostly ICU staff, family members, friends, and visiting clergy. The intensive care unit, Paula thought, was a busy place with the ten sickest patients in the hospital, always seriously ill, each and every one with a life-and-death drama—sometimes a miracle and sometimes a disaster. Paula's patient, the retired minister, was critical, and the next twenty-four hours would tell if his personal drama would be a success or failure.

One of the ICU nurses walked up to the counter across from Paula and waited for her to finish her note. Paula looked up.

"I believe Mr. Pettigrew," the nurse said, "needs more furosemide."

The nurse, Toni Perkins, looked to be in her early twenties, probably fresh out of school. She wore green scrubs rather than a nurse's uniform, which was a common practice among the intensive care nurses.

Paula didn't particularly like ICU nurses. They were the best nurses in the hospital, no one disputed that, but were as a rule difficult—aggressive, sometimes even abrasive. Paula rested forward on her elbows and waited. The nurse had more to say.

"He sounds wet to me," Toni continued. "I hear rales in both bases."

The nurse's tone was condescending. She was implying that Paula had failed to notice her patient needed a diuretic to remove the fluid from his lungs. Paula had spent hours and hours in intensive care training at her pulmonary medicine residency program in Oklahoma City and had daily rounded on the most complex, intensive patients for the two years she had practiced in Tulsa. This case, though his infection was significant, was actually fairly basic. One of her absolute pet peeves was some new-grad nurse telling her how to practice medicine.

"He sounds wet in both bases because he has bilateral pneumonia," Paula said patiently. "Furosemide would dry out his lungs, which would make his pneumonia worse."

"So you don't think there's a chance of heart failure?"

"Not very likely, Ms."—Paula paused as she read her name tag—"Perkins. Not impossible, but the fluid sounds you hear are common with pneumonia."

"Are you ordering an echocardiogram?"

"Not at this time. We'll see how he does."

Nurse Perkins stood for a moment as if she wanted to say something else, but instead she turned and walked away.

Paula shook her head, returning to her note. She glanced up and saw Toni talking with the nursing supervisor near the stairwell while pointing in her direction. She took a deep breath. The nursing supervisor's name was Sally Carpenter. Paula recalled several conversations with her, and none had been pleasant. Originally a nurse on the night shift, she had risen quickly, an assertive and confident manager, through the ranks of the nursing staff to become the supervisor of the intensive care unit. She wasn't particularly liked by the medical staff, and she knew it. The rumor was that she tended to call physicians multiple times at night for minor problems, targeting those doctors who had crossed her. Paula didn't doubt it.

Paula's shoulders stiffened as Sally left Toni and walked toward her.

"Dr. Barrett?"

"Yes, Ms. Carpenter?"

"Your patient in room three with pneumonia is in critical condition."

"Yes, I know that." Paula pushed away the computer keyboard and straightened in her chair. "Reverend Pettigrew is progressing as expected."

"Are you on call tonight?" Sally said. "Ms. Perkins is on the night shift, and I'm sure she'll contact you if there's any change."

"That would be fine," Paula said calmly.

"Then you don't mind if we call you."

"Of course not. If there's a problem that needs my attention, since I'm the physician in charge of the case, I should be called. Don't you agree?"

"Then that's what we'll do."

"Thanks. Anything else?"

"No, Doctor. That's all...for now."

It was a threat, and Paula didn't like it, but she held her tongue. No point in creating an issue.

Paula watched the nursing supervisor walking away, and then turned back to the computer screen. When she started to type, her pager began a soft, steady beeping. As soon as she heard it, she knew she had forgotten to call. She entered the number on her phone and waited.

"Bureau of Alcohol, Tobacco, and Firearms," a female voice said.

"Is Matt Nicholson there?"

"Just a moment. I'll check."

Paula had been dating Matt Nicholson for almost six months. They had met through a mutual friend who had set up a blind date, and she had almost backed out. The last thing she wanted then was a relationship—she had sworn off men—but he was intelligent, charming, and entertaining, and she had enjoyed his company. Besides, as her friend had assured her, he was actually good-looking—tall, trim, and handsome, with stunning blue eyes. She liked him, which was exactly the consequence of dating she had feared in the first place.

Now she wasn't sure where their relationship was going. She sensed Matt wanted to discuss their future, a subject she was trying to avoid. Fortunately for her, when he acted ready to broach the topic, their schedules never seemed to match. She worked eighty hours a week, was on call every fourth night and weekend, and had an erratic, unpredictable life.

His was as bad. He was a special agent with the Bureau of Alcohol, Tobacco and Firearms, and he worked as many hours as she did, always on duty, taking emergency calls twenty-four hours a day. Before joining the Tulsa ATF office, he had served ten years in Washington—the first five years undercover with illegal gunrunners and the last five as a hostage negotiator. Though now based in Tulsa, he often traveled around the country, negotiating some of the ATF's most serious hostage situations.

Tonight was one of the rare occasions when their schedules coincided, and he had invited her to dinner. They had planned to meet at the restaurant at seven. She was embarrassed. She had forgotten.

"Hello?" Matt's voice came on the line.

"Hi. It's Paula."

"Hey, I was just checking. Are we having dinner?"

"I'm so sorry. I got stuck in the intensive care unit."

"I just finished with a meeting myself. Can you get away?"

"Not until eight or so. Maybe we should pass tonight."

"You might as well come and eat. They'll still be cooking food when we get there."

"Are you sure you don't mind waiting?"

"No problem. But it'll be tough on me. I'll have to go save us a table, eat those chips, and stuff down some salsa."

"Sounds terrible."

"Come on, let's go. The change of pace will do you good. Besides, it's your chance to have dinner with the best-looking guy in the restaurant."

She laughed. "Okay, you're right. See you there in a few minutes."

Paula hung up. She typed a few lines to complete her notes and entered a couple of orders before clicking on the sign button to close the chart. Before leaving the intensive care unit, she stopped by room 3 for a final check on a sleeping Reverend Pettigrew.

My life is unsettled, she thought. She preferred stable, predictable, even ordinary. Though her friends often joked she was just plain boring, she saw herself as dedicated and focused. Her medical career came first. Years of study, long nights on call, the mental abuse of senior residents, the financial sacrifices—all were wasted if she didn't apply her knowledge and skills to practice medicine. More than that, she thrived on it. She loved the gratification of helping others, the intellectual stimulation, and the prestige. What else could she want?

Every once in a while when she was on call, wide awake and all alone in the quiet darkness, she felt an overwhelming sense of emptiness. She was missing what so many others took for granted—a part of life she thought would be natural and beautiful. She was missing the feeling of closeness, of commitment, and even of passion.

Matt was likable enough, and she enjoyed being with him. But was she ready to commit herself? Was she falling in love?

She didn't like her life unsettled.

Paula watched the ventilator breathing for Reverend Pettigrew for a few moments. *He'll be fine overnight,* she thought. The nurse's threats to call her didn't bother her. They'd call if they needed her, and she hoped they'd leave her alone if they didn't.

She expected a long night.

CHAPTER 2

The women of the Church of the Redeemed Believers sat rigidly in worn wooden pews, stern-faced, waving at the heat with cardboard fans, their eyes fixed on Harper standing at the pulpit. The women wore plain cotton dresses, and their hair was braided and pinned up under simple hats or head coverings. Children of various ages were permitted, but were required to sit quietly. The men were dressed identically in white shirts and thin black ties, each man clean-shaven with hair cropped short military style. They outnumbered the women, which was uncommon for a Sunday evening religious service in rural Oklahoma. Sober and unsmiling, the men were silent except for an occasional forceful affirmation of the preacher's fire-and-brimstone sermon.

Sam Harper stood immobile with his hands gripping the sides of the pulpit, having paused for a good thirty seconds. His eyes were diverted upward, as if he were communing directly with heaven. Small beads of sweat on his forehead formed larger drops that rolled off his face, splattering the pages of his open King James Bible.

Suddenly, he raised his fist and slammed it down. "Eternal damnation!" he shouted, "Eternal damnation for the God-haters!" With his left hand Harper thrust his Bible high above his head as he slowly swept his right index finger across the church. "Who will escape God's anger?" he asked. "You are sinning against God with your deceit. You are rejecting his truth." Harper stepped from behind the pulpit and approached the pews, his eyes burning.

"God hates sin," he said. His voice thundered over the congregation. "The Bible says in Romans, 'For the wages of sin is death.'"

"Amen!" several called out.

"God hates disobedience! As in First Corinthians, 'Every man's work shall be revealed by fire!'"

"Preach it, Brother Sam!" they cried out, clapping. "Praise the Lord!"

"Tear away your rotten flesh," the preacher said, raising both hands toward heaven, "the flesh that the maggots eat, infesting you, leaving you spoiled. Cut it away!"

Harper held his arms in the air, his Bible upward, his dark eyes darting back and forth, his face showing his disappointment, displeased by their failure, weak and unworthy. Disgusted, he slowly turned his back on them, shaking his head, and returned to the pulpit.

"The prophecy of the Lord is clear to the anointed," he said, leaning forward. His voice was calmer. "'Thy wrath is come and shouldst destroy them which destroy the earth.'"

"Amen!" the people cried out. Several women jumped up with their hands raised, speaking in tongues. The men stood and clapped loudly, and within seconds every person was on their feet, clapping, praying aloud, and uttering unrecognizable words.

"God *will* destroy those who dishonor their own bodies," he shouted over them, "men who lust after other men, women who lust after other women. God will destroy the abortionists who murder babies. He will destroy them all!"

Harper again grabbed both sides of the pulpit and stopped, and the people immediately grew quiet. He pulled a handkerchief from his rear pocket and wiped the sweat from his forehead. He motioned for them to sit. A quick glance signaled the pianist, sitting in front of an ancient upright Baldwin to his right, and she began playing "Onward Christian Soldiers." As Harper's faithful pianist, Jane Harper had heard her husband preach three services a week for three years. She sat straight, her braided hair knotted into a bun, dressed plainly, unadorned with jewelry or other pagan ornaments. She was the perfect preacher's wife, supporting him without complaint, just as she had been the perfect farmer's wife for more than thirty years, since the day he married her, a shy young girl of fifteen.

Harper wiped his face again before stuffing his handkerchief back into his pocket.

"God has sent an angel," Harper said, his voice now almost a whisper, "to keep thee in the way." He shook his head. "Who will listen to the angel? Who here will obey the word of the Lord?"

Harper rushed toward them, his jaw clenched tight, his eyes narrowed, his hands drawn into fists beside him. Sweat flew from his face.

"Who will destroy the God-haters?" he roared.

"We will!" they yelled back.

"Stand up," he said, motioning upward with his arms. "Stand up if you're willing to obey God!"

Instantly, the congregation was on its feet, clapping and cheering.

"God will bless the anointed! He will bless the Redeemed, the defenders of God! You are the true patriots!"

As his wife pounded out the chorus, Harper waved his arms back and forth like a choir director, singing, "Onward Christian Soldiers, marching as to war…"

The people joined in, clapping their hands as they began the familiar hymn. Harper sang the loudest, walking in front of the pulpit, pumping his arm in the air with every word. When the congregation finished all four verses, Jane stopped playing. In silence Harper returned to the pulpit and bowed his head in prayer.

"Almighty God," he prayed, "God of the New Israel, give us the strength to follow your perfect will. Make us fearless when your mighty sword delivers your perfect justice, *smiting* the flesh of the spiritual forces of evil, *destroying* those who hate you. Bless your anointed ones, the true believers, and bring us into your eternal light. Amen."

The people called out, "Amen!"

Harper lifted both of his arms over the congregation for the benediction. "Now may the God of power and justice reign over the lives of the Redeemed. In the name of the Father, and the Son, and the Holy Ghost. Amen."

As the congregation repeated the hymn's last verse, Harper walked down the side aisle to the back of the church. At the end of the song, the forty men, women, and children quietly filed past the preacher as he greeted each of them and shook their hands, exhorting them by name to be faithful. His wife packed her music in a vinyl folder and sat on the back pew.

Three men hung back, stopping near Harper, waiting for the others to move past and out the door into the evening sunlight. The men were in their late twenties and dressed identical to the other members.

When the entire congregation had left, the tallest of the three men spoke first. "Is it ready?" he asked in a low voice, glancing around.

"Almost," Harper said, whispering. "I'm going to test it soon."

"Do you need help?" the second man asked. "We could—"

"No," Harper cut in. "If I need your help, I'll ask for it." Harper glared at the three men and said nothing. They stood still, increasingly uncomfortable, until Harper was ready to break the silence. "Is that clear?" he said finally.

"Yes, Pastor Harper," the tall man said quietly. "We will follow your orders. When do we meet next?"

"Tomorrow night," Harper said. "Nine sharp." He gestured toward the door.

The three men immediately understood that both the Sunday evening church service as well as their conversation with Harper were over.

⋏

Paula found her car in the doctor's parking lot, worried for a moment that she had forgotten where she had parked it so early in the morning. She opened the door and felt the rush of hot air. Even though she had parked in a covered garage, the temperature inside the car must have been 120 degrees. Having spent the entire day in the air-conditioned hospital, she hadn't remembered it was one of the hottest days so far in July. Someone had told her 107. She slid in, started the car, and turned the air on high to cool the interior as quickly as possible, knowing that by the time the temperature was reasonable she'd already be drenched in sweat. It was typical for summer in Tulsa.

Paula needed to call Matt but hated picking up the phone. She wanted to go to dinner with him, not disappoint him, but it was too late, and she was exhausted. An unexpected issue with an asthma patient on the general medical floor had delayed her. She dialed the number of his pager and entered her phone number. Within a few seconds he was calling.

"Hey, Matt," she answered.

"So it's a no go?"

"How did you know?"

"I figured it's late, and you must be completely beat."

Paula laughed. "I'm so predictable."

"No, unfortunately your circumstances are predictable. Instead of a restaurant we could go fast food if you want. You may not know it, but it's still light outside."

"I'm so sorry, Matt. I just can't."

"No worries. Are you doing okay?"

She appreciated him asking. "Just tired is all. Busy weekend, very little sleep, I'm still on call tonight, and tomorrow's office is already packed."

"Then a rain check, okay?"

"Sure."

"So how about tomorrow night? I don't mean to be corny or anything, but I sure enjoy our time together."

"That's sweet."

"Then it's a yes? Tomorrow night? My treat?"

"I'd like that," she said. *If only I could make definite plans*, she thought, *like an ordinary person. Say yes and be certain it would happen.*

"Me, too," Matt said. "I'll call you."

"Okay, talk to you tomorrow."

After they both disconnected, she sat a moment feeling the cold air blowing on her face. She knew she was right about tonight. She was running on fumes as it was, and there was no guarantee she'd get a minute of sleep on call. It was the nature of her chosen occupation.

Yet a simple dinner. A night out with a friend. A chance for a relationship. Was that so much to ask for?

Paula backed her car out of its space and headed for the exit of the parking garage. *Yes, tonight,* she thought, *the best I can hope for is a good night's sleep.*

⟡

Sam Harper slid the thick cardboard box to the center of the plywood and Styrofoam raft. He checked the electrical wires of the detonator attached to the radio receiver on the box's top. Green to black. White to red. Each wrapped tight. Careful—no mistakes. After meticulously examining every connection to confirm it was correct, only then was he satisfied. All was set. He extended the radio receiver's antenna to its full height and gave the raft a gentle shove. It floated away from the bank of the pond and out toward the middle.

The summer evening had little breeze, and the surface was glassy smooth, disrupted only by the motion of the awkward raft. The water reflected the fading sun, its pink light broken and scattered on the surface, filtering through the branches of the surrounding scrub oak forest.

The raft stopped in the dead center of the pond, about twenty yards from shore. Harper scrambled up the bank and positioned himself behind an ancient blackjack oak about thirty yards from the water's edge. Its trunk was thick and stout and would protect him.

Harper looked around and listened carefully. The leaves of the dense forest rustled softly all around him. A lone whippoorwill cried sweetly in the distance. Besides these typical sounds of a country woodland, he heard nothing.

In his hand he held the radio transmitter that would send the signal. The red light indicated it was on. Harper pulled the transmitter's antenna to its fullest position, looked and listened one last time, and then pushed the button.

A flash like a bolt of lightning rushed past him, immediately followed by a blast that knocked him backward. Leaves and water from the sky rained down around him. His ears roared, and he lay still on the ground, his hands covering his head. Gradually, the roar softened to a high-pitched whine. He stood slowly, testing his balance. At first unsteady, he regained his equilibrium, and then headed for the edge of the water to look at the result.

The pond was half empty. Dead fish were floating on the surface and lying around the perimeter. The leaves of the nearest trees were missing, and several large branches had broken off. The raft and bomb packaging were gone.

He had used what he thought was a small amount of nitrate fertilizer and fuel oil in his test. Impressive. What pleased him most was that the radio-controlled detonator worked perfectly—an essential part of his plan.

He sat on the bank, his skin tingling, soaked with water and covered with leaves, and he smiled. This was perfect. This was absolutely perfect.

Chapter 3

Paula's Monday morning office schedule was completely full, and she was glad she wasn't running late. Rounds at Saint Luke's had gone smoothly. Reverend Pettigrew was holding his own, still on the ventilator and still receiving antibiotics. The intensive care nurses had called only once during the night, and she had slept pretty well.

The Monday after an on-call weekend was more hectic than a typical Monday, or at least it seemed so, probably because she was unusually tired. Today was no exception. The patient schedule was on her desk, and it looked like she'd be working through lunch and into the late afternoon before traveling again to the hospital in the evening. She hoped her rounds wouldn't take too long because she really wanted to go to the restaurant with Matt. After canceling their dinner the night before, she felt terrible about it. The last time she and Matt had been on a date, she had spent the entire evening laughing at him and his stories. The time had flown, and the laughter had felt good. She couldn't remember when she had felt so happy.

All she did was work. Life should be more than that.

Paula's office was across the street from Saint Luke's on the twelfth floor of a physicians' office complex. She shared the space with eight other pulmonary doctors, and the nine of them were a reasonably good fit. They argued only occasionally, covered each other's calls, and practiced good medicine. Though she was the newest member, so far she had been treated as an equal, unlike what she had experienced in her training. With her current group, she was on a guaranteed salary that would only last a few more months. Working long hours in medicine, and she was definitely doing that, didn't always equate to making more money. The most lucrative part of a pulmonary practice was the procedures—bronchoscopies, thoracenteses, and sleep studies—but those came with larger patient panels that took time to build. In a private practice of medicine, every doctor pulled his or her own weight, and she'd be no exception. So far, she had only warranted one meeting with the business manager. She hoped it'd be the only one.

Somehow, after a senior partner retired, she had lucked into a corner office with a view of Tulsa to the south and west: today clear, blue skies and rolling hills clothed in lush green, and with the sandy Arkansas River winding off into the distance. Oklahoma was known for its massive thunderstorms, and she had watched several roll in, following along Interstate 44 from Oklahoma City to Tulsa. Several months earlier a powerful storm with a wall cloud headed straight for their building. The tornado sirens sounded, and they evacuated to the basement. Tornados were something no Oklahoman took for granted, and the whole thing was a bit frightening.

Her office was glass windows on two walls. The other two walls were filled with bookshelves decorated with her collection of antique medical textbooks and a variety of personal knickknacks. Her desk, neat and clean without the clutter of most physicians, occupied the middle of the room. A leather chair, brown with brass studs, sat behind the desk. Paula had bought the chair in Oklahoma City at a garage sale for thirty bucks when she was a poor medical student. It was one of her most prized possessions. Paula was sitting at her computer checking her e-mails when Wendy Garcia, her nurse since the day she started practice, stepped in from the hallway.

"Looks like a busy day," Wendy said.

"Thank goodness," Paula said. "I was afraid I'd be bored today."

Wendy smiled. "Not likely." She held up the schedule. "Jerry Cook is first with COPD. Your second is Lulu Martin. She turned a hundred since we saw her last."

"Amazing!"

"A couple of asthmas, several more with COPD, and three hospital follow-ups. Two new patients."

"That's good." Paula stood. "Then we'd better get started."

"How is Reverend Pettigrew?" Wendy asked.

Wendy was asking because Thomas Pettigrew was her pastor. Though Paula had never met Pettigrew before he had arrived in the emergency room, he had asked for her because Wendy was in his congregation.

"No worse," Paula said. "He seems like he's holding his own, but I'd prefer that he'd show more improvement."

"I hope the pastor does okay. He's a nice man."

"I think he'll be fine," Paula said. "At least I hope so."

Reverend Pettigrew, though seemingly stable, hadn't looked all that good to her on morning rounds. The antibiotics should have kicked in by now. If the medication didn't start working pretty quickly, Reverend Pettigrew would be in big trouble.

She didn't want that.

Paula walked out into the hallway and picked up the slip for her first patient. Jerry Cook was only fifty-five years old but had the lungs of an eighty-year-old, a result of three packs of cigarettes a day for twenty-five years. He stopped smoking with his first hospitalization for pneumonia ten years earlier, but it was too late to save his lungs. Now, despite oxygen, home nebulizers, and eight medications, he was disabled. With constant shortness of breath, he seldom went longer than a month without being hospitalized for what was medically called a COPD exacerbation, an acute and sometimes dangerous worsening of his condition.

Paula opened the exam room door. Cook was sitting in a chair, a portable oxygen tank on the floor beside him.

"Good morning, Jerry."

"Good morning, Dr. Barrett. How are you?"

"Fine, Jerry. How about you?"

"I'm actually having a pretty good day. I think that new antibiotic you gave me when I went home last week has really helped."

"I'm glad."

Paula recalled how sick he had been, spending the first two days on a ventilator this time. He was doing everything right now, taking his meds, not smoking, but the damage had been done.

"So this should be an easy visit, Doctor."

"Exactly what you deserve."

Paula reviewed the medications, the vital signs, and listened to his heart and lungs. "Sounds pretty good," she said. "A few wheezes and mucous sounds, but nothing unexpected."

"Thanks, Doctor."

"I think we should see you back in three months," Paula said as she stood up.

"That's great. Thanks, Dr. Barrett."

Paula heard him hesitate and knew he had something else to say. She stopped and waited.

"Can I ask a question?" he said.

"Sure, Jerry. What is it?"

He paused. She would be patient. It was likely important. Patients many times waited until the very last minute of the visit, getting up the nerve to discuss what troubled them the most. If she was impatient or rushed him, she'd miss his most serious concern.

"The last time I was in the hospital, you know, I was just..."

Paula sat back down, nodding, waiting for his next comment. She saw his eyes tear up.

Cook shook his head. "Dr. Barrett, the ventilator was tough." He lifted up the oxygen tube that ran from his tank to prongs in his nose. "And I feel trapped with this bullshit oxygen on me constantly."

Paula couldn't recall that he had expressed his frustration with his illness before. She saw the sickest of the sick, and it wasn't too uncommon to hear patients upset with their condition, expressing their hurt and sadness and fear. It wasn't ever a comfortable conversation.

"I know it's tough," she said.

"I don't think I can do it anymore."

"What do you mean?"

"I want to talk to you about one of those advance things."

"Advance directives?"

"Yeah, one of those. I never want to go back on a ventilator…ever!"

"You know the ventilator saved your life."

"But for what?" Cook looked down and paused. After a few seconds composing himself, he was ready to go on. "I'm not fatalistic. I don't have a death wish."

Paula shook her head. "Of course not."

"But I'm a realist. It's not the money, though God knows how much it costs to be in the hospital so frequently."

"The money's not important."

"It is for someone, I'm sure. The insurance company probably hates me. I cost a fortune."

"I promise that your money issues don't guide my treatment. I try to do the right thing."

"Of course. It's not the money. It's the pain. I just can't do it anymore. I'm not afraid of dying."

Paula wondered if it was really true. She thought most people were. "What do you want me to do? You know I'll respect your wishes."

"I want to look into hospice. I talked to my family."

"Are you sure?" He was fifty-five years old, after all, she thought. She wanted him to be certain.

"Absolutely. I've thought a lot about it. I want to die at home, Dr. Barrett, not at the end of the hallway in the hospital."

Paula couldn't blame him. She wouldn't want that either. She had seen enough pulmonary deaths already in her short career to know it was a horrible way to die—struggling for every breath, essentially suffocating, no hope for a cure.

"Jerry, I understand. We can arrange for that."

"No heroics."

"Okay."

"Keep me comfortable."

She could see his tears coming. He was tough, but life-and-death conversations weren't easy. "I promise," she said softly. "You'll be as comfortable as possible. I promise."

"Thank you." Cook was done. He had said all he would say.

"I'll order hospice. They'll contact you today."

He nodded.

Paula stood, left the exam room, and closed the door behind her. The tough job of being a pulmonologist was taking care of terminal patients. Oddly, he was fine today. He was dying nonetheless, standing at the very edge of a cliff, his feet on the slippery wet grass, waiting for the slightest breeze to blow him over.

Nothing in her training prepared her for visits like Jerry Cook's. Nothing in her life made her an expert in dealing with the dying, particularly with a younger person like Cook. Unfortunately, the longer she was in practice, the more experience she was gaining, definitely one of the parts of medicine she enjoyed the least.

She'd order hospice for Jerry Cook. The nurses would see him in his home. If he died at home, she might not even see him again.

Tobacco had killed him, as certain as a bullet to his head.

⅄

The white frame house, loaded on flatbed trucks in three separate pieces, had been hauled to the center of the compound on a moonless night and reconstructed at the site by hand. The trucks were a tight fit on the narrow road built through the trees behind the church. The road, hidden from view by the sanctuary, served as the only approach to the compound. Neither the house nor any of the compound's other structures was visible from the church's parking lot or from any of the adjacent public roadways. Dense virgin scrub oak with thick underbrush made the perimeter of the property nearly impenetrable. The house, barn, and outbuildings stood in an open area in the center of the compound only seen from the air, but great pains were taken by the membership to have the entire compound mimic exactly any other rural farm property in the region when photographed by a satellite or drone or helicopter that might fly over.

The house was modest, consisting of four small rooms and a screened-in front porch, and was used as the parsonage. The larger meetings were held at the church, but the smaller ones—those that were the most important—were held here.

The living room, where the four men would meet, was the only room of any size. On one side, the room opened into a tiny kitchen, and Harper stood amid dirty dishes and peeling wallpaper, brewing a fresh pot of coffee. On the other side, a short hallway led to the bathroom and a small bedroom. The bedroom door was closed, and behind the door Jane Harper was reading a book, minding her own business.

Three of the men huddled around a coffee table, peering at a diagram and waiting for Harper to return from the kitchen. The oldest of the three was Carl Joe, a lanky twenty-nine-year-old, fresh from working his family farm north of Muskogee, wearing dirty denim coveralls and a white T-shirt. He was the first to speak up when Harper sat down. "How much longer before we know the target?"

Harper let the question hang for a few seconds, and Carl Joe knew he should have waited.

"Carl Joe," Harper said slowly, "do you think you need to know before I'm ready to tell you?"

The other two men shifted uneasily. Tommy, the newest member, sat closest to Carl Joe and moved slightly away at the preacher's comment. He was a couple of years younger than Carl Joe and had grown up outside of Taft, the small town near the compound. Tommy was currently unemployed. He usually worked odd jobs around the county but frequently seemed to butt heads with his bosses. He seldom held a job for more than six months.

Buddy, sitting on Harper's right, had been a member for two years. In his late-twenties, he was muscular, slightly overweight, and wore a Nike cap turned backward and a faded gray Oklahoma State polo. He was a cous-in of Harper's and had been born near Taft, but moved to California as a young child after his mother was divorced. He hated California and moved back to Taft, saying he was suffocating from the stench of the "faggots and communists."

"No, Pastor Harper," Carl Joe said carefully. "I wasn't saying that."

"Good," Harper said abruptly, looking at the three men. "Then I can get on with some details."

Harper pushed the diagram aside and set down the coffeepot and four cups.

"If any man here can't do this," Harper said, "say so now."

Harper poured each man a cup of coffee while he waited for a reply. No one spoke.

"Time is running out," he continued. "If you watch TV for a few hours, you know that our country is rapidly disintegrating." Harper's voice was calm, a steady monotone. "The federal government has violated the sacred sovereignty of the people. It is unauthorized, unaccountable, and anti-Christian, an irresponsible, unlawful bureaucracy planning to destroy our Constitution and the God-given rights we hold true as patriots. At this very moment, an international conspiracy led by the United Nations is infiltrating our government under the banner of the 'New World Order'—a sickening cry for socialism and communism. Federal agents are training in house-to-house, forced-entry, and no-knock search and seizure. A massive gun confiscation is planned to strip the last defenses from law-abiding Americans. Then they'll take our Bibles."

"Over my dead body!" Carl Joe said.

"Everywhere, in living rooms and churches," Harper continued, "at gun shows and lodges, plain people like you and me are taking up the task, preparing to stand against the forces of evil. They think we are divided. They think we are weak. We have an opportunity, God help us, to make them know, to make them hear, to make them scared."

"God save America," Buddy shouted.

"God save us all," Harper said. Harper stood and walked to the window, sliding the curtain to the side and peering out into the darkness. When he turned back he was frowning. "Federal agents are everywhere." Harper looked out the window a second time, and then returned to the couch and sat down. "We have definite proof the FBI blew up the Murrah in Oklahoma City. One of our patriot groups had exposed illegal drug running by the FBI and the ATF. The FBI bombed the federal building to cover up their operation in South America." He paused as he drank his coffee and poured a second cup. "The FBI put the nitrate and fuel oil instructions out on the Internet. Anyone can make a nitrate bomb. It's simple. Why would the FBI put it on the Internet unless they needed to cover their tracks?"

"I heard it was a conspiracy," Carl Joe said. "Just like the Kennedy assassination."

"That's right. So it's up to us. We must restore our country, our Constitution, our government. We must restore our way of life to this godless nation." Harper reached for the diagram and held it up. "This is the bomb."

"Is it ready?" Tommy asked.

"We have all the ingredients," Harper said. "Buddy, did you pick up the radio-controlled car from the toy store?"

"It's in the sack by the door," Buddy said as he pointed.

"What's that for?" Tommy asked.

"Tommy, you ask too many questions," Harper snapped. "Why don't you shut up and listen!"

"Yes, sir. I'm sorry."

"We're using ANFO on this operation," Harper said, ignoring the apology. "Ammonium nitrate fuel oil."

"Like Oklahoma City," Carl Joe added.

"Right, we're going to use a radio-controlled electronic detonator."

Harper described his bomb while they listened. He chose ammonium nitrate, a high-order explosive, which was easy to prepare but difficult to detonate. Ammonium nitrate, he said, had a low impact and friction sensitivity and thus was safer than many other explosives. The purpose of the fuel oil, mixed 6 percent by weight, was to prevent the ammonium nitrate from absorbing water vapor. The water vapor inactivated its explosive potential. Harper explained that he had selected the ammonium nitrate fertilizer and kerosene as the fuel oil because both were impossible to trace, especially since the feds were using tagging agents to trace the manufactured high-order explosives to their source of production. Harper had specifically sought out nitrate fertilizer that was several years old, which wasn't difficult in this part of the country, stacked up and forgotten in one of the many old barns in eastern Oklahoma. Such a product was truly untraceable, and better yet, when stolen, had no record of purchase.

Earlier that day, Harper had crushed the fertilizer to a fine powder and mixed it with kerosene; then he loosely packed the mixture in plastic containers. He expected the main charge to have a velocity of detonation of nearly 13,000 feet per second. The tough part of an ANFO bomb was finding an appropriate detonator, but Carl Joe had provided them with blasting caps and sensitized detonating cord.

"I borrowed them from a jobsite a few years ago," Carl Joe said proudly.

"We once could buy them at gun shows," Harper said, "but the feds have cracked down."

"Because we know how to use them," Buddy said.

Blasting caps, Harper told them, were designed to explode when an electric current ran through them, which then ignited the detonating cord, which in turn detonated the ANFO. In his bomb, the electric current was provided by a radio-controlled toy car. It was simple. He would detach the solenoid that controlled the motion of the front wheels of the toy Buddy bought and connect the blasting cap to the contacts for the solenoid. He could be a quarter of a mile away and control exactly when the bomb exploded. He had considered using a cell phone for the signal, but the feds could block a cell phone, not a toy's remote.

"And it really works?" Tommy asked.

"Of course," Harper said. "I tested it yesterday. My ears are still ringing."

"Then we're good to go?" Carl Joe asked.

"Pretty close," Harper said. "I have just a few details left to work out."

"We should hit a federal installation," Carl Joe said, "but if we do, we can't let some Middle Eastern terrorist get the credit."

"I decide the target," Harper said sharply. "Is that clear?"

"Yes, Sam. Of course."

"Okay," Harper said. "I want us to meet here Wednesday night. I'll give you the final details. Don't expect to go home until we're done. Is everyone on board?"

They nodded.

"Do you need some help mixing the ingredients?" Buddy asked.

"No, that part's done."

"So the bomb's here on site?" Tommy asked.

"Does that make you nervous, Tommy?" Carl Joe asked.

"I was hoping to see it."

"It's in a safe place," Harper said. "A place where even the feds can't find it. I've been preaching that each of you needs a safe place—hidden from the black helicopters and the infrared satellites—and now you know why. Your ammo and your guns should be there, along with food and provisions for you and your family. Not at your house. Better off in an outlying area." He pointed his finger at them. "And tell no one about it. Not even your best friend. Your survival depends on it."

"I've got mine," Carl Joe said.

"Good," Harper said. "None of us can be too careful." Harper stood, indicating the meeting was over. "Okay, we meet back here Wednesday night. Don't talk to anyone. Not a soul. Do you understand? The feds are near. I just feel it. Don't trust anyone, especially someone asking questions."

Harper watched through the kitchen window as the three men left in separate vehicles. Their lights cut across the grassy field in front of the house as they headed for a small break in the trees on the opposite side. The opening led to the road connecting the compound to the church. The men would replace the locks and chains on the gates to secure the property, as they had been told, but Harper would check to be sure before going to bed.

Jane opened the door to the bedroom and switched off the light. She came up close behind him and stood a moment. Harper didn't move.

"So the bomb is ready?" she asked softly.

"It worked perfectly," he said, staring intently out into the darkness.

"And you have chosen the target, haven't you?"

He turned and smiled. "Yes, I have. You know me better than any."

"And?"

"The target is the US attorney general."

"Ronald Montgomery?"

"Yes," Harper said. "He's giving a speech at the Merrimac Hotel in Tulsa."

"I thought our target would be an abortion clinic," Jane said. "I thought that's what you had decided."

"This target is better. I've been thinking about it for weeks."

"Abortion clinics are of Satan," Jane said, "where heartless mothers offer up their innocent babies to murderous doctors. They deserve to be destroyed. God *demands* they be destroyed."

Jane had raised her voice, which was unlike her, and Harper leaned back on the window sill, waiting a moment before he responded.

"I don't disagree with you about that," he said finally, "but this is an opportunity we can't miss. Montgomery is one of the masterminds of the federal conspiracy, corrupt and ungodly, and a traitor to the true patriots. He is the instigator of the plan to monitor every conservative group like ours, calling us domestic terrorists, a blatant attack on any American who challenges the government's authority. We must destroy him before he destroys us. He is the perfect hostage."

"When is this going to happen?"

"Tomorrow night. Seven o'clock."

Jane sat on the couch near him. "Why didn't you tell the others?"

"I think you and I can do this alone," he said. "If it doesn't work, they'll be ready."

Harper took a seat next to her and explained his plan. The attorney general's meeting was a private fund-raiser, he said, not a government-sponsored event, and he expected security to be lighter. He would use two bombs. The first was the size of his test device, and it would be hidden in the trunk of a car parked near the front of the hotel. The explosion, though relatively small, would attract a lot of attention. The second would be much larger and hidden in a van parked in the hotel's garage next to an exterior wall adjacent to the ballroom. He had checked out the exact location a week earlier. The second bomb's blast would be substantial, possibly collapsing the entire ballroom and most of the garage.

"I would expect," Harper said, "a significant level of collateral damage. It's a dinner full of rich people, and I heard the privilege of seeing Montgomery is costing them five hundred dollars each."

"Their cost may be higher than they anticipated."

"Exactly," Harper said. "You'll be near the ballroom, and when Montgomery starts his speech, you call me. I'll be observing from Saint Luke's Hospital across the street. If the FBI doesn't respond to our demands in fifteen minutes, I'll detonate the first device."

"Instant pandemonium," Jane said.

"No doubt. Montgomery will be our hostage. If he tries to leave, we'll detonate the second device. You'll have to be clear of the building."

"Yes, Sam. I understand."

"Montgomery would no longer be a hostage," Harper said dryly, "but he'd be dead."

Harper stood and walked back to the window, again looking outside. "Do you know what's ironic?" he asked.

"No, Sam. What?"

"Montgomery's speech is on victims' rights!"

Jane's face showed a glimmer of a smile. She stood up and moved next to him at the window. "Then this *is* an opportunity," she said close to his ear, "and I pray to God that a victim is *exactly* what Ronald Montgomery becomes."

⋀

It was nearly nine o'clock when Paula turned into the parking lot of her favorite restaurant to meet Matt. She could already taste the pasta she liked with the marinara sauce lightly touched with garlic, and of course the cheesecake, creamy smooth, smothered in strawberries. The perfect end to a busy day.

Paula saw Matt's car but no Matt as she walked in, suspecting he had gone inside to secure a table for them. It surprised her that he had beat her there, the restaurant located only a couple of miles from the hospital, next to Tulsa's largest mall. He must have been close when he called.

As soon as Paula entered the lobby, she saw Matt waving at her from a table for two near the front. He jumped up as she approached to give her a kiss and hug.

"Glad you could make it," he said as they sat down.

"Thanks for getting a table."

"No problem. I thought you'd appreciate me being efficient. Are you done for the night?"

"Should be. I'm not on call, and I turned off my pager on the way over."

"Great."

"Sorry about last night. I wanted to come."

"I understand. It's our lives."

Of course he was right. Neither of them had much control over their schedules.

"I thought tonight would work out better anyway," Matt said. "Yesterday would have been so late." Matt glanced at his watch. "But actually it looks like we're getting a bit of a late start tonight, too."

She was glad he had said it. Last night, exhausted after a weekend on call, she had fallen asleep the instant her head hit the bed. Tonight her energy level was almost as bad. "So how was your day?"

"Mine was pretty standard, working fervently to catch the bad guys." Matt grinned. "You know, being a hero and all that."

Paula laughed. "In all modesty, you mean to say."

"I call it like I see it. How was your day?"

"Busy, you know, saving lives and all that."

"I wouldn't have expected less."

Paula felt herself smiling. She smiled and laughed a lot around Matt. That part was a good thing.

The waitress approached their table offering to take their drink order. Both of them knew what they wanted for dinner, so the waitress jotted down their selections and left.

"So," Matt said, "do you think we might be able to make a movie this weekend?"

Paula loved movies, virtually a cinema fanatic since she was a child, and Matt would always indulge her. "Oh, that sounds fun."

"There are a couple of new ones being released this weekend."

"Really? I hadn't checked."

"One's a big-dollar, highly rated technoblockbuster."

"That sounds great," Paula said, rolling her eyes.

"The other is one of those silly romances."

"Either is fine with me."

"Okay, okay. Romance it is!" Matt raised his hands in mock resignation. "It was my first choice."

Paula shook her head. "You're a mess."

Matt liked to talk about the movies or the arts or the latest novels they'd read. They seldom discussed work, and she appreciated that. What she needed, not that she always recognized it, was an escape from work. Medicine was all consuming, a constant pressure, squeezing in one last appointment, checking one more lab test on a critical patient, studying another important journal article. The job was never done, always more the doctor could do. Sometimes she needed a break, and Matt seemed to understand that.

The waitress brought out their meals. The portions were huge, and Paula would box up half of hers, particularly since she wanted to save room for cheesecake.

"You talk to your dad?" Paula asked.

"Couple of nights ago."

Matt was originally from Aurora, Illinois, not far from Chicago. His parents still lived there, both in their early seventies. His mother had recently been diagnosed with Alzheimer's and was rapidly deteriorating, eating poorly, losing weight, only occasionally recognizing close friends and family. It was heartbreaking. Matt had always been close to his mother—not so much his father—and Matt was taking his mother's illness hard. He had occasionally asked Paula about his mother's medical situation, not so much for advice but for information. As was often the case with caregivers, Matt's father was facing exhaustion, considering putting Matt's mother in a nursing home. Matt was struggling with that decision, the thought of such a facility difficult, yet understanding the reality of an old man, fragile himself, trying to battle his wife's impossible circumstance. Paula didn't want to pry but rather wanted to be supportive, a delicate balance.

"You don't mind me asking?"

"Oh, no. Of course not."

"So has your dad made a decision?"

"Not really. He went to a couple of memory support units, saw how bad some of them were, and thought he could wait a bit longer."

"Tough situation."

"Yeah. To be honest, he's doing a better job than I thought he would."

In Paula's experience, the spouse almost always bore the greatest burden. Matt, an only child, wanted to help, but he lived seven hundred miles away and had a full-time, challenging job. For a child unable to effectively help, like Matt, there was always some guilt.

"Your dad will do the right thing."

Matt didn't answer. The waitress stepped up and asked about dessert. They'd share a piece of cheesecake, they told her. She scurried off. While they waited, Matt seemed quieter, like his mind was somewhere far off. She was the one who had brought up the hard topic. Maybe it was a mistake.

"I was thinking," Matt said after a few minutes. "It'd be good for me to visit my mom pretty soon."

"That's a good idea."

"You like baseball?" Matt was smiling.

Matt had changed subjects, ready to move on.

"I don't know anything about baseball." Paula was smiling, too. Matt had asked her this question a hundred times, and her answer was always the same. He was a baseball fanatic, and it was true she was completely ignorant. Someday she'd need to learn.

"When are you coming to a Driller's game with me?"

Tulsa had a new downtown ballpark, and Paula wanted to go sometime, just to make Matt happy, but it always seemed to be talk and no action. "We'll do that soon, okay?"

"Sounds great."

If the truth be told, she really preferred movies to baseball.

They finished dessert, and Matt picked up the check. Paula insisted on splitting it, but he'd hear nothing of it. Matt walked her to her car. The evening was still warm, even at ten thirty, with no breeze. The parking lot had thinned out. It was later than she would have liked.

As she opened her car door, Matt pulled her close, and they kissed. He held her a moment, but not too long, because he knew she needed to go home. Paula wished it were different. She slipped into the front seat.

Matt leaned in. "What's the chance of dinner tomorrow night?"

"I'd love to."

"Me, too. See you then."

Matt stepped away, and Paula backed out of the parking spot. He waved as she drove off.

She'd be home late, but fortunately she wasn't on call. She thought a moment about Matt deciding to go see his parents. It was important to him, and she would encourage him to go, but the circumstances weren't ideal—very ill mother, exhausted father, tough life decisions. She was thankful her parents were healthy—a blessing not to have that stress in her life.

Paula pulled into her condo complex. *Busy day*, she thought, *good dinner, great company.*

She was ready for bed.

CHAPTER 4

Paula stepped into Reverend Pettigrew's room and noticed he was sleeping. As she approached his bed, he awakened and turned toward her, as if he knew exactly when she was coming.

"Good morning, Reverend," she said as she took his hand. His skin felt cool, yet slightly warmer than the previous day.

Reverend Pettigrew smiled at her. The tube in his trachea prevented him from speaking, but the smile was a good indicator that he was improving. Paula had changed the ventilator settings based on his blood gases earlier that morning. He was breathing better, and the ventilator was doing less of the work. Paula found no reason to change his antibiotics. So far they were doing fine.

"Let me listen to your lungs," she said, as she removed her stethoscope from the pocket of her white jacket.

He nodded.

She pulled down his bed sheet to his waist so she could lift up his gown. She slipped her stethoscope in her ears and held the diaphragm on his chest, listening a few seconds as the air entered and exited his lungs. The sounds were some better, but the pneumonia was not gone.

"We'll get a chest X-ray today," she said. "You'll need the antibiotics a few more days. I'm hoping we can wean the ventilator over the next twenty-four hours and extubate you tomorrow morning."

Pettigrew winked. She was sure he understood her plan.

That'll be the plan, she thought to herself, *if all goes perfectly*. She wanted to be realistic. He wasn't out of the woods yet.

Paula said her good-byes as she left Reverend Pettigrew. She found an empty seat at a computer in the nurses' station to complete his chart, and she'd spend a couple of minutes typing in her morning progress note before leaving for the office.

"Dr. Barrett."

The voice was to her right. She turned to see Sally Carpenter. Sally was frowning, a disapproving look on her face. About what, only Paula could guess.

"Yes, Ms. Carpenter, can I help you?"

"The unit is full. What are your plans for Pettigrew?"

Paula let out her breath. *Does this nurse not believe in simple pleasantries?* "He's still on the ventilator."

"I can see that."

"Of course you can. I'm hoping to wean him off by morning. It all depends on how he does. Fair enough?"

"I'll let you know." Sally turned her back and walked away.

Sally Carpenter, Paula thought, *is a disagreeable woman. This is the intensive care unit, but does the head nurse of the unit need to be so intense?* Paula couldn't imagine it was essential.

Paula finished her progress note and logged out. She had another full schedule at the office. The best thing about her office was seeing her patients...and not having to see Sally Carpenter.

⅄

Harper followed close behind Jane on Sheridan Road as they approached the Merrimac Hotel. Its gray granite and glass exterior rose prominently between two modern, high-rise office complexes at the corner of Seventy-First Street and Sheridan Road, a thriving South Tulsa location, directly across the street from Saint Luke's Hospital. The forty-mile drive from Taft had taken well over an hour in the morning's rush-hour traffic, but Harper thought parking a couple of cars at the hotel would be less suspicious early in the day. As the time for the attorney general's speech grew nearer, the security would likely increase.

Jane pulled to a stop in front of Harper in the left-turn lane at the entrance to the hotel and waited for the traffic to clear. She was driving a ten-year-old Honda Accord, new enough to avoid attention parked in front of a luxury hotel. Harper's van, a full-size white 1982 Chevrolet panel van, was trickier. To a trained security eye the van would look suspicious, even more so if parked alone or left for long in a hotel garage. But these two cars were all Harper had. Both had been stolen two years earlier and hidden in a barn on the property to be used for just such an occasion.

That morning, he and Jane had loaded the two bombs into the vehicles. The bomb in the Honda was the simpler of the two. Harper had mounted the device in a plastic carton the size of a dress box, positioned in the trunk directly over the gas tank. Only the small antenna wire coming out the trunk near the rear window gave away the Accord's true purpose. For the van, Harper had calculated the necessary amount of nitrate fertilizer and fuel oil and placed the mixture into three large plastic trash cans. After securing the cans in the back, he attached a sensitized detonating cord of equal length to each can, twisting the ends into a single cord before connecting two blasting caps, one for backup. The toy solenoid would receive a signal from Harper's radio transmitter from the Saint Luke's parking lot and trigger the explosion. He had slipped the receiver's antenna wire through a tiny hole he had drilled through the van's metal roof and hidden its six-foot length along the top of the van's rear door. The antennas would be in his direct line of sight from the hospital. Both bombs had been carefully wrapped three times in plastic, washed down each time with chlorine water, to lessen the chance of discovery by the bomb-sniffing dogs.

Before leaving the church compound, Harper had wiped the vehicles free of fingerprints inside and out. He had placed disposable covers on the chairs and paper mats on the floor in an effort to eliminate any incriminating evidence, even though the blast should rip everything to shreds. The feds were clever. He had to be careful.

A break in the oncoming traffic allowed both Jane and Harper to turn left into the hotel driveway. The driveway was six hundred feet long, lined with white oaks along each side and a mass of red begonias down the median. Jane pulled over and allowed Harper to pass. Harper drove down the driveway until the road opened up to the front of the hotel as a circle drive for the arriving guests. The entrance to the multistory parking garage abutting the hotel structure was to his left. To his right was a small ground-level parking lot that normally held about fifty vehicles for guests and visitors, but so far the small lot was only about half full. Harper didn't see many people milling about, precisely what he had hoped for by coming early in the morning.

Harper turned right. As he passed an empty spot in the second row, he paused a moment, his signal for Jane. Harper moved forward, and he saw Jane in his rearview mirror pull into the vacant space. He circled around the lot a second time to pick her up.

"So far, so good," she said as she climbed into the van.

Harper nodded in agreement. He followed the main drive a short distance to the parking garage entrance and wound his way up the spiral ramp until he reached the second floor. The placement of the van here in the garage was critical so the blast would destroy the wall adjoining the hotel, collapsing the entire parking garage into the ballroom several stories below. He hoped that at least one spot was vacant along the wall he had chosen. As he pulled around the corner, he felt a moment of anxiety but then smiled in relief. Only a few cars were parked on the entire floor, and the spot perfect for his purpose was open. He pulled into the space and turned off the engine.

"Now both devices are in position," Harper said.

"It seems almost too easy."

"The feds are here somewhere. We must be alert."

After scanning the second floor to be sure no one was near, both he and Jane exited the van. He wadded up the paper seat covers and the disposable floor mats, locked the doors manually, and wiped off his fingerprints with his handkerchief. Jane waited quietly by the front of the vehicle.

"This spot is perfect," he said softly as he approached her.

They walked about a hundred feet on a narrow sidewalk to the hotel entrance. Before entering, Harper stopped to stuff the wadded paper to the bottom of a trash can, confident no one would think his trash significant. He pulled open the hotel door, holding it for Jane, and felt a rush of frigid air. As Harper followed Jane inside into the coolness, he noticed the richness of the entryway—dark, wood-paneled walls, brass fixtures, an Oriental rug on the floor.

"There is no one here," Harper said. "This is good." He pressed the down button for the elevator.

"God is with us," Jane said.

A bell chimed, and the doors opened. He and Jane entered. The inside of the elevator was also plush, with beveled-glass mirrors covering the three interior walls, accented by railings of brushed brass. Harper looked at himself in the mirror and straightened his tie. He had chosen to wear a black suit and white shirt. Jane wore a plain dress. He had hoped the two of them would look like regular hotel guests, but he was already feeling uncomfortable. He prayed to God no one would notice them.

When the elevator reached the first-floor lobby, the doors slid open. The Merrimac lobby was possibly the most extravagant interior of a building he had ever seen. A crystal chandelier hung from the ceiling, a hundred lights like candles illuminating the glass. Brown leather sofas and matching chairs were arranged in neat groupings underneath, centered around an ornately carved wooden table, ten feet square, very old and expensive. An elaborate floral arrangement extended at least six feet into the air.

Jane was frowning at him. He had stopped directly in front of the table and was gaping at it, and she was unhappy with him, a country farmer in a fancy hotel. He looked at Jane and nodded. She was right—he should be more careful.

"Need a taxi, sir?" A man standing to his right was talking to him. He was dressed in a bell captain's uniform.

"No, thanks," Harper grumbled, looking away so the man wouldn't see his face.

Harper gently grabbed Jane's arm to guide her toward the front entrance. *We should avoid further encounters*, he thought. He had been distracted, and it was not a time to be careless.

Once outside, they crossed the circle drive, walking past the Honda in the parking lot, and then up the driveway until they reached Sheridan Road. They followed Sheridan Road north two miles on foot until they reached Sheridan Hills Mall. Carl Joe would be waiting with a car, just as they had planned. Harper would tell him they had been shopping, and he would believe them.

Harper *had* been shopping. He had been shopping for a target. And now his target, the attorney general of the United States, would pay Harper's price, the full measure for the evil he had caused. He'd pay, or he'd be dead.

CHAPTER 5

The emergency room at Saint Luke's was packed, all too common for a Tuesday evening at nearly six thirty, and Paula wasn't one bit happy she was there. A few minutes earlier she was finishing her evening rounds, confident she'd be done in time to meet Matt for dinner, but then the emergency room physician, Dr. Frank Hunt, paged her. He was recommending admission for one of her patients, a forty-five-year-old male who had begun having an asthma attack after hitting the local smoked-filled casino. Though severely short of breath, he had initially refused to leave, winning big at blackjack. The aggressive treatment in the emergency department failed to relieve the wheezing, and Hunt had called her to admit the patient to the hospital.

As soon as Paula walked into the exam room, she knew he was in trouble.

His name was Randy Booker, and she had treated him at least three times in the emergency room in the last two years for asthma attacks. This time was by far his worst. He was breathing forty times a minute, a rate that would quickly exhaust him, and he had that wide-eyed look of panic on his face. The respiratory tech had seen it and was standing ready at the head of the bed, having had the foresight to bring a ventilator into the room, predicting it would soon be needed. The patient had a rebreather, a mask and bag that covered his face, delivering oxygen. A nurse in the room was hanging an IV with the tubing running to the back of his right hand.

"Hi, Randy," Paula said. "Sorry to see you struggling."

Booker half waved at Paula.

Too short of breath to talk, Paula thought. *Bad sign*. Paula turned to the nurse. "What have you done so far for him?"

"Continuous nebulizer," the respiratory tech said, answering first. "One hundred percent rebreather, big dose steroids. Getting worse. Pulse ox 86 percent and dropping. Matter of time."

He meant matter of time before the patient would need the ventilator, and Paula knew he was right.

Paula moved next to the patient and listened to his lungs. His lungs were tight. He was moving so little air that she heard almost no wheezing. Again, a bad sign.

"Randy," Paula said, "we need to put you on the ventilator."

Booker shook his head.

"I know, I know. We don't have a choice. We're doing everything we can, and you're getting worse. It's inevitable. If we do this, I'll give you some sedation."

"Dr. Barrett?" Booker said.

Paula leaned forward. She could barely hear him. "Yes, Randy?"

"If it's…absolutely necessary. I trust…you."

"Thanks, Randy." Paula glanced up at the nurse.

"I'll call anesthesia," the nurse said, heading out the door.

"I'll be ready," the respiratory tech said, already moving the ventilator into position.

Booker looked worse by the second, and Paula was glad the anesthesiologist arrived quickly. Within minutes the sedation was given, the patient was intubated, and the ventilator was breathing for him.

Booker would be going to the intensive care unit. Asthma was taken lightly by so many patients, but at times it became extremely serious, even life-threatening. Booker was in trouble. Paula left the exam room and dragged a chair up to the crowded doctors' desk to sign on to the computer so she could write her admission orders. The sights and sounds of a busy emergency room surrounded her—babies crying, patients moaning on stretchers, and some confused elderly woman screaming profanities in a nearby exam room.

Saint Luke's had the busiest emergency room in Tulsa, and this was the last place she wanted to be tonight. For a moment her thoughts drifted to the solitude of her condo—a warm bath, soft jazz in the background, a glass of white wine—

"Your guy is a tough case."

She turned to see Hunt. He was tall and thin, about forty, wearing a white lab coat over a polo shirt and khaki slacks. His stethoscope was slung around his neck, which she hated, giving him the I'm-a-stud look.

She smiled politely. "He needs to be here," she said. "I'm sure he'll need a couple of days. It's not his first time."

"This guy has terrible asthma. The pollen count is the highest in months. We have an ozone alert today. And yet this guy heads to a casino filled with smoke. Can you believe that?"

"So you think this will make him stop gambling?"

Hunt laughed. "Sure. About the same chance of me winning the lottery." Hunt sat down in the empty chair beside her. "I'm sorry to dump this one on you."

"That's okay. He's my patient."

"Most docs avoid the emergency department. We see you down here way too often, don't we?"

"I do my very best to stay away. No offense."

"None taken, and I bet we'll be seeing you again tonight. I see you're on pulmonary call." He reached out for an X-ray report a nurse was handing him.

"I know," Paula said. "I saw the schedule." It was her bad luck. She had just been on call for her group and now the hospital pulmonary call.

"Well, good luck," Hunt said as he stood, seeing a nurse waving at him that another room was ready.

Unassigned patients, those without established doctors, were a hassle, and the hospital staff rotated on a call list to cover them. Paula clicked on the computer to start her admission note. "I doubt you'll need me," she said over her shoulder.

"Maybe not," Hunt said as he started down the hall. "You never know."

"One can always hope, Doctor. One can always hope."

⚓

Harper had chosen the west edge of the Saint Luke's parking lot. He backed up his 1993 Ford van, gray with tinted windows, so the rear of the van faced toward the Merrimac Hotel. He shut off the engine. The western half of the parking lot was basically deserted, which suited him fine. Tuesday nights, he thought, apparently weren't the biggest night for visitors at the hospital. *Praise God!*

Harper cracked open the back door and assessed his position. Just down a small incline, the hospital service road ran parallel to the edge of the parking lot, and beyond the service road was a large grassy area that dropped to Sheridan Road. Across Sheridan was the entrance to the Merrimac Hotel where Jane and he had been earlier that morning. His view was perfect— straight down the entrance road to the hotel, framed on each side by the two tall office towers.

He scanned the complex with field binoculars. From his position his views to both the front of the hotel and the garage were unobstructed. The white 1982 Chevy panel van he had left in the garage was parked in a direct line he estimated to be about three hundred yards. Panning the binoculars across the top of the roof of the hotel and both office buildings, he saw neither snipers nor SWAT team members. His position was excellent. Better than he had expected. In fact, with a high-powered rifle he could have easily picked off the attorney general should Montgomery have taken a stroll out the front of the hotel.

Two local news vans were parked in the circle drive. They'd be in a good position for the top news story of the day.

He glanced at his watch, and it showed ten of seven. The attorney general's speech was scheduled to start at seven, but he expected it might be late. He reached into a green cloth bag and pulled out the two radio transmitters, each the size of a pack of cigarettes, laying them side by side on the bed of the Ford. The transmitter on his right was marked with a large number one on its front, and it was for the Honda. The second had a number two for the Chevy van. He picked up the first transmitter, slid open the back, and slipped in two fresh AA batteries. He pulled the antenna out to its fullest extent before placing it gently back on the floor. The procedure was repeated with the second transmitter. Each one would be switched on when it was needed. He laid two cell phones between the transmitters—one was his and the other a throwaway—and reached into his pocket to pull out a crumpled piece of paper. He smoothed out the paper and then placed it carefully beside the phones. He would need the phone numbers he had written on the paper in just a few minutes.

For the next several seconds he stared at the four electronic devices, and then slowly he smiled. This would be a great day. A day many would remember.

Jane would be calling shortly. He was ready.

⟁

Ronald Montgomery looked in the elevator mirror and straightened his tie.

"Why did I let you talk me into another conference?" he asked. He was tall, almost six feet four inches, distinguished, and immaculately dressed, with thick brown hair graying at the sides.

"Because it's good for the country," Jennifer McLaughlin said, holding up his suit jacket, "and it's good for you, too."

Jennifer stood a foot and a half shorter than he and had to balance on her tiptoes and extend her arms upward for him to slip into his jacket. She helped him into it and then smoothed the wrinkles on the back and shoulders. Sliding the strap of her purse onto her shoulder, she bent over to pick up his briefcase.

"Don't let me go four weekends in a row again."

"Yes, sir. Even if you insist?"

"Even if I insist."

Ronald Montgomery, the attorney general of the United States, and his secretary, Jennifer McLaughlin, rode down the Merrimac Hotel elevator. Two plainclothes FBI agents, Rick Simmons and Mike Asher, his security detail, stood silently behind them.

"Do you have your notes?" she asked.

He tapped his breast pocket.

"You look a little pale. Are you feeling all right?"

"Yes, I'm fine."

"Are you sure?"

"I'm just tired. It's all this traveling you're making me do."

"I'm going to check on a later flight for tomorrow. You need to sleep in."

"You're such a mother hen."

Jennifer laughed. She turned to Simmons, the older of the two agents, and became serious. "You have any locals?" she asked sharply.

"Yes, four. Two on each side. We'll stay at the front."

"Good."

They rode the elevator to the lobby and then the escalator down to the ballroom level. Entering the back of the ballroom, they were joined by the conference's coordinator, a friendly, attractive woman who had escorted and assisted them since they had arrived from Dallas. The conference was on victims' rights, and Ronald Montgomery was the keynote speaker. Victims' rights were his personal crusade, and he was considered by many to be the country's leading expert. Five hundred people were seated, having just finished the first course of a $200-a-plate formal dinner, waiting for him to speak.

At the front of the room on a raised platform, the conference moderator, Jim Black, began listing the attorney general's impressive credentials and background.

"Mr. Ronald Montgomery was born and raised in Chicago, Illinois. After graduating third in his class at Harvard Law School, he practiced at one of Chicago's most prestigious law firms for fourteen years. He was elected to the office of state attorney general of Illinois and was reelected four times. Two years ago, he was nominated by the president of the United States for attorney general and has been a spokesman for the president's war on crime. Long a supporter of victims' rights and author of two books on the subject, we are fortunate to have the attorney general as tonight's keynote speaker. Without further delay, ladies and gentlemen, let us welcome the attorney general of the United States: Mr. Ronald Montgomery."

The audience rose to applaud, turning to the door as the spotlight flooded on Montgomery. He strolled down the center aisle to the podium at the front and stood in the spotlight for a moment. Then he raised his arms and waved for the audience to take their seats.

"Thank you, Jim," Montgomery began as they quieted down. "Thank you for that wonderful introduction. I see my mother has been writing your material."

The audience laughed. Simmons and Asher took their positions at each side of the podium, their eyes scanning the crowd. The four local agents covered the corners of the ballroom.

"I appreciate your invitation to this great conference," Montgomery said. "Victims' rights are a topic I can talk hours and hours on…and Jim told me I had as much time as I wanted." Montgomery smiled as they laughed again. He took a small computer tablet with his notes out of his pocket, placed it on the lectern, and waited for them to become quiet. "I always start by telling a joke, and this is it: where did the cow and the horse go on their date?" He paused briefly. "They went to the moo-vies."

The audience laughed politely.

"That sounds like a five-year-old's joke, doesn't it? In fact, it is. I was told this joke by a young boy, I'll call him Timmy, last month in a children's hospital in Boston. Timmy was in the hospital recovering from a bullet wound to his head. He had been left for dead by the same intruders who had killed his father and mother and his eight-year-old sister. Timmy was a victim. A small, fragile, orphaned child left alone in this cruel world. And as I looked at Timmy, this precious child, and laughed at his sweet, innocent joke, I realized something—something that tore my heart out, that ripped at my guts. I realized that we could give Timmy food, a home, an education—even find someone he could grow to love. But we could never fix Timmy. We could never make him whole. We could never bring back his mother or his father. Or his sister. Or his innocence. Timmy is a victim." He paused for a moment. "Ladies and gentlemen, the sad truth is that there are hundreds of little Timmys out there. Maybe thousands of little Timmys."

Montgomery stopped and closed his eyes.

"Please excuse...I seem to be...I can't—"

Montgomery suddenly grimaced and leaned forward into the lectern. He rose sharply upright and clutched his chest hard with both fists. He stumbled a few steps backward, his face revealing his agony. For a brief moment, he stood still as a statue, frozen and motionless, but then he fell back, crumpling in a heap onto the floor.

⅄

Harper's phone rang, and he picked it up.

"It's Jane," she said.

"Yes, Jane," he said. "Are we ready?"

"We are. I walked by the ballroom a minute ago and glanced inside. Montgomery was at the podium ready to start, so I'm sure he has by now. The dinner guests are all there. From what I could see, the ballroom is packed."

Harper noticed the calmness of her voice. She was the right person to help him.

"What's the security like?" he asked.

"I saw two men in front and one Tulsa uniform in the hallway. Of course, there may be some in the back or undercover I can't see."

"There are two cops outside in the circle drive," Harper said, "but none on the roofs. I expected some security, but this isn't the Capitol or the White House. It's a hotel and a public place. This level of security is acceptable to me."

"Just as you said it would be."

"I think it's time we began," he said.

Harper set his cell phone on the floor of the Ford and reached for the first transmitter. A small red light lit up on the front when he turned it on. He opened the back of the van a couple of inches. The Honda Accord sat in his direct line of sight in the lot near the front of the hotel. He slid the tip of the antenna through the opening of the van's door until it protruded a few inches beyond the doorway. The tip was pointed directly at the Honda. He picked up the cell phone and held it to his ear.

"Jane," he said, "I'm ready. Are you?"

"Yes, Sam," she said. "I'm ready."

Harper set the phone back down. He held out the transmitter and placed his thumb lightly over the button. Harper felt the pressure of his thumb on the plastic, the smooth surface of the transmitter. He was ready, the first of the two bombs, the warning no one could ignore. Montgomery deserved this. Harper was tempted to push down the button and hear the blast. He wanted to see the Honda explode, erupting in flames and smoke, but his warning was first.

Harper set the transmitter down and picked up the throwaway phone. He entered the top number on the paper and pressed the call button.

The phone rang four times before a female voice answered. "Federal Bureau of Investigation, Tulsa office. How may I direct your call?"

Before he could answer, Jane's voice came from his phone on the van's floor. "Please, Sam. Pick up the phone!"

"Hello? This is the Federal Bureau of Investigation. Is anyone there?"

"Wait, Sam," Jane said. "Please!"

Harper hung up with the FBI. He reached down and picked up his cell phone.

"What is it, Jane?"

"You need to wait, Sam. Something is happening here. There's a terrible commotion."

"What is it?"

"People are running out of the ballroom—a lot of people. Something is going on, Sam, and I can't tell what, but it's something major."

He could hear the tension in her voice. "Jane," he said softly, "you know I trust you. What do you suggest we do?"

She took a breath and let it out slowly. "Let me listen a moment."

Harper picked up the binoculars. He scanned the front of the hotel. Nothing had changed.

After a few seconds, Jane was back on the line. "It's the attorney general."

"What, Jane? What about the attorney general?"

"They're saying…they're saying he has collapsed. He could be dead."

Harper again scanned the front of the hotel. This time, a number of people were running outside, and the police were trying to clear the circle drive of cars. Harper slid in the antenna of the transmitter and turned it off.

"Okay, Jane. You stay there and call me back if anything changes."

"Okay, Sam," she said. "I will."

Harper hung up the cell phone. *Damn it*, he thought. *Damn it to hell! What's Montgomery trying to pull?*

This confusion, whatever was causing it, was spoiling his plans. He had Montgomery. Everything was set. Montgomery was his!

He'd know soon enough if Montgomery was dead or alive. How could he be dead? God couldn't allow him to die now. And if Montgomery was alive, as Harper trusted God he would be, he would wait patiently for him, for as long as it took, for as long as it was necessary.

For he was a patient man.

Montgomery's face was gray-blue. A fine cold sweat covered his body. Within seconds of his fall, Jennifer was at his side, dashing from the back of the ballroom before anyone else had reacted.

"What's wrong, sir?" she asked as she quickly loosened his tie and collar.

"I think it's my heart. I feel like an elephant is standing on my chest." He pushed himself up with his arms, attempting to sit.

"Just don't move," Jennifer said. She knelt beside him and slipped her arm under his head. "We'll get some help."

A crowd was gathering around them. Jennifer looked up and saw Simmons standing over them.

"Call 911!" she shouted at Simmons. "We need an ambulance immediately! And move them back!" She waved her hand at the crowd. "Give us some room."

Simmons and Asher stretched out their arms and urged the crowd back.

"I think I'll be fine," Montgomery said. "It's probably indigestion."

"I don't think so," Jennifer whispered in his ear. "You need to go to the hospital."

"I've never had a heart problem."

"Please, sir."

"Okay, okay," he said. "You win."

"Thank you, sir."

"The ambulance shouldn't take long," Simmons said over his shoulder. "Saint Luke's Hospital is just across the street."

"Call their emergency room," Jennifer ordered. "Tell them the attorney general of the United States is having chest pain and is coming now! Tell them we need the chief of cardiology in the emergency room immediately!"

"Yes, ma'am. We'll take care of it. I'll call the emergency room."

Jennifer felt the crowd closing in. "Get them back! The attorney general needs some air!"

Two paramedics pushing a stretcher entered the ballroom at the back, and the crowd parted to allow them to reach Montgomery. While the younger of the two paramedics moved the stretcher into position, the older one knelt and leaned in toward Montgomery.

"What have we got here?" the older paramedic asked.

"This is Attorney General Ronald Montgomery," Jennifer said. "Mr. Montgomery just collapsed while giving his speech."

Montgomery looked terrible—pale, sweating profusely, obviously in pain.

"It's my chest," Montgomery said. "The pain is crushing me." Montgomery started to sit up again. "But I think there's no need for a stretcher. I can ride in a wheelchair."

"Yes, sir," the paramedic said as he gently pushed Montgomery back down. "We'd better be safe and use the stretcher."

He nodded to the younger paramedic, who quickly began attaching electrodes for a cardiac monitor and applying an oxygen mask to Montgomery's face. After turning on a portable oxygen tank, he pulled up Montgomery's sleeve to insert an IV line.

"Have you ever had any heart issues?" the older paramedic asked.

"No, sir."

The crowd noise had increased, and the paramedic leaned close to hear Montgomery.

"On any meds?" he said, raising his voice.

"No, sir."

"Good. We'll have you at the emergency room shortly."

"They should be waiting for him," Jennifer said to the paramedics. "We called the hospital."

Both paramedics nodded as they loaded Montgomery on the stretcher and strapped him down. Asher and Simmons separated the crowd as the paramedics pushed Montgomery toward the exit. Several people were holding cell phones, videoing Montgomery as they passed. Simmons roughly pushed them back.

"Have some decency!" Jennifer snapped as she moved alongside the stretcher, trying to block their view of Montgomery.

Outside the entrance, the ambulance was waiting in the circle drive with its lights flashing. Two police cruisers had also arrived, and the officers were directing traffic to keep the crowd away. Reporters attending the conference had already called their news departments, and the TV news vans parked near the ambulance had their video cameras rolling. The paramedics loaded Montgomery into the ambulance, and Simmons and Asher climbed in. The ambulance's siren let out a low-pitched whine that quickly cranked up to full volume. Jennifer approached the ambulance, ready to join the two agents.

One of the paramedics standing at the back cupped his hands and leaned to Jennifer. "The emergency room is on standby for him," he shouted. "You can drive over and park—"

"No way," she yelled back. "I'm riding with you."

"It's against our policy—"

"He's the attorney general," she said forcefully, pushing past him to take a seat. "I'm not leaving him. You got that?"

"Yes, ma'am."

"Ms. McLaughlin," Asher yelled over the siren, "there's not enough room."

"Then *you* get off. I'm going."

Jennifer glared at Simmons. He shrugged and motioned for Asher to get out. The second paramedic climbed in and pulled the two back doors shut. The first paramedic opened the cab door and started the engine. The ambulance began moving slowly as it swung around the circle drive, but was running "hot," with siren blaring and lights flashing, by the end of the hotel driveway.

"The hospital is just across the street," the driver said. "We'll be there shortly."

As they turned south onto Sheridan Road, the traffic pulled over and stopped. Jennifer peered out the window at the ten-story hospital they were approaching. The sun behind them to the west lit up the building, reflecting bright off the light-gray exterior. Jennifer hoped the staff at the hospital was ready for them.

Suddenly, the alarm on Montgomery's heart monitor screeched out a warning.

The paramedic looked up at the monitor. "He's in V-fib!" he shouted.

"Dammit!" the driver said. "Check his pulse."

The paramedic felt the carotids. "No, nothing here."

"Then shock him."

He reached up to charge the defibrillator. "It's set at two hundred."

"What the hell are you doing?" Jennifer asked sharply.

"We're shocking him, lady. He's having a serious irregular heart rhythm." The paramedic pressed the paddles against Montgomery's chest. "Everyone stay back! Don't touch the bed." He glanced around before pushing the buttons.

Montgomery's body jerked upward, his back muscles in spasm from the electrical jolt. After a brief moment, he fell limp. All eyes turned to the monitor.

"He's still in V-fib. I'll increase to 360."

"Do I need to pull over and help?"

"Is he all right?" Jennifer asked. "Is he going to make it?"

"No, keep going," the paramedic called up to the driver, ignoring Jennifer, "but we should let the emergency room know that we're coming in, in a full code."

"Our ETA's only a minute or two."

The paramedic in the back glanced at the defibrillator. "It's ready. I'll hit him again."

He positioned the paddles.

"Clear!" he yelled.

The paramedic shocked Montgomery again. His back arched off the bed and went limp. Montgomery's face was turning a bluish color.

"I'm going to bag him at 100 percent oxygen until we get to Saint Luke's. We'll be there before I can get him tubed. Should I start the thumper?"

"No, start manual compressions. We're almost there."

The paramedic began pushing on his chest.

"I know CPR."

"Lady, you just sit there and be quiet," the paramedic snapped. "You're along for the ride, remember?"

"ETA in one minute," the driver yelled back. "I've called the ER."

"Hold on, you bastard," the paramedic said, pushing hard on his chest. "Don't die on us now."

⅄

Paula finished entering her note and logged off the computer. She swung her chair around and watched as an orderly pushed a stretcher with her asthma patient down the hall to transport him to a room upstairs. She would see him again on her morning rounds.

She had called Matt a few minutes earlier and apologized for messing up dinner plans twice in the past three days. He was still at the ATF office doing paper work himself and said he understood. He always seemed to understand, which was the problem. Paula suggested they postpone, but he persuaded her to go. They agreed to meet at eight.

Paula looked up as Hunt walked up beside her.

"The ambulance is bringing in a respiratory arrest," he said. "Looks like your unassigned patient is on its way."

"At least the timing is good. Unlike Elvis, I haven't left the building."

Hunt laughed. "Must be your lucky day."

"Dr. Hunt," a nurse called out from across the desk. She was holding up a red phone. "EMT is calling. That patient is in V-fib. They're coding him now. He's some governmental official. Attorney general or something. He'll be here any minute."

"Hell of a deal," Hunt said. He turned back to Paula. "Looks like I could use your help."

"I'm not going anywhere."

The emergency room doors burst open, and two orderlies rushed in with the stretcher. The two paramedics continued CPR, with one pumping on Montgomery's chest and the other holding the Ambu bag over his mouth to deliver oxygen.

As the ER staff directed the paramedics to the nearest cardiac room, cleared of a patient moments earlier, Paula and Hunt both stood to make their way to their new arrival. A man in a dark suit crossed in front of them to position himself beside the door outside in the hallway, and Paula was sure he was some sort of federal agent there to guard the attorney general. Paula followed Hunt into the room as six or eight of the staff began to gather around Montgomery to assist. Hunt moved to the foot of the bed, and Paula positioned herself at the head of the stretcher, preparing an endotracheal tube while a respiratory tech set up the ventilator next to her. She leaned over and listened to Montgomery's lungs. The paramedic continued the chest compressions until a male nurse pushed him aside and took over. Paula quickly intubated Montgomery and connected the tubing to a ventilator. The EKG technician began a tracing and placed defibrillator pads on his chest.

"Breath sounds are bilateral," Paula said, "with rales halfway up. He's in pulmonary edema."

A nurse took his blood pressure. "Pressure's seventy over fifty."

"Oxygen saturation 60 percent," the respiratory tech said after clipping a gray plastic gauge on Montgomery's finger.

"Is he on 100 percent O_2?" Hunt asked.

"Yes, sir."

"We need to get him out of V-fib," Hunt said. "How many times did you shock him?"

"Twice," the paramedic said.

"Give him amiodarone 300 milligrams IV bolus now. Also, I want furosemide 160 milligrams IV push and morphine 4 milligrams."

"Are you a cardiologist?" Jennifer asked. She was standing at the foot of the bed.

"Who are you?" Hunt asked.

"I'm the attorney general's executive assistant."

"Sorry, ma'am, you'll have to leave," he said firmly, pointing toward the hallway.

"I'm not going—"

"Oh, yes, you are," he interrupted. "Secretaries aren't allowed."

"I insist—"

"*I* insist. We'll call security, ma'am, if that's what you want."

A nurse lightly grasped her arm. Jennifer shook loose from the nurse's grip but then reluctantly followed the nurse outside, demanding to speak with the hospital administrator.

"Okay, let's hit him at 360," Hunt said. Hunt took the paddles from one of the nurses. He positioned the paddles on Montgomery's chest. "Clear," he yelled and then waited a second for the staff to move away before triggering the defibrillator. Montgomery's back arched upward then fell limp. The monitor's previous erratic pattern changed to a steady beeping. The electric discharge had converted Montgomery's heart to a normal sinus rhythm.

"He's got a pulse," Paula said, gently touching his right carotid artery.

"Good," Hunt said. He turned to a nurse. "Let's get some lytes, blood gases, a CBC, cardiac enzymes, and a chest X-ray. Start an amiodarone drip at 1 milligram per minute."

Paula turned to the two paramedics. "Now, what's his story?"

"He's the attorney general," one the paramedics said. "I think of the United States."

"You don't say?" Hunt said.

"He was giving a speech at the Merrimac," the paramedic continued. "Apparently he was fine. During the speech he clutched his chest and fell over. When we arrived four minutes later, he was complaining of chest pain and nausea. He was stable at the scene but went into V-fib in the unit."

"History of heart disease?" Paula asked.

"No. In fact, he specifically told us he had no heart issues."

"Smoker? Diabetic? High blood pressure?"

"No, don't think so. He doesn't take any meds."

Dr. Terrance England pushed the curtain aside as he entered. "What's up, guys?" England was around sixty, short and stocky, his thick hair graying at the sides. He wore a starched white lab coat cut to below his knees. The chief of cardiology at Saint Luke's for eleven years, he was capable and cool in a crisis. Paula was glad he was there. He nodded at her.

"It's Ronald Montgomery, the attorney general," Hunt said.

"That's what I heard."

"Looks like an MI," Paula said, "and now he's in cardiogenic shock." Paula briefly updated him as England began his exam.

The EKG tech picked the cardiogram off the machine and held it up for England to review.

"ST elevation in the inferior leads," he said, pointing. "He's having an inferior infarct."

Hunt looked over England's shoulder. "ST segment is four to five millimeters. Looks big."

"What's his pressure?" England asked.

"Sixty over forty," a nurse said. "Still low and going down."

"Okay," England said to the nurse, "give him another 160 of furosemide and start a dopamine drip." He turned to the two doctors. "He's crashing. I think he needs a balloon pump."

"We called the cath lab," Hunt said. "One crew's in, but Dr. Reynolds is doing an angioplasty. The second crew will take forty-five minutes to come from home. Dr. Reynolds said he'll be through in thirty."

England turned back to the nurse. "Okay, then," England said, "give tPA 15 milligrams IV over two minutes and then 50 milligrams over thirty minutes. Start it now! Call the cath lab to bring in the backup crew from home if they haven't already, and tell Reynolds to get the hell out of my room!"

"You want the attorney general to stay here?" Hunt asked.

"No, I prefer not in the ER. Let's go directly to the cath lab."

"No one's there."

"Then can we take him to the ICU? It's closer."

"It's your call."

"He should be in the unit, particularly if there is any delay."

The staff quickly prepared Montgomery for transport. After strapping him in, two orderlies guided the stretcher out of the room and started down the hallway. Three nurses strained to keep up while carrying or pushing various pieces of equipment. England walked beside the stretcher, writing notes on a clipboard, oblivious to the staff's near panic. Paula stayed a pace or two behind the entourage.

The attorney general of the United State of America, Ronald Montgomery, was her patient, and he was deathly ill. This person was in all the newspapers and on TV, his face famous, and it seemed particularly odd that he was actually here, just another unassigned patient. But attorney general or not, national celebrity or not, his situation was extremely serious. And it looked like she might be up all night.

⅄

Matt Nicholson shut down his computer and started for the door.

"Meeting your girlfriend for dinner?" Stan Gill asked.

"Yeah," Matt said, smiling. "Fortunately."

Stan's desk was across the room from Matt's, in the office they shared as partners for two years. Stan was eight years younger than Matt and had served with the ATF for five years to Matt's twelve. The two were as different as they were alike. Matt's athletic, six-foot frame towered over Stan's shorter, somewhat rounded body. Stan's thick beard and long hair, T-shirt, and blue jeans, undercover requirements, contrasted with Matt's short brown hair, chinos, and polo shirt. Yet both were meticulous, relentless, and dependable, and they matched perfectly as partners. They had saved each other's butts more times than they cared to remember.

"The doctor?" Stan said. "If you marry her, you can retire on easy street."

"She's a pulmonologist," Matt said, laughing. "Not a neurosurgeon."

"A pulmono…a what?"

"Pulmonologist. A lung doctor."

"So she's broke? I should be so broke."

"I'm going to dinner. If I keep looking at you, I may lose my appetite."

"That ain't no gastric juices you got flowing."

Matt laughed. Matt put his hand on the door to leave but then stopped and turned back to Stan. "Listen," Matt said, turning serious. "I haven't heard from Jake. If Jake calls, page me."

"Hasn't he checked in?"

"No, and it worries me."

"He's with that militia group?"

"Yeah, and getting pretty close. His last contact was a week ago. He thought they were preparing to go."

"Is Reese on your ass about it?"

Jeffrey Reese was the resident agent in charge, their boss, and Matt had been careful to update Reese on every single aspect of this case. So far, nothing was going as Matt had planned, and it was making him nervous. Reese was unhappy Jake was still out there, still alone, not checking in. The agency had a major weapons and drug bust planned for two weeks, a four-month effort with local authorities, and Reese wanted every agent immediately available. Jake being out undercover so long was a sore spot for Reese, and Matt knew sooner or later he'd catch hell for it from Reese.

"I updated Reese," Matt said, answering his partner's question.

"So Jake thinks it's an abortion clinic this time?"

"That's what he said."

"If Jake doesn't call, will you go find him and bring him in?"

"No, not yet. He should be safe. At least we think he should be. He'll call...soon...I hope. Jake said he's being careful—they're extremely paranoid."

"He'll call. Go have dinner. I'll page you."

"I hope you do."

Chapter 6

Three nurses, two orderlies, and a respiratory tech from the ER hustled Montgomery into room 4 of the intensive care unit. England was barking orders, pointing to the staff as he assigned duties. They quickly replaced Montgomery's clothes with a hospital gown, attached electrodes to his chest, started a second IV, and inserted a catheter into his bladder.

Several other nurses working in the unit wandered to the doorway to watch the action. Paula stood at the foot of the bed and tried to stay out of the way. Though Montgomery was in respiratory failure, the main issue was cardiac. It was England's show. The tension was obvious. The patient was trying to die.

"What's his pressure now?" England asked.

"Terrible," Toni said. "Forty systolic."

"Double the dopamine in his IV." England turned to the head nurse, Sally Carpenter. "Call the cath lab. I want the lab up and running in five minutes, even if Reynolds has to finish his case by himself. I'm going to insert a balloon pump and squirt his arteries. How far out are we?"

"It's eight fifteen," Sally said. "He went down about forty-five minutes ago. The ER just called, and his first CPK is over a thousand."

"I was afraid of that," England said. "This is a big infarction, so we need to get moving. Tell the cath lab we gave the first dose of tPA in the ER. Also, notify cardiovascular surgery. I want them on standby."

Sally nodded and left.

"I'm having trouble getting any pressure now, Dr. England," Toni said.

"Okay, that does it. Let's go!"

"Dr. England," Jennifer McLaughlin spoke up. She was standing just outside the room. "I'm the attorney general's executive assistant. What's his condition?"

"Are you a family member?" England asked, approaching the doorway.

"No, but—"

"He's had a heart attack. He's in shock. He's dying, and we are trying to save his life. Anything else?"

"I have a couple of questions. I want to call the president and give him an update."

"His blood pressure is zero. Every second that I stand here and talk to you, he's losing brain and kidney cells. Any other questions?"

"No, sir." Jennifer moved aside.

"Toni," England said, turning abruptly, "tell the cath lab we're on our way. I want a balloon in his aorta in three minutes."

The small crowd of staff outside the room stood back. Two orderlies pushed the stretcher out of the room and raced the patient down the hallway.

Paula followed England out.

"We'll be in the cath lab," England said to her, "for an hour or so—at least."

"I'm happy to stay and help."

"I'll call you if I need you," he said over his shoulder as he turned to chase the stretcher down the hallway.

Paula watched England and company disappear around the corner. He was right. There wasn't much more she could do.

"He'll be fine," the hospital administrator said to Paula.

The administrator, Howard Parrish, had rushed from home to the emergency department at Jennifer McLaughlin's demand and then followed Jennifer up to the unit. He was a peculiar, thin-necked man of fifty with thick horn-rimmed glasses and an oversized suit covering his slight frame. At the helm of the hospital for a mere two months, his sole purpose was to be a benign replacement after the cost-slashing marauder who had preceded him.

From what Paula had seen, the crisis of a national dignitary was out of his league. "I've assured Ms. McLaughlin that he's in the best of hands."

"Yes," Paula said, turning to Jennifer, "Dr. England is an excellent doctor."

"Mr. Parrish," Jennifer said, ignoring Paula, "I want your security guards available under the command of the attorney general's FBI detail." She pointed to the two agents. "I want to set up an office nearby with a door that locks. I want a desk, a private phone, and two fax machines. And I want possession of all his personal effects."

"Yes, ma'am. I'll see to it." Parrish hurried off.

She turned to Paula. "Are you a nurse?"

"No, I'm a doctor."

"Oh, I'm sorry."

"I'm Dr. Paula Barrett." She reached out her hand. "I'll be Mr. Montgomery's attending physician."

Jennifer shook hands. "I'm Jennifer McLaughlin, the attorney general's executive assistant."

"Does he have any family?"

"His only living relative is his son, Jeff. He's working at the US embassy in China." She paused briefly. "May I ask you...what is an aortic balloon?"

"Of course. It's actually called intra-aortic balloon counterpulsation. Dr. England will insert a tube, which can be inflated like a balloon, in his groin artery and slide it up into the aorta. When it inflates, it creates back pressure which pushes blood into his coronary arteries. The increased blood flow will help his heart."

"And teepee? I'm not sure what he said."

"It's tPA, a thrombolytic. It lyses, that is, it breaks up a clot if that's the cause of the blockage in his coronary artery."

"Oh, I see." Jennifer quickly looked away.

Paula could see the tears forming.

"Tell me honestly, will he make it?"

"It's hard to know," Paula answered softly. "It looks pretty serious."

Howard Parrish returned to inform Jennifer that the staff was clearing a room for her near the waiting room at the end of the hallway. He assured her the phone would be private, and the faxes would be installed shortly. He scurried away to assist.

"I appreciate your explanation, Doctor. May I call you Paula?"

"Sure you can. I hope he does okay."

"Me, too," Jennifer said. She glanced at her cell phone and began walking down the hall. "I'd better call the president." She was talking mostly to herself.

As Paula watched her go, her pager started beeping. It was Matt. She dialed his number. It only rang once. "Hi, Matt," she said when he answered.

"So how's your evening going?"

"It's been pretty busy."

"Sorry to hear that. Hope it gets better."

"Thanks. Me, too."

"I sure had a great time last night. I was thinking maybe we could repeat."

"I can't. I've just admitted two patients to the intensive care unit. It's really crazy."

"I'm sorry. It doesn't have to be dinner. How about some dessert?"

"Sorry, Matt. Tonight's really impossible. I wish I could."

"That's cool. Hey, if you can, give me a call when you get home. I'll be up."

"I'll try."

"Great. Talk to you later."

Paula hoped Matt understood. Missing dinner was the last thing she wanted, but she wasn't done with her work at the hospital. She still needed to make rounds, delayed by the two admissions, on a couple of patients up on the floor. It would likely take at least another hour. Dessert was out of the question. Sleep was beginning to look doubtful.

Paula pulled out her phone to check the time. Before she left the intensive care, she decided to check in on Reverend Pettigrew and listen to his lungs. He appeared more alert and was beginning to fight the nasotracheal tube in his throat. His lungs sounded slightly better, but he continued to have prominent rales and expiratory rhonchi at both bases, evidence of severe pneumonia. Despite the ventilator and Toni's frequent suctioning, he had improved less than she had hoped. Still, it seemed reasonable to consider weaning him off the ventilator in the morning. Nurse Carpenter would be happier. Yet if she altered her medical practice every time a nurse complained, she wouldn't be much of a doctor.

Every single day in the current medical environment, it seemed to Paula, someone was trying to tell her how to practice medicine—an insurance company, the hospital case managers, the government, and even the nurses. Everyone thought they knew what to do—that was the easier part—but no one wanted to take the responsibility. That was always completely on the doctor. She should discharge patients from the hospital quicker, order fewer tests, prescribe generic meds, and even avoid admitting the patient to the hospital in the first place. But absolutely don't make *any* mistakes. Angry patients made for happy lawyers. Challenge the doctor's decisions again and again, but make him or her totally responsible for the outcome, especially the bad outcomes. It was a no-win.

If Pettigrew was better by morning, she'd consider weaning him, but not because the ICU was full, or because his length of stay was too long based on some computerized statistic, or because some nurse was trying to boss her around. It'd be because she was the doctor and would decide what was best.

Paula slipped the stethoscope out of her ears. She didn't even have time for a quick dessert, but she knew Matt would likely forgive her. It wasn't the first time.

The intensive care unit had grown quiet, and she was the only doctor. As she started down the hallway to leave, her pager started beeping. It was Hunt in the ED. Not what she would have wanted.

When she dialed the extension, a female voice answered. "Saint Luke's emergency department."

Paula could hear the usual commotion behind the receptionist. "This is Dr. Barrett. Dr. Hunt paged me."

"Just a moment."

As Paula waited for Hunt, the elevator music played in the background.

"Dr. Barrett?"

"What have you got?"

"One of yours. A Jerry Cook, fifty-seven-year-old male with COPD."

"Yeah, I know him."

"Sorry, he's DOA."

"Oh, goodness. What happened?"

"Apparently his brother was with him. The patient slumped over in his chair, and the brother called 911. They coded him on arrival at the home. The paramedic said it was really too late when they started, but they hated not to try. We stopped it when he got here."

"I just saw him yesterday. We talked about hospice."

Paula recalled his office visit. He had seemed fine but talked about his final wishes, maybe a premonition or something. *How odd,* she thought, *dead a few hours later.*

"Then he was in bad shape?" Hunt asked.

"In and out of the hospital. He was tired of it."

"Then I'm glad we didn't intubate. He was really too far gone anyway."

"He wouldn't have wanted it."

"I can pronounce him. I'm down here…unless you want to."

"That's okay," Paula said. "I'll do it."

Pronouncing a deceased patient wasn't one of her favorite tasks, and it always included talking to the family. If she didn't do it, though, she would always feel a little guilty.

"I ran the code. No family here. I really don't mind."

"His brother left?"

"Guess so. That's what the nurse said."

Hunt was giving her an out. "That's fine," she said. "I appreciate it."

"You'll sign the death certificate?"

"Sure."

"Have a good night."

"You, too."

Paula hung up. She saw Jerry's face as he was the day before at the office. She never would have dreamed he'd be gone so soon. Life had its odd twists. Jerry was a patient she had seen many times in the office and several times in the hospital. For most of his visits, he was alone. They talked in snippets about his life—a musician on the road, drummer in a rock band with a couple of record albums, a stint in the navy, never married, parents long dead. He especially hated lawyers and insurance companies. That much they had in common. Over time she had gotten to know him and like him, and now he was gone.

Few professions had such constant reminders of the fragility of life.

She'd need to remember to send his brother a card.

Paula picked up her purse. She still had a lot of work to do, and it was time to get started.

The parsonage was cooled by a single window unit in the bedroom. A floor fan in the doorway blew some of the colder air into the living room. It made it almost tolerable. Harper picked up his Bible. Jane was sitting at the kitchen table waiting with her Bible open in front of her. Harper sat down across from her.

"Let's pray," Harper said.

Both bowed their heads.

"Heavenly Father," he said, "Almighty God, Creator of all things, we ask that you prepare our minds and bodies to do your will. Help us understand your word, in Jesus' name we pray. Amen."

"Amen," Jane said.

"Where were we?" Harper asked.

"First Chronicles 13:9."

"Would you read it?"

"Certainly, Sam. 'And when they came unto the threshing floor of Chidon, Uzza put forth his hand to hold the ark; for the oxen stumbled. And the anger of the Lord was kindled against Uzza, and he smote him, because he put his hand to the ark: and there he died before God.'"

"Behold the power of God," Harper said.

"He killed the Israelite for steadying the ark?"

"Yes, woman. He was defiling God's perfection."

"A big penalty. In today's world, it would seem such a minor infraction."

"God's ways are clear, even now. His anger is upon our nation, and his servants have been called to carry out his will."

"He is a God of justice."

"So it is time for us to prepare ourselves."

"Yes, Sam. I am ready."

Harper gently closed his Bible. "I'm planning to stay up for a while and study. You should go to bed."

"Okay, Sam. I will be waiting for you."

"I'm not sure how long I'll be."

"That's fine. Awaken me."

Jane stood to leave. She closed her Bible and left for the bedroom. Harper would finish reading the rest of the chapter and spend several minutes meditating. He wanted to better understand this scripture, though he thought the meaning was obvious. He must follow God's will exactly. Montgomery was vile and unclean, and God would smite him for his impurity.

Montgomery had escaped his fate tonight, and Harper was disappointed. The attorney general's sudden collapse and transportation to the hospital had upset his plans. After the commotion subsided, Harper had locked the Ford at Saint Luke's and walked across the street to the hotel. He and Jane had driven the Accord and the panel van back to the compound, hiding the two vehicles for now in the large barn. It was all a big disruption. Montgomery should be his hostage at this moment. He had missed a golden opportunity.

Harper bowed and prayed. *Montgomery is the enemy of God*, Harper thought, *deserving God's wrath*. "'And there he died before God.'"

Harper was deep in prayer when he heard Jane's voice calling out from the bedroom.

"Sam, you need to watch this," she said. She was watching the evening news on a portable television.

"What is it?" Harper asked, stepping into the doorway.

"Montgomery had a heart attack and is in an intensive care unit at Saint Luke's."

Harper sat on the side of the bed and listened as a reporter rattled on about Montgomery's past achievements. "Have they listed his condition yet?"

"Critical. They're not sure how bad. Several local news stations have reporters at the emergency room, but the hospital officials aren't commenting. The president issued a statement."

"Then he must be in bad shape." Harper watched quietly as the reporter read the president's statement. "He's the president's henchman," Harper said, "and I hope he rots in hell." Harper stood and began pacing back and forth in the small bedroom. "We almost had him, and now he's going to die."

"He's the enemy of God, and I'll pray he suffers a painful death."

Harper stopped pacing. "Yes, you're right," he said, turning to Jane. "May God destroy his enemies, and may Montgomery die a slow and agonizing death."

⅄

It was almost ten o'clock in the evening before Paula unlocked the front door to her condo and was greeted by her two cats. A fat yellow tabby named Bobcat purred and rubbed her ankles, more a display of the cat's hunger than of his love. Tomboy, a gray Persian, waved a paw at Paula from her perch on the bookshelf, the most emotion the female cat could muster. Both had wandered into the courtyard of her apartment when she had lived in Oklahoma City. After making the mistake of feeding them twice, they had refused to leave. They all had benefited. She fed them, and they had kept her company—a small-town Tahlequah girl living in her first big city.

She had always loved strays. As a child, her adoptive mother chided her about her assortment of animals, all strays: dogs, cats, birds, rabbits, lizards, and once an injured opossum that she nursed—no, she told her mother, she was *doctoring* it—back to health. She was nine years old. Their small house in Tahlequah resembled a makeshift zoo, housing her odd menagerie. Good thing she was an only child.

Paula's adoptive parents couldn't have children of their own and adopted Paula as a baby. They told her she was a full-blooded Cherokee, so she knew both of her biologic parents had to be full-blooded, which wasn't particularly uncommon in Tahlequah, Oklahoma. The Cherokee Nation, which had authority over such matters, had insisted she be adopted into a Cherokee family, and since both of her adoptive parents were full-blooded, they perfectly met the requirements.

The only information Paula had about her birth mom was that she was sixteen and unmarried when she had her. Paula often thought about her birth mom, wondering what she looked like and where she lived. When Paula was a child, she'd occasionally see a woman in Tahlequah whom Paula thought she resembled, and she wondered if it was her mother. How could someone ask that? Hey, lady, are you my mother? She supposed every adopted child had such thoughts.

When she was a teenager, Paula had even more difficulty understanding how a mother could give up her baby. How could a woman give away her flesh and blood? How could she never again see the child that had grown inside her?

Paula had read once in medical school that most all adopted children have some degree of attachment disorder—difficulty developing close relationships, afraid of being abandoned. She hated to think it might apply to her, taking the form of intense dedication to work rather than to family or friends...or Matt.

Paula walked into the kitchen and opened two cans of a tuna mix as both cats scurried under her feet. Bobcat and Tomboy were fat and happy, luckier than her houseplants. At least she remembered to feed the cats. All her plants died—a slow, waterless death. Then she'd buy new ones. If she practiced medicine the same way she did horticulture, she'd be deadly.

Paula left the cats to enjoy their dinner. In her bathroom she unwound her braids and gently shook her head, causing her thick brown hair to fall to her waist. She washed off her makeup, what little she wore, and slipped into a robe, ready to plop on the couch and turn on the television, hoping to catch some news on the attorney general. He probably wouldn't make it through the night, his condition so critical. What a shame.

She thought about calling the nurses in the ICU for an update, but they probably had their hands full. They'd page her if they needed her.

Matt had asked her to call, but all she wanted was to go to bed, still feeling some fatigue from her weekend on call. And she had no guarantee, with Montgomery so critical, that she'd get any sleep. She sent Matt a quick text with her apologies. Within a second he answered. He understood. Paula hoped so.

When they had been at dinner on Monday, Matt had kept the conversation light, and she had appreciated it. Matt was good to her, yet at times she felt herself pulling away. She thought his intentions were serious, maybe even marriage. But at thirty-three, single, starting a new practice, and paying off seventy thousand dollars in school loans, Paula decided marriage wasn't in her immediate plans.

And she hated that Matt's work was completely secret. He never uttered a word about any case or project, but she suspected his job was dangerous, something to do with drugs, guns, or bombs—she could only guess the details. She had never once touched a gun, much less shot one, and to think Matt's whole life was about such things made her wonder. She had a good friend from high school whose husband was in the military, and the constant worry took its toll.

It was difficult for her to make the emotional investment right now. She was in too much debt and working too hard. Her parents thought she was frugal to a fault. No vacations. Few new clothes. A cheap condo near the hospital—she'd move to a bigger place when the loans were paid. No social life. Few friends outside of medicine. She was sick of feeling poor, scraping by on every penny. For goodness' sake, she was a doctor! Her adoptive parents weren't especially rich, yet growing up, she felt she had everything she needed. Her dad taught math at an elementary school. Her mother stayed at home mostly and played the piano part time at their Methodist church. Only when Paula was in medical school did she realize her dad struggled financially on her account. He told her he found a second job as a carpenter because he enjoyed working with wood. She now knew better.

She'd be out of debt in a few years. Then she could get the life she was missing.

Bobcat curled up in her lap. Paula could hear and feel the soft purr of the cat's contentment. He pushed his spine back up against her hand as she gently stroked him. Her cats were her only real responsibility, and they didn't expect much, nor did they give much in return.

The ten o'clock news blared on the television, and Montgomery was the lead story. The newscaster didn't say he had died, so England's balloon must be working—for now, at least.

A story about some political scandal came on next. She turned off the television, brushed her teeth, and slid into bed. The nurses hadn't called her all evening, so maybe they wouldn't.

It wasn't three o'clock in the morning yet, either.

⚓

The cell phone startled Matt awake. He rolled over and glanced at the clock. Two-fifteen! *What the crap?* He picked up his phone and answered.

"What is it?" Matt said it gruffly and meant it. He hated being awakened from a sound sleep, and every time he was, it'd better be for a good reason.

"It's Stan."

Matt sat up. Stan never called unless it was important.

"What's up?"

"Weapons bust. East Tulsa. Bunch of arrests. They need us."

Stan was a man of few words.

"Give me thirty minutes. Where do you want to meet?"

"Make it ten. I'm in your driveway."

Of course he was. "Be out in a second."

Matt hung up the phone. He took less than ten minutes to toss some water on his face and get dressed.

Stan's car sat in the driveway, running. The car, a ten-year-old Ford, was battered and bruised, with hail damage unrepaired, major dents, and peeling paint. The inside was worse. Matt had to push trash to one side—hamburger wrappers, coffee cups, and God knew what else—to find room for his feet. Stan claimed his car had to look like crap because, like him, it was undercover. Matt told Stan both he and his car were full of crap.

"Sara let you out this late?" Matt asked as he buckled up.

"She didn't care as long as I didn't wake up the kids."

Stan was drinking a cup of coffee. He handed Matt a cup.

"Starbucks open?"

"I wish. McDonald's."

"Works for me. What's going down?"

"Got a call from Reese. The boss said that one of our informants called about a cache of weapons being moved. He thinks it's part of the operation."

"That's in two weeks."

"It is, but they singled this one out based on the informant. It may be gone. Have to move fast."

"Risky info. That's trust."

"Reese said no choice. Tulsa PD SWAT on scene. Reese wants us there."

"Where's there?"

"East Tulsa somewhere? I put the address in the GPS."

Stan raced down Eighty-First Street heading for 169th North. The side streets were deserted, everyone in bed. *We should be in bed*, Matt thought.

"Slow down," Matt said. "You'll get us pulled over."

"You worry too much."

It had happened before, Matt remembered. Stan's long hair, undercover look, beat-up old Ford, speeding at three in the morning. What cop wouldn't pull them over? The last time it happened, it took thirty minutes to prove their identification to the patrol officer's satisfaction.

Matt sipped his coffee. The operation Stan had mentioned was the agency's current all-consuming top priority. If this weapons movement was a part of the operation, it seemed good but could be a disaster. If it was a coincidence, it still put everything they'd worked for at risk. The media publicity about big busts was never good for undercover operations. Worse, if it was related, the bad guys would realize that they had an inside info leak that had tipped the good guys.

Stan drove the six miles on the expressway at over ninety miles per hour, but mercifully they were not pulled over. He turned east on Twenty-First Street and slowed down to a more reasonable speed. Stan's police scanner had been mostly quiet the entire time, but they both expected radio silence until it was over.

The GPS took them straight to the location, a small, rundown frame house surrounded by a dozen police cars with two cruisers in the driveway, all with lights flashing. *Obviously*, Matt thought, *the bust is over.*

"Damn," Stan said, "we missed it."

Stan pulled up to the curb a few houses away, and they exited his car to walk to the house. Matt knew most of the local cops, and most knew him, but he pulled out his badge in case he needed it. An older officer, a captain whom Matt had known for years, was one of the uniformed officers standing in the front yard, and Matt approached him first.

"Hey, Thomas," Matt said. "What happened here?"

The officer turned. "Hey, Matt. Hey, Stan. You should have been here."

Matt could see his excitement.

"We fired several rounds of pepper spray through the front window and within five minutes a suspect came out of the front door. He said he was alone, and he was." The officer pointed toward the suspect in the back of one of the patrol cars in the driveway. "We found a pile of stuff—guns, drugs, you name it. You should check it out."

"Thanks," Matt said. "I think we will."

Matt headed for the house with Stan a couple of steps behind. They showed their badges to a patrol officer guarding the front door who waved them past.

Once inside, Matt guessed the whole place was about fifteen hundred square feet total with the living room in front, opening up to a combination eating space and kitchen on the right. A short hallway on the left ran down to two bedrooms. A dozen uniformed officers were standing around in the front of the house. One pointed Matt toward the bedrooms.

Matt could see the house was a mess. Trash covered the living-room floor and nearly buried a broken-down couch in the center of the room. Paper sacks of fast food, opened bags of chips, and dirty paper plates were piled high on a dining table in the kitchen.

"It smells like crap in here," Stan said, making a face.

More specifically, Matt thought, *it smells of feces*. He decided he'd watch where he stepped. He also picked up the scent of marijuana and the slight chemical smell of methamphetamines. Someone had been cooking, growing, or smoking.

The first bedroom down the hallway had a blow-up mattress in the midst of garbage and rotting food. A couple of officers had the unenviable job of sorting through it. The next room was pay dirt. Jeffrey Reese was standing facing away from them, talking to a police captain as Matt and Stan entered.

"Pretty good haul," Matt said.

"Won't complain," Reese responded.

The entire floor was covered. At a glance Matt counted four AK-47s, two high-powered rifles, five shotguns, eight or ten handguns, and an assortment of clips, boxes of ammo, and a couple of Kevlar vests.

"Besides this," Reese said, "we found several bags of marijuana, some meth, maybe heroin, with cash, scales, and drug paraphernalia in the kitchen."

"Great," Matt said. "Stan and I thought you'd wait for us."

Reese shrugged. "It was quick and easy."

"It's a good bust," Stan said.

Matt put on a pair of gloves from a box on the floor and picked up one of the AK-47s. He checked to be sure the weapon was empty and held it up, looking down its sights to the corner of the ceiling. "Glad this is off the streets," Matt said.

"One of too many," Reese said.

Matt scanned the room, checking out the assortment of weapons in more detail. He and Stan would help with the processing, and it would take hours. Stan was right, it was a good bust, but Matt knew that, unfortunately, it was just the tip of the iceberg. He worried it might be all they'd get. The news media would have a field day. It'd make the evening news—twenty-one illegal weapons and drugs worth a fortune confiscated, credited as usual to the Tulsa

Police Department. But every thug in town would lay low, and the agency's operation after months of preparation would be postponed, yet on the street for the most part it would be business as usual.

Another big day fighting the war on crime.

CHAPTER 7

The intensive care unit had continued nonstop since Paula had left the previous evening. The heart monitors beeped, the warning lights flashed, and the overloaded staff rushed about, just as they did twenty-four hours a day.

Her pneumonia patient, Reverend Pettigrew, had pulled out his nasotracheal tube during the night and Toni had called her, as she should. He had breathed well on his own, so the tube stayed out. His condition was improving. Pettigrew's broad smile highlighted the thick wrinkles around his eyes, but his thinning gray hair and the paleness of his skin caused him to appear older than his seventy years.

"My pretty young doctor here has delayed this stubborn old man's meeting with his Maker," he told her. "Yet I am grateful."

"I'm glad to see you're better," Paula said, "but we still have some work to do, Reverend."

"Nonetheless, I'm here because God has provided me with such a good doctor."

"You're too nice."

"I'm just telling the truth."

"Thank you," she said.

She carefully explained his current situation. He was still on two antibiotics until the cultures grew the specific bacteria invading his body, and he would need frequent suctioning and breathing treatments. He'd probably require intensive care for another twenty-four hours. He asked only a few questions.

Paula stepped out to the desk to write her morning note.

"He looks better."

Paula looked up and saw Toni Perkins standing in front of her. She was smiling, a surprising change from their conversation on Sunday. "He does," Paula said. "I was worried."

"His lungs sound clearer. I guess you were right about the furosemide."

"Thanks. It can be confusing."

"I'm sorry I had to call you last night…about the tube."

"You needed to."

"I know, but you're nicer than most at two in the morning."

"What was I thinking?"

They both laughed.

Sally Carpenter and Dr. England walked out of Montgomery's room and began talking in the hallway. Their discussion was intense.

"Was she here all night?" Paula asked Toni, pointing at Sally.

"Never left. She took personal charge of the attorney general's case."

"I'm rounding on him next. How's he doing?"

"Bad. They think he may be brain dead from the lack of oxygen."

"That doesn't sound good."

Dr. England left Sally, and he walked toward them at the doctors' desk, taking a seat a couple of chairs away from Paula. He logged onto the computer and scrolled through several screens as if looking at something important. It didn't escape Paula's notice that he hadn't said a word to her. She and England were both on staff at Saint Luke's and often shared mutual patients in the intensive care unit. England was thirty years her senior, and though a skilled cardiologist, he was a humorless man, often sullen and withdrawn. Paula respected yet didn't particularly like him. She suspected England didn't like anyone.

"So Montgomery is doing poorly?" Paula asked.

England spoke but didn't look away from the computer. "He occluded his right coronary and had a large inferior infarction. I opened him to 50 percent, and the tPA may have helped, but his cardiac output is terrible, and he wouldn't have a blood pressure without the balloon." Finally England turned toward Paula. "Sorry I didn't call you last night. There wasn't much to do."

"The nurse said he may have anoxic brain damage."

"I hope not. Neurology should see him today. Would you mind paging them? He really wasn't in V-fib that long, I wouldn't think."

"I don't mind," Paula said. "What a shame, a man as smart as he is."

"It's possibly a moot point. He may not survive his infarction."

England turned back to the computer and began typing, obviously done with the conversation. Paula spent a couple of minutes finishing her note on Pettigrew before picking up the phone to call her office to check her morning appointments.

"Paula," England said, turning to her. "You could do me a favor."

"What's that?" She replaced the receiver.

"Montgomery's secretary—she said she met you last night—is in the room."

"I talked to her briefly."

"You seemed to have developed some rapport. She intimidates all the nurses, except for Ms. Carpenter, and she's even had a couple of conflicts already with her."

"What's the favor?"

"It'd help me if you'd talk to her and explain the medical issues. She asks so many questions. I think she'd relate better to you."

"Sure, I can do that." Paula would've done it anyway. She was the attending on the case, not England. Besides, in this situation, who wouldn't ask questions?

"Good. I appreciate it. I'll explain the essentials, and you can elaborate the details."

England had turned back to the computer before he finished his sentence. "Happy I can help," Paula said. She didn't intend it to be sarcastic, but if she had, England missed it anyway.

Paula took a few minutes to review Montgomery's chart, checking the lab reports, vital signs, and nurses' notes. None were good. As she entered

Montgomery's room, she noticed Jennifer sitting in a chair beside the bed, holding his hand. Montgomery was hooked up to every imaginable piece of medical equipment, a common fate of ICU patients.

"Jennifer."

"Oh, Paula," she said, standing. "How are you?"

"I'm fine, Jennifer. I wish Mr. Montgomery was doing better."

"Thanks for your concern. He'll make it. He's a fighter."

Jennifer was polite and friendly, often difficult in such a situation. Obviously dedicated and intelligent, she also clearly cared personally for this man. The attorney general was fortunate to have her. Paula pulled over a nearby chair and sat next to her. "Dr. England asked if I could answer any questions for you."

"The nurses think I'm a bitch." She grinned as she said it. "And Dr. England would rather talk to an X-ray machine. Oh, I'm grateful. He seems competent enough."

"He's good. Trained at Harvard."

"No kidding. That's where Mr. Montgomery went to law school. He'd like that." Jennifer's eyes were tired, but her voice was upbeat. "Are you from here?"

"Nearby," Paula said, impressed that Jennifer would even care. "From Tahlequah, Oklahoma."

"Headquarters of the Cherokee Nation."

"That's right. Not many people know that."

"Not many from east of the Mississippi, you mean."

Paula laughed. "Yes, exactly. And how do you know about the Cherokees?"

"I was a history major. I thought forcing thousands of Cherokees to march on foot from Georgia to Oklahoma in the 1830s was one of the greatest tragedies in American history."

"The Trail of Tears. It must have been terrible."

"A fourth of the men, women, and children died."

"Yes, I know."

"Then you're Cherokee?"

"I'm adopted, but we think I'm full-blooded."

Jennifer smiled at her. "You must have an ancestor who's a healer."

Paula shrugged. "Funny you should say that. Because I'm adopted, I really couldn't say, but I hope that's true. Even when I was a young child, I used to have dreams I was a tribal healer. Isn't that odd? Among our people, the tribal healer is held in the highest esteem. The healer is responsible for every soul, from the least to the most noble. When I was older, my friends would bring me their sick pets and any strays they might find for me to doctor back to health. I had a knack."

"You still have a knack."

"Thank you." Paula felt her face flushing. "I'm sorry to talk so much about me. Did you have some questions?"

"Yes, of course, thank you. I appreciate the time you've spent with me."

Jennifer asked quite a few questions about Montgomery, but Paula didn't think any seemed inappropriate or out of the ordinary. The attorney general was near death. If Jennifer cared for him, she would certainly ask questions.

And Paula sensed, just a womanly instinct, that Jennifer's concern was more than that of a typical assistant. Not that it mattered to Paula, but she would file it back. It wouldn't be the first time that a powerful man was involved with his secretary. In this case, if Montgomery survived, Paula could see it adding an interesting dimension to the situation.

Paula said her good-byes to Jennifer and sat back down to write her note. She glanced at her watch. She still had Booker to see and several on the floor before going to the office. She'd definitely be running late today, the last thing she wanted or needed.

ᛉ

Matt had been soundly sleeping when Stan had called during the night, but he had no hope of returning home or resting or doing anything that didn't resemble work. After the weapons bust in East Tulsa at three in the morning, Matt and Stan had been working nonstop. The whole thing was one big sensational rush—what every federal agent lived for—and he felt wired. The six cups of coffee hadn't hurt. Now because of the bust he had tons more work to do. The paper work alone would take weeks.

Matt took a sip of coffee, black exclusively, and turned back to his computer screen. The sun had been up an hour and was brightly shining through his office window onto his monitor. He stood up to close the blinds when his private line rang.

"Hello?"

"Matt, it's Jake."

"Jake, are you okay? You haven't called in a week."

"Listen, I only have a few seconds. He's made a nitrate bomb that works, and he's dangerous. He's very cautious. Paranoid, actually."

"Do we have probable cause?"

"Yes, soon, maybe...but I haven't seen anything. It's all hidden."

"Has he named the target?"

"He won't tell us yet...probably tomorrow. Could be tough to get you a message."

"This whole operation is making me nervous."

"I'm safe."

"I'm not so sure, Jake. We should bring you in."

"No, please don't. If I'm not on the inside, we'll never know. We have nothing yet on him and won't likely find the bomb."

"It's not worth the risk."

"Matt, I'm okay. I'm the only one who could do this."

"Don't make me regret this."

"I won't. And Matt?"

"Yes, Jake?"

"This one's for real. Harper's serious. We need to put everyone on alert."

"I'll get the word out. Don't go a week again without calling. We'll be sorry we sent you in by yourself."

"I'll try."

"You be careful."

"I will. I know how to duck."

Matt hung up the phone and leaned back in his chair. Jake might be as cautious as possible, but was he in over his head? Jake had insisted he would be safe alone, despite policy. Now Matt wasn't so sure. It sounded like he was with a real nut case. If Jake couldn't call back, he'd missed his last chance to pull him off the assignment. If he pulled Jake off now, they might not get this close again. Matt needed to decide. This case was becoming complicated— and Matt didn't like complicated.

Jake wanted him to put everyone on alert. It wouldn't be easy, especially with all that was going on, but he could trust Jake. He hoped his friend could give him some advance warning.

⋏

Jennifer was nervous. They were in Oklahoma—far from civilization, far from the competent protection of the Washington agencies. She had complained from the outset that the two agents who had been assigned on the trip weren't stellar. Mike Asher was her least favorite. She had been unimpressed with him since the moment they had left Washington. He was cocky and overconfident. The second agent, Rick Simmons, was tolerable. He was older and seemed dependable, at least more respectful to her than Asher. She had heard rumors he had once been a heavy drinker, but she had never seen any evidence. The two agents argued constantly—never in front of the attorney general, of course, but they made little effort to hide their disagreements from Jennifer. She worried that they had little experience in their current unfortunate situation. Hopefully, the attorney general would be stabilized today and transferred to Bethesda. A military air ambulance was on standby. A few more hours and with any luck at all, they'd be back home.

In the meantime, she was challenging the territory of the unit's head nurse, Sally Carpenter. Simmons had set up a security desk to screen visitors at the entrance to the intensive care unit, and Jennifer insisted on strictly enforcing the hospital's policy of one visitor per patient. Sally said her patients were seriously ill and needed their family members. Jennifer didn't care. She was certain the curious would soon invade the unit, especially the unscrupulous press.

Jennifer also had demanded that all the staff and visitors show photo IDs and wear name tags or not be allowed in. Sally argued that impeding the flow of hospital personnel—respiratory techs, nurses, lab techs, and the multitude of others involved with the patients—would interfere with the intensive level of care. Jennifer, with more than a little sarcasm, informed Sally that she was a big girl and would compensate. Sally was furious. Jennifer didn't particularly like to ruffle feathers, but at least now the pecking order was established.

Jennifer sat at a small desk, leaning forward on her elbows. Simmons stood against the doorframe of her cramped office, holding a cup of coffee, his arms folded against his chest. She could feel her face flushed with heat.

"How many agents are you planning on the detail?" Jennifer asked. They had been arguing about security for several minutes. Her control was slipping.

"Four should be plenty."

"Just four? Besides you and Asher?" He probably thought she was questioning his judgment. She was. She sat back and waited.

"Four total," Simmons said. "We'll bring in two locals. Without any threatening intelligence, I can't see tying up the agents. He's in a hospital."

"So you think that's enough? The FBI is usually more cautious."

"The hospital is basically secure. The intensive care unit has little traffic and poor access. I doubt we'll have much of an issue."

"I'm not so sure."

"Honestly, it'll mostly be keeping out the media."

"I agree that's a must. The media is relentless. So otherwise, you're not worried?"

"I'm always worried."

"Good."

"They may have some crazies here in Oklahoma," he said, "but I think we've got it covered."

"I want him protected."

Simmons suddenly frowned. "You take care of his cards and flowers. We'll handle his security." He opened the door.

"No!" Jennifer said, raising her voice as she stood. "We're *both* responsible for his welfare. Your director plays racquetball every week with Mr. Montgomery." She jabbed her finger at him. "You'd better not screw this up."

Simmons smiled. "Okay, Ms. McLaughlin," he said, barely suppressing his anger. "For a moment I forgot who was in charge of his detail."

"Don't get smart. I could make a phone call..." She let the words hang.

His smile vanished. "We take our job seriously. We'll protect him. You worry too much."

Yes, she was worried. She had good reason to be. "I want to know about every request to see him. No visitors will see him unless approved by me personally."

Simmons finished his coffee and tossed the cup in the trash. "Sure. Whatever."

"I hear Senator Blair is coming—full entourage of media. He probably wants to garner a few votes from his local constituents."

"I'll be on the lookout."

"I guess we'll allow the mayor to visit. He's asked."

"Your call," Simmons said. "Are we through now? I have work to do."

"I want all the belongings of all staff and visitors searched with a metal detector."

"Yes, ma'am. I'll see if that can be arranged."

"And a full report every two hours."

"Sure. Is that all?"

"That's all."

Simmons walked out the door, shutting it softly behind him.

Simmons is tough, she thought, *and for the most part he stayed under control. No yelling or slamming doors. He'll be reasonable. He'll protect the attorney general. It's his job.*

Only now, Montgomery's worst enemy was his own heart.

Jennifer next would call their office in Washington. She'd secure a list of all hospital employees through tax records and order background checks on everyone—all the doctors on the case, the security guards, Howard Parrish, the nurses, and especially, of course, Sally Carpenter.

⋏

"You won't be able to spend the night again, Mrs. Hyatt," Sally said.

Laura Hyatt had slept next to her husband in a chair in the intensive care unit every night for the past two weeks. Her husband, Arthur Hyatt, a fifty-three-year-old truck driver, never sick a day in his life, had suffered a massive stroke and was now totally paralyzed on his left side. He had spent the first two weeks in the ICU on a ventilator and had been extubated the previous day, now breathing comfortably on his own. His blood sugars were over five hundred, despite a continuous infusion of insulin, yet other than his hyperglycemia, his general condition was slowly improving.

Laura, a petite Irish redhead with a quick wit and a temper to match, had demanded to stay at her husband's bedside. Sally, typically not one to bend the rules, had allowed Laura to stay rather than confront her. Now Jennifer was insisting that visitors' hours be strictly enforced, and Sally didn't cherish the task of informing Laura of the new restriction.

"And why is that, Nurse Carpenter?" Laura asked politely.

"The attorney general's FBI detail is asking that we enforce the visiting hours."

"I have as much right to be here as they do."

"Actually," Sally said, "they're not asking. They're insisting."

"I'll not stand for it," she said, the politeness quickly leaving her voice.

"Honey," Mr. Hyatt said, "I'm doing better." His speech was slightly slurred. "Go home tonight and sleep in our bed."

"That would be a good idea," Sally chimed in.

"I'll sleep where I choose," Laura said sharply.

"No, sweetheart," he said, "don't make a fuss. I don't need you here now. I'm doing fine."

Laura looked up at Sally. "I'll think about it and let you know."

Sally returned to the nurses' station. Just what she needed. Make an exception and pay the price. It never failed.

⅄

Wes Baskins would rather have walked his usual rounds—helping patients in and out of their cars and hanging around the emergency room, gossiping and drinking coffee—than sit at the ICU security desk. A security guard at Saint Luke's for five years, Baskins had retired from the Tulsa Police Department at the age of sixty because of his bad knees, old football injuries worsened by years in a patrol car. He was a burly man, over six feet tall and nearly three hundred pounds, entirely bald, with a thickset chin and broad nose, looking more like a retired linebacker than a cop. Simmons had assigned him to the security desk at the front of the hallway that led to the intensive care unit. Behind him the hallway ran about fifty feet, with doors to three or four offices along it, including the one set up for Ms. McLaughlin, before opening into the unit. The ICU secretary sat at a counter at the end of the hallway greeting the visitors who entered, processing doctors' orders, and answering the phone. Beyond the ICU secretary, a large nurses' station opened up with desks and computer terminals.

Baskins was the only non-fed on the security detail. Simmons had said that Asher and he would rotate two-hour shifts sitting outside Montgomery's room, one agent guarding Montgomery while the other made rounds checking the unit and surrounding areas. The only other entrance to the unit was the back stairwell. It connected to the medical staff offices on the first floor, the chest pain unit on the second, the surgical ICU on the fourth, and the pediatric ICU on the fifth. When the two local agents showed up in an hour or so, Simmons would assign one to sit at the stairwell and the other to the security desk with Baskins.

The desk was the toughest spot with dozens of staff entering and exiting the unit during a twenty-four-hour period. The job of monitoring every single staff member had proved overwhelming, so since Baskins personally knew most of the regulars, he waved them through, keeping their handbags or packages at the desk. Every visitor, however, he diligently scanned with the handheld metal detector Simmons had provided and searched their belongings, following the procedures exactly.

The visitors complained bitterly about the searches. Several visitors refused, vowing to write their congressman or the mayor, jotting down Baskins's name, as if he might care. If their family members were really sick, would they throw such a fit? More than likely, Baskins had reasoned, they were reporters attempting to sneak in. A retired police officer, especially one his size, wasn't easily intimidated by threats or pressured by status.

Baskins was conducting one of the mandatory visitor searches, his hands in an elderly woman's purse, looking for a loaded gun or a Bowie knife or whatever, when a familiar voice called out.

"Hey, Wes. How's about a coffee?"

Baskins looked up at John Hays, who was standing in front of him, grinning and holding two Styrofoam cups of coffee, both steaming hot.

"You're the best, John."

"You weren't in the coffee shop this morning. Thought you might be sick or something."

"I should be so lucky. But no, I've been assigned to protect some bigwig lawyer."

"Some lawyers need protecting, and some ain't worth spitting on."

John Hays was a janitor at Saint Luke's and had been employed at the hospital longer than any other employee. He was known by everyone as John, even the doctors. Raised by a single mom as one of nine, he had dropped out of school in the eighth grade and worked odd jobs until at the age of twenty, he had landed a job at Saint Luke's, at the time a brand-new hospital. John's back was now bent by arthritis, but his eyes were still bright. He had rarely if ever missed a day of work in over forty years and was never heard to utter a single complaint.

John handed Baskins his coffee. "Besides," John said, "if it's something important, you're the man to do it."

Baskins took a sip as he waved through a couple of staff members hauling a portable X-ray unit. "Thanks, John."

"No sweat," he said. "Hey, my cart's downstairs. I'll bring it up so you can search it."

Baskins laughed. "Of course I will. You look like a terrorist."

"No, really. My supervisor said you were supposed to. Then I'll leave it in the unit. I'm the only one that'll be cleaning the ICU while the governor is here."

"Attorney general."

"Whatever." He shrugged. "Anyway, I can come and go—unlike you— so I'll keep us supplied with coffee."

"Thanks for reminding me."

As John walked away, Baskins picked up the metal detector to scan a ninety-year-old man who said he was visiting his wife with heart failure. Though Baskins screamed the reason for the search several times in his ear, the old man never understood what he was doing. For Baskins, it would be a long day.

CHAPTER 8

Harper was awakened by the smell of bacon, eggs, and grits, his usual breakfast. He slid out of bed and stretched, wondering what time Jane had left their bed. Most mornings he would have noticed. As he crossed through the living room into the kitchen, he saw the sunlight streaming through the single kitchen window, bathing the brown card table and metal chairs they used as a makeshift dinette with a bright, morning light. Seeing the sun already up was a rare sight for a farmer. He seldom slept this late.

Harper sat facing away from Jane and waited for her to serve him. Without a greeting, she poured his coffee and then returned to the stove to finish making his breakfast. She stirred the grits and poured in a dab of milk. Crisp pieces of bacon drained on a stack of paper towels beside her. A transistor radio on the counter softly played gospel music from a local religious station.

Jane had laid out the previous day's paper that Buddy had brought him— no deliveries ever to the compound, not even a newspaper. News from twenty-four hours ago in today's world was good enough for him. He found an article about Ronald Montgomery delivering the keynote speech at a victims' rights conference at the Merrimac Hotel. No mention of the heart attack, of course, since it hadn't yet occurred when the paper was printed.

Harper shook his head while reading the article, the writer praising Montgomery for his many accomplishments. *No,* Harper thought, *Montgomery isn't some great public servant. He's the enemy—just one more lying, deceitful bureaucrat without morals or a conscience. He's the worst of the worst, a government lawyer who manipulated the law, purposefully and deliberately crushing the common man.*

Harper had seen the government at work firsthand, stealing his daddy's land, a farm that had been in his family for three generations. They had taken away his daddy's livelihood on a legal technicality, an honest oversight, and left him broken, penniless, destroyed. The bureaucracy had showed no mercy—not the kind, helpful government officials portrayed to the voters, but vicious and vile, with evil intent and motives.

His daddy never recovered. Once a proud and strong man, he died shriveled and spent.

Where was Montgomery then? Was he touting his victims' rights propaganda? Was he seeking fairness? Or was he pushing some button or signing some form that ruined the life of a law-abiding citizen?

He'll reap what he sows, Harper thought. "For whatsoever a man soweth, that shall he also reap." Montgomery had sown the seeds of evil and would reap the harvest of destruction. *He'll pay for his sin*, Harper thought, *and he'll be destroyed by the angel of God.*

"God grant me strength," Harper said.

Jane flipped off the radio and waited.

He turned to face her. "We still must destroy Montgomery," he said. "He *should* be our target."

"Why, Sam?" she asked. "Why must we destroy him? He may be dying."

"We don't know that."

"'Vengeance is mine, saith the Lord.'"

"God's word says we must destroy the God-haters."

"I am praying for his death to be painful."

"Me, too, but God demands we follow his will. We must do his will."

Jane filled Harper's plate and placed it on the table in front of him. She reached back for the coffeepot to refill his half-empty cup. "Are you sure the abortion clinic shouldn't be our target?" she said. "Satan's work is done there. The mothers, instead of protecting their babies, allow them to be murdered. The doctors commit the murder. Destroying them makes sense to me. Besides, Montgomery is in a hospital."

"To heal this man is to commit sin. They are defying God by saving him."

Harper folded his hands in prayer, said grace over his food, and then began eating.

He continued. "They have chosen to participate in the sin that prevents God's will. We must use their weakness to God's advantage."

Jane watched him as he ate and did not speak until he finished. "You're my husband," she said when he was done. "I'll pray that God grants you wisdom."

"Then I choose the hospital," Harper said. "The hospital is our target, but we can't do this one by ourselves. I'll have to call the others."

"So when?"

"We'll begin tonight."

⋏

Matt propped his feet on his desk and dialed Paula's cell phone. He hoped he'd catch her between her hospital rounds and the office. He wanted to ask her out to dinner again, knowing two evenings in one week was unlikely, particularly two weeknights. Yet even if she could come, which was always a challenge, and even though he was the one making the invitation, he could never guarantee he'd be there. Such was the life of an agent. Too many unexpected events. Too many criminals inconsiderate about the hours of their crimes. Drug deals that went down at night. Bombers who didn't keep banker's hours.

She understood. She knew the meaning of an emergency.

Paula was unlike any woman he had ever met. Smart, really smart, but also funny. He loved how bright her eyes got when she laughed, and when she smiled, it knocked him over. She had a serious side with a calmness and confidence, and he saw her caring and sincerity, a doctor dedicated to her profession.

Too dedicated, actually, he thought, *and possibly too absorbed in her career to give him a part of her life.* He sensed she was battling with her choices, torn by all her responsibilities, trying to decide what was most important.

He found himself thinking about her all the time. Last week, crawling on his belly through mud and poison ivy, busting a meth lab with the DEA, all he could think about was her. Would he be crawling in the woods if they were married? Would he be willing to risk it all when it counted? Or would he ask for a desk job? Be finished with field work. He'd done his fair share of the dangerous stuff. More busts than most. He had even done some things he didn't like to think about. Not that he felt guilty. Choices made in a split second that saved his life or his partner's life came with the job.

Matt sensed Paula was pulling away, and he wasn't sure why. He wanted to ask her, but worried that by asking, it'd make it worse, expose the possibility, and he didn't want that.

Even if she did, even if Paula turned out not to be the one, maybe he should consider the desk job anyway. Twelve years in the trenches was a long time. Most agents burned out in ten years, and sometimes he wondered if he was, too. No, he was just tired. He just needed a couple of days off, that's all. He and Stan still had plenty of important work to do—important enough to stay on the job. Even if he got married. Even if he had kids. Just like Stan.

If only she wouldn't pull away from him; if only she'd give him a part of her life.

Paula's number rang, but no one answered. He glanced at his watch. Time for the meeting with his boss. He'd have to call her later.

A

Harper loaded the thirteen jacketed hollow points into the clip of the Springfield Armory 9 mm and pulled back the slide, chambering the first round, before handing the weapon to Jane. Jane took the semiautomatic pistol and held it in both hands, pointing it down range, taking careful aim at the silhouette target thirty feet away.

"Slow, gentle trigger pull," Harper said. "So slow that it surprises you when it goes off."

Jane squeezed the trigger. The gun blast caused a burst of fire from the nozzle as it recoiled upward in Jane's hands. Her hit was center target, midchest in the silhouette, a perfect shot. She continued to hold the weapon facing toward the target but turned and smiled at Harper.

"He's dead," Jane said.

"Good shot. A bull's-eye."

Jane's definitely doing better, Harper thought. Both of them would fire twenty-five rounds at thirty feet and an additional twenty-five close range at ten feet. Jane was going first.

After practicing regularly for six months, Jane had improved greatly. She had never expressed any interest in firing a weapon in the past, and she didn't explain to Harper why the change. He didn't ask. Now she wanted to practice all the time, and he was pleased with her newfound enthusiasm. No one could predict, Harper knew, when proper firearm techniques might be lifesaving. He believed every woman and older child should know how to defend themselves and their families. He preached about it on Sundays to his congregation of Redeemed Believers. It could be essential in the future—the unpredictable, chaotic future of America.

Harper's Browning sat loaded and ready to use on the lane next to Jane's, but he wanted to watch her shoot. She was using a weapon he had purchased on the black market a few months earlier, its serial number filed off, untraceable. Hers was a three inch semiautomatic, small enough to carry in her purse. Oklahoma had a concealed-carry law, but none of the Redeemed would ever register for a concealed-carry license, never voluntarily agreeing to be fingerprinted, nor would they ever pay the government a license fee for a God-given constitutional right to bear arms. It was unconscionable.

Jane lifted the weapon into position, aimed carefully, and squeezed off a second shot, this time striking dead center in the head of the silhouette.

"Perfect," Harper said.

"He's dead," Jane said.

"Certainly is," Harper said.

"It's loosening the trigger pull. That helped."

"I knew it would. I want you to use only the silhouette targets from now on. I want the target to look like a human outline, and I want you to think you are hitting a real person every time you pull that trigger. You shouldn't be shooting at someone unless you intend to kill them."

"I can do that."

"I'm sure you can. It'll be essential when the day comes."

"I know that, Sam."

"Good. Now finish up, and I'll follow you."

Jane fired her next five shots. The third shot hit the target in the right shoulder, and the next four hit in the center of the chest. Over the next several minutes she finished the first twenty-five rounds and then waited as Harper moved the target to ten feet. She rapid fired at close range, a realistic distance for most combat situations, and Harper counted the number of shots near the center of the chest. He was pleased.

"You did good," Harper said.

"Thank you, Sam."

Harper took his position in the firing lane next to Jane's. His first target was a silhouette at thirty feet. He would practice with his Browning 9 mm, because it was the weapon he had decided to carry on the mission. He would only use bullets with jacketed hollow points, the same he always loaded, designed to mushroom in the victim's flesh to cause the greatest impact and internal damage. The feds were preparing attacks on all the militia groups. It had become common knowledge. He would be ready.

Harper squeezed off his first shot, and it hit dead center in the silhouette's head. He was a good shot. He had a steady hand.

"They better not underestimate us," Harper said.

"It'll be their fatal error."

Harper smiled a moment and returned to his business at hand. He fired three more at the head and two at the chest. All hit center.

Harper finished his first twenty-five, and Jane moved the target. He rapid fired three clips of eight, quick changing each of the clips, creating a ragged hole in the dead center of the silhouette's chest.

"Good work, Sam," Jane said. "Yours is dead, too."

Harper nodded. He wanted every shot perfect.

⚔

The Tulsa field office resident agent in charge, the RAC, had the largest and nicest office in the division, a corner office with floor-to-ceiling windows on two sides, fancy walnut furniture, and a splendid view overlooking the Williams Plaza Green and the downtown pedestrian mall.

Jeffrey Reese was a twenty-five-year veteran of the agency. After fifteen years out of the Chicago ATF office, one of the nation's busiest, he had been promoted to head the Tulsa field office five years earlier. Tough, intimidating, and controlling, he was obsessed with details and demanded his agents provide him a comprehensive report every single day, weekends included. He had convened this meeting specifically to discuss Harper and what they were now calling the Redeemed Believers Militia.

Reese, it seemed to Matt, sat all day behind his desk, isolated from the rest of them. How Reese knew which cases were their hottest, Matt could never figure.

Reese waved Matt and Stan into the two chairs across the desk from him. Three agents sat in the three chairs behind them. Matt would be the lead. The other agents would not likely say a word. Reese slid his half frames down his nose and peered at the report on his desk. Matt had prepared the report for Reese's review. They had been monitoring Harper's militia group for almost two years, and Matt had outlined everything he knew.

The Redeemed Believers were an organized, independent militia group with over forty men. Well funded from as-yet-unidentified sources, they owned substantial property, including 120 acres of land near Taft with the church and other buildings, and a few acres and several buildings scattered throughout eastern Oklahoma. They had never paid taxes on the properties, alleging they were sovereign citizens, rejecting Social Security numbers, ZIP codes, and the authority of the IRS. They also claimed they were a legitimate religious organization and that Harper was an ordained minister.

Despite their paramilitary training exercises and high-level security systems, the agency thought they were unlikely dangerous, until an undercover agent was successfully infiltrated into the group, and the talk of making explosives, stockpiling guns and ammunition, and selecting bombing targets heightened the ATF's interest.

Harper's background was unimpressive. He had been raised on his father's farm a short distance from his own. The research hounds thought he had only completed the eighth grade, but his school records were lost as the result of a fire that destroyed the one-room school he had attended. For thirty years he had farmed his own property in Muskogee County but had sold it three years earlier and dropped out of sight for six months until he resurfaced as a minister at the Church of the Redeemed Believers. His file was basically empty, boring, with not so much as a parking ticket. How he became a preacher and the head of the militia group was still a mystery. So little information always worried Matt.

Matt was convinced from the very beginning that Harper could make a bomb. Jake didn't think so at first, but Matt was sure, just a gut feeling that Harper was dangerous. Now Matt would have to bust him.

"Do we have enough to arrest him?" Reese asked.

"No, sir," Matt said. "Nothing concrete. He's been cautious."

"Are we waiting for him to blow up a few buildings before we're ready to act?"

"I hope that won't happen. Jake is undercover. He'll get us a warning."

"You'd better hope so. If we were to drag their self-righteous butts in here now, we might not be able to hold them, but at least we wouldn't have a bunch of dead doctors and patients in a bombed-out abortion clinic."

"If we don't make it stick, they'll be right back at it."

"I want an agent on every abortion clinic in our jurisdiction," Reese barked and pointed directly at Matt. "I can't put everyone on alert with basically nothing, but I do want a daily update. A written report. No detail is too small."

"Yes, boss."

This case is becoming a real pain, Matt thought. *Jake had better give me a warning.*

CHAPTER 9

Saint Luke's Hospital sat on the top of a hill overlooking all of Tulsa to the north. The jagged outline of the downtown skyline peeked above the thin blanket of brown summer haze lying along the horizon. Harper parked in the north lot, picked up the gift bag sitting on the passenger seat, and walked slowly to the main entrance. Automatic sliding glass doors opened into a vestibule of gray granite and tiled floors. Ahead, revolving doors slapped out a rhythm from the constant stream of late-morning visitors.

Harper waited a moment for a larger group of adults to follow in, ducking his head slightly as he passed under a smoked-glass globe suspended from the ceiling, likely housing video surveillance equipment. He headed down a hallway to the escalators and started to go up, but noticed a doorway marked EXIT STAIR #23 to his right. He waited a moment until the hallway was empty and then went in. A single flight of stairs led down to a small area with two doors. Both were locked. *No entry here, a dead end, but yet,* he thought, *knowing a few out-of-the-way places in the hospital might come in handy.*

Harper returned to the hallway and proceeded up the escalator to the central lobby. He passed a volunteer information desk to his left but avoided eye contact with the two older women in pink ancillary outfits who were smiling and greeting visitors. The lobby opened onto a large area with walls of walnut paneling, visitor seating in groups of maroon upholstered chairs, and a long line of people at the back, mostly employees, waiting at a coffee bar. A glass wall along one side housed a gift shop, and Harper wandered in.

He picked up a magazine in a rack near the door and held it up, appearing to read it, occasionally peeking over the top to check out the lobby to see if he was being followed. After ten minutes of thumbing through magazines and get-well cards, he purchased mints and left.

In the center of the lobby was a directory with a map of Saint Luke's. He examined the map for several minutes, studying every detail, noticing that the hospital was shaped like an X. The intensive care unit was clearly marked, a wing off one of the arms like an appendage of a deformed X chromosome. The intensive care unit was connected to the other floors at the front by a staircase and two banks of elevators, and at the rear by a single staircase. Harper noted the two floors above were the surgical ICU and the pediatric ICU. The two floors below were the chest pain unit and the medical staff offices. He decided the rear stairwell on the third floor appeared to be the best spot, assuming the TV reports were correct about Montgomery's location in the ICU.

A large family, grieving and crying, moved as a group as they left the lobby, and he tagged behind them down a long hallway, his head leaning forward, looking sad. He passed a wall covered with the hospital's accreditation certificates. He was unimpressed.

At the end of the hallway, the family continued straight-ahead while he ducked into a men's restroom. No one was there. He chose an empty stall and waited, thinking it was unlikely he would be followed, but he wanted to be sure. After fifteen minutes, he stepped to the door. The restroom doorway was recessed in the hallway, allowing him to see in both directions without being observed. No one seemed to be watching or waiting. He turned to casually walk down the hallway toward the specialty wing, the direction he had seen outlined on the hospital map.

His sneakers squeaked noticeably with every step on the shiny, tiled floor. They'd need quieter shoes tomorrow.

As he reached the specialty wing, he passed in front of the medical staff offices. Double doors spanned the hallway and were closed. He quickly realized it would be too risky to access the rear stairwell on this floor through the medical staff offices. A different floor would be better. Opposite the double doors were two banks of elevators with several staff members waiting: two doctors in white coats and three nurses in scrubs. The elevator doors opened, and the hallway emptied. To the right of the elevators was a stairwell door labeled with a sign STAIRWELL #4. Harper slipped in and went down the stairs.

At the bottom he had two choices. The first was a doorway that led to the basement. The second was a hallway that circled around to the back of the staircase. He looked through the basement door window and saw only a storage area with twenty or thirty old beds. The storage area was likely a dead end, especially since the map didn't show a connection from this area to the rear staircase.

Rather than enter the basement, Harper turned around and followed the narrow hallway that circled to the back of the staircase. After a couple of sharp turns, he discovered a door that exited to the outside of the hospital, likely required as a fire escape route. The door was not alarmed. A No Smoking sign was posted on it, Harper thinking the area once serving as an employee smoke hole. Outside was a loading dock. Nearby sat three large industrial containers holding trash and metal waste. The door had a push-bar opener that would automatically lock when the door closed, yet allowed easy entry into the building when opened from the inside. Harper checked the ceiling and all the outside walls for cameras and saw none. No surveillance equipment guarded the entrance. *This is too good to be true*, Harper thought. He had found an unsupervised back doorway into the hospital!

Harper waited. Several times he heard the basement door opening and closing, but no one entered the rear hallway. He stood quietly for ten minutes and was about to leave when a female employee quickly rounded the corner. Startled to see him, she passed with an exchange about the weather.

"Is it going to rain?" she asked, hardly looking at him.

She was outside and gone before he could answer.

Was she looking for a place to smoke? Would others smoke there, too?

Harper waited nearly thirty minutes, but no one else came. Satisfied, he returned to the staircase and climbed up two flights. The chest pain unit on the second floor might provide the easiest access and would tend to have the most visitors coming and going. As he entered the chest pain unit, he noted it was designed with a nurses' station in the center of two long hallways, flanked by rows of patient rooms lining each side.

A secretary at the nurses' station greeted him. He half waved then chose the hallway to the left. At the end of the hallway a second nurses' station faced the doorway to the back stairwell exit. He walked past a nurse and into the stairwell as though he belonged. No one called out or followed him.

After climbing up and down the stairs to check out all the floors, he stopped on the third floor. To his amazement, he saw no video surveillance and no guards. His presence was undetected. Yet if Montgomery was in this part of the hospital, why wasn't the stairwell guarded? How could someone walk around so freely, the security so lax? It didn't seem possible.

Harper stood in the stairwell outside the intensive care unit and listened for several minutes. He could hear the noise from the unit—people talking and an alarm beeping. The metal door separating him from the inside had a small window near the top, and without looking through it he could see the reflections of people walking by. His heart began to pound. He was inches away from the intensive care unit. *This has to be the right place*, Harper thought. Yet without guards or security, how would he know? Had Montgomery's illness caught them unprepared? Had Montgomery already died?

Harper had to make a choice and make it now.

Montgomery was here, Harper knew it, and very much alive.

For now.

Harper surveyed the situation. Behind him were the stairs; in front was the doorway. To his lower left was an air vent. Four screws, one at each corner, held the vent cover in place. He was glad he had brought his tools. He set down the gift bag beside him and reached in for a screwdriver. Kneeling in front of the vent, he removed the four screws and started to lift off the cover.

The stairway door on the second floor below him opened. He froze. Footsteps proceeded down the staircase away from him instead of up, eventually exiting the first floor. He sighed and took a deep breath. He waited a second for his pulse to drop before he quietly lifted the vent cover off.

The space inside the vent appears sufficient, he thought, guessing three and a half feet wide by two feet deep with plenty of height. He could stack several boxes easily. The back of the vent was only inches away from the interior of the intensive care unit. This was lucky. The blast would blow this wall inward, possibly collapsing the entire floor.

He lifted the cover to replace it. Would his radio detonator reach inside? Without its signal, the bomb would be worthless.

He set the cover back down. Inside his bag was the radio receiver in case he needed to test it. The receiver was attached to a small toy car, which when activated would roll forward. After placing the toy car inside the vent, he again lifted the cover to replace it. If the car moved, he'd know his signal had reached. He quietly screwed in the first three screws and then picked up the fourth.

The door on the second floor opened again, but this time the footsteps were coming up.

Harper's heart jumped. His presence in the stairwell would be difficult to explain. Racing to finish, he fumbled the screw and dropped it. The screw clinked repeatedly as it bounced.

The person's footsteps were rounding the corner and continuing upward, now approaching more quickly.

The vent cover only had three screws. But who would notice? He wouldn't wait to find out. With a man dressed in a white coat, probably a doctor, coming up behind him, he slipped the screwdriver in his bag, opened the door to the unit, and walked in.

⋏

The intensive care unit was a spacious, open, and bright area. The patient rooms were on the perimeter, separated from the center by sliding glass doors and blue curtains. Monitors and other equipment were beeping. Harper could see patients in each of the rooms. The stench was of alcohol and disease.

Harper attempted to cover his face with his hand. The staff, occupied with their tasks, never looked up. He was a visitor, a family member, a person who belonged, not unusual, not suspicious.

I'm right about Ronald Montgomery being here, he thought. *He's in this unit. No guards. No security. No protection. He is arrogant to think he is safe.*

Harper walked briskly through the unit, unnoticed. He continued down the long hallway, noting two doors on each side, all closed. At the end of the hallway, an old man in a security uniform sat at a desk, searching a woman's purse. *The security must be for Montgomery's benefit. He's definitely here*, Harper thought. Harper moved quickly past before turning to his right and down the common hallway. The guard never saw him.

In the parking lot, Harper removed the transmitter from the gift bag and raised the antenna. The wing of the intensive care unit rose up directly in front of him. The toy was supposedly long-range. He would see.

The location he had selected would work. They would not look in the vent unless they knew and searched.

The red light was on. He pushed the button.

Harper retraced his exact steps through the hospital. He cautiously entered the stairwell on the second floor and proceeded to the third. The screw he dropped lay in the corner, and he picked it up.

He unscrewed the three screws and gently pulled the cover away from the wall. If the receiver moved, his plan would be foolproof. He would be unstoppable.

Harper peered into the vent. The receiver was gone!

No, there it was. It had rolled across the entire width of the vent. The receiver had moved!

Praise God, he thought. Now he was ready.

CHAPTER 10

Reverend Pettigrew coughed frequently during Paula's chest exam. He was her last patient in the unit on her evening rounds. Randy Booker, her gambling asthmatic, had improved some but was still on the ventilator. He'd be in the unit two or three more days. Montgomery, whom she had seen with Dr. England, was doing poorly. So poorly, in fact, he would be unlikely to survive the night. Jennifer was in her office, and Paula wanted to update her, but first she needed to finish her rounds.

Pettigrew looked better. He was sitting sideways with his legs dangling off the edge of the ICU bed, two nurses holding his frail body, one under each arm. A thin, light-blue tube delivered oxygen through nasal prongs from a humidifier attached to the wall above the head of his bed. Two small clear-plastic bags, each holding a broad-spectrum antibiotic, hung on an IV pole, and two IVACs pumped the powerful medications through his IV lines.

"You still have congestion in both lungs," Paula said, slipping her stethoscope back in her pocket.

"I'm coughing a bunch of it up."

"That's good," Paula said. "Ralph will give you a treatment in a few minutes." She looked out toward the nurses' station and could see the respiratory tech fidgeting, waiting impatiently for her to finish so he could give his last respiratory treatment and go home. "We'll continue the IV antibiotics and breathing treatments for twenty-four hours. I'd like to keep you here in the unit until morning."

"Okay with me. The nurses are treating me really well."

The two nurses smiled as they swung him around and laid him back in the bed. They glanced at Paula, confirming her approval, and then left.

"And how are *you* doing, Dr. Barrett?" Pettigrew asked when they were alone.

"I'm doing fine. Thank you for asking."

"I've been praying for you."

"No offense, Reverend, but you're the one needing prayer."

"No, my child. We all need prayer."

Pettigrew reached out his hand toward her, and she took it. His skin felt thin and wrinkled, the surface cool and clammy. He gently held on to her and closed his eyes.

"Heavenly Father," he began praying, "merciful and full of grace, thank you for the gift of every precious moment. Thank you for your generous love, which is beyond all our understanding. Most gracious Father, I ask your blessing on Dr. Barrett. Grant her the wisdom to heal through your goodness with mercy and kindness. In Jesus' name we pray. Amen."

"Amen, Reverend," she said softly. She smiled at him. "And thank you."

"Peace be with you, child."

Paula left his room and crossed to the physician's desk. As she slid out a chair to sit down, Sally Carpenter approached her.

"Is Pettigrew ready to move to the ward?" Sally asked sharply.

"No, I don't think so."

"What are you doing for him?"

"Reverend Pettigrew continues to need a substantial amount of care."

"He's the least sick patient in the unit, Doctor."

"He's on two antibiotics and respiratory treatments every four hours, and he requires suctioning every hour. He's too sick to move."

"That's nursing care. It can be handled on the floor." Sally gestured over her shoulder. "With our celebrity, our nurses are stressed to the max. We're trying to clear out as many as we can."

"I don't think Reverend Pettigrew is ready, Ms. Carpenter. He's fragile, and of course it is my decision."

"Yes, Doctor. Obviously."

Paula thought she said it with a snarl. This nurse didn't like being challenged.

"So, Doctor, I may call you if we need the bed."

Paula turned away and flipped on the computer. "Fine," she said. "Call me if you wish, and I might reconsider my decision." She began writing her progress note.

Paula didn't look up as Sally walked away. She had tried to be friendly with Sally, but Sally was difficult. What was it? Was she envious? They weren't playing dolls. Paula was the authority, and whether Sally liked it or not, she had to follow Paula's orders. Sally would be happier if Paula would be nice and play along, but Paula had done that for too many years. The male doctors during her training had their subtle ways of intimidating her. They'd forget to send her a memo to an important meeting, or exclude her from the best cases, or even once called for patient rounds in the men's room. She had fought intimidation for four years of medical school and three years of residency. But she had won. She had finished and had finished well.

Would she now take grief from some nurse? Not likely.

Paula typed her note and electronically closed the chart. She would talk with Jennifer before meeting Matt for dinner—incredibly, it looked like they might go out twice in one week—and the last thing she needed was to be upset. She absolutely refused to play Sally's silly games.

Why then, she wondered, *do I feel so angry?*

⋏

Paula knocked on the door of Jennifer's office and waited. After only a second or two, she heard Jennifer calling out for her to enter. She stepped inside and pulled the door closed behind her.

"You missed Dr. England on his evening rounds," Paula said, "and he asked me to update you on Mr. Montgomery."

"The good doctor should have known I was here."

"Sorry," Paula said and shrugged. "What can I say?"

"You're right. Thank you." Jennifer stood up to greet her and offered her a chair. "Please come sit and tell me how he's doing."

"Thank you," Paula said as she stepped forward, accepting the offer. Paula sat quietly for a moment, gathering her thoughts. Delivering bad news was always difficult, but Paula knew to hear it was worse. She wanted to get the words right. "The truth is, his condition is deteriorating." Paula said it as gently as she could. "His blood pressure is no better, despite the balloon and the medications. He's still requiring the ventilator. It's difficult to know if his mental status has improved or not, since he's getting some sedation because of the ventilator."

Jennifer was watching her intently, taking it all in, listening to Paula's every word. Paula paused briefly to see if Jennifer wanted to ask a question. She didn't.

Paula took a breath and then continued, "And now he's developing some complications."

"What complications?"

"His kidneys are beginning to fail. His urine output is dropping, and his creatinine is climbing."

"How bad is that?"

"If it gets much worse, he may need kidney dialysis." Paula leaned forward, clasping her hands together. "And we're afraid he might be developing pneumonia. The chest X-ray is showing some new changes."

"How would he get pneumonia?"

"Unfortunately, it happens to the sickest of patients. He can aspirate. His immune system is challenged. I worry that sometimes a patient's lungs can go into a kind of shock."

"Is he on antibiotics?"

"Two, in fact. I started them this evening." Paula paused. "I'm sorry to tell you, but his prognosis is very poor. He may not make it through the night. We're doing all we can."

For a moment there was an awkward silence as Jennifer's eyes began to fill with moisture. Paula waited. Jennifer needed a moment.

"Thank you for coming," Jennifer said. "I do know you are trying everything, and I appreciate it."

"I'm going out to dinner with a friend, but I'll be on my pager and immediately available."

"I know you will be."

"And I'll keep the attorney general in my prayers."

"Thank you. Prayer may be what he needs the most right now."

Paula saw Jennifer fighting back the tears, and she stood to leave.

It's a tough situation, Paula thought, *when saying a prayer is the most a doctor has to offer.*

🙽

Jennifer entered Montgomery's room as Sally was hanging a plastic bag of antibiotics and connecting it to his IV.

"I understand he has pneumonia now," Jennifer said, moving beside Sally.

"Yes, that's what his X-ray showed." Sally didn't look up as she slipped the needle in the IV line and opened a plastic valve.

"Both Dr. England and Dr. Barrett made evening rounds," Jennifer said, "and I was right down the hall, yet no one bothered to come get me. At least Dr. Barrett was professional enough to give me an update."

Sally turned to face her. "Ms. McLaughlin, I'm not sure we need—"

"I don't care if you're confused," she interrupted, "so I'll make this simple for you. I'm acting as the attorney general's guardian, and I want to know everything that's done for him. Every medication. Every test. *Everything.* And I'm called for physician rounds. Is that understood?"

"Legally, we must—"

"I can have a federal court order here in five minutes, if you prefer." Jennifer paused and moved a bit closer. "Shall I call your administrator?"

"No," Sally said flatly, not backing off. "I'll come fetch you."

"Exactly."

Jennifer's attention was drawn to the television. The screen showed a picture of the attorney general with his name underneath. A news anchor was speaking but the sound was turned off. Jennifer reached for the remote control to increase the volume.

"And now," the anchor said, "to our reporter in the field, Cara Beeson, for a special report."

The scene changed to an attractive blond woman holding a microphone. She was standing outdoors, and Saint Luke's Hospital filled the screen behind her.

"We have an exclusive report tonight on the medical condition of Ronald Montgomery, the attorney general of the United States, who is hospitalized at Saint Luke's Hospital," she turned and pointed, "in this wing. As we have reported here on Alert Three News, Mr. Montgomery suffered a massive heart attack early yesterday evening at the Merrimac Hotel and was brought here by ambulance to the emergency room. Tonight we bring you an exclusive report from a confidential source that Ronald Montgomery is being treated for heart failure with a device called a balloon pump and may have irreversible brain damage."

Jennifer turned the volume up higher.

"We have been informed that he has developed several complications, including kidney failure and pneumonia, and there is concern he might not survive the night. We will bring you further details as they are available. This is Cara Beeson, Alert Three News, reporting."

"What the hell was that?" Jennifer snapped.

"I...I...don't know," Sally stammered. "I can't believe that report."

"Where did it come from?" Jennifer said, her face instantly red. "Who's her source?"

"I don't know. It could be anybody. One of the doctors. A nurse. I can't believe my staff would—"

"I don't care what you believe," she said, cutting her off. "You plug the leak. This is the attorney general we're talking about. His medical condition is confidential."

"Yes, of course. I just—"

Jennifer leaned to within inches of Sally's face. "Plug the leak! Your job depends on it. Is that understood?"

人

The crowd at the sports bar was rowdy as the baseball game moved into the bottom of the ninth, tied three to three. Matt had hoped to catch a few innings of the Texas Rangers on the big screen before Paula arrived, but she had been only a few minutes late. Occasionally he peeked over her shoulder for the best plays, but mostly he tried to listen to her conversation. She told him he could finish watching the ball game. He knew better.

Paula's pager had been quiet all evening until the moment they had brought out her food, but of course then she had three calls. While she stepped out to answer the last call, he had watched the bottom of the seventh when the Rangers had scored two runs, tying the game. Now she was done, back at the table, and the game was still tied in the ninth. He'd probably miss the rest of the game, the most exciting part, but it was just baseball.

Matt definitely felt distracted, but it wasn't really the game. It was the fact that Jake hadn't called. Every few seconds, as much as he'd try to push the thoughts away, whether talking to Paula or watching baseball, he'd think of Jake. Why hadn't he checked back in? Was he okay? Jake had talked about a bomb. He wanted them to cover every abortion clinic, basically an impossible task. Yet based on what? Jake's intuition? His gut feeling? Where was the proof, the evidence? What was Jake waiting for?

Matt was sick of worrying about Jake. He'd feel better if Jake would call.

Matt watched Paula's face as she talked, enjoying how animated she was when engaged in conversation. Paula didn't often complain about her work, but tonight she spent the evening harping on the ICU nurses, especially the nursing supervisor she had been arguing with earlier. There wasn't much he could say, and he tried to listen intently, occasionally nodding in agreement. He had seldom seen Paula upset. She was usually calm, almost passive—he thought it must be a Cherokee trait—but tonight she was angry, tightly twisting her napkin and talking nonstop.

"That nurse has a problem with female authority figures," Paula said. "She may be the charge nurse, but I write the orders."

The Rangers' third baseman cracked a homer over the center-field fence. The bar crowd roared, and Matt jumped to his feet before he realized. Paula was looking up at him, smiling.

"I'm sorry," he said, sitting. "I was listening to you. I promise."

"I'm talking your ear off," she said. "Why don't you tell me about your day?"

He slid his hand across the table to gently touch her arm. "Mine was not nearly as important."

"I'll be nauseated if I talk any more about Sally Carpenter. I'd really rather hear about you."

He wanted to tell her. He knew some of the agents talked to their wives or their girlfriends, but rules were rules. If he told her about the drug bust last week or the gun traffickers yesterday or the foot chase today, she'd only worry anyway. If he told her about Jake, how much danger Jake was in, she'd worry even more, since he also occasionally went undercover. "It's been exciting," he said, smiling. "The new fiscal year started on the first, and I ordered a year's worth of office supplies. Last month I couldn't requisition a battery for my pager, but with the new budget this month, I could order a hundred."

"You're not going to tell me anything, are you?"

"You know I can't," he said softly. He wished he could. "Say! How's Montgomery doing?"

"Well," she said, hesitating. "Actually, it's confidential."

"So," Matt said with a big grin, "you're not going to tell me anything, are you?"

Paula laughed. "Our conversations are pitiful, aren't they?"

"There's a report on the news now." Matt pointed to a television behind her.

They both turned to watch. A blond reporter was talking.

"Tonight we bring you an exclusive report," the reporter said, "from a confidential source that Ronald Montgomery is being treated for heart failure with a device called a balloon pump and may have irreversible brain damage. We have been informed that he has developed several complications, including kidney failure and pneumonia, and there is concern he might not survive the night. We will bring you further details as they are available. This is Cara Beeson, Alert Three News, reporting."

The television switched back to the news anchor. "Thank you for that exclusive report," he said absently and moved on to the next topic.

"So there you go," Paula said, turning back to face Matt. "That's exactly what's going on. Yet, to be honest, I'm surprised they released that to the press."

"That is pretty specific."

"I talked with Montgomery's secretary earlier this evening, and she's been very selective about what's released."

"And I thought I'd get the inside scoop."

"Apparently not," she said, shaking her head.

Paula's pager beeped. She reached into her purse and lifted it up. "Looks like the ER," she said, "and I'm on call."

Paula left to answer the page, and Matt watched a few minutes of the news. He thought it was unusual to hear such specifics on a media medical report, even someone as well known as Montgomery. Odd.

Paula returned and sat down. "Sorry. Looks like I have to go."

"Business before pleasure."

"For you and me," she said, standing to leave, "that's our motto."

Matt escorted Paula to her car. The orange glow of the streetlamps cast long overlapping shadows on the parking lot. As she reached to slip her key in the car door, Matt gently placed his hands on her waist. She turned and embraced him, kissing him tenderly. Matt pulled her tight and felt her soft lips on his. He didn't want her to leave his arms, didn't want the moment to end. He wanted to spend the rest of the evening with her, not always feeling rushed, not torn apart by their careers. But it wouldn't be tonight. She was needed in the emergency room, off to the hospital to save a life or cure a disease.

Paula gently pushed him away, smiled, and slid into the front seat of her car. Matt shut the door and watched her drive away.

Not that his pager might not go off just as Paula's had done, calling him to a different type of emergency, always involving the worse of the worst. For him it was drug dealers, bombs, and guns. In a way just like Paula, he also dealt with disease—the sickness of a decayed, decadent, and troubled society.

Did they have a future? He hoped so. He'd be patient. She was worth the wait.

CHAPTER 11

Harper had called the meeting for eight o'clock, and the three men were precisely on time. For the first hour they practiced with automatic pistols at the range, firing a hundred rounds each. They brought their own weapons—all unidentifiable with the serial numbers filed off. Carl Joe carried a blue-steel Colt M1911 .45 caliber, military issue, bought under the table at a gun show many years ago. The others carried 9 mm weapons. Harper's was a Browning 9 mm in excellent condition, though over twenty years old. The Browning had been his father's. Tommy and Buddy both carried Rugers.

Harper was a good shooter. Tommy was an amateur. He had never shot a pistol before joining the militia group. Carl Joe was a crack shot after serving three years in the army. Buddy was the best—an excellent marksman. Harper had taught Buddy himself, starting when he was five years old.

When it had grown too dark for them to see the targets, Harper instructed them to leave their weapons in the parsonage and return to their cars. He drove his van, and they followed him to the twenty-four-hour Wal-Mart in Muskogee, ten miles away. Each would park their car in a different location in the parking lot, leaving all their personal belongings in their vehicles, and then return to the van to give him their keys.

Carl Joe climbed into the front passenger seat, and Buddy and Tommy slid into the back. For the next thirty minutes, Harper drove slowly through nearby residential areas, circling and backtracking several times. By the time they left Muskogee for the compound, it was after ten o'clock, and the moonless summer night was pitch black.

"I've selected a new target," Harper said, once they had returned to the parsonage.

Carl Joe, Buddy, and Tommy sat together on the couch in the living room. Harper sat in a recliner across the coffee table, holding a brown plastic bag on his lap. Jane offered each a freshly brewed coffee before she sat nearby on a folding chair in the kitchen, listening.

"Before we go over the details," Harper said, "I want Carl Joe and Tommy to change into these." He reached into the plastic bag and threw both of them several articles of clothing. "All the workmen at the target site wear the same thing: white slacks, polo shirts, and sneakers. Sleep in them tonight so they looked used." He turned to Buddy and tossed him the plastic bag. "Wear these street clothes, Buddy, so you'll look like a visitor." Harper handed them each an empty paper sack. "Put your own clothes in the sacks after you change. I'll store them in one of our closets. Any questions?"

No one spoke or said a word. One by one they changed in the bathroom, and after returning to the living room, they laid the paper sacks with their clothes on the floor next to Harper's feet.

"I put your weapons on the kitchen counter," Harper said. "You'll carry your own weapon tomorrow." Harper spread out some papers on the coffee table. "I have some rough drawings to show you. We're placing the item of interest internally."

"You mean inside a building?" Carl Joe asked.

"It's required."

"Isn't that risky?" Tommy asked.

"Is everyone on board or not?" Harper said angrily. "Why all these questions?"

The three men shifted uneasily.

Carl Joe pumped his fist. "We're just ready to blow away some baby-killers."

"Then let's continue." Harper put his finger on a spot on the diagram. "Jane will drop me and Buddy off here in front of the target building." He pointed at Carl Joe and Tommy. "You two will carry the item inside from the van at a loading dock in the back. After I let you in, we'll initially split up to get into position, but then we'll join up to proceed together to the placement area."

The men listened without asking questions. Harper never mentioned the target site, and no one asked. He would be more specific in the morning when they were on their way.

"Are we detonating during the daytime?" Carl Joe asked. "We'd have the greatest body count, like in Oklahoma City."

"I haven't decided when we'll detonate, but I'll be able to choose the timing."

"We want destruction of the guilty," Buddy said, "but not the innocent."

"No one there is innocent," Carl Joe said. "You should know that, Buddy."

"We don't know where 'there' is yet," Buddy said. "Let's kill those who are destroying our country, but killing children like at Murrah is wrong."

"You've developed a conscience?" Carl Joe asked sharply. "Brother Sam will guide us—"

"God will guide us," Harper interrupted. "Throughout history, destroying the wicked puts the innocent at risk. It's evil that makes victims of the innocent."

"When are we going to see the bomb?" Tommy asked.

Harper glanced at Jane sitting quietly in the kitchen and smiled. "I told Jane that none of you would notice. You've been looking at it all evening." Harper pointed to the corner of the living room. "The bomb's been sitting right there all the time."

Four cardboard boxes, each measuring thirty inches wide, eighteen inches deep, and fourteen inches high, occupied one corner of Harper's living room. The boxes originally had held intravenous supplies, and Harper had picked them up empty from the basement storage room before he left the hospital. Not a soul had noticed.

Harper opened the top box and proudly displayed the arrangement of the detonator wiring. The radio receiver was taped to the inside of the top box, which was otherwise empty except for several wires entering a small hole to the boxes below. The bottom three were filled with the nitrate and fuel oil mixture in plastic containers. All four boxes were taped together as a unit. Harper attached two blasting cap detonators, one as insurance, to the mixture in the second box. The initial blast would ignite the explosives in the other two. Once placed in the stairwell vent, the receiver's antenna would be raised to its full height through a tiny hole in the lid, the only indication the stack of boxes wasn't actually medical supplies.

Harper rested his hand on the top of the stack. "You didn't even think about these being the bomb."

"That's ingenious," Buddy said. "Intravenous fluids."

"I'll carry the transmitter in my pocket. Buddy will carry the tools in a knapsack. Carl Joe and Tommy will carry in the boxes on a hand truck. It'll look completely innocent."

"A lot of the militia is just talk," Carl Joe said. "They're gonna see us rock!"

"Is that enough explosives?" Tommy asked. "McVeigh used a Ryder truck."

"It's enough to do the job. The result will be impressive."

"It'll be the sign to call the militia to arms," Carl Joe said.

"Hasn't nitrate become hard to find?" Buddy asked.

"Not if you know where to look," Harper said. "I had some kid steal it out of old barns for me. Told him it's for the old women's gardens. Nitrate fertilizer is untraceable if you pick it up at the right places."

"The feds are stupid," Tommy sneered. "They won't figure that out."

"We can't be too cocky," Harper snapped back. "The feds are smart. We can't be too careful."

Harper tied a string to the antenna and guided the string through a quarter-inch hole in the top box. He taped it down to use later to pull the antenna out. Harper then taped the box closed.

"You three will sleep on the floor here in the living room. I know there's not much space."

"I don't mind sleeping outside," Tommy said.

"No one sleeps outside," Harper said sharply. "No one leaves the house. Is that clear?"

The men nodded.

The three men laid out blankets and pillows that Harper pulled out of a closet. Harper and Jane went into the bedroom and shut the door. Harper had set two alarm clocks for 5:30. He stripped to his underwear. Jane dressed in white cotton pajamas.

"I was watching the news," Jane said softly, her voice low so the others wouldn't hear. "It came on before you all returned from the Wal-Mart."

"And?"

"The reporter said Montgomery may not live through the night. What will we do if he dies before morning?"

"I'm certain the media will report his death shortly after it happens. They're a bunch of vultures. If he's dead by morning, we'll postpone and change targets. If we can place the bomb before he dies, then I really don't care if he is alive or dead."

Harper lay on top of the covers. Jane slipped under a light blanket.

"His dead body," Harper said, "makes almost as good a hostage as his live body. One thing's for sure."

"What's that?"

"You can quit praying for his death."

⅄

The emergency that interrupted Paula's dinner with Matt was a drug over-dose: a fifteen-year-old attempting to manipulate her mother in a fit of anger by taking thirty of her grandmother's sleeping pills. The girl had not real-ized the drug was dangerous, and now was comatose in respiratory failure on a ventilator heading for the pediatric intensive care unit. Paula had spent over two hours in the emergency room, and though she was fading fast, she decided she'd check in on Pettigrew and Montgomery before heading home.

The emergency department was at the opposite end of the hospital from the intensive care unit, but she was very familiar with the route, having walked it many times. After midnight the hospital floors grew much quieter, the lights dimmed, the patients asleep, and the nurses huddled in small groups, talking softly. It was her favorite time in the hospital, peaceful and less harried. Even the patients tended to appreciate the nighttime visits, recognizing only the dedicated few roamed the hallways at such an hour.

The intensive care unit, on the other hand, she thought as she arrived, *never stops, never slows for a moment, always busy, loud, and bright.* When she entered Reverend Pettigrew's room, he was sleeping soundly. His monitor showed a normal rhythm, and his vital signs were stable.

Down the hall outside Montgomery's room, Simmons, the FBI agent, sat in a chair. He nodded as Paula passed by him. Jennifer was reclined in a chair near Montgomery's bed. Her eyes were closed. Paula decided not to disturb her. Montgomery's ventilator clunked as it pushed air into his lungs. The balloon pump whirled softly, forcing blood into his heart arteries through a tube in his aorta. He had three IVs running, one in each arm and one in his leg, and a catheter in his bladder with only a few drops of urine in the bag. His eyes were closed, and he was deeply sedated—not even a twitch of movement. A host of vital signs were displayed on a screen above the bed—all were bad. He was barely alive.

As reported, he might not survive the night. Paula wondered how the news reporter knew about his condition. The report had been too accurate. If Jennifer hadn't released it, then it must have come from someone in the unit.

Paula walked to the doctors' desk and as a matter of habit wrote a brief entry in both of the patient records.

"What are you doing here at this ungodly hour?"

Paula turned and saw Sally Carpenter standing next to her. "What are *you* doing still here at this ungodly hour?"

"Don't you have enough common sense to go home? It's after midnight."

"Look who's talking."

Sally smiled. Paula had never seen Sally smile.

"I probably won't call you to move Mr. Pettigrew," Sally said. "He's sleeping pretty good…and you're not."

Paula chuckled. "You're funny when you're sleep deprived."

"I'm going home in a few minutes. I want to make sure the attorney general is okay first."

"Did you see the television report tonight?"

"It made my evening," she said sarcastically. "Someone here is leaking information. That McLaughlin woman is ticked off and wants me to find out who. Even you're not above suspicion."

Paula, despite her best judgment, couldn't let it go. "And neither are you."

Sally's response surprised Paula. Instead of anger, Sally laughed.

"You're not the pushover everyone says you are," Sally said, grinning.

"And *you* actually have a nice streak."

"I try to hide it."

A decent conversation with Sally Carpenter in the wee hours of the morning was not what she had expected.

Paula was about to respond when a loud alarm screeched from Montgomery's room. Instinctively, Sally sprinted to Montgomery's bedside. Paula was right behind her. The alarm startled Jennifer, and she jumped to her feet.

"What is it?" Jennifer demanded.

"He's in V-fib again," Sally said, looking at the monitor.

"What does that mean?" Simmons was standing in the doorway.

"It's a serious heart irregularity," Paula said.

"Any orders, Doctor?" Sally asked.

"Let's defibrillate him," Paula said. "We need to be quick."

Toni and two other ICU nurses rushed in to help. Knowing the drill, they brought in the crash cart. The respiratory tech moved next to the ventilator and checked its settings.

Sally began barking orders. "Call a code blue. We'll need the help. Page Dr. England stat." One of the nurses nodded and left.

"Jennifer," Paula said, "you'll need to wait outside."

"I'm not leaving. I want to be here."

"Please, Jennifer. You shouldn't see this."

Simmons gently took Jennifer's arm, and she reluctantly followed him outside the door.

"Give me the paddles," Paula said. "Set the defibrillator on two hundred."

Paula took the paddles from Sally and placed them on Montgomery's chest. Toni flipped on the defibrillator, and it charged with a high-pitched whine. "Everybody clear!" Paula yelled. She waited a brief moment and pushed the buttons. Montgomery's body arched upward.

Every eye in the room turned to the monitor.

"Still V-fib," Sally said. Sally dropped the bedrails and pulled up a small footstool to begin chest compressions. "You want some meds, Doctor?"

"Let's repeat the shock, and then we'll see."

"Code blue ICU," the overhead speaker announced. "Code blue ICU."

"Try it at 360," Paula said. Paula positioned the paddles as Toni turned the dial. "Clear!" Paula said.

Sally and Toni stood back, and Paula defibrillated him. Montgomery again arched upward with the electrical charge.

"Meds, Doctor?" Sally asked firmly. "Amiodarone? Epinephrine?"

"He's on an amiodarone drip already, right?"

"He's on two drips—dopamine and amiodarone."

"The amiodarone is 1 milligram?"

"Yes, that's right."

"Then give him an additional 75 milligram bolus."

"Thank you, Doctor," Sally said.

Toni deftly drew up the amiodarone, slipped the needle in the IV line, and pushed the medication in.

"Did you call Dr. England?" Paula asked. "Is he coming in?"

Toni nodded her head. Paula waited a few seconds for the drug to circulate.

"Okay, let's hit him again at 360." Paula placed the paddles on his chest. "Clear!"

When Paula pressed the buttons, Montgomery's back spasmed briefly, and then he fell limp.

"Sinus rhythm!" Sally shouted.

Paula watched as the monitor etched out a steady, regular rhythm. For a few seconds no one breathed and no one spoke. All eyes remained on the monitor as it continued to maintain a normal pattern. Montgomery's heart had converted.

"I've got a pulse," Sally said. "His pulse is fine."

"Fantastic, guys," Paula said. "Good job! Let's check his vital signs, and I want lytes, enzymes, a set of gases, and a cardiogram. He may have reinfarcted."

"You've got it," Sally said as she climbed down from the stepstool. "Dr. Barrett, good job to you, too."

"Thanks."

They had run, all of them, a successful code and brought the attorney general back from certain death.

Paula stepped outside the hallway. Jennifer and Simmons were waiting.

"His rhythm is normal now," she said. Paula could see the relief on their faces. "We had to shock him three times."

"What does that mean?" Jennifer asked.

"Well, it's not good. His heart muscle is sick. We'll be giving him some medication that hopefully helps."

Jennifer nodded. She understood. "Thanks. I'll go sit with him."

Paula sat down at the nurses' station and flipped on the computer to write a note. Montgomery's heart rhythm was normal, but the sobering truth was his condition had not changed. In fact, each time they coded him, his chances grew slimmer. The next time he might not be so lucky.

Paula looked up as Sally left Montgomery's room and approached the counter in front of her. Sally likely also knew, just as Paula did, that Montgomery's reprieve from death was almost certainly temporary. But for Paula, even if it was only for now, it felt good. Success was sweet. Paula smiled, and Sally smiled back. They had done it.

CHAPTER 12

Harper was awakened by a soft sound in the kitchen. Though typically a heavy sleeper, he had tossed and turned most of the night, reviewing in his mind the upcoming day's events. The plan would be risky. Should he have allowed the three men to know the target? Could he trust them? Was an hour of final review in the morning too little time for them to grasp the details? Their failure could mean disaster.

Harper heard the sound again, barely. He listened carefully into the darkness. After a few seconds, he quietly opened the bedroom door and scanned the living room. A dull light from the kitchen cast odd shadows on the floor and outlined the shape of a man's profile against the open refrigerator.

"What are you doing?" Harper asked.

Carl Joe turned, startled, shutting the door. "I was…uh…looking for a… uh…beer," he stuttered.

"There's no beer in there," Harper said with an icy stare. "We don't drink beer in this house. Now go back in the living room. You're not welcome to rummage through the kitchen."

"I'm sorry," Carl Joe said. "I thought it might help me sleep."

Harper stood waiting, not answering, as Carl Joe returned to the living room. Harper glanced around the kitchen. The handguns lay neatly in a row on the counter where he had left them. Nothing seemed amiss. He reached to the wall and touched the phone receiver and it moved slightly. Had the phone been used? Had someone not replaced it properly in their haste?

Harper unplugged the receiver and carried it with him.

Something wasn't right. If he could trust anything, it was his own instincts. The three of them would only be given the information on a need-to-know, and if he was smart, he'd watch his back. And he was smart.

⋏

The pink glow of the morning sun inched its way into the stillness of the kitchen, illuminating Harper sitting at the table reading his Bible. His huge shoulders and arms held the small, frayed book he had seen his father read one hour each day since he was a boy. His eyes strained in the dim light as he read the fifteenth chapter of Revelation:

And I saw as it were a sea of glass mingled with fire: and them that had gotten the victory over the beast, and over his image, and over his mark, and over the number of his name, stand on the sea of glass, having the harps of God.

And they sing the song of Moses the servant of God, and the song of the Lamb, saying, Great and marvellous are thy works, Lord God Almighty; just and true are thy ways, thou King of saints.

Who shall not fear thee, O Lord, and glorify thy name? For thou only art holy: for all nations shall come and worship before thee; for thy judgments are made manifest.

Harper pushed the Bible away and closed his eyes. Yes, I must remember these verses, he thought. I must learn them. I can do this.

"And I saw as it were…" Harper paused; then after a moment pulled the Bible toward him and reread the passage. He closed his eyes again.

"And I saw as it were a sea of glass…"

His mind went blank.

I can do this! He held the Bible in both hands. He read it again then shut his eyes.

"And I saw as it were a sea—"

You stupid idiot! You're too stupid to do this. It's God's word.

I'm not an idiot. I can do it, Daddy. Yes, I can.

Harper's eyes jerked open. He looked around him, and he was alone. The room was still. Harper's breathing was rapid, and he inhaled deeply to calm down. *My daddy had meant no harm,* he told himself. He had meant no harm, and he had been forgiven.

A

At 5:30, both alarm clocks began ringing, one in the bedroom and one in the living room. Harper had brewed a pot of coffee, and the three men wandered into the kitchen to pour themselves a cup, joining Harper at the card table. Jane cooked breakfast for the men and served them. The four men talked constantly, mostly about firearms and munitions, government conspiracies, and federal agencies. Jane busied herself, washing the dishes and cleaning the kitchen without saying a word.

At six, Harper instructed them to load the van. The drive to Tulsa would take forty-five minutes, and he would wait until they were en route to discuss the plan. Once they were in the car, none of them would be out of his sight.

Maybe he was wrong to suspect a problem. The three men's background checks were clean, according to militia sources. Yet could he trust them? Harper would watch carefully for a slip or a false word or a small mistake. Every militia leader feared infiltration by the feds. If one of these three men was an infiltrator, then he was good. *Damn him!*

Should he postpone? Change the target? Montgomery was the opportunity of a lifetime. The attorney general of the United States, virtually unprotected, was a patient in a Tulsa hospital. An opportunity he couldn't miss. The plan would work.

Harper instructed them to load the boxes in the van. Buddy brought in the hand truck. Carl Joe and Tommy gingerly lifted the edge of the boxes upward, and Buddy eased the hand truck into place. Buddy slowly tilted the hand truck until the boxes lifted off the floor before starting to push it to the living-room door.

"It's supposed to be intravenous fluids," Harper said. "You boys act like its liquid nitro. The ANFO is stable unless you put a little electrical juice through it with this." Harper held up the transmitter.

"We don't want to take no chances," Tommy said.

"You handle the package like that, and everyone will wonder what's in there."

Despite Harper's reassurance of safety, they nervously carried the bomb through the doorway and down the three steps. They opened the back of the van and lifted the bomb in. Carl Joe cut off several feet of yellow rope to strap the boxes down. Buddy shut the door, and they followed Harper back into the house.

Harper was dressed in a pair of navy slacks, white shirt, and a thin black tie—a preacher on visitation rounds. Buddy would look like any visitor in a denim shirt, blue jeans, and white sneakers. Carl Joe and Tommy had slept in the uniforms, now sufficiently wrinkled to pass as used. Harper loaded the knapsack with tools—pliers, tape, flashlights, screwdrivers—and gave the knapsack to Buddy. Harper slipped a leather holster over his left shoulder and slid in his Browning 9 mm. A blue sports coat covered the weapon, and Harper would disguise it further by holding a Bible pressed close to his chest. Buddy stuffed his Ruger in the knapsack. Carl Joe and Tommy taped each other's weapons on their backs. Jane came out of the bedroom wearing a flower-print dress, her hair tied into a bun with a thin red ribbon. She carried a clear glass vase in one hand and a bouquet of yellow mums and daisies in the other.

Harper gathered them into the kitchen. "O Lord," he prayed, "Lord God Almighty, grant us the power to destroy thine enemies and bring glory to thy name. Allow us, O Lord, to reveal thy judgment as we set out to battle the spiritual forces of darkness. Grant us protection from all harm, and keep us safe from evil. Amen."

Harper asked the three men to go to the van, and he watched them carefully through the window, observing every detail. Jane started to leave, but he pulled her aside and handed her an envelope.

"We need a contingency plan," he said in a low voice. "I plan to hide the bomb in the stairwell. Then we'll leave on the second floor and out the main lobby. You pick us up in the front of the hospital and drive us to the north parking lot. I tested the transmitter from there, and I know it will work. We'll wait a few minutes before using a pay phone in the lobby to call our demands to the hospital and also to that reporter at Channel Three. If they try to evacuate the hospital, we'll blow it up. If they bring in the bomb squad to search the building, we'll blow it up. The plan is solid, but I want a contingency." He pointed to the envelope. "Putting the bomb in the stairwell will take about fifteen minutes. If we're not out in forty minutes, you call this number on the pay phone in the lobby and read this letter. Then go to the van and wait."

"Yes," she said, "that's clear." She slid the envelope in her purse.

"The portable television is in the van so we can watch and see if our demands are met. If they're not, we'll detonate the bomb and drive away." Harper's voice dropped even lower. "But I'm worried. I'm not sure I can trust these men."

"Why do you say that?"

He told her about the kitchen phone and Carl Joe searching for a beer in the refrigerator. "I may be overreacting. I could be wrong."

"We can't be too careful."

"Then help me watch them. Is your weapon in your purse?"

She patted her purse.

"Keep it handy."

She nodded.

Harper and Jane joined the others in the van. Harper drove. The van followed the narrow road through the trees, leaving the compound behind. Harper looked back in his rearview mirror. He had worked hard for all this— an enormous investment in time, energy, blood, and sweat. He hoped he would see it again.

Chapter 13

Mist steamed the walls of the glass shower as the warm droplets soothed Paula, massaging her aching neck and shoulders. Up early this morning, she allowed a few moments of luxury, soaking up the heat and relaxing.

Reverend Pettigrew was improving. She'd transfer him to the floor today if all went well. The nurses hadn't called about Montgomery, which probably meant he was alive. Her other twelve patients weren't in the intensive care unit so they would be easier. She hoped rounds would be quick.

She turned off the water, leaned forward, and squeezed her thick hair, milking it downward, the water flowing to the shower floor. After wrapping it in a towel, she stepped out and slipped into a terry-cloth robe. She dried her hair before nimbly braiding it into a single plait. At the end she tied a small bow. It was a style she had worn since childhood, taught by her mother, a ritual every day before school.

Paula pulled up a chair to put on her makeup. She still felt the excitement from the early morning episode in the intensive care unit. They had saved Montgomery's life—a nationally famous person and, even more, a patient who was very ill. Jennifer had told them how grateful she was. She knew they had nearly lost him.

They might not be so lucky next time.

The entire code blue team had arrived shortly after Montgomery converted to a normal rhythm. Dr. England came in from home, grumbling and disagreeable. Paula talked to the nurses for a good two hours to unwind—Sally had actually been civil—and didn't go to bed until three. The alarm jarred her awake at six. Three hours of sleep. Not enough. Tonight she'd catch up, since she wasn't on call. She'd curl up in bed with her cats next to her and read a romance novel, her favorite, and fall asleep in the middle of a chapter, her usual.

Paula finished her makeup, dressed, fed the cats, and left for the hospital. With three hours of sleep, she hoped the day would be simple, routine. With her luck, it wasn't likely.

⅄

Jennifer wearily slumped in the chair next to Montgomery's bed. Being near his code blue last night had snapped her back into reality. He would likely die, and she had not allowed that thought to enter her mind. He was strong, the strongest man she had ever known. How could he die?

She looked at the equipment keeping him alive—ventilator, IVs, monitors, aortic balloon, oxygen, catheters—and realized how accustomed she had become to it all. She knew every piece of equipment and what it was supposed to do. She knew all the bells and alarms, which ones were serious, and which were a nuisance. She had learned much in only two days.

Two days. Had it only been two days? Incredible! The last two days had seemed like a lifetime.

Sally stuck her head into the room. "How's he doing?" she asked.

Jennifer started to answer, but the emotion choked her, and the tears began forming.

"I brought you a cup of coffee," Sally said softly. "You look like you need one."

"Thanks," Jennifer said, reaching for it.

Sally crossed to her and handed her the cup. "You can never give up hope," she said. "I've seen patients worse than this do well."

"I won't give up on him."

"We won't either. We're doing everything possible to give him the best chance."

Jennifer held the cup in both hands and took a sip. The warmth felt good as she swallowed. She appreciated Sally's thoughtfulness. A slight movement in Jennifer's peripheral vision caught her attention. She turned and saw Montgomery's eyes open. His eyes were looking straight at her. She jumped up and nearly dropped her coffee.

⚔

"Have you heard anything from Jake?" Jeffrey Reese asked Matt.

An early morning phone call at home from his boss was a bad omen. Matt had been worried that Jake hadn't called, and now his boss was worried, too.

"I haven't heard a word," Matt said. "I hope he's in a place where he can call."

Matt pushed away his bowl of cereal. He'd normally be in the office within the hour. He wondered why Reese's sudden rush.

"I read your update on Harper," Reese said. "This is one serious loon. Do you have all the abortion clinics covered?"

"Night and day."

"I was thinking," Reese said. "We may want to knock on his front door so he knows we're watching him."

Matt poured himself a cup of coffee and took a sip before he answered. "It could blow the undercover operation," he said. "Maybe even put Jake's life at risk."

"Jake should be safe. We may save some lives."

"It's your call."

"Why don't you take Stan and a couple of agents and check out the church and the property."

"A couple of agents? Shouldn't we use the special response team?"

"Do we have probable cause?"

"We may have enough for a warrant. We just don't know where the stuff is. I'm sure it's on his land there somewhere."

"If we brought in the SRT, it could quickly get out of control, and we'd still probably find nothing." Reese paused for a moment. "I just want to knock and talk. Let him know we're on to him. I'm hoping he'll back off."

"It's a militia group." Matt hated to state the obvious. He waited for Reese's response but didn't really expect one. "Okay, we'll do it," Matt said finally, "but it's your neck."

"I want four agents," Reese said quickly, "including you."

"Yes, sir. So no search warrant?"

"No, knock and talk, and make it snappy. I have a bad feeling about this."

"Me, too."

Matt's feelings were beyond bad. Jake was a professional. He would have called if he'd had half a chance. In the past three years they'd worked on multiple undercover cases where Matt was his contact. Jake had never failed to get the word to him. Something was wrong. Definitely wrong.

⚔

John Hays had coffee with the same four men every workday for the past eight years. They hogged the corner of the Saint Luke's coffee shop for an hour every morning before their shifts started, tackling the topics of religion, politics, sports, and hobbies, telling a few jokes, mostly clean, and solving to their satisfaction the host of ills that troubled the hospital and medicine in general.

John and Wes Baskins had started the tradition ten years earlier. John would meet Baskins after loading his janitor's cart and moving it from the basement to one of the wards, and then they'd sit for an hour drinking coffee. One by one over the years the other three had joined them. This morning the five men huddled around a table sharing a freshly brewed pot and eating breakfast. Steven Pinson, a heavyset forty-year-old with Elvis-styled hair and matching Elvis gut, had worked in the respiratory therapy department for fifteen years and through attrition was now the supervisor. Clark Arnold, with a beaked nose, receding hairline, and horn-rimmed glasses, had been stuck in the basement at the same low-level accounting position for ten years. Nathan Heinemann, an odd man, anorexic and pale in appearance as long as they had known him, had worked in purchasing for nine years and was the newest member of the morning coffee group. He aspired to be a true-crime writer and was continuously pumping Baskins for stories, much to Baskins's irritation. Wes Baskins was especially irritable today. He said his knees were killing him, and if he spent one more day at the security desk outside the intensive care unit, he'd need both knees replaced.

John ate the only healthy breakfast—granola cereal, skim milk, and decaf coffee. After an episode of angina a couple of years earlier, he had quit smoking and lost thirty pounds. His arthritis prevented him from exercising much, so he took his medicine and ate carefully, hoping to live long enough to enjoy a little retirement and see his grandchildren grow up. Heinemann and Arnold only drank coffee. Baskins was working on a cinnamon roll. Pinson was stuffing down bacon, fried eggs, sausage, milk, and a couple of doughnuts.

"That breakfast there's gonna kill you," John said.

"I'll take my chances," Pinson said. He pointed at John's bowl. "I couldn't choke that granola down if I was starving."

"With that tire around your belly," John said, "it doesn't look like starving would happen anytime soon."

The other three laughed.

"Very funny," Pinson said as he shoveled in a mouthful of fried eggs.

Heinemann was sitting next to Baskins. He leaned over and whispered, "I heard Montgomery was poisoned. Any inside scoop?"

"Give it a rest," Baskins said.

"How long you be guarding the governor?" John asked.

"Attorney general." Baskins reached for the coffeepot and poured a second cup. "They're hoping to send him back to Washington soon. The sooner the better, as far as I'm concerned. And I'm sick of that secretary of Montgomery's. She threw a fit when she noticed we weren't searching the employees."

John tossed Baskins a packet of sugar. "So you're back at it today?"

"Yeah, but I'm hoping I can switch with Harry Wilansky this morning so I can get up and walk around."

"They may have no one to guard," Pinson said. "I heard they coded him again last night."

"How did you hear about that?" Baskins asked. "You haven't been to work yet."

"I know everything that's going on in this hospital."

"I'm sure I'll hear all about it," John said. "They don't pay me no mind when they're talking when I be cleaning the intensive care unit."

Arnold looked at Pinson. "You still have your lottery going?"

"Yeah, I've got five bucks on today between two and three."

"What's this?" Baskins asked.

"The respiratory department has a lottery. We're betting on Montgomery's date and hour of death."

"That's sick," Baskins said.

"Is it doubled if he dies on your shift?" Heinemann asked, grinning.

"Now *that* would be unethical." Pinson feigned disgust.

"Remind me not to get sick anytime soon," John said. He looked at his watch. "It's six forty-five. I best be going up to the unit."

John stood to leave. Pinson stuffed the rest of his breakfast into his mouth. The coffee drinkers had already switched to Styrofoam cups, ready to carry.

"Same time tomorrow?" John asked.

They nodded in agreement.

John smiled. He never missed their morning coffee.

Chapter 14

The forty-five-minute drive to Tulsa was quiet. The plan was basic, and Harper explained it to them in fifteen minutes. None of the three men asked any questions, which worried Harper a bit, thinking it was because they didn't understand or know enough to ask. Just to be certain, he outlined the plan in detail a second time. He knew he was obsessing, but it was important. A mistake would be costly. Yet he would be present throughout, so if they became confused, they could follow his lead. The placement would take fifteen to thirty minutes. Fifteen minutes later they would be safely in the van.

Harper turned right into the main entrance of the hospital and followed the service road to the back. He drove by the loading dock slowly. The area was empty, just as he had seen it before. Satisfied, Harper continued on the service road circling the hospital to the covered drive at the front entrance. Several cars were waiting, with people loading and unloading. A couple of elderly patients were waiting in wheelchairs, attended by orderlies or nurses. Harper noticed only one security guard, and he was helping a young mother holding a newborn climb up into a minivan. After about ten minutes, Harper had moved up to the front of the line.

"You go on around," Harper said to Jane, glancing around to be sure no one was close by, "but wait for my signal before you back up to the dock."

Jane nodded.

Harper lowered his voice. "And as soon as the men finish unloading the package, you leave, park the car, and come in the front entrance. When we're done, I want you in the car sitting here in the covered drive. Understand?"

"I understand."

"Good," Harper said. He opened the car door to get out, but then hesitated, leaning back toward Jane to kiss her gently on the cheek. "You be careful," he said.

"You be careful, too, Sam." Jane reached out and pulled his ear close to her. "Your daddy," she said in a whisper, "would be proud."

"No," he said softly. "He would never be proud of me." Harper stepped away and pointed to Buddy. "You come with me."

Buddy nodded and followed Harper into the hospital. They entered through the revolving doors, ducking their heads as they passed under the video camera. Harper clutched the Bible tightly to his chest and looked like a visiting pastor. Buddy, casually dressed with the knapsack over his shoulder, walked a few steps behind Harper, close by but to all onlookers separate.

Harper noticed that the lobby was fairly crowded with visitors. Several people were lined up at the information counter on his left and others at the admissions desk on his right. There seemed to be enough commotion for Buddy and him to blend in.

Harper retraced his steps to the specialty wing, followed the stairwell to the basement, and circled around the staircase to the hallway underneath. A moment later, Buddy joined him. No one else was in the hallway. No guards or surveillance equipment. Not even a single smoker sneaking a quick drag at the smoke hole. Harper thought his good fortune would be Montgomery's bad luck.

Harper cracked open the door and looked out to the dock, watching for Jane. After a couple of minutes he saw her driving slowly by. He signaled, and she turned into the dock area.

Jane backed up the van. Carl Joe and Tommy opened the pair of rear doors and carefully lifted the hand truck and boxes to the loading dock, looking more nervous than Harper would have liked. As soon as they closed the van's doors, Jane drove off. Carl Joe and Tommy rolled the hand truck into the hospital entrance.

"Put the boxes by the wall," Harper whispered to Carl Joe and Tommy, "then stand by the entrance with these cigarettes, like you're about to light up. Buddy and I will be over by the stairwell. We need to wait about ten minutes before going upstairs to meet Jane on the second floor."

Harper timed the ten minutes on his watch and then signaled them. He and Buddy walked to the elevator. Harper pressed the button and waited. The doors opened with a chime to an empty car, and Harper waved them all on. They rode to the second floor without stopping. At the second floor they stepped out into a large hallway outside the entrance to the chest pain unit. The four men separated again into pairs. Carl Joe and Tommy pushed the hand truck a few feet down the hall before stopping to lean against the wall. Harper moved with Buddy in the opposite direction, acting like they were having a conversation. After a couple of minutes, Jane strolled by, holding a vase filled with cut flowers, pausing to read a sign near the elevator before nodding and turning toward the entrance to the chest pain unit.

"Okay," Harper said in a whisper to Buddy as Jane walked by. "Now is the time. Let's go."

⋏

Reverend Pettigrew had been coughing bright-red blood for half an hour when Paula arrived. She had expected him to be improved today, ready to move to the medical floor. Instead, he was much worse. His face was gray and his lips were blue, and he was sweating profusely, sitting up in bed, holding the handrails, struggling for air.

Toni had started her shift at six o'clock by checking Pettigrew's vital signs. She was taking his pulse when he sat up sharply, cried out, and suddenly coughed, spraying blood all over his bed. In the next few seconds, his condition had quickly deteriorated—his blood pressure plummeted, oxygen saturation fell below 60 percent, and his breathing became shallow and rapid. Toni had increased his oxygen, turned up his IV, and then hurried out to page Paula.

Paula had just parked her car when she received the page. She had rushed to the unit and immediately knew Pettigrew was in trouble.

"Looks like a pulmonary embolus," she said to Toni, "or possibly a pneumothorax, but a pneumo wouldn't account for the blood."

"What do we need, Doctor?"

"I want a stat portable chest X-ray, blood gases, CBC, and lytes. And bring in the ventilator. Let's move quickly!"

The monitors' alarms warned of his distressed vital signs.

Reverend Pettigrew turned his head toward Paula. "Dr. Barrett," he said, his voice barely audible.

Paula didn't hear him at first. "Get respiratory in here!" she said to Toni. "And I want a CT scan of the chest as quick as possible."

"Dr. Barrett," he said again, reaching out for her arm.

Paula felt the tug on her sleeve and turned to him. "Yes, Reverend?"

"No ventilator," he said, each word a whisper as he struggled for air.

She leaned forward. "I'm sorry. Say again?"

After resting a moment to gather his strength, he lifted his head toward Paula. "No ventilator," he said. "It's my choice."

"Reverend Pettigrew, we must put you back on the ventilator. It's your only chance."

"Please," he gasped. "I can't."

"If we don't," she said softly, "you may die."

"I know. It's in God's hands."

"Dr. Barrett," Toni said, "he wrote a handwritten letter for you last night after Mr. Montgomery's code. He said no code for him."

Paula turned back to Pettigrew. "Is that what you want?"

He nodded.

"Toni, I want a 5,000-unit bolus of Heparin IV now."

"Yes, Dr. Barrett."

"Then start a Heparin drip. Let's do it now."

"Yes, ma'am."

"I still want that chest CT." She turned to Pettigrew. "No ventilator, but I'm not ready to give up yet."

Reverend Pettigrew was as close to death as any patient she had seen, as pale and gray as a ghost, struggling for every breath, but at that moment he looked directly at her and smiled, his eyes clear and very much alive.

⋏

Baskins tossed his coffee cup in the trash as he stepped into the specialty wing elevator, not at all eager to begin his shift at the security desk. He had covered for Wilansky when he had pulled his back playing softball a month ago. He would remind him of the favor and suggest a switch. Hopefully, the attorney general would be in Washington by the end of the day; then his routine would return to normal. No more complaining families. No more of that slimy Asher hanging around drinking coffee, bragging about his FBI exploits and bitching about Montgomery's secretary.

Montgomery will be in Washington, or he won't. If Pinson was right, he might even be dead. A lottery on Montgomery's death. That was disgusting. Baskins shook his head. These medical people were morbid, maybe even more morbid than cops.

Baskins rode the elevator and exited into a small third-floor lobby. To his left, cutting off at a right angle, was the hallway to the intensive care unit. Twenty feet down the hallway the security desk straddled the entrance, blocking the ICU's access.

To his right was the family waiting room and an unexpected disturbance. A news crew was filming a female reporter holding a microphone in the face of Howard Parrish, the administrator. She was talking to Parrish but looking at the camera. Fifteen or twenty people crowded behind the camera, watching the impromptu event. The reporter had positioned Parrish so the hospital's logo was directly behind them on the window of the waiting room.

Parrish appeared nervous, and his answers sounded defensive.

"I don't know where you obtained your information," Parrish said sharply, "but the hospital has no official position on Mr. Montgomery's condition.

The attorney general's office in Washington has been releasing a daily update, and the hospital declines to comment further."

"Mr. Parrish, our source informs us that he underwent a code blue last night. Is this report true?"

"The hospital neither confirms nor denies that report."

"We've heard a report that he required three electrical shocks to revive him."

"Ms. Beeson, you know I can't comment on that. I think the interview is over. Thank you."

Parrish stepped out of the lights, and Cara Beeson turned fully to the camera.

"And there you have it. The hospital does not deny the report that the attorney general was brought back to life last night after suffering from a near-fatal abnormal heart rhythm. The hospital also does not deny that he required three electric shocks to revive him. We continue to bring you the latest on the medical condition of Ronald Montgomery. This is Cara Beeson, Alert Three News, reporting live from Saint Luke's Hospital. Now back to you, Terry."

The reporter remained still for a moment.

"That's a wrap," the cameraman said. He lifted the camera off his shoulders and turned off the floodlight.

Baskins watched a few seconds as they loaded their equipment and the crowd dispersed. He wondered who had allowed the news crew in the hospital. He wouldn't have expected Parrish to agree to an impromptu news conference.

Baskins looked down the hallway and noticed Wilansky sitting behind the security desk. Standing behind Wilansky was a man in his midthirties, dressed in a dark suit, shifting uncomfortably from one foot to the other. Baskins thought he must be an FBI agent fresh from the academy. They were easy to spot.

"Harry," Baskins said, walking up. "They didn't interview you on camera?"

"No, they wanted to, but Parrish wouldn't allow it." Wilansky pointed to the man next to him. "Wes, meet Bob Godfrey."

The two men shook hands.

"He's local FBI."

"Glad to have you," Baskins said. He turned back to Wilansky before the agent could respond. "Harry, you look pretty damn comfortable sitting there."

"I'm fine, Wes. Why don't you walk the rounds this morning."

"Suits me." *Wilansky is too easy*, Baskins thought. *He's allowing me to switch duties without calling in a favor.* "I'll make the rounds for you and check back on the hour."

"That works. Bring me a cup of coffee when you come back by."

"No problem," Baskins said, looking serious, holding back a smile.

A slender, redheaded woman started past Baskins.

"Excuse me, ma'am," Baskins said. "We need to check your handbag."

"And why is that?" she asked sharply.

"We've increased the security of the intensive care unit."

"My husband had a stroke two weeks ago, and I've been here every day. I'm more familiar to the staff than half the temp nurses they've hired."

"That may be, but we need to search your handbag." He pointed toward her.

She tossed her purse on the desk. "Some asswipe from Washington comes in and changes the routine for everybody."

Baskins slid the purse to Wilansky, who opened it and began digging through it.

"What's next?" she snapped. "Searching body cavities?"

Baskins stiffened at the comment. "Are you hiding something that would make that necessary?"

"Depends on how horny you are, doesn't it?"

Baskins quickly glanced up and down at her. "I'm not that horny, ma'am."

"You're a prick!"

And you're a bitch, Baskins thought, and wished he could say it out loud without losing his job. "We're just following orders, ma'am."

"Yeah, just like the Gestapo."

"It's clean," Wilansky said, shoving the purse toward Baskins.

Baskins grabbed the purse and held it up. She snatched the purse from him and turned down the hallway, raising her middle finger in disgust.

"Have a nice day," Baskins called out as she walked away.

"Luck o' the Irish, eh?" Wilansky mumbled.

"I'll bring you that coffee," Baskins said quickly, hoping Wilansky hadn't changed his mind.

"Cream and sugar."

"You've got it," Baskins said and smiled.

Baskins turned down the hallway toward the specialty stairwell. *Maybe knee surgery isn't so likely after all*, he thought. He'd stroll around the hospital, avoiding the host of unhappy visitors like that woman, then hike up and down a couple of staircases and come back for coffee. If Montgomery went to Washington, the rest of the day might require a visit to the ER or possibly the coffee shop. No problem.

⅄

Jennifer squeezed Montgomery's hand every few seconds and smiled broadly. Little had actually changed. He was still on the ventilator, still on the balloon pump, still critical and potentially near death. Little had changed, except now his eyes were open. His brain was working. There was a glimmer of hope.

Montgomery looked at her for a few seconds, and then his eyes shifted to Sally. Jennifer asked him to look back at her, and his eyes instantly turned toward her. Jennifer both laughed and cried. She squeezed his hand again, and then on her command she felt him gently squeeze hers.

Sally quickly tested all four extremities. He was able to move them, but only weakly. Jennifer stood and crossed over to the opposite side of the room, and he could follow her with his eyes. Sally asked him if he could blink once for yes and twice for no. To their amazement he blinked once and then also nodded his head.

Sally left to tell Paula. Jennifer slowly and carefully explained what had happened to him in the past two days, beginning with the Merrimac Hotel and ending with the present. When she paused and asked if he understood, he blinked. He understood.

There was hope. Finally there was some hope!

CHAPTER 15

The two-lane blacktop road wove through the oak, cottonwood, and hickory, snaking its way into unfamiliar territory. Reflections of dark-green foliage flashed on the black hood of the speeding automobile. A dusty gray haze rose from the road as the first morning heat burned off the overnight blanket of condensation.

"How much farther to Harper's?" Stan asked. Stan drank the last bit of his coffee and threw his cup on the floorboard.

Matt glanced at the cup. His car was spotless, immaculate, always perfectly detailed—*just like*, Matt thought, *a car should be*. He couldn't tolerate Stan's trashed-out vehicle, so he had insisted they use his car for the trip to Harper's compound. If Stan made a mess, he might regret it.

Stan noticed Matt's grimace and laughed. "Hey, I'll pick it up when we're done." He smiled widely and crossed his heart. "I promise."

Matt ignored his comment and answered the question. "ETA's five minutes. Baker and Rice should be waiting at the turnoff."

"A militia group, right?" Stan said, shaking his head. "I bet they have an arsenal—the latest and the greatest."

"We're going to walk up in plain view. No SWAT teams or ambushes. We don't want a Waco."

"Our plan is to stroll right up to their front door?"

"Knock, talk, and go," Matt said. "We're sending a message."

"Reese approved this? Isn't this ignoring standard operating procedures? Worse, risking Jake's cover?"

"It was Reese's call."

They approached a black sedan parked on the shoulder, and Stan pointed. "There's Baker and Rice."

Matt felt his heart jump with anticipation as he watched the two men climb into the backseat. Harper's compound was just a couple of minutes away now. His gut was churning and twisting in knots on this one. He was sure—he felt it deep down—this day would be a disaster.

▴

When John Hays arrived at the security desk, Wilansky was looking harassed. Wilansky had just informed an irate family member that the intensive care unit was closed to visitors. As one of Jennifer's latest attempts to improve security, she had decided that no visitors would be allowed. The family member hadn't taken the news well.

"So Wes talked you into switching?" John asked, stopping in front of the security desk. Asher was standing next to Wilansky.

"Wes tricked me," Wilansky said. "It was quiet when he was here a few minutes ago. Now he's out doing me a *big favor* by walking my rounds."

John laughed. "Wes is good at tricks."

Asher glanced over his shoulder. "I wish Godfrey would hurry up," he said sharply. "I need my cup of coffee."

Besides Wilansky and Baskins, the unit had a detail of four FBI agents. Two local agents, Godfrey and Harrison, had arrived shortly before noon the previous day. Asher, having just returned from breakfast, sent Godfrey to fetch him some coffee. The second local agent, Harrison, was assigned to the back stairwell to guard the rear entrance. Simmons would be waiting impatiently for Asher to relieve him outside Montgomery's room so he could go to breakfast. Only Simmons and Asher guarded Montgomery. Jennifer had insisted. Wilansky would stay at the front. Baskins was making rounds somewhere; exactly where was anyone's guess.

A gray-haired, elderly woman carrying a huge purse in one hand while navigating a cane in the other approached the desk. Wilansky informed her of the new policy then listened to a five-minute barrage of angry insults.

"McLaughlin's policy sucks," Asher said as the woman walked away. "McLaughlin thinks a few visitors will interfere."

"She should be out here taking the abuse," Wilansky said.

"Not very likely," Asher said sharply. "She'll stay in her office and pretend she's in charge."

Wilansky shrugged. "Baskins said he'd be back in an hour with my coffee. I'm gonna give him hell."

"He deserves it," John said, smiling.

A young man, another family member, dressed in a gray, pinstripe suit, a banker or a lawyer, approached the security desk, anxious to see his father in the unit. Wilansky informed him of the policy, and the young man cussed and screamed, demanding an exception.

Wilansky would have a steady stream of visitors, and they would all be unhappy, but not as unhappy as Wilansky was with John's friend Baskins. John gave Wilansky a short wave and entered the unit to start his day.

⅄

Harper was ready to go. The chest pain unit's nurses' station faced an open space that served as a reception area, but this early in the morning, a few minutes after seven, the chairs were empty. Harper glanced at Carl Joe and nodded slightly, his signal to move. Carl Joe and Tommy had positioned the hand truck in the hallway just outside the chest pain unit. Tommy was casually leaning back against the wall. Carl Joe knelt down and tied his shoe.

Harper nodded at Buddy and watched as he threw the knapsack over his shoulder and entered. Harper followed close behind. Directly ahead of them was the nurses' station, dividing the floor into two long hallways. The unit secretary's face was in the morning paper, and she never looked up. Buddy's instructions were to proceed down the left side, walk slowly to the end, and wait for Harper.

Harper had purposely chosen to begin a few minutes after seven—the night shift had just ended, and the day shift staff were preoccupied with their morning chores. It seemed too early for many of the doctors.

Harper took a position at the beginning of the left hallway. Grasping his Bible in one hand, he slipped a small piece of paper out of his pocket as though he were looking at a list of patients. He tilted his eyes upward as Buddy walked slowly down the hallway away from him, nearing the end. In the opposite direction Carl Joe and Tommy were in his line of vision just outside the chest pain unit. They hadn't moved. Several nurses were going in and out of patients' rooms up and down the hallway, but none had entered the nurses' station. No doctors appeared to be on the floor. He had chosen the time well.

Jane followed behind her husband and turned down the right hallway. He pretended not to notice. Jane walked briskly, her head erect, stride full, carrying the glass vase of flowers. Halfway down the hallway, she stopped, fumbled in her purse, and removed a tissue, gently wiping a supposed tear from her eye. She dabbed her eyes as she glanced around. The patients' doors were closed. No nurses were in the hallway. No doctors. No staff.

Jane held out the vase and turned it over, dumping the flowers and water on the floor. She lifted the glass vase high and threw it down hard, shattering it into pieces. After hiking her dress up above her waist, she fell to the floor.

"Help me," Jane cried out. "Help, help."

Within seconds five nurses were standing beside her, coming from all directions.

"Are you all right?" one of the nurses asked, leaning over her, out of breath.

Jane pulled at her dress, trying to cover herself, and began crying. "I slipped on some water," Jane sobbed. "I think I broke my back."

"Don't move," a second nurse said. She seemed to be in charge. "We'll get some help."

"I can't believe someone left water on the floor," Jane said sharply.

"I didn't see any water a second ago," the first nurse said.

"What are you saying?" Jane said, acting insulted.

"She's not saying anything," the charge nurse said quickly. "We're going to call the house doctor."

"No, no," Jane said. "Give me a second."

"I'm going to call the doctor."

"No, please. Let me see if I can move my legs." She began to move her legs slightly.

Jane glanced toward the far end of the hallway, and Harper was standing there. He looked at her and nodded slightly. Buddy would have secured the nurses' station at the back of the unit and signaled Carl Joe and Tommy into the stairwell. The plan was proceeding. Harper disappeared around the corner. They were all in position.

Jane immediately stood up. "There," she said. "I think I'm fine."

The nurses backed away a bit.

"Are you sure?" the charge nurse asked, surprised.

Jane looked around at the floor. "Oh, I'm so sorry for the mess. I think I jarred my back. It seems fine now."

"You should go to the emergency room and see our doctor," the nurse offered. "I'm sure the hospital will pay for it."

"I'm fine now. I don't need a doctor."

"I should call the house supervisor," the charge nurse said. She reached into her pocket for a note pad and pen. "May I have your name? We need to write up an incident report."

"I'm fine now. Really I am. I don't need to fill out any forms."

"It'd take just a second. It'd be best for you to document your injuries."

"But I'm not injured. Thank you so much." Jane smoothed her dress and picked up a few of the cut flowers from the floor. "You're all so nice. Thank you for your timely assistance." She turned her back to them and briskly walked away.

Chapter 16

Reverend Pettigrew was breathing more comfortably, probably because of the oxygen, Paula thought, rather than the heparin thinning his blood. His color remained a pale gray, and a cold sweat covered his face and chest. He was teetering on the edge of death.

Paula suspected a pulmonary embolus, but the diagnosis required a CT scan of the chest. The nurse had just informed her that due to a multiple-vehicle accident in the ER, the earliest the radiology department could schedule a CT scan was eight o'clock, forty minutes away. The CT scan would define the size and location of the blood clot, and if it was a clot, a radiologist could inject it directly with a powerful blood thinner. Paula believed his chances without the CT scan were dismal. Forty minutes might be too long.

"His pulse ox is only 60 percent," Toni said, "and that's on 100 percent rebreather."

"That's the best we'll do without a ventilator," Paula said, mostly to herself. Paula was struggling with Pettigrew's decision about the ventilator. His pulmonary embolus, though sometimes fatal, was treatable. His oxygen could be improved optimally with the ventilator, allowing time for the medicine to help the clot. Yet Pettigrew had decided and signed the legal papers. She was required to respect his wishes, regardless of her personal feelings.

His eyes were shut, but she thought he was awake. She wanted to argue with him. *Give me the chance to save your life*, she wanted to say. *I can't help you if you insist on dying.* She fought the impulse. It was his life. She was just the doctor.

Attachment wasn't an emotion she was accustomed to. She hadn't even met Reverend Pettigrew before she had admitted him, but she liked and respected him, and now seeing him dying in front of her was difficult—more difficult than she would have expected. When she was in training in the unit in Oklahoma City, patients died every day, but she had only known them a few days, at most a few weeks, and often they were too sick to be anything more than a patient assigned to her. But with Pettigrew it seemed different. He was a minister. Her nurse loved him, and she could see why. He was kind and caring, a person whose life made a difference.

Let me save you, she wanted to scream. *Let me save your life.*

He was so sure of his mortality, his belief in eternal life so real, his confidence in his God so complete. She envied him. The thought of death had always scared her. Though she knew intellectually that she believed in God, a by-product of her Methodist upbringing, her heart often struggled with the concept. Pettigrew's unwavering joy at death was filling her with unexpected, perplexing emotions.

Concentrate on your patients. They come first. You don't have time for this.

No ventilator for Reverend Pettigrew. She'd live with his decision. Would he?

"Doctor, are you all right?"

Toni's question brought her back to reality. "Yes. I'm fine," she lied.

"I asked if you want any more lab. The tech's here."

"No. It won't matter. We'll wait for the CT."

Paula walked toward the doctors' desk to write a progress note. Sally and Jennifer were outside Montgomery's door drinking coffee. Jennifer was animated, laughing and telling Sally a story. Jennifer noticed Paula and started toward her.

"Did you hear the news about the attorney general?"

"No, what?"

"He's awake," Jennifer said with a broad smile. "He's out of his coma."

"That's great. Maybe now he's—"

"Ms. McLaughlin?"

They both turned as Asher walked up. Anticipating official business, Paula waited to finish.

"Yes, Mike," Jennifer said. "What is it?"

"The security guards are complaining about the no-visitors policy we instituted."

"You mean the families are upset?"

"Yes, but of course I told them the policy was essential to the attorney general's safety."

"They'll get over it. Why don't you switch with Simmons so he can get some breakfast."

"Yes, ma'am."

Jennifer turned back to Paula. "Sally called Dr. England, and he's going to wean him off the aortic balloon."

"That's a remarkable improvement."

"He's going to make it. He's really going to make it!"

Paula was glad. Two deaths today would be too much tragedy.

⋏

Sally Carpenter stepped into Arthur Hyatt's room.

"Mrs. Hyatt," she said, "I'm sorry to tell you, but the FBI has closed the unit to visitors. We're asking the visitors to leave."

Laura Hyatt was in a chair next to her husband, holding his hand. He was awake and sitting in bed, eating breakfast.

"I heard that," she said. "It's ridiculous. My husband needs me here."

"I threw a fit myself, but I was overridden."

"I'll call the administrator," she said firmly.

"He was the one I complained to."

She folded her arms across her chest. "What if I refuse?"

Sally shrugged. "They'll probably arrest you."

Arthur Hyatt spoke up. "It's not worth the trouble, Laura. As soon as my sugars come down, they'll be moving me out anyway."

"It's been challenging for all of us," Sally said. "They're talking about moving the attorney general to Bethesda later today."

"See, honey," he said. "It'd just be a few hours. I'll be fine. The nurses will take good care of me."

Laura didn't look convinced.

"I promise I'll keep an eye on him."

Laura stood. "This is total crap," she said loudly and pointed her finger at Sally. "If anything happens to him, I'll have my attorney on you so fast—"

"We'll try—"

"I'm not intimidated," she interrupted, "by you or your goons out front." Her finger stabbed the air as she spoke. "Either I'm sitting next to my *seriously ill* husband tomorrow, or I'll be at the courthouse getting a judge's order."

"I hope that won't be necessary."

"You'd better be right."

Laura leaned over her husband and pecked him on the cheek. She grabbed her purse and stood a moment in front of Sally, as if ready to make another threat. Instead, she quickly turned and winked at her husband.

"I'll see *you* tomorrow," she said.

Neither her husband nor Sally had any doubt that she would.

⋏

Jake eyed the three men as they stopped to rest. Allowing the plan to proceed this far was a mistake. He had been careless. He had wanted to bring in Matt days ago to catch Harper in the act, but Harper was careful, much too careful, and Jake never had the opportunity. Harper was one paranoid bastard.

The hospital was a complete surprise. The target was supposed to be an abortion clinic, and Harper had told him it would be unoccupied. Every abortion clinic in the region would have ATF surveillance, and he expected he'd have backup. The hospital had nothing. Harper had tricked him. Now the situation was desperate. These rank amateurs could blow this place up and kill hundreds of innocent people. And the attorney general. The stakes had risen enormously. Jake needed to make his move and make it quick. They'd plant the bomb and be gone in five minutes.

"Jane was perfect," Harper laughed, breaking the silence.

Harper's laugh jarred Jake from his thoughts. Harper was peering out the small square window into the chest pain unit. The other two stood across the stairwell from Jake, so close he could smell their sweat. The bomb was in the middle of the four men, inches away from Jake's touch, yet miles from his control. He should have made a move downstairs in the stairwell, but he wasn't sure then how Jane figured in the plan. He even worried she might have a second detonator. He had been wrong to wait.

"They didn't suspect anything," Harper said, turning to face them. "Buddy, hand me the knapsack."

Buddy handed Harper the knapsack.

Jake saw Harper's hard face and empty eyes. He had underestimated how dangerous Harper was. Harper's plan was meticulous, cold, calculated. *He'll blow up this hospital*, Jake thought. *Sure as hell, the bastard will blow it all up. It's up to me—against the three of them. No mistakes. Stay close and be ready.*

Harper pointed to Jake. "I want you here to guard our rear."

Jake couldn't believe what he was hearing. Staying behind was a big problem.

Harper pointed to the other two. "You follow me."

Harper began climbing up the stairs to the third floor. The two men gently lifted the hand truck and followed.

Jake had to decide quickly. A couple of minutes were all he had.

They rounded the corner and were out of his sight.

Jake was glad he had taped an extra gun to his leg, taking a risk that Harper would discover it. He quietly peeled the tape off and held the weapon in his hand. He took a deep breath and let it out slowly. He might have to kill them all.

He couldn't hear any noise above him, but he wouldn't have expected any. They were there, one flight up, preparing enough explosives to obliterate this wing of the hospital. Jake took one stair at a time, silently, cautiously, ready for anything. He pressed against the wall, his weapon pointing up the stairs, creeping upward toward his target, trying to ignore his pulse pounding in his ears. When he reached the first turn, he saw them.

The vent cover had been removed and was resting against the wall. The two men were facing away from him, lifting the boxes into the empty space.

Jake stopped. Harper was blocked from his view by the staircase. He couldn't proceed without knowing Harper's position. Was Harper just around the corner, or was he guarding the fourth floor? Jake held his breath and inched up the wall, searching for Harper while anticipating the slightest reaction from the others.

The two men slid the boxes into place, and then one of them reached for the vent cover. As the man moved to the side, Jake saw the boxes sitting there, placed in the middle of the vent, antenna raised to its fullest height. The bomb was ready.

Then he heard Harper talking in a whisper.

"Put the cover back on, and we're gone," Harper said.

The voice had come from just above him, a few feet away on the staircase to the fourth floor. Jake moved slightly up the stairs, noticing the two men intently focused on the bomb. He cautiously advanced, hugging the wall, until he could see the smallest tuft of brown hair. The top of Harper's head was barely visible over the railing.

Now was the time. He had just seconds left. He had to act now!

Jake lunged forward, swinging his gun upward at Harper. "Don't move!" he yelled. "ATF!"

Harper turned to face him.

"Don't move, you bastard," Jake said, grasping his weapon with both hands, his arms outstretched. The gun was pointed specifically and exactly at Harper's head. "If you move, I'll kill you."

Chapter 17

Stan's lighthearted humor did little to lessen Matt's apprehension. Stan chattered continuously about the weather, his dogs, his kids, and his pitiful golf game, yet at the same time he nervously tapped his fingers on the dash and checked the ammo in his .40 caliber clip three times. Matt knew his partner well. They both needed to calm down. They couldn't afford any mistakes. At least when they were crawling through the underbrush busting a meth lab, most of the time they knew exactly what to expect, some stupid meth-heads, stoned and preoccupied, with at most a chained-up pit bull and a couple of handguns for security. Harper's militia compound was different. Militia groups were organized, prepared, high-tech, and completely unpredictable. Though Jake had been undercover for months, he had managed to provide Matt with only a sketchy description of the layout. The Washington office had procured a few aerial photographs, but the images were nearly useless because of the dense forest. The only area seen well was an opening in the center of the compound showing a house and some outbuildings. They were going in almost blind.

Rod Baker and Rick Rice were quiet in the backseat. Matt had chosen the two agents, fresh from the academy, because they were smart, aggressive, and confident. They looked like new graduates, both trim, muscular, with their hair buzzed short. Neither appeared nervous—too new to know better.

All four men wore dark suits. Matt preferred the business look, yet underneath the jackets were bulletproof vests, shoulder holsters, and .40-caliber

Glocks. He'd avoid a fight if he could—just say a few words to Harper—but they'd be ready for anything.

Matt followed an asphalt county road for almost a mile and slowed as they approached the gate to the Church of the Redeemed Believers. Just a church? *My ass*, thought Matt. The compound was surrounded by a ten-foot-tall chain-link fence topped with barbed wire. The gate was closed and padlocked. Inside the fence a gravel parking lot led to the front of a single-story white country church. The view from the church to the gate was unobstructed—a clean, easy shot. Tulsa's ATF field office was less secure.

Dense scrub oak surrounded three sides of the building, obscuring the entrance to the main compound behind the church. Only by the aerial photographs were they aware of its location. If the church was empty, the next objective was the main compound, but they knew next to nothing about the area in between.

"No mistakes," Matt said, saying aloud what they all were thinking.

Stan jumped out and grabbed an oversized bolt cutter from the trunk, snapped the chain, and kicked open the gate. Matt drove the car to the middle of the parking lot and positioned it at an angle. All four agents exited the vehicle and scanned the property nervously. Stan and Baker, on the side of the car closer to the church, approached the front door. Matt and Rice remained behind the car to provide cover, each with a hand in their jackets, touching the butts of their weapons. Except for the four of them and Matt's sedan, the parking lot was vacant.

Stan knocked on the door and waited for a response. He knocked again. No answer.

Stan pointed to one side, and he and Baker split up. They proceeded down the sides of the church building, peering in the windows. Inside were several rows of wooden pews, a pulpit at the front, and an old upright piano off to one side. The building was otherwise empty. They continued around to the rear of the church and noticed a gate blocking the narrow road they knew led to the parsonage, a seemingly pleasant country lane cut through the Oklahoma woods. Stan sent Baker back for the others.

Matt maneuvered the sedan down the side of the church and up to the gate. Baker pulled the bolt cutter out of the trunk and cut the heavy chain. Stan swung the gate open wide, and Matt drove the sedan through. Matt slid out of the car and scanned the surrounding trees.

"I think we can assume we're being watched," Matt said.

The two younger agents stared up in the trees, turning circles to identify the cameras.

Matt left his weapon holstered—it was essential to appear nonthreatening. The others followed his lead. They'd know when to use them.

Stan tore open a pouch of Redman and stuffed a wad in his cheek. "Need a chew?" He held out the pouch to Matt.

Matt's frown answered Stan's question. "That stuff will kill you," Matt said.

"Better than dying of old age."

Stan only chewed when he was nervous. Matt had seldom seen Stan nervous. "I'll check out ahead," Matt said seriously, gesturing down the road. "You wait here."

Rays of light filtering through the oak trees cast broken shadows on the dirt road. A hot south wind rustled the leaves, and an unseen cicada sang from a nearby tree. The only human sound Matt heard was his own footsteps.

Matt distrusted the militia intensely. Common criminals seldom used surveillance equipment, trip wires, or attack dogs. Anything was possible with the militia, especially Harper's. He felt his heart race. His shirt was soaked.

The narrow road continued two hundred feet through the trees and thick underbrush before angling to the right. When Matt reached the angle, he could see into the compound. No gate. No fence. Only a single-story white house located in the center of several smaller buildings. A firing range extended out from the left of the house, the only structure that gave a hint that it wasn't typical for an Oklahoman farm property. Not a soul was visible outdoors. No cars that he could see.

Matt wanted to hide behind the trees, to take cover using their protection. Or crawl to a secure observation position. Better yet, return in the dark with the ATF special response team with raid gear and night-vision goggles. He was vulnerable. Unprotected.

He was here to deliver a message—not risk death.

Matt fought back the nerves inside him. He would never become accustomed to the awkward feeling at the beginning of a raid. Once he started, he lost the emotions and functioned on adrenaline. If any of them thought or felt too much, it could be dangerous. A moment's distraction could be costly.

Matt scanned the trees again. If they were observing him, he couldn't identify the cameras. He signaled Stan and the other agents to bring the car to his location. If they pinned them down, at least they'd have the protection of the car. But if they brought the car too close to the house, the militia might perceive their action as an offensive move. Matt didn't want that. He knew he should go to the house alone. Risky enough for him, but the best chance of avoiding a firefight. Matt waited briefly for Stan to bring the sedan up before proceeding.

One hundred feet of clearing separated Matt from the buildings. Except for a pair of tire ruts in the dirt, the clearing was an open field with recently mowed grass. The early morning sun was already unbearably hot, and his feet kicked up a small cloud of dust as he ventured forward. The dry dust clung to his clean suit like a fine powder.

At the front of the house was a screened-in porch. Twenty-five feet from the porch, he stopped, lifting both hands so they were clearly in view. He approached the house slowly, and when he reached the screen door, he knocked firmly, rattling the door against a wobbly frame. He waited. No answer. He knocked harder, and the door rattled even louder. They would hear.

Matt waited several minutes before motioning the three agents over. Without turning his back, he eased away from the porch. Stan brought up the vehicle. Matt removed the Glock from his holster, pointing the nozzle upward, and signaled the three agents out of the car.

"What do you think?" Matt asked as Stan approached. "Seems no one's home."

Stan shrugged. "A quick look around wouldn't hurt, would it?"

"No, I wouldn't think so. You and Baker take the outbuildings. Rice and I will take the house."

"You got it, boss."

Stan spit a wad of tobacco toward Matt, and it landed a few inches from his foot. Matt shook his head. Stan unholstered his weapon and started toward the outbuildings. Baker followed, carrying a knapsack of equipment over his shoulder.

"Stan," Matt yelled after him, "be careful."

Stan glanced over his shoulder at Matt. "Yes, Mother"—he laughed—"you know I will."

⅄

"I don't think you'll kill me, Jake," Harper snapped, "because I have this." Harper pulled his hand from inside his jacket. He was holding the radio transmitter.

"I'll kill you, Sam, so help me God."

"Then you'll kill us all. The bomb is armed. It was armed the whole time."

Jake reached out his hand. "Give me the transmitter, Sam, or I'll blow your head off. I mean it."

Harper didn't flinch. "I tested the transmitter from the parking lot, and it worked from there, so I know it'll work from five feet. You may be able to put a bullet in my head, but can you stop me from pushing this?" He held the transmitter upward, his index finger hovering over the button. His stare was icy. He talked through his teeth with a hissing sound. "You can blow my head off, but we'll all be vapor before my dead body hits the ground."

Harper saw Jake's hesitation and smiled.

"I thought it was you all along, Buddy. I should have expected as much—as worthless as your momma, whoring around in California."

"Shut up, Sam."

"You didn't think I was suspicious of you," Harper said, "coming to the church every Sunday, acting like one of the Redeemed?"

Jake "Buddy" Jackson was Harper's cousin but had lived in California since he was nine years old. The ATF had made the connection during Harper's background check and had brought Jake in from the Los Angeles office to go undercover.

Jake pointed to Carl Joe and Tommy. "You two, get down!" Jake yelled. "Get down, you bastards, and put your weapons on the floor!" Jake swung his gun back and forth between them and Harper. "I said get down!"

Carl Joe and Tommy looked at Harper and didn't move.

"Do you think I'd let the likes of you stop me?" Harper continued calmly.

"Give me the transmitter, Sam," Jake said. "You don't want to hurt anybody."

"Is that what you think? Then that's where you're wrong."

"You don't want to kill these innocent people before you've had a chance to tell your story."

"No one here is innocent. How many innocent babies have our enemies killed? No one cares about them. Did they have a chance to tell their story?"

"Don't do this, Sam. Listen to me. We're family."

"You're not my family," he snarled.

"Give yourself up now before someone gets hurt." Jake glanced at Carl Joe and Tommy. "If you don't quit right now, he's going to take you down with him."

Neither of the two men answered.

Harper smiled again. "Then it looks like to me," he said, "that we have a genuine Mexican standoff, don't we?"

Jake moved his weapon rapidly back and forth, first at Harper, then at Carl Joe and Tommy, aiming at their heads.

"What the hell is going on here?" The voice came from behind Jake.

The unexpected sound startled Jake, and he jumped. Harper reacted instantly, kicking his leg out into Jake's knee. Jake, off-balance, went sprawling down the stairs, landing crumpled at Baskins's feet.

Baskins staggered back a step, his eyes wide, his mouth falling open. He froze in panic for a second and then began fumbling for his gun, trying to pull it from his holster.

Crack! The sharp discharge echoed in the stairwell.

The force of Carl Joe's bullet knocked Baskins backward, ripping through his abdomen and out his flank. His hands instinctively grasped his abdomen and were soon covered with the blood pumping from the wound. Baskins cried out in agony, his face blanched white. His eyes rolled upward, and he slumped to the floor next to Jake. Jake lay completely still, unconscious, blood oozing slowly from his mouth.

"Grab their weapons," Harper said.

As Harper swung back around to the stairwell door, Harrison, the local agent, peered in the window to check out the noise.

The glass shattered, exploding violently, as Harper's weapon discharged. The top half of the agent's head disintegrated, and the impact thrust his body backward out of Harper's view.

"No choice now," Harper said calmly. "We're going in."

Chapter 18

Matt slipped the hard drive out of the back of the PC and placed it in the duffel bag with a half dozen flash drives he found next to it. The sweat was accumulating inside the tips of his latex gloves, causing his fingers to slide back and forth. *The temperature in the house*, he thought, *must be 120 degrees.* No air conditioning, but he'd live with the heat. He had work to do. Even if he avoided contaminating all the evidence with the sweat dripping constantly off his forehead, what they discovered probably wouldn't be admissible in court without a search warrant. Yet at least they'd know what Harper was up to. And it wasn't likely something good.

Rice searched the house while Matt concentrated on the computer. Rice dumped the contents of the kitchen cabinets on the floor and flipped the mattresses in the bedroom against the wall. He checked for secret compartments in the walls and floor but found none. He looked in the toilet, under the furniture, behind the picture frames, and beneath the rugs. Rice wasn't polite. In the bedroom, he discovered paper sacks with men's clothing of different sizes. Matt and Rice briefly speculated as to the importance of the clothing. They could only guess.

Little of interest was found. Matt hoped the flash drives and the computer's hard drive would prove useful. The system was substantially more sophisticated than he would've expected for a rural farmhouse—a fast CPU, high-speed modem, large hard-drive memory, two printers, a fax machine, and a flatbed scanner. He didn't bother booting up the system. It likely would be encrypted, and he'd defer to the boys at the lab. They hadn't yet found a militia code they couldn't crack.

"Are we done?" Rice asked. "I'm about to have a stroke from this heat."

Matt wiped his forehead. "Me, too. I doubt we'll find much more." He tossed Rice the duffel bag. "We'll throw this in the car and then go help Gill and Baker."

⋏

Stan hated the smell of manure. And though he could detect a slight whiff, it had been many, many years since manure of any significant amount had been found in Harper's barn.

Stan and Baker had checked out two other outbuildings before entering the barn. All three resembled typical rural structures with gray weathered wood, corrugated-metal roofs, and wide double doors. The barn, the largest of the three, leaned sharply to one side, as though waiting for the next thunderstorm to dump it over.

Inside each structure, though, was an efficient storage system with stacks of supplies on rows of wooden shelves. The interiors were fortified with wood posts and four-by-eight beams. The barn's outside appearance was the most deceiving of the three. On the outside it appeared to be on the verge of collapse, yet its inside construction could probably withstand gale-force winds.

They had searched the outbuildings and noted only ordinary supplies: water in large containers, coffee, K-rations, some gasoline, fuel oil, light bulbs, toilet paper, soap, laundry detergent, two electric generators, and other standard provisions. Each section was covered with plastic and clearly marked for rotation. No weapons or ammo. Nothing suspicious. Just enough supplies for a year or two of independent existence.

This was their secondary stash, Stan was certain. Their weapons, ammunition, electronic equipment, radios—militia essentials—were hidden someplace else. Stan thought most likely those items were buried in an underground bunker somewhere on the property, camouflaged and undetectable.

"This is incredible," Baker said softly, turning a circle in the barn. "I've never seen anything like this."

"You're not going to often, either. We're treading in a parallel world."

"I've only read about this in the manuals."

Stan pointed to the doorway. "Let's check the perimeter."

Stan gripped his weapon with both hands and glanced out the door in both directions before stepping outside. Baker followed. Stan spit out a wad of tobacco and then hand motioned Baker to proceed down one side of the barn. Stan took the opposite side.

Around the corner, Stan noted tire tracks leading to the back. He cautiously moved along the barn, occasionally peering into the woods for movement. The dense underbrush obscured a view of more than twenty or twenty-five feet. Were they out there watching him? He was fully exposed against the flat walls of the wooden barn. He felt his pulse quicken and his palms moisten with sweat. He gripped his weapon a bit firmer.

Stan reached the back as Baker rounded the opposite corner. In front of them, adjacent to the rear of the barn, was a new metal storage shed, approximately ten feet square and eight feet tall, sitting on a cement base.

Stan raised his hand as a signal for Baker to listen for a moment. Not a leaf rustled. No birds chirped. No dogs barked. Not a sound—complete silence.

"What the heck is this?" Baker whispered, lightly touching the shed.

"Beats me," Stan said aloud. "Odd that it's back here, isn't it?"

"This one's locked."

Baker's right, Stan thought. The three outbuildings were unlocked, which on second thought, seemed unusual. The shed was secured with a heavy combination padlock.

"Get the bolt cutter," Stan said.

While Baker fished around in the knapsack, Stan carefully examined the shed. He checked all sides and then ran his hands over the surface. He noted an odd odor, but otherwise nothing appeared suspicious.

"Smell that?" Baker asked.

"Yeah. Stinks. Smells like something died."

"Is it coming from the shed or from the woods?"

"I'm not sure. Hard to tell."

Baker reached out to Stan. "I have the bolt cutter."

Stan took a breath and let it out slowly. *Calm down*, he told himself. *Watch the nerves.* "Okay," he said, "we need to do this."

⋏

Harper pushed open the heavy metal door. "Everybody down!" he yelled as he stepped into the intensive care unit, brandishing his weapon high.

Harper stood erect in the doorway while Carl Joe and Tommy crouched down on each side of Harper, their weapons pointed into the unit.

The staff was completely panicked. They scrambled in all directions to find safety, ducking behind counters or falling to the floor and covering their heads. Harrison's body was sprawled out near the doorway, half his face and the top of his head gone, a large pool of blood forming where they had been. Asher was twenty feet away outside Montgomery's door. He had jumped up when they had entered, spilling a cup of coffee in front of him. Asher stood reaching into his jacket for his weapon, but before he could pull it out, the three men were aiming at his head. Ghostly pale and trembling, he slowly raised his hands over his head.

"On the floor," Harper shouted to him.

Asher fell to the floor.

"I'll cover him," Carl Joe said as he stepped over Harrison's body. He moved next to Asher and pushed his weapon against the back of Asher's head.

Two orderlies down the hallway bolted for the front. Harper aimed his 9 mm toward the ceiling and discharged a round. The sharp pop echoed loudly in the unit. A fluorescent light shattered and sent a shower of sparks and glass onto the nurses' station. The two orderlies dropped to the floor and froze.

"I said everybody down!" Harper shouted, sweeping his weapon across the room. "And I mean *everyone!*" He pointed toward Asher. "Carl Joe, check his weapon."

Carl Joe held his gun on Asher's head and slid the agent's weapon out of its holster. He took a gun in each hand and raced around the perimeter, pointing at the heads of any of the staff who might act defiant.

Harper reached down and pried Harrison's gun from his hand. He tossed it to Tommy. "Secure the front," Harper said to Tommy, gesturing toward the doorway. "Be careful. A guard is down the hall."

Tommy positioned a gurney near the entrance and turned it over to block the doorway. Fifty feet away at the end of the hallway, the security guard had already flipped the wooden desk over for protection.

"How about a warning shot?" Tommy asked.

"Sure, show him we're serious."

Tommy aimed carefully and fired a single shot, splintering the corner of the desk. The security guard quickly crawled from behind the desk to the safety of the adjacent hallway. Tommy laughed, his voice carrying down the hall. "The next one's for real!"

Harper moved forward to cover the front while Carl Joe and Tommy dragged in the two wounded men from the stairwell and dumped them near the nurses' station. Baskins rolled back and forth on the floor, holding his abdomen and moaning. Jake was still unconscious. After signaling Tommy to return to the front, Harper and Tommy fortified the front barricade.

"This is a pretty narrow hallway," Harper said. "It'll provide you a very good defensive position. Keep your eyes open. They may be stupid enough to try to overrun us."

"Yes, sir."

"Of course they won't be nearly as likely when they receive the information about the bomb. That will change their strategy dramatically."

Tommy nodded.

"Be sharp, Tommy."

"Yes, sir. I will, Pastor Harper."

Harper returned to the nurses' station to join Carl Joe.

"Tie up Buddy and the FBI agent," Harper said as he threw Carl Joe duct tape from the knapsack.

"Gladly," Carl Joe said, his head nodding.

"I've got Buddy's Ruger from the knapsack. You take the weapon he had in the stairwell and give Tommy the guard's gun. That's three for each of you."

"Sure, Sam."

Harper looked around at the staff. "Do exactly what I say, and you won't get hurt," he said, his voice without emotion. "God's true believers will destroy the unrighteous. Who here wants to die?" Harper held the radio transmitter high. "We have a bomb with enough explosives to destroy this unit. Remember Oklahoma City?" He pointed to the transmitter with his pistol. "I touch this button here, and we'll all be destroyed. Anyone here a hero?"

Harper waited for a response. No one spoke. "I didn't think so. Follow my commands, and you may be saved. Defy me, and you will die."

Carl Joe grasped Jake's shoulder and flipped him over, face down. He pulled Jake's arms behind him and wrapped the tape tightly around both his arms and his legs several times. He did the same for Asher. He gagged and duct-taped both their mouths.

"Secure that guard, too," Harper said, pointing at Baskins, "then we'll move the bomb in."

Baskins moaned loudly as Carl Joe touched him. He clutched his abdomen with both hands, his abdomen, chest, and hands completely covered with blood, and a pool of blood began forming on the tile floor around him.

"Let me attend to him."

Paula was standing a few feet in front of Harper. She had been sitting at the nurses' desk. She stood erect, shoulders back, looking directly at Harper. His eyes met hers with a cold stare.

Carl Joe jumped up, grabbed Paula's hair braid and jerked her head backward. He pressed the nozzle of his gun against her temple. "Looks like we've got a hero, Sam," he said, grinning.

Paula's knees nearly buckled, but Carl Joe hung on to her.

"Please," she said softly, "let me attend to him...or he'll die."

Harper didn't blink. "God knows we all die," Harper said coldly. "Sooner or later, we all die."

⋏

Matt checked the compound from each of the windows inside the house. Now they were invaders, easy targets for a high-powered rifle once they stepped outside. Ruby Ridge flashed in his mind. He shook off the thought.

The entire compound appeared empty, deserted. Was Harper expecting them? Everything was entirely too neat, the house too clean with the dishes lined up in the cabinets, the bed made, the refrigerator nearly empty. Was this how they were supposed to find it?

Matt glanced around the house one last time. They had found nothing. All they had to show for their efforts were the computer disks and a hard drive. And they were probably worthless. The flash drives looked new— unlabeled and stacked in neat piles next to the computer. Maybe they were blank. Maybe the hard drive was a decoy. Did Harper anticipate their raid? Was he ready for them?

Matt unholstered his weapon, nodded at Rice, and swung open the door.

ᛣ

Baker eased the bolt cutter onto the lock and started squeezing.

"Be careful," Stan warned.

Baked nodded. Stan heard Baker grunt as he applied pressure to both handles, and after some effort the bolt cutters slid through the metal of the padlock. Baker cautiously removed the lock from the handle and tossed it on the ground.

"Now open it slightly," Stan said, "and I'll check for wires."

Baker slowly lifted the handle and then, using two hands, moved the door a fraction of an inch.

Stan heard the soft click—a rather high-pitched, nondescript, barely audible click. He knew immediately what had caused it.

ᛣ

Matt stepped outside. Rice followed him out. The heat was almost as bad as indoors. He removed his latex gloves and emptied the sweat on the ground.

Nothing's here, he thought. *Harper was waiting for us.*

He turned toward the barn and started to yell at Stan.

The force of the blast blew Matt and Rice backward off their feet. Matt rolled over and instinctively covered his head as pieces of the barn and shed showered around them. A cloud of dust engulfed them, cutting off their air, choking them. Matt felt the sting of metal and glass pelting his body. His ears roared.

In a few seconds it was over.

Matt knew the instant he heard the explosion that Stan and Baker were dead.

CHAPTER 19

Paula's head snapped back sharply as Carl Joe squeezed his fist around her hair and jerked it backward. He pressed the gun tightly against her temple.

"Are you eager to die, Florence Nightingale?" he asked sharply.

"The officer needs help," Paula said, her voice stronger than she expected. "We can save him."

Paula felt the grip on her hair tighten. The man holding the gun had wild eyes, like one of the transients high on drugs she had seen during her training. Unpredictable. Dangerous. The older man next to him was calm, emotionless. A disturbing contrast.

Baskins would die, she knew. He lay in a pool of his own blood, bleeding to death as they watched. The FBI agent's skull was blown off with most of his brains gone. He was dead.

"Let her go," Harper said.

Carl Joe pulled back on Paula's hair before releasing her. His weapon remained pointed at Paula. "Nurses trying to be heroes," he said, "become dead nurses."

"I'm not a nurse. I'm a doctor," Paula said, pulling her shoulders back. Paula grabbed a couple of cloth towels and moved toward Baskins. She knelt down and pressed the towels against his abdomen and flank, the blood quickly saturating them.

Paula turned to face the older man. She was guessing, hoping, that he was in charge, not the crazy man with wild eyes. The older man had done the talking when the three men had burst into the unit. He had fired the first shot into the ceiling, and he was holding the radio transmitter. He appeared to be the leader. "Are you sure you want him to die?" she said to him. "Is that what you want?"

Paula felt John kneel beside her. She knew that Baskins and he were good friends, yet John wouldn't provide any medical help and might make matters worse. She wished he had stayed with his janitor's cart.

"No good's done," John said, "if he dies."

Carl Joe gripped his weapon with both hands and moved directly in front of John. He pushed the weapon against John's forehead, forcing him to fall backward to the floor.

"Back off, asshole," Carl Joe yelled at John. Carl Joe straddled him and placed the barrel against John's forehead. "A smartass doctor and this badass. Not a particularly healthy combination."

"Carl Joe," Harper said. "Let him go. You made your point. And watch your mouth." He turned to Paula. "Okay, Doctor. Tend to the guard." Harper pointed to the back stairwell. "Carl Joe, secure the stairs."

Carl Joe didn't budge. He pushed the gun harder against John's head. "We should pop them both, Brother Sam. Quit wasting our time with them. The guard's going to die anyway. As for this one, I don't trust his shiftless black ass."

"Carl Joe," Harper repeated slowly, "I said secure the stairs."

Carl Joe hesitated a moment, staring at Harper briefly before withdrawing to the stairwell. John slid closer to Paula. She felt his calmness—not at all the emotion she had expected.

Harper turned his gaze to Paula. She felt a shiver race down her spine. It took all her strength not to turn her eyes away.

"We're not murderers," Harper said. "Exodus chapter twenty, verse thirteen says, 'You shall not murder.' We have not come to murder but to bring judgment to the murderers."

Paula turned her attention back to Baskins. Despite her constant pressure, the towels were quickly soaked. She felt an arm reach across her as Sally dropped more towels next to Baskins.

"Doctor," Harper said from behind her. "Are you in charge?"

Sally stood and faced Harper. "I'm the supervisor of the intensive care unit. I'm in charge."

Harper stepped up to Sally and pushed the radio transmitter in her face. "Okay, then," he said, his voice icy. "Where is Ronald Montgomery?"

⋏

Jane Harper had been instructed to bring the van to the circle drive and wait, and she had done exactly as she had been told. Jane was pleased with how her part went. She had followed her husband's instructions exactly, and her ploy had worked. Her husband and the three men had crossed to the back stairwell undetected, her diversion a success.

Jane chuckled softly as she recalled the nurses' faces. She jumped up, and they were bewildered, stunned that she wasn't injured. She had walked away and left them standing there, stammering and confused.

Her husband was a genius.

Harper had planned for several contingencies, and he had insisted Jane memorize them. She played the contingencies over and over in her head. Her initial instructions were to park the van in the north parking lot and wait ten more minutes. If they didn't arrive, she would return to the hospital by foot and, assuming no unusual commotion, make a telephone call on the pay phone in the lobby to read the statement Harper had given her. Harper had said that even if the men were killed or captured, as would be according to God's will, her actions would advance their cause.

As the time passed, she grew more worried. She prayed the contingency plans would not be required.

Jane removed the envelope from her purse and opened it. She read the note quickly. She understood. She would do as instructed.

A large fist rapped sharply on the window beside her, and Jane jumped, turning quickly to see a uniformed security guard standing outside the van. The guard was a burly linebacker of a man, his frame filling most of her window. A steel-blue revolver hung on his belt, brushing lightly against the glass. Jane dropped her arm to her side, releasing Harper's note and envelope, allowing them to slip to the floor. She took a deep breath and exhaled slowly, attempting to appear calm.

Jane lowered the window. "Yes, Officer?" she said, smiling sweetly.

The guard's oversized head leaned into the window. "Ma'am," he said firmly, "you'll have to move your vehicle."

She acted surprised. "But I'm waiting to pick up my mother," she said. "She's being discharged."

"I'm sorry, ma'am. We have an emergency and need to clear this area. You'll have to move."

"I was told to pick her up here."

"I'm sure you were, but we have a police emergency."

"What emergency? Has something happened in the hospital?"

"Ma'am, I've been instructed to clear this area," he said, the patience leaving his voice. "You need to move now."

"Is it something serious? Is my mother okay?"

"I don't know any details," he said. Now the officer's voice became stern. "I just know you can't park here. You have to move your van and move it now."

"Yes, sir. I understand. Thank you, Officer."

She raised the window and shifted into gear. She knew what she had to do.

CHAPTER 20

Matt stepped across a charred, splintered board that had once been a two-by-four and gazed into the bomb crater. The crater was twenty feet across and eight feet deep. Around him in all directions were pieces of debris flung as faraway as two hundred yards. The blast reduced the trees in the adjacent woods to stumps for thirty feet. For the next fifty feet, ugly skeletons of bare, twisted trunks and leafless, broken branches protruded awkwardly from the blackened earth. A few small fires burned nearby.

The muscles in Matt's legs stiffened, drained of strength, tightening to prevent his legs from buckling. His brain fought for clarity. The cloud of dust that had choked him had settled, but his brain was hazy, dazed, confused. He stood on the edge of the crater without moving, his shoulders slumped forward. Flying glass had ripped holes in the sleeves of his suit, but he wasn't cut. A fine layer of dirt covered his face, mixing with sweat to create a crust around his eyes and mouth.

Matt stood unbelieving. Seconds earlier he'd been yelling at Stan. In a moment everything had changed. He'd been at many bombing sites, including a few he'd seen explode at a distance, but never this close. He gazed into the bottom of the crater, empty except for a few small pieces of debris. This was the spot where Stan and Baker had been standing only a few seconds ago. Now an empty hole.

Since Matt had called for backup, agents from Muskogee would be arriving shortly, and they'd likely insist Rice and he go to the Muskogee emergency room. He would refuse. No sense going to Muskogee when Tulsa wasn't much farther. He'd go to Saint Luke's. Maybe Paula could see him there. He seemed fine. No broken bones. No major gashes or gaping wounds. No serious injuries from projectiles. He was lucky. He was afraid his eardrums might be ruptured, though. His ears rang, and the ringing drowned out the silence that he thought should be there. Surely no living thing within a mile would be making any noise after such a blast. Instead of silence, he could only hear the ringing.

Matt surveyed the wreckage. The senior agent on the phone from Muskogee had asked him—more accurately, had ordered him—to leave the site. Near-victims, as he was now, who wandered through a crime scene were known to destroy the evidence. Even law enforcement officers stunned by an explosion used poor judgment. He had seen it more than once.

Rice sat underneath a nearby tree, his hands over his face, sobbing. Rice lost his stomach first then fell to his knees and began to weep loudly. Matt helped him to the shade before he left him to inspect the site. It would be good if Rice finished before the backup arrived. Rice needed to pull it together, or he'd be destined for a menial desk job in some podunk city. He wasn't the first agent to lose a partner, and he wouldn't be the last.

The way to make it right was to make Harper pay.

Harper had set them up—the computer, the flash drives, the property, the bomb. Harper had planned this. He had fully intended to kill a law officer, or anyone else, searching his property.

The layer of dust had turned to a thick coating of mud on his face. He wiped off the mud with the back of his hand and brushed his hair, knocking out small shards of glass.

Sam Harper, he thought, *you're not so smart. Killing my partner was a mistake. Now you've made this personal, and I swear you'll pay.*

His thoughts were clearer now. The anger was growing inside of him, turning confusion into resolve, pain into purpose.

Matt heard the rumble of an approaching car and instinctively crouched with his gun drawn. He could hear the sound clearly. The ringing had stopped. Rice was kneeling behind the tree with his weapon ready. Matt signaled Rice toward the entry of the compound before swiftly taking cover.

Two black SUVs raced onto the compound and stopped near Matt's sedan. Eight men jumped out in full raid gear, taking positions around the vehicles and the buildings.

Backup had arrived.

The agents secured the compound. The Tulsa PD bomb squad and the army EOD would be arriving shortly to search the wreckage. Matt briefed the agents. They insisted that he and Rice seek immediate medical attention, but both refused. Matt would stay at the scene until the preliminary work was completed, however long it took. Rice could go back if he wanted.

Reese had called earlier, one of the agents told Matt, asking for an update. Reese wanted Matt to call. Matt slipped into the front seat of his car and reached for his cell phone. He rapidly dialed Reese's phone number and heard it ring three times. Reese answered.

Matt started to talk, but his voice failed, a lump sticking in his throat. He hung up and gently laid the phone on the car seat beside him as he felt the tears flow down his face.

On the floorboard, tossed there an eternity ago, spoiling his spotlessly clean car, was Stan's empty coffee cup.

⚔

Paula tore open Baskins's shirt. She started to push him to roll him onto his side, and John helped her. Baskins weighed nearly three hundred pounds. As they moved him, even as gently as possible, Baskins moaned in agony. Paula briefly observed the blood oozing from his two wounds before replacing the towels. The entry wound was located in the right lower abdomen. The opening was only a centimeter, but the wound was bleeding briskly. The bullet exited out the right lower flank, ripping open a larger area. The flank wound was bleeding worse than the abdomen. Paula suspected injuries to the intestines and probably the kidney. A liver injury was less likely—the entry too low. She hoped the vena cava or one of the other large blood vessels wasn't hit, or he'd be dead soon. His skin was pale and clammy, and he was quickly going into shock. *He may be dead soon anyway*, she thought. She held pressure on both wounds simultaneously, hoping the pressure would slow the bleeding.

"Help me, Doctor, please," he said. "I think I'm dying."

"Don't worry," she whispered in his ear. "We'll get you out of here."

Toni kneeled beside Paula to help. She expertly slipped a large-bore IV in his left arm. She hung Lactated Ringer's from an IV pole and ran it wide open. She removed a portable oxygen tank from a nearby stretcher, attached the tubing to its nozzle, and slipped the nasal prongs into Baskins's nose.

Paula, with John's help, gently rolled him onto his back. He cried out in pain.

"John," Paula said softly, "lift his legs onto that chair. We need the blood in his legs to flow to his heart."

John lifted his legs, and Baskins again cried out.

Harper was two or three feet away, standing in front of Sally, and Paula watched as he questioned Sally about Montgomery. Was that what this was about? Were they here for Montgomery? Had they brought a bomb to the hospital, killed an FBI agent, and shot this guard over the attorney general?

"Sally Carpenter," Harper said, reading her name tag. "So you're in charge?"

"Yes, I am."

"Then, Sally Carpenter," he said, holding the transmitter close to her face, "you're responsible for all the lives here, right?"

She nodded.

"Then I'll only ask one more time. Where is Ronald Montgomery?"

"He's not here," she said, lowering her eyes. "You have the wrong unit."

"I want a complete list of all the patients, their room numbers, and their medical problems. I want a list of all the staff—their names and positions."

On the floor near Paula, the other injured man she had seen brought in from the stairwell moaned as he regained consciousness from his fall. He appeared alert now, Paula thought, he eyes jerking around, taking in a view of the unit. He began to struggle at his restraints, but Carl Joe had wrapped him tight and covered his mouth with duct tape. He wouldn't be going anywhere.

"Let me help him," Sally said, stepping toward him.

Harper's weapon was instantly in her face. "No one helps him," he snarled. "The guard is one thing. This man is another."

Sally stepped back. "Yes, sir. I understand."

Paula continued the pressure on Baskins's wounds. Despite her efforts, the guard was dying.

"Helping the guard," Paula spoke up, "means immediate surgery. Without surgery, he'll die."

Harper didn't turn around. "Nobody is leaving to have surgery."

"Then he'll bleed to death right here in front of us."

"We can put him on a stretcher and move him," Sally offered.

"I'll think about it." Harper's words were without emotion.

"Don't let him die," John said softly in Paula's ear. John's statement was calm, not anxious, and it helped her.

"What is your name, sir?" Paula asked Harper.

"Why do you ask?" Harper said, turning to face her.

"We should call you something, don't you think?"

"Okay, fair enough. My name is Pastor Sam Harper."

"Well, Pastor Sam Harper, my name is Dr. Paula Barrett, and it's my medical opinion that if we don't take this man to surgery in five minutes, he's going to die. It's a medical certainty. You said you weren't a murderer. Now prove it."

Before Harper could answer, Carl Joe walked the several steps from the stairwell and placed his gun on Baskins's head. "Let's just shoot this fat bastard, Sam. If we start giving away our hostages, it'll weaken our position."

"A dead man," Paula said, "is a poor hostage." Paula looked up at Harper and held up the bloody towels. "He needs to move now."

"Let me shoot the bastard!" Carl Joe yelled. "Letting him go is a mistake."

"Shut up," Harper snapped. "I decide who comes and goes. You follow orders."

Paula watched as Carl Joe's eyes grew wide, and for a moment Paula thought he'd defy Harper's order. At first, Carl Joe didn't move, but then he slowly swung his weapon forward off Baskins's head, lifting it upward, briefly pointing at Harper as he raised the weapon toward the ceiling. Harper glared at Carl Joe until his weapon was straight up. For a few seconds Carl Joe held Harper's glare, but after a moment Carl Joe dropped his eyes downward. When he did, Harper abruptly turned his back on him.

"Okay," Harper said. "Move the guard out."

CHAPTER 21

Jennifer peeked out through a tiny crack in the closed curtain to watch the three men outside Montgomery's room. When the men had searched earlier, she had hidden in the bathroom, expecting they'd find her. After waiting until she thought it was clear, she had tiptoed out to see what she could learn.

Jennifer watched the intruders for several minutes before returning to the bathroom, shutting the door quietly. Removing her cell phone from her purse, she cupped her hands around the phone and dialed nine-one-one.

"This is nine-one-one," the voice on the phone answered. "Do you have an emergency?"

"Yes, I do," she whispered. Jennifer explained the situation to the operator. She had few details to give, but it was clear to her what was happening—they were here to do harm to Montgomery. She was certain, without any doubt. "So you understand what I'm saying?"

"Yes, ma'am. I understand. I'll notify the police immediately."

"It's imperative to coordinate with the local FBI. You know this *is* the attorney general, Ronald Montgomery, right?"

"Yes, ma'am. You said that."

Jennifer paused at a sound outside the bathroom. An alarm on Montgomery's ventilator was beeping, but it quickly stopped. She waited and heard nothing else. "I'll call the Washington office," she said, "if I can."

"I think you should stay on the line with me. You can update the authorities."

"No," Jennifer said. "I'll call Washington. You call the local PD. I have some critically important things to do here and very little time. Thanks for your help."

"Are you sure?"

"Yes, I'm sure," Jennifer said and hung up. She dialed the Washington office of the FBI next.

"You've reached the Federal Bureau of Investigation." It was an automated system. "If you know your—"

Jennifer punched in the extension number. After a couple of rings, a female answered. "Office of the director. How may I help you?"

Jennifer identified herself and explained the situation.

"The director's not in at the moment, but we'll page him immediately."

"The attorney general is in grave danger. He's been taken hostage."

"Yes, I understand. The highest priority."

"Good," Jennifer said, "but don't call me here. Too risky. I'll call you back…if I can."

"Be safe, Ms. McLaughlin."

"It's *his* safety I'm worried about. Act quickly. His life is in your hands."

After finishing the two phone calls, Jennifer listened for any noise outside before cracking open the door and slipping out of the bathroom. She removed Montgomery's nameplate from above his bed and cut the ID bracelet off his wrist. She removed his name from every item in the room: the monitor, IV bags, and equipment. She tore up the medical papers and graphs that identified him. If they weren't in the unit for the attorney general, which she thought highly unlikely, they'd still recognize his name. Without any identification, and if they didn't recognize his face, he might be safe.

Montgomery's eyes followed her as she scurried around the room. She noticed him watching her, so she leaned over the bedrail to whisper softly into his ear, explaining to him the serious situation outside the room. He nodded. He understood.

The last news reports had indicated he was in a coma. The news leaks might now prove useful. Once again she leaned over and whispered. She begged him to keep his eyes closed and to remain absolutely motionless—no matter what. The more he appeared helpless, the more useless he would be to them.

Washington would send the SWAT teams, but Jennifer couldn't wait for them. Montgomery was in danger, and every second counted. She'd do all she could to protect him.

⚔

"Okay," Harper said, pointing across the unit, "load him on that stretcher. But only one person takes him. You there." Harper motioned toward a lanky young man sitting on the floor. "Are you an orderly?"

Paula saw the young man nod. His head was cast downward, and he didn't look at Harper. He was a student, hired for the summer to transport patients. He was in the unit to take a patient to radiology.

"Bring that stretcher over here and help load him."

The orderly rolled the stretcher next to Baskins. Four of the staff loaded Baskins on as Paula continued to hold pressure on his wounds. Baskins moaned loudly, rocking back and forth in pain. Paula felt helpless. He was still bleeding, and she could do nothing. If she were in the ER, he'd have a large-bore IV in each arm, MAST trousers on his lower extremities, and a couple of units of blood hanging. The surgeons in the operating suites would be preparing for immediate exploratory surgery. She couldn't even give him morphine because his blood pressure might plummet. She felt the urgency, but all she could do was stand next to Baskins, holding the towels soaked red with his blood.

The orderly started to push Baskins toward the door.

"Wait," Paula said. "Someone needs to apply pressure."

"Only one goes," Harper snapped.

"Look at these towels. He'll bleed out before he hits the door."

Harper shook his head as he smiled at Paula. "You can't go, Doctor."

"I wouldn't go," she said, indignant. "Let this nurse go." Paula gestured toward Toni.

Toni was sitting on the floor in the nurses' station where she had been since helping Paula with Baskins's IV. Harper glanced at Toni briefly and looked at the bloody towels.

"Okay," he said. "I'll let her go."

"No, I refuse," Toni said, folding her arms.

"You refuse?" Paula said. "Why?"

"I won't leave my patients, Dr. Barrett. Send someone else."

"I order you to go," Sally said.

"No, I won't go. Send Jackie."

"Send someone," Harper said, "or I'll—"

"Jackie, you go," Sally ordered.

Jackie Wallace was sitting next to Toni on the floor. A single mother with four children, she had worked as the unit secretary for ten years. Jackie quickly stood, slipped on a pair of latex gloves, and slid in close to Paula. Paula took her hands—they were noticeably trembling—and placed them on the wound, showing Jackie how to apply pressure, forcing them down hard into Baskins's flesh.

"Tell them," Paula said, holding each of her hands in place, "that he needs surgery immediately."

"Yes, Doctor," she said.

Paula saw her fear and felt her trembling and wondered if her own fear was as evident. After positioning Jackie's hands, Paula stepped aside. "Okay," she said. She looked back at Harper. "Can they go?"

"Hold it," Harper said, abruptly stepping toward them. Reaching between them, he removed Baskins's two-way radio from his belt. He slipped the radio in his pocket and waved them on.

The orderly eased the stretcher forward with Jackie along the side, holding the towels. As they approached the doorway, Harper directed the staff to clear a temporary opening so they could pass.

Baskins probably will die, Paula thought. She watched as the two employees pushed the stretcher down the long hallway to the overturned security desk at the end. He was losing too much blood. If they rushed him to surgery, it'd still be thirty minutes before they could clamp the bleeders. He didn't have thirty minutes.

If Baskins died, as he likely would, these intruders had murdered him. In her training, she had seen more patients with gunshot wounds than she cared to remember, and several had died. Some were self-inflicted. Others were accidental. But many were deliberately caused by a third party, and though she hadn't thought much about it at the time, those patients had been murdered. She held up her blood-covered hands, and they started to tremble. She had witnessed one murder and possibly another. She had touched Baskins's wounds and may have heard his last words. Paula could not stop her hands from shaking.

"Carl Joe," Harper said loudly, "I'll cover the back door. You clear the rooms. I want everyone out of those rooms and into the nurses' area. All the patients, too. Everyone."

"Yes, sir," Carl Joe said, starting for the first room.

"Pull the curtains open so we can see in every room, and close the shades on the outside windows. Be careful of snipers."

"Yes, sir." He disappeared into the first room.

"You can't move the patients out," Sally spoke up. "They're connected to monitors, IVs, and other equipment. They'll die."

Harper ignored her.

"You picked the wrong unit," she continued, sounding braver. "We can't stop taking care of these patients. They're too sick."

Harper turned to face her. "I want you to shut up and get me the list I asked you for ten minutes ago. You do exactly what I tell you, Nurse Carpenter. Understand?"

Sally nodded and looked away.

"Carl Joe," Harper called after him, "the patients stay."

"Whatever you say," Carl Joe answered from inside one of the rooms.

Harper demanded the entire staff assemble in the nurses' station. Paula washed the blood off in a nearby sink before joining the rest of the staff. As she sat on the floor, a loud noise erupted from inside Montgomery's room. Carl Joe was dragging Jennifer out, screaming at her, holding his weapon against her forehead. Jennifer was pleading that her patient, a Mr. Johnson, needed her help. Mr. Johnson was comatose, she complained. Carl Joe forced her to the nurses' station and pushed her to the floor.

Harper pointed his gun at Jennifer. "I want you to be quiet, you understand?"

Harper had said it calmly but with a force everyone understood.

"My patient is in a coma—"

"You don't listen well," Harper said, interrupting Jennifer, now raising his voice. "I said quiet!"

Jennifer nodded at Harper as she slipped in next to Paula.

"I'm not asking anyone twice," Harper said. He slipped his weapon into the shoulder harness under his jacket and held up the radio transmitter in his right hand for the staff to see. "You'll do exactly as I say. No one moves. No one talks. I will not tolerate it."

Harper glanced over his shoulder at Carl Joe standing behind him. "Carl Joe," he said, "take Tommy and bring the bomb in. I don't want to leave it out there since we let the guard go. Here," he said. "Use the good doctor." He kicked his foot toward Paula. "She'll make a good hostage."

Paula briefly considered resisting but thought it useless. She stood up before Carl Joe had a chance to grab her. Carl Joe moved next to her and held a gun to her head, the cold steel of the weapon pressed hard against her skull.

"You heard him," he said roughly. "Move!"

Carl Joe pushed her toward the doorway, and she shuddered at his touch. Tommy came from the front to join them.

"Be careful out there," Harper said. "We're a man short because of Buddy. And be quick!"

The hand truck sat empty in the stairwell near the wall next to the vent. Tommy squatted down to unscrew the vent cover, turning his back to Paula and Carl Joe. Carl Joe leaned his tall body over Paula's petite frame, reached around her chest, and cupped her right breast. He squeezed it firmly several times. She felt his hot breath stinging her neck.

"Wouldn't want you to escape," he said in her ear.

Paula was tempted to pull away, but remained still. She turned her head slowly until she made eye contact. "Take your hand off me, pervert," she said, trying to sound calm, "or I'll tell your preacher friend."

"I'm not scared of him."

Tommy glanced in their direction, and Paula felt Carl Joe's hand slide off her breast down to her ribcage. She felt him tighten the pressure, compressing her chest wall, exerting his control over her.

He *was* in control. How close was he to being out of control?

Tommy set the screws on the floor as he removed them one by one before lifting the vent cover off, leaning it against the wall. The four boxes were stacked neatly inside. Tommy reached in, attempting to slip his fingers under the bottom box. He was struggling to lift them by himself.

"Hurry up," Carl Joe snapped.

"I'm hurrying," Tommy snapped back. "Just watch my back."

Tommy swung the corner of the bottom box to the edge of the vent space and tilted it up over a four-inch metal strip lining the opening along the floor. As he pulled the stack out into the stairwell, the bottom box slipped off the strip and dropped hard to the floor.

"Dammit, you idiot," Carl Joe snarled. "You want to kill us all?"

"Shut up, Carl Joe!" Tommy's face was red with anger.

Paula felt Carl Joe's gun leave her head and saw him move it until it pointed straight at Tommy.

Tommy's demeanor remained unchanged. "What are you going to do, asshole?" Tommy said. "Shoot me?" Tommy slowly rose up and stood facing Carl Joe, the barrel inches from his chest. For at least thirty seconds, neither man moved.

Carl Joe blinked first. He pulled the gun back to Paula's forehead. "No," he said, letting out a laugh. "Not you, Tommy. But I'm not as certain about the good doctor here."

Tommy glanced at Paula and then looked directly at Carl Joe. "You're the idiot, Carl Joe." He turned his back to them and lifted the boxes onto the hand truck.

"Just get them inside," Carl Joe said.

Paula heard Tommy curse under his breath as he passed by them, dragging the hand truck through the doorway.

Carl Joe shoved Paula back into the unit and pushed her along until they reached the nurses' station. Paula saw that the hospital staff, fourteen in all, were lined up in two rows along the inside. All looked grim-faced and scared. Some were sobbing quietly. Paula slipped in between Toni and Sally. John made eye contact with her and smiled briefly. Paula didn't think there was much to smile about.

Carl Joe and Tommy returned to the stairwell door and spent ten or fifteen minutes blocking both sides of the doorway with empty beds, chairs, IV poles, and metal bedside tables. On the inside, the pile towered higher than the doorway, a formidable barricade. Harper had instructed they leave the window unobscured so they could monitor the stairwell. When they returned, Tommy unloaded the boxes next to Harper at the nurses' station.

Paula knew the bomb was legitimate. Everyone, including her, was fixated on the boxes Tommy had just unloaded. It was hard not to be. Maybe Harper had brought the bomb in to secure it, but Paula thought there was a second purpose—the threat of the bomb became all too real. The cardboard boxes themselves weren't all that unusual, the type used for IV supplies every staff member had seen. It was instead the antenna projecting from the top box, matching the one on the transmitter Harper was holding only a few feet away. Paula had no doubt it was exactly as Harper had said.

For the briefest moment she saw the bomb explode with a massive bright light, instantly destroying everything. She shuddered at the thought.

While the two men had been gone creating the barricade, Harper had paced back and forth in front of the staff the whole time. He waited until Tommy and Carl Joe were positioned at the two entrances before he spoke.

"Here's the rules," he said. "No phone calls. No one in or out. No one near these boxes." He pointed. "No one gets out of our sight at any time. Understood?"

Harper waited a moment for a response, but no one spoke.

"Now, I want everyone to empty all their pockets and purses in the middle of the floor here." He made a circle with his finger as he spoke. "Anyone who doesn't will be very, very sorry."

Everyone did as they were told. Harper spent several minutes sorting through the pile. He confiscated the cell phones. The rest he dumped into a plastic bag he pulled out of a nearby trash can.

"No one touches this," he said as he tied the top shut and tossed it on top of the counter. He pointed at Sally. "I want your list of staff."

Sally held out the list, and Harper took it from her. He read off the list, identifying each one of the fifteen staff members by calling their names and their positions: five nurses, including Sally and Toni; John, the janitor; Jennifer, listed as a visiting nurse; one orderly; two respiratory techs; one EKG tech; and three nurse's aides. Paula was the only doctor.

Harper turned back to Sally. "Now I want to see a list of all the patients."

Sally stood and moved to a computer terminal. In a few seconds she had prepared the list, printed it, and handed it to Harper. Sally stepped back into her spot. Harper stood facing them, studying the list he had just been handed.

Paula knew that since Montgomery was a high-profile patient, he wasn't on the list Sally pulled up. The unit normally held ten patients, but two rooms were empty—one patient had died during the night, and one had required emergency surgery earlier that morning. Paula watched as Harper's eyes scanned the list as he started to pace back and forth. He didn't speak for a full minute.

"Is the list complete?" Harper said.

"Yes," Sally answered.

Harper stopped pacing. "Ronald Montgomery is not on the list."

He was talking to Sally. No one answered him.

"Is Ronald Montgomery under an assumed name?" He slowly turned to face Sally.

"He's not here," Sally said, looking down.

"Uh-huh," Harper said softly.

Suddenly, Harper flung the paper into Sally's face. She jerked back and let out a short cry.

"You think I'm stupid?" he yelled, inches from her face. "You think this will protect him?"

Sally cowered, unable to withdraw, forced against a cabinet door.

"God has sent his angel to avenge the deaths of his children." Harper's face was red with rage, his neck veins protruding. "God has sought out his enemy to be punished for his sin. Are you willing to obstruct God's justice, risking your life to protect the enemy of Almighty God?"

Sally covered her face with her hands.

"Tell me *now*," he screamed.

"He's not here!" she cried out.

Harper stepped back. "He's not here?" he repeated sarcastically.

"No…no, he's not," Sally said, shaking her head, sobbing, refusing to look at him.

Paula thought that with Montgomery as sick as he was, he actually appeared very different in his hospital bed compared to his photos in the news. Would Harper recognize him? Had Jennifer removed the items that would identify him?

"That's right," Paula said, taking a risk. "He just left a few minutes ago for Bethesda."

"You are both liars," Harper snapped, "and I *hate* liars!" Harper removed his gun from his shoulder holster and pressed it into Sally's forehead, raising her head upward until her head stopped on the cabinet door. "Then why is the FBI still here?"

Neither Paula nor Sally answered.

"No more chances," he said. He pushed harder against her head. "I'll count to three. One…"

Paula looked at Sally. Her face was blanched white, her eyes wide.

"Two…"

Paula had to tell him. It wasn't worth this. "He's—"

"You harm the attorney general," Jennifer said loudly from behind Harper, "and you won't leave here alive."

Harper wheeled around. "And who are you?"

"I'm his personal assistant," she said, pushing herself upright.

Harper laughed loudly. "Montgomery's secretary? I'm being threatened by his secretary? Do you have an Uzi in your pocket?"

Harper laughed again then instantly frowned. The change was chilling.

"We're not frightened," he said, squatting in front of Jennifer, his voice again a flat monotone. "We're ready for the black helicopters and the SWAT teams and the unaccountable, unelected federal agents that have violated our Constitution and oppressed our people. We're fighting to the death to restore our freedom, to protect our country against tyranny. We're ready." He stood up and stepped back. "But are you? Are you ready to die? Take me to him now. Your silly games are risking the lives of all those here."

Jennifer didn't move.

Harper grabbed her by the hair, jerking her upward, shoving his gun into her throat.

"No more games," he said, raising his voice. "Take me to Montgomery now!"

CHAPTER 22

J effrey Reese's stomach churned despite the four antacid tablets and a glass of
milk. Matt Nicholson's telephone call had left him feeling sick to his stomach—two of his agents killed in an explosion at Harper's compound. Sitting
at his desk, he stared blankly out the window, past the pedestrians on a mid-
morning downtown stroll, past the view toward South Tulsa, and into the
cloudless blue sky. In his twenty-five years with the agency, he had not had a
more distressing day.

Reese dreaded his next responsibility. In a few minutes he'd be leaving to
inform Stan Gill's widow of her husband's death—a widow with two small
boys, eight and ten years old. After he finished there, he would go to the
home of Rod Baker's parents and inform them. Both families would be dev-
astated. He would try to see them before the story hit the news media.

He had just wanted them to deliver Harper a message. Instead, Harper
had sent the agency one.

Reese's secretary knocked and entered. "The administrator at Saint
Luke's is on line one."

"I'm leaving the office. Can I call him back?"

"You'll want to take this call."

Reese waited until his phone rang, and he answered.

"My name is Howard Parrish. I'm the administrator of Saint Luke's
Hospital. We have an emergency." Parrish talked rapidly. His voice sounded
frantic. "We have a terrorist takeover of our intensive care unit. Three men

killed an FBI agent, shot a security guard, and are holding the staff and pa-tients hostages. We think there's a bomb. We've called the police and the FBI."

Parrish described the scene at the hospital. The security guard's wounds were serious, Parrish said, and the surgeons were operating on him now. Before his anesthetic, Baskins had described the three men in detail.

The description, Reese immediately thought, *matches Harper and his men perfectly.*

Baskins guessed twenty to twenty-five people, including patients, were still in the unit. "I'll get a list. The attorney general, Ronald Montgomery, is one of the patients."

"Montgomery is there? The attorney general? He's in that particular unit?"

"Unfortunately, yes, we are positive. Baskins was assigned to patrol the back staircase. He came up on them on his rounds and saw a fourth man holding a gun on the other three. It was all confusing. They pushed the fourth man down the stairs, knocking him out. That's when they shot Baskins. Inside the unit two agents were guarding the attorney general. You may know this."

"They're FBI. We're ATF."

"Oh, okay. Anyway, Baskins said they shot one agent in the head as he looked out a window into the stairwell. Baskins saw him dead on the floor. The other agent inside surrendered without a shot."

Stupid bastard, Reese thought.

"Since it's a bomb," Parrish went on, "I was told by the local police that you should be called."

"That's right," Reese said. "That's exactly what you should have done. Now listen carefully. I'll send agents immediately. The hospital security staff shouldn't do anything without my specific instructions. Understand?"

"Yes, sir, I understand."

"Good. I'll be touch with you shortly."

Parrish thanked him, and they hung up.

His secretary opened the door. Of course she knew the conversation was over.

"We have a serious situation," he said to her. "Call in every available agent."

"Yes, sir."

"Call the Washington office. I want to update the director immediately. And call Matt Nicholson at Taft. I'm pulling Matt off Taft. He won't like it, but I need him at the hospital. Tell him we might need him to negotiate a hostage situation."

"Yes, sir. Right away, sir." She closed the door behind her.

Reese's gut feeling about Harper had been right. He should have moved more quickly against him. He should have anticipated this. Now they had a lunatic who had a bomb. Bad combination.

And the fourth man? Was it Jake?

Reese slipped on his jacket to leave. His secretary could patch the director to his cell phone. Every agent in his jurisdiction would be at the hospital in a few minutes, and so would he, but first he'd make two stops. He owed his agents and their families that much.

λ

Harper rested his arms on the side rails of the attorney's general's bed and gazed down at Montgomery. A white sheet covered him to his waist. His eyes were closed. A clear plastic tube extended from his nose and attached to tubing from the ventilator. Three EKG leads applied to his chest connected to a small rectangular box at his side, sending signals to the monitor hanging from the ceiling. An intravenous line ran from his left hand to a large bag of fluids and three smaller bags of medications on a pole beside the bed. The ventilator triggered when he took a breath, and his chest rose upward with the oxygen-rich air. The aortic balloon was still inserted in his groin, but the nurses had weaned him off the device earlier. Now, assisted only by a small dose of dopamine, he was almost maintaining his own blood pressure.

Harper had insisted that Paula accompany him. She had chosen to stand opposite Harper, and she tried to read Harper's emotion as he watched Montgomery. Harper was hard to read.

Montgomery's color is better, she thought. Though mostly an ash gray, a hint of pink touched his cheeks. His face sported a two-day stubble, and his hair was in disarray. His breathing on the ventilator no longer appeared labored. He was definitely improving. She suspected Montgomery understood everything they were saying.

"So tell me, Doctor," Harper said. "What's his condition?"

"He's in critical condition, like every patient in this unit."

"I'm not concerned about every patient in this unit. I'm only concerned about him. What's his condition?"

"Like I said, his condition is critical. He had a major heart attack. He went into congestive heart failure, acute respiratory failure, and renal failure. He developed pneumonia and probably suffered brain damage. He's comatose." Paula hoped that no one had written in the medical record that he'd awakened from his coma, or she'd be caught in a lie. Harper might well try to read Montgomery's computer chart, but she doubted he was sophisticated enough to understand the medical record. "This patient's condition is extremely serious, and he'll require continuous intensive care."

"Is he going to die?"

"I don't know," she answered honestly. "It depends how we're able to care for him. The nurses can't sit out there and not care for any of these patients. Every patient in this unit will die without constant attention. We need lab. We need X-ray. The patients need respiratory therapy treatments, especially those on ventilators. Some need dialysis. Some may need echocardiograms or pacemakers or a whole host of things we don't have here in the unit." Paula stopped. She was surprised she had been so verbal.

Harper listened without comment. He continued to stare at Montgomery, watching him breathe. "Does he need a pacemaker?" he said finally.

"No, not right now."

"Does he need dialysis today?"

"No, but he might if his kidneys get worse."

Harper looked up at her and leaned over the bedrail. "Are you the only doctor here?"

She nodded.

"I don't care what you do with the other patients. Do as you wish, but so long as everyone stays in the open where I can see them. No one comes in the unit, and no one leaves. No echograms, X-rays, or the other tests you mentioned."

"They must have lab and X-ray," Paula said. "The patients will die without them."

"You'll keep them alive, Doctor. I know you will." Harper leaned farther over the bedrail. "And let me add this. The attorney general is your priority. If he dies, he will have escaped his just punishment. If he escapes his just punishment, you and the others will pay the price." Harper abruptly turned and left.

Pay the price? Keep Montgomery alive without lab or X-ray? Not knowing a patient's blood sugar or sodium level or kidney function. Not having a clue as to the status of a patient's heart or lungs on a chest X-ray. No help from any other doctors. Harper was asking the impossible. She'd be lucky to keep any of the patients alive without the use of the usual diagnostic tools. Montgomery especially. He had been at death's door since his admission. He could crash and die at any moment. So could any of the patients in the unit. That's why they were here.

She was dealing with a madman. A madman with a death wish for everyone.

⋏

Jane followed closely behind a large group entering the pedestrian tunnel into the hospital, ducking her head as she passed under the video surveillance equipment in the ceiling. As she looked around the lobby, there didn't seem to be any particular disruption. An elderly couple sat about fifty feet away in a small grouping of chairs, both reading magazines. On the opposite side, several people were waiting for an elevator. Through the front automatic doors she saw that the two security guards outside had cleared the circle drive and were standing at each end, their arms folded across their chests. The guards were obviously making preparations.

Jane obeyed her husband's instructions, finding a pay phone near the gift shop in a quiet area off the lobby. She inserted a coin and dialed the hospital operator. When the operator answered, Jane asked for the administrator. After several rings a female voice answered, "Saint Luke's Hospital… administration."

"May I speak to the administrator, please?" Jane said politely.

"He's tied up at the moment," the voice responded. "May I ask who is calling?"

"It's about the bomb," she said sharply. She smiled as the woman became instantly quiet.

"Just…just a moment," the woman stammered.

Only a few seconds passed before the administrator was on the line. "This is Howard Parrish. How can I help you?"

Jane suspected they were recording her. At the very least the police were likely listening in on her phone call. Harper's message was brief so her call could not be traced.

"The patriots of the Redeemed Believers have planted three bombs in Saint Luke's Hospital." She read the message slowly and precisely. "They are radio-controlled, and their whereabouts are being observed continuously. If the bomb squads are brought to the hospital, or if there are any attempts to evacuate the patients, the bombs will explode. If any of the patriots of the Redeemed Believers are shot or killed, the bombs will explode. There will be no compromise. Do you understand this message?"

"Yes, yes. Let me ask you—"

Jane hung up the phone, cutting him off. Harper had instructed her, and she had followed his instructions exactly.

Now they would fear her husband. Now they would fear the patriots of the Redeemed Believers. God's power was made plain to them. If they see his power and do not fear the Almighty God, they will be destroyed.

She removed a handkerchief from her purse and wiped the phone clean of fingerprints. Harper had told her to do this. She entered the gift shop and flipped through several magazines, occasionally looking out into the lobby for any sign that someone was coming. No one came.

She left the lobby, following closely behind a young couple with children, and walked through the pedestrian tunnel into the bright, hot sun. Several sirens wailed in the distance, approaching the hospital from different directions. She hurried to the van and crouched down in the back. Now all she could do was wait.

⅄

Reverend Pettigrew seems to be holding his own, Paula thought. His color was gray, a result of the poor oxygenation from what she expected was a blood clot in his lung, but he wasn't gasping for air as he had been when she was with him earlier.

A lot had happened in the intensive care unit since she had seen him last.

"How are you doing, Reverend?"

"As well as can be expected. I'm praying for everyone. Toni told me what's going on."

"Thanks. We need the prayers."

"Wish I could help."

"There's nothing to do. You just need to get better."

Pettigrew nodded his head. "I'll do what I can."

Paula checked his IV lines. *The blood thinner might be working,* she thought. *He does seem better. Of course, he's still on antibiotics for the pneumonia.* A ventilator would help him for both issues, maybe even save his life, but she knew better than to bring it up

Paula examined him, listening to his heart and lungs. She heard no arrhythmia or murmur, but he still had rales and rhonchi, sounds of congestion in his lungs.

"Your exam is about the same," she said.

"I appreciate you."

The old man was suffering, his condition critical, yet his eyes showed his kindness.

"I appreciate you, too, Reverend. I'll be back in a little while."

He smiled and weakly waved at her as she left.

His condition was precarious. She needed every tool of the trade, but she had nothing. It would be a long night.

The next patient was Arthur Hyatt with a stroke. His room was next door to Pettigrew's.

"Mr. Hyatt," Paula said as she entered, "it looks like you're going to be stuck with me."

"It's Arthur, please. No one has called me mister in years."

"Sure, Arthur, I can do that."

He had a worried look on his face. "What's going on?" he asked. "Sounds pretty bad out there."

"Pretty crazy."

"Do you think anyone knows they're here?"

"Oh, I'm sure they do."

"What do you think will happen?"

"I have no idea. What I want is to concentrate on your medical condition."

"I appreciate it, but I'm probably the least sick one here. They were ready to send me out to the floor."

"I heard that. Toni filled me in. I plan to review your records on the computer. The stroke was pretty tough, huh?"

"Would never have believed it'd happen to me. Bagged my entire left side. Completely dead. Useless. Damn!"

"The nurses will have to do your physical therapy. He won't let anyone else in."

"Sure."

"We'll only be able to check finger sticks for your blood sugars. He won't let us send out lab or get X-rays. We have plenty of strips."

"Doc, I'm broken up about not having blood drawn."

Paula smiled. "Blood sugars will be the only lab we can get."

"I'll survive."

"How's your breathing?"

"It's fine."

"Let me take a look." Paula listened to his heart and lungs. She tested the muscles on his left side—completely paralyzed, just as he said. "Hopefully, you'll get some of your function back," she said as she was checking him. "You can't give up. Sometimes it takes months."

"That's what I heard."

"Take care, Arthur. I'll be back."

"Go help the others. I'll be fine."

Paula nodded. She left the room. Strokes were the worst. The patient was normal one second and paralyzed the next. Despite what she told him, he might not get anything back. It was hard to tell at the beginning. Paula headed for the desk to type in a note and check Mr. Hyatt's records. They would likely be extensive, with his complex hospitalization. All the patients in this unit were complex.

As Paula approached the desk, she saw Carl Joe leaning over one of the computer units holding the power cord in his hand. With a brisk movement he ripped the cord from the receptacle. The monitor screen went blank.

"What are you doing?" Paula asked.

"What do you think I'm doing? You're not stupid. I'm unplugging the computers."

Paula looked around the nurses' station and saw that all but a couple of the monitors were already off.

"You can't do that!"

"I just did."

"Sir, that's how we take care of the patients. All their records are on the computer."

Carl Joe shrugged. "Harper's orders."

"It's impossible," Paula said. "It's dangerous. We can't check their records or review their reports. I can't begin to adequately provide medical care for these sick patients without their records." Paula was raising her voice. "This is unbelievable!"

Carl Joe stood straight and moved closer to her face. "I'm following orders, Doctor. Security reasons."

"You can't do this!" Now she was angry.

"Why don't you shut up, bitch!"

She was just pissing him off, she realized. "Come on," she said. "Without the medical records, I'll be flying in the dark. I won't know their diagnoses or the medications they're on." Paula moved away from Carl Joe, sliding along the desk, positioning herself between him and the next computer, trying not to look defiant. "Please, please let me have one computer. You can watch while I'm on it. It's critical for the care of these patients."

Carl Joe moved toward her. "Out of the way. We're *not* leaving them on."

Paula stood her ground. "I can't let you do this!"

Paula barely saw Carl Joe's hand as he jabbed his open palm forward, striking her hard on the cheek. Instantly she felt the sharp pain, and she let out a cry as she stumbled back and fell.

"I told you to back off, bitch!" Carl Joe said as he stood over her.

Paula held her cheek and felt the burning.

"What the hell!" It was Harper's voice behind Carl Joe. "What's going on here?"

Carl Joe turned toward him. "She was blocking me from turning off the computers."

"So you hit her?"

"She had it coming."

Harper was shaking his head. He pointed to the back door. "Go guard it."

"Pastor, she wants to get on the computer. I was only trying—"

"Go now," Harper interrupted.

Carl Joe looked down at Paula on the floor. He was shaking his head as if he was justified. Paula turned her eyes away, refusing to acknowledge him, and was glad to hear his steps as he left. She kept her hand on her cheek and slowly moved her jaw back and forth. She didn't think it was broken. She had lost her balance and had fallen. She didn't think she was hurt.

"Pastor Harper," Paula said, still holding her face, "the medical records on the computer are essential. I know nothing about the patients here. Caring for them without their records is an impossibility."

"No computers. Medicine has done fine without computers." Harper was constantly looking around the unit as he spoke. His voice was calm.

"Yeah, but that was when we had paper charts. I have nothing. *Nothing!*"

"I've decided. No computers. Do the best you can."

"But Pastor, I can't—"

Harper leaned forward and looked directly at her, his dark eyes empty as a void. Then without another word, he turned his back on her and walked away.

Paula knew the answer. There would be no compromise or concessions. There would be no computers. No lab, no X-rays, no medical records. It would be much more difficult than she had thought.

She took a breath and gently rubbed her sore face. She had done it before. Sometimes during her training program, and even occasionally at Saint Luke's, a psychotic homeless person or a patient comatose from a drug overdose would arrive at the emergency room and be admitted to the hospital. No history. No idea of medications or allergies or previous medical issues.

She'd get by. It wouldn't be modern medicine by any stretch, but she could only do what she could do.

Do her best.

Keep them alive. Keep everybody alive.

CHAPTER 23

Matt's thoughts raced past like the flashing of the white center line of the turn-pike as he and Rice rushed back to Tulsa. He felt wretched. Stan and Baker were in his charge. He was responsible for their safety and should have anticipated the possibility of explosives. Why didn't he insist on the special response team? Why hadn't he trusted his own instincts? If he had, Stan and Baker might still be alive.

Neither Rice nor he spoke during the drive, both quiet, reflecting, lost in their own thoughts.

The traffic was sparse until they reached the outskirts of Broken Arrow, a suburb to the southeast. Matt proceeded into Tulsa and turned south onto Memorial Drive, and as the traffic slowed to a crawl, he wondered what Reese thought was so urgent that he had to leave the bomb scene. *I should be there now*, he thought, *sifting through the clues, finding the evidence to hang Harper.* Watertight case. Jury verdict. Lethal injection.

"Die, you bastard!" Matt yelled and thumped hard on the steering wheel.

Rice jumped. He looked at Matt with an odd smile, and Matt nodded.

Rice knows what I want, Matt thought. Rick Rice had lost his partner, too. They both should be at Taft.

Despite the heavy traffic, Matt and Rice arrived at Saint Luke's within forty minutes of receiving the secretary's call to come to the hospital. She didn't provide any details, but had insisted Matt meet Reese on site. Matt counted no fewer than six police cars and two fire trucks in front of the hospital. Fifteen or twenty uniformed officers were milling about, and Matt sensed their apprehension. Their strained faces and tense movements suggested a serious reason for their presence.

For a moment Matt's stomach sank. Paula practiced at Saint Luke's, but as he thought about it a moment, at this time of day she should be back at her office. Whatever might be happening, she should be okay.

Inside the hospital the lobby was swarming with a crowd of people wandering around—nurses, doctors, visitors, police, firemen, and even a few patients in hospital robes. A policeman approached Matt and Rice, telling them that no one would be admitted. Matt flashed his ATF badge.

"Oh, okay," he said. "Follow me. I'll take you directly to the administration boardroom."

"What's going on here?" Matt asked the officer.

"Beats me," he said and shrugged. "Somebody said a bomb scare."

The officer showed them to the administration wing, and they entered through two leaded-glass french doors, passing through a small reception area before turning right into the administration boardroom. Ornate mahogany paneling lined three walls. On the fourth wall, floor-to-ceiling windows overlooked the Tulsa skyline. Twenty or thirty people, clustered in small groups of two or three, were engaged in intense conversations. Most were in dark suits, others in police and fire department uniforms, and a couple in raid gear. Reese was one of the suits standing across the room talking to two men, the Tulsa chief of police and an odd-looking, small man in a baggy, oversized suit. Matt had met the chief several times, but the smaller man he didn't know. All three looked up as Matt and Rice approached.

Matt looked terrible. His jacket was filthy and ripped in several places. Black soot smeared his white shirt. His slacks, only hours earlier pressed perfectly, were wrinkled and torn. His face was smudged with mud, and his hair was a mess, even though he had stopped at a gas station to wash his face and comb out as much glass as he could from the explosion. It had only helped a little.

"What's up?" Matt asked, as he walked up to Reese.

"We have a problem," Reese responded. "Three perpetrators in the hospital's intensive care unit. An FBI agent killed on detail and one captured. Multiple hostages—both patients and staff—probably twenty or twenty-five. We think Ronald Montgomery is one of the hostages."

"The attorney general?" Matt said.

Reese nodded and unrolled the map. "They accessed the unit through this stairwell." He pointed at the map. "Apparently they were planting a bomb in the vent shaft. A security guard surprised them on his routine rounds, and they shot him in the abdomen. He's in surgery now and may not make it. Fortunately, he's a former cop and gave a good description. He saw four large boxes in the stairwell, and one of the perpetrators was holding what he thought was probably a radio-controlled detonator."

"If it's a bomb," Matt said, "and if it's that size, you'd have to consider a nitrate fuel-oil bomb."

"It's a possibility," Reese answered.

"At Taft," Matt said, "the lab boys are thinking the explosion was caused by a fuel-oil bomb."

Reese looked up from the map at Matt. "Yes, I know. We think this is Harper."

Reese's words took a moment to register. Harper was at Saint Luke's! He had been here the whole time they were at the church and property. He *was* setting them up, expecting them to search his place and trip his detonator. He had specifically planned everything.

Reese was talking to him, but Matt's mind was elsewhere. The compound. The bomb. Stan.

"Matt," Reese said, "are you following me?"

Matt nodded blankly. *Harper is here*, he thought, *holding hostages in the hospital, threatening to explode a bomb like the one I just witnessed, like the one that had killed Stan and Baker. Harper is holding hostages, ready to kill again.*

Matt told himself to settle down. He had to focus. Harper was too clever to make many mistakes, and Matt had seen none so far.

"Matt?"

"Okay," Matt said, standing straight. "I'm listening."

"Three men," Reese continued, "are holding the unit: an older man who is probably Harper and two younger men. They're all armed but apparently with just handguns. The older man is constantly holding a radio transmitter."

"That sounds like Harper."

"It gets worse. When the security guard surprised them on the stairwell, a fourth man had his weapon drawn on them. The older man knocked the fourth man down the stairs. Apparently they beat him pretty badly and tied him up. We don't know his condition, and we're not certain of his identity…" Reese hesitated and then added, "but we think it's Jake."

No wonder Jake hadn't called. He couldn't.

"I should have ended the operation," Reese said, "but Jake's a cowboy. He assured me Harper didn't know."

"Yeah, me too. Now we have a mess. Have they made any demands?"

"None so far," Reese said. "How many times have you negotiated hostage situations?"

"Thirty-five, maybe forty."

"That's good. We're going to need your help."

Reese turned to the man beside him. "This is Harold Parrish, the hospital administrator."

Matt and Rice both shook hands with Parrish.

"Tell Matt about your call," Reese said.

Parrish recounted his phone conversation with the anonymous female caller in great detail, and it seemed to Matt he was enjoying a bit too much being the center of attention.

"Of course," Parrish said as he finished, "the bomb in the unit is probably real, but the others could be a hoax."

"Better to assume he's serious," Matt said.

"Oh, yes," Parish said. "Of course."

"They're capable," Matt said. "They've already killed two of our agents." Matt turned to Reese. "Jake told me that Harper will be cautious, and I believe him. I think Harper's crazy enough to blow up this hospital with himself in it."

"You're more familiar with Harper than anyone," Reese said. "Are you up to handling the negotiations?"

"Yes, sir. I'm ready."

"I hope we're given an opportunity."

An administrative secretary had entered the room and was speaking. "You all should see this," she said loudly.

The secretary lifted a remote control and turned on a television suspended in the corner. On the screen was Cara Beeson, the reporter from Channel Three. Behind her was Saint Luke's Hospital.

"Repeating, a source at the hospital informs us that three terrorists have taken over the intensive care unit at Saint Luke's Hospital, killing an FBI agent and seriously injuring a security guard by wounding him in the abdomen. Fourteen staff, one doctor, and eight patients are being held hostage. We'll bring you more when available. This is Cara Beeson, Alert Three News."

"How the hell?" Parrish said, saying aloud what they all were thinking.

"If this is accurate," Reese said, "at least we have a report on the hostages."

"Only one doctor?" Matt asked.

"Only one was in the unit," Reese said, "and we're not sure of her identity, but the security guard said she saved his life by defying the terrorists."

"A female?" Matt asked.

"We're checking the records now," Parrish said. "The guard said she's a young, Native American female with long braided hair."

Matt instantly felt sick to his stomach. In his mind he saw Paula standing among the faceless hostages, Harper holding a gun to her head. "It's Dr. Paula Barrett," Matt said softly.

"You know her?" Reese asked.

"Yes, sir," he managed. "I definitely know her."

CHAPTER 24

Harper smiled to himself as the TV news report concluded. The report had come from inside the intensive care unit, he was certain. It was too accurate. But how? Someone must have called out after they secured the unit. This person was brave...but foolish.

Harper and Carl Joe stayed in front of the TV, away from the staff. Harper had allowed the nursing staff to resume caring for the patients, but he could monitor their every move through the glass partitions. One staff member at a time for each patient, he had told them, unless he was present in the room with them. The remainder of the staff sat on the floor, huddled in the center of the nurses' station.

"I told you we should have popped that guard," Carl Joe said softly.

"No, all the better," Harper said. "The news will be international within an hour. We have Montgomery. Soon the world will know."

"What about him?" Carl Joe motioned toward Jake.

"Nothing. He's almost as good a bargaining chip as Montgomery."

Jake had struggled against his bindings when he first regained consciousness, but he had since quieted down.

Carl Joe left Harper to take his position at the back. Harper walked to Jake and bent over him to remove his gag.

"I didn't think someone from my own family would rat me out."

"Sam, what you're doing here is wrong."

"If your comrades try to burst in to save you, you'll be the first to die. I promise."

"You're in a hospital, for God's sake."

"God's work takes us wherever he requires."

"Don't expect any sympathy for your choice of targets. Too many innocent people will get hurt."

"There are no innocent people here."

"Yes, there are, Sam. Look around you. These people are innocent. Do you want to be another Timothy McVeigh or Osama bin Laden?"

"My judgment is from God, not man, and I am prepared to be judged. For you," Harper said, pointing his finger in Jake's face, "your judgment will be harsh. Your day of destruction is near."

"Sam, this is wrong."

Carl Joe stepped up behind Harper. "I'm tired of hearing this pig squeal."

"Then put the gag back in," Harper said, turning away.

The radio in Harper's pocket crackled with voices. He pulled it out and turned up the volume. As he listened for a few minutes, he suspected the chatter was false, initiated for his benefit. Lifting the radio up, he spoke into the mouthpiece. "This is the intensive care unit," he said. "I want to talk to the chief of security."

⅄

Matt was in the boardroom with Reese and Parrish when he heard Harper's voice on one of the officers' radios. He slipped the radio off the officer's belt and answered Harper.

"This is Matt Nicholson, ATF. I'm in charge. Who is this?"

"This is the man who is holding the attorney general prisoner for his crimes against the people."

"Then you're the one we need to talk to. I've given you my name. If we're going to have a conversation, tell me who you are."

"You know who I am."

"No, sir, I don't. You need to tell me."

"Mr. ATF man, I am confident you know who I am. In fact, I have one of your comrades with me as we speak. Unfortunately, he's tied up at the moment."

Matt looked at Reese and shrugged. All the men and women in the boardroom had come to a complete silence as Matt talked on the radio.

"Okay," Matt conceded. "You're Sam Harper."

"See, I was right. The ATF knows everything."

Harper strolled around the unit as he talked on the two-way radio, watching the staff carefully in each of the patients' rooms. He pointed to Carl Joe and Tommy, motioning them to be alert at the front and back entrances.

"I hope you're not as stupid as most ATF agents."

Matt didn't answer him immediately. The others were beginning to gather around him as he talked to Harper.

Matt dropped the radio to his side. "Let's confirm where this signal is coming from," Matt said in a whisper to no one in particular. "We can't just assume he's in the unit. And clear all other traffic off this channel." He lifted the radio back to his mouth. "Sam, we have some important business to take care of. We'd like to move some of those sick patients out of the intensive care unit. It'll make this whole situation easier for everyone."

"We're not moving anybody out."

"Sam, I'm sure that's your first thought. Those patients are much too complicated. You don't have enough staff to take care of them. Sam, I don't think you want them to die for lack of medical care."

"We have several bombs planted throughout the hospital. I have one here with me in the intensive care unit. I can destroy this unit with the touch of my finger. We have observers on the outside who can detonate any of the explosives if we need to."

"I can't see any reason we would need to, Sam. We're willing to work with you on this. You need to work with us, too. Give us three patients as a sign of good faith."

"I don't think you heard me. No one is leaving. We are in control. You're going to follow *our* rules."

"We're willing to follow the rules, Sam. We don't want to see anyone get hurt. We can end this peacefully."

Harper listened to Matt and shook his head. He settled into a chair in the middle of the nurses' station and leaned over, resting both elbows on his thighs.

"Okay, Matt Nicholson," Harper said, cradling the radio in both hands. "Now I want you to shut up and listen to the rules."

"Okay, Sam. I'm listening."

"These are the rules." Harper paused, and then spoke slowly into the radio. "No one is leaving the unit. If I see any SWAT teams, any snipers, or any black helicopters, we will destroy this unit."

"Okay, Sam, I hear that. Your rule is no SWAT teams, snipers, or black helicopters. What other rules?"

"All the patients stay where they are in the hospital. No evacuation. No patient is moved."

"I hear you, Sam. What else?"

"No microwave beams or radio blockers. I want the TVs to stay on. I want the phone lines, electricity, and water. If anything turns off, a hostage will die."

"No microwave or radio blockers. Of course, Sam, the TV, phone lines, electricity, and water will stay on. It's an intensive care unit, Sam, so we couldn't turn those off anyway. We wouldn't want to hurt the innocent."

"You all think they're innocent. No one here is innocent. All may die."

"We don't want anyone to die. We want to settle this."

"Good, so these are the rules. It's not a negotiation."

"Okay, Sam. Then let's talk about the patients."

"In one hour I'll announce my demand. I want a live TV interview. In one hour I want Cara Beeson from Channel Three at the front entrance to the unit. Just her. She brings the camera in, and we'll run it. It must be live."

"I'm not sure we can do that. We don't have control of the TV stations. I'm willing to work on your request, but you have to show us a sign of good faith. Send out a hostage, your sickest patient, as a sign of good faith, and we'll work on your request."

"One hour…Beeson…by herself…or we'll send out a hostage—a dead hostage. One less hostage…one dead federal agent."

Harper clicked off the radio and dropped it in his pocket.

⅄

Matt expected Harper to end the conversation abruptly. He had seen this tactic frequently in similar situations. The gesture would allow Harper to feel in control, and Matt had no reason for Harper to think otherwise for now. But it was his job to be sure Harper didn't stay in control.

"What's on the other floors on that wing?" Matt asked anyone listening.

Howard Parrish rolled the map back out on the table. "That wing has five floors. They're on the third. The floor above them is the surgical ICU, and the floor above that is the pediatric ICU. The floor below them is the chest pain unit. The medical director's offices are on the first floor. There's a basement, but it's just a small storage area."

"The first thing we do," Reese said, "is move everyone we can out of that wing. All visitors. Everyone. We move all unessential staff. He may have someone planted on other floors. I'd believe him." Reese pointed to a spot on the map and looked up at Matt. "We should secure those stairwells front and back with undercover agents now. No media. No TV cameras. We should tap their phones. No calls in. None."

"Okay," Matt agreed.

"It's risky to evacuate that wing," Reese said, "but we really don't have a choice. Murphy?"

Franklin Murphy was in charge of the SWAT team. He was standing across the table listening to Reese. "Yes, sir," he answered.

"As soon as the visitors are out, we can move you here…and here." Reese pointed. "Be invisible."

"Yes, sir."

"And the plan for the rest of the hospital?" Matt asked.

"Fortunately this wing extends out separately from the main hospital, so that helps. We'll evacuate the specialty wing and then sweep the entire hospital for bombs. If there aren't any others, we'll begin the evacuation of the nonserious patients first."

"It could take days to evacuate all the patients," Parrish said. "We can't just discharge them all. Many of them will require transfer to other facilities."

"Then we'd better get started," Reese said firmly. "I'd recommend a skeleton crew of volunteers—nurses, lab, X-ray, surgery. Of course, you should close the ER."

"We can do that," Parrish said, nodding, "if we have to."

"Harper's capable," Matt said. "We have two dead agents to prove it."

"Three."

The voice came from behind Matt. He turned to see a short stocky man in a suit.

"Rick Simmons," the man said, holding out his hand, "FBI."

Matt, Reese, and Murphy introduced themselves and shook hands. They updated Simmons with the latest information. He had heard about Harrison's death, but not the specifics.

"Thanks for the info," Simmons said. "Now..." He paused and looked back and forth at each of them. "Since I'm in charge of the attorney general's detail, I'll be taking over the situation."

Reese laughed. "Taking over?"

"This should be an FBI operation," Simmons persisted. "We have six agents from the Tulsa office on the way and thirty coming from Dallas and Kansas City. The director himself is flying in from Washington. This *is* the attorney general."

Matt could see Reese stiffen. Reese's voice remained steady, but Matt saw his anger building.

"We've been following this bomber for eighteen months, and he's killed two of our field agents. Matt here knows everything there is to know about him."

Simmons folded his arms across his chest. "The AG is *our* detail," he said firmly. "This is the FBI's jurisdiction."

"I would disagree," Reese said.

Simmons face grew red. "I'm not trying to step on your toes, Reese, but since this is simply a jurisdictional disagreement, I'll call my director. He can decide."

"Hey," Matt said, "we have a bomb in a hospital, with patients and staff as hostages. What we need here is cooperation."

Reese moved closer and pointed his finger at Simmons. "I'm the RAC, and I'm in charge until *my* superior tells me otherwise. You'll help where I say you'll help."

Simmons didn't move. "Whatever you say," Simmons said through clenched teeth. "At least...for now."

The two men stood facing each other.

"What about the interview?" Parrish asked.

Parrish was still leaning over the table, holding the map open. Matt thought he must be oblivious to their discussion, but his interruption was timely.

"Harper wants Cara Beeson," Matt said quickly, hoping to change the topic. "We should call her. Since she apparently knows so much, maybe we can tap into her source."

"We need to decide how we'll handle this interview," Reese said.

"It's your call," Matt said. He took a sideways glance at Simmons.

"Get Beeson in here," Reese said.

Matt nodded. *Whatever we do*, he thought, *we'll have to be more cautious this time.* Harper was smart and tough, and they had underestimated him. Also Jake was there as a hostage, and that complicated the situation. So did the hospital employees. And the patients. *And Paula.*

Matt thought about Paula standing up against Harper. She had defied him to protect a security guard. As proud as he was of her, he hoped she wouldn't push Harper too hard. Harper wasn't likely fond of female authority figures, yet Paula was the only doctor in the unit. If Harper was as smart as Matt thought he was, he'd use Paula to keep the patients alive, including Montgomery. Now if only Matt could find a way to save her.

Matt needed to stop thinking about her. He had work to do.

If only he could push her image from his mind.

⋀

Sally's brow was tense and her eyes heavy with fatigue as she propped her arms on Montgomery's side rails across the bed from Paula. Paula and Sally were left by themselves for a few minutes. Paula didn't think Harper's rule about two in a room applied to her, and Harper would have to tell her otherwise. Sally had assigned each of the nurses and nurse's aides a patient on Harper's instructions. The three aides were assigned to the patients who were the least ill and the registered nurses to the most ill. Sally took Montgomery.

Paula knew the medical history of Montgomery and her own two patients, Reverend Pettigrew and Randy Booker. She wanted to review the charts of the five other patients, but of course she couldn't, because Harper had dismantled the computers. All five would be quite complex medically, or they wouldn't be in the intensive care unit in the first place. Most of their records, if she could see them, would be extensive, with pages and pages of lab reports, X-rays, and notes to examine. To make matters worse, Harper had said no phone calls, so she couldn't call their personal physicians or their specialists. And no Internet to search for answers. The nurses could fill her in on some aspects of their medical issues, but a nurse's perspective differed from that of a doctor's. A doctor typically diagnosed a disorder and planned the treatment. A nurse administered that treatment and helped to monitor the progress. Paula could rely on the nurses for some historical information but would have to determine most on her own. She would quickly round on Montgomery, Pettigrew, and Booker before moving to the five patients she didn't know.

"What are we going to do?" Sally whispered.

Paula glanced out at Harper in the hallway. He was looking in the opposite direction. "We do exactly what he says, that's what. We have little choice."

"We need a plan of care for these patients."

"I'll do a complete evaluation on every patient. You should assign the nursing duties in addition to Montgomery, if you can."

"I'm sure I can."

"Good. Then we should ask Harper if you and I can supervise all the care together."

"How are we going to do anything without lab or X-ray or the electronic record?"

"Poorly, that's how."

Harper turned around and looked in their direction. Paula pointed to the monitor as though she was commenting on its reading.

"Maybe he'll let us do lab," Paula said. "We could send the blood through the vacuum system. I doubt he'll budge on the X-ray."

"It's impossible without the lab. He doesn't understand."

Paula lifted Montgomery's IV line off the bed. "Is he still on the dopamine?"

"Yes," Sally said, "but we've tapered the dose down."

"So his blood pressure is better?"

"Much."

"How about the balloon pump?"

"I weaned him off a few hours ago."

"I'm not sure what's next with the balloon," Paula admitted. "Do we pull it out?"

"Dr. England would probably leave it in for a few hours," Sally said, "in case his condition worsens."

Paula looked down at Montgomery. "This is a tough case," she said. "How are we going to keep Mr. Montgomery alive? He's been on the ventilator and pump for forty hours, basically without a blood pressure."

"And our lives depend on it," Sally added.

Montgomery opened his eyes, and they both saw him wink.

"Sorry, Mr. Montgomery," Paula said, embarrassed. She had forgotten he was conscious. "We'll do our best."

"I know." Montgomery mouthed the words. The nasotracheal tube prevented him from speaking. "Thank you."

Paula heard her pager begin beeping, and she reached in her pocket. She lifted the pager to read the message.

"Late for dinner? I understand. Love, M."

She smiled. Matt knew she was here. He must be in the hospital. If Matt was on the case, he'd think of a way to save them. She could depend on it.

Paula looked up. Harper was staring directly at her, and he was frowning.

Chapter 25

Carl Joe handed Harper a cup of coffee. "No live interview," Carl Joe said in a low voice. "The feds won't let it happen."

"Doesn't matter," Harper said, accepting the cup. "We'll get our interview."

Harper and Carl Joe stood together against the wall near the stairwell, drinking coffee. Moments earlier, Harper had effortlessly lifted Harrison's dead body and propped him in a chair, positioning his feet so they were partially showing in the doorway. The feds would think Harrison's feet belonged to one of the militia guarding the unit. Harper dragged Jake and Asher, bound and gagged, through the pool of Harrison's blood and brains on the floor, and then positioned them about fifteen feet inside the door. Harrison's feet in the doorway and the two blood-covered agents on the floor might provide a moment's distraction when the feds stormed the unit—a couple of extra seconds Harper could use to detonate the ANFO.

The unit was quiet. The staff in the nurses' station dared not speak, which of course suited Harper. In each individual patient room was a nurse, separated by Harper's explicit instructions. The doctor and head nurse were in Montgomery's room. Harper watched them closely.

Harper had stationed Carl Joe at the back and Tommy at the front. Harper held the transmitter. The feds could come anytime. He was ready.

Harper smelled the coffee and took a sip. "It's too good of a news story," he said to Carl Joe. "Attorney general. Bomb in a hospital. It'll be international before Cara Beeson gets here."

"Militia brothers throughout the nation will unite to help the cause."

"Maybe, but we can't depend on them."

Harper leaned forward toward the stairwell and listened in the silence. "They'll come in from this direction when they come," he said, barely a whisper. "Even with the barricade."

"After they negotiate first?"

"Maybe. Maybe not. I'm afraid we've angered a few people."

Harper pointed toward the front entrance. "This long hallway is easily defensible. One person can hold them off here."

"Even Tommy?"

"Yes, possibly even Tommy." Harper finished his coffee and then tossed the cup on the floor. "They'll come in force."

"We have five extra guns and a few clips of ammo thanks to our law enforcement officers."

"The bomb is our key…maybe the hostages."

"We'll use the hostages as shields."

"Maybe, if we have time." Harper stepped away from the doorway. "Normally they'd come at us with smoke, tear gas, and flash bombs, but with the patients so ill, it'll limit their tactics."

"I'll be ready."

"I'm sure you will be." Harper leaned into Carl Joe's ear. "I'll blow the bomb if I have to. You know that, Carl Joe."

"Yes, Sam. I know."

"Good. Keep an eye on the staff—especially the nurses and that doctor. I don't trust them."

"We should keep them scared."

"Fearful, yes. But unharmed."

Carl Joe nodded. "Yes, Pastor. I understand."

"As the Bible says, 'Let all the earth fear the Lord: let all the inhabitants of the world stand in awe of him.'"

"Amen, Brother Harper."

"We're doing his will," Harper said softly. "He'll protect us from the unholy."

Jennifer ran her index finger along the rip in her silk stocking, gently caressing the large bruise forming on her right thigh. Carl Joe had thrown her on the floor, and she was sore with bruises all over. She shifted uncomfortably on the hard tile floor, her back aching as she leaned against a cabinet door.

Jennifer eyed Harper and Carl Joe talking at the back entrance. Harper gestured as he spoke, and she carefully studied his movements, observing his appearance, memorizing everything. She had an eye for detail and a near-photographic memory. Harper looked like a low-class bully—squat body hunched over, poor-fitting clothes, dirty nails. The lanky man they called Carl Joe stood next to Harper. He had been unnecessarily rough with Jennifer, tearing her stocking, bruising her legs and arms. *He's also a bully*, she thought, *but unstable and thus more unpredictable.* The two of them talked quietly, seriously, likely talking tactics, defense. Tommy, the third man, guarded the front entrance. He was the weak one, a follower, almost looking out of place to her. Harper had barely acknowledged him.

Five grim-faced staff members sat with Jennifer in the nurses' station. The orderly and two respiratory techs had their faces buried in their knees. The EKG tech, a young girl who couldn't be twenty-five, appeared to be the most frightened, wringing her hands and sobbing quietly, sometimes crying out with a loud sigh. She'd be worthless. Sitting directly across from Jennifer was John Hays. He appeared less tense than the others, almost relaxed, which seemed odd since Carl Joe had just threatened to kill him.

John glanced over his shoulder at Harper and Carl Joe. Both were facing the stairwell door, engaged in an intense conversation. John leaned forward to Jennifer and softly whispered, but she shrugged, not hearing him. John looked again over his shoulder and kept a constant watch on the two men as he inched forward. He waited until he was within a couple of feet and whispered again.

"We need a plan," he said, his voice barely audible.

Jennifer quickly pushed back, shaking her head. "No! No!" her lips mouthed.

John slowly crept toward her. She waved at him to move back. He was too close. Harper and Carl Joe were still facing the doorway but could turn at any second.

"They're going to kill us," John whispered. "We need a plan."

Jennifer shook her head. The other staff members were looking at them.

"No," Jennifer whispered back. "It's too risky. We can't do anything that risks Mr. Montgomery's life."

John slid back to his spot. "They have a bomb," he mouthed. "They'll kill us anyway."

Jennifer shook her head and cast her eyes downward. John tried to engage her, but she refused.

"Hey!"

Jennifer jumped. All heads turned to the voice coming from behind them. A few feet away stood Tommy, holding out an empty coffeepot.

"We're out of coffee," Tommy said loudly. "Isn't that nurse making coffee?" Tommy lifted the pot up.

Several of the staff pointed to one of the rooms, and Tommy headed toward it.

"Is someone making coffee?" he yelled outside the doorway.

Harriet Sampson, a nurse's aide, stepped out of the room, apologizing profusely. Harper had charged her with the coffee duties.

"I'm so sorry," she said as she took the pot from Tommy. "I got busy with the patient."

"You need to pay better attention."

Harriet set a paper filter in the funnel and scooped in fresh coffee. After pushing the funnel into the machine, she filled a container with water at the sink and poured the water in. She stood by the coffee maker a couple of minutes as the dark fluid began to drain into the pot. When it was about half full she called out that the coffee was ready and returned to her patient.

Jennifer watched as Tommy filled his cup and walked back to the front. He startled her. If Tommy were more observant, he would have seen her and John communicating. Not good. Jennifer glanced briefly at John. He gave her a wry smile and nodded. Jennifer shook her head again. The best plan was to wait for help. Help would come. They should wait. Wait to be saved. Anything else would be foolish.

"Montgomery must be pretty sick."

Harper had walked into Montgomery's room and was directly behind Sally when he spoke. Paula had seen Montgomery flinch slightly and hoped Harper hadn't noticed.

"You've been in here a long time," Harper continued. "I thought you said you had a few other patients."

"We're here because he's seriously ill," Paula said, "and we *do* have other patients."

"Oh, really? Who's taking care of them?"

What is this about? Paula thought. *Isn't Montgomery Harper's only priority?* She *did* have other patients, as if he cared.

Paula wanted to challenge him, to yell at him that he was asking the impossible. How could they care for these patients under these conditions? How could they keep *anyone* alive? She was on the verge of tears but pushed them back. He wouldn't see her cry. She could feel the hatred rising up inside of her, an emotion she had only rarely felt.

Paula dropped her arms to her sides and remained completely still. She cast her eyes down, avoiding eye contact. "I'm sorry, Mr. Harper," she said softly. Her voice was a monotone, like a schoolgirl to an unhappy teacher. "We're just trying to stabilize these patients the best we can. Our staff is stressed to the max, and our patients are getting sicker."

Paula didn't look up and waited for his response.

"I'm sure you'll get it done."

"We need lab tests."

"No lab tests."

"Whatever you wish, but it's hard to treat them without lab tests. We could send it through the vacuum tubes. Wouldn't have to leave the unit."

"No one leaves the unit."

"Thank you, sir," Paula said, glancing briefly up at his eyes before looking back down.

Harper smiled. "Okay. But you try anything...try to sneak something by us...and one of you dies." Harper pointed back toward the nurses' station at Jennifer. "Her. She's dispensable. Anything screwy happens, and she dies."

Paula had no doubt he'd kill Jennifer.

"We'll need at least one computer terminal to review the results. The lab is all digital."

Harper's response was immediate. "Absolutely not."

"But we can't—"

"Doctor, I said no. Send the results back in the tubes, but I look at every tube first. Understood?"

"Yes, sir."

"And any attempts to communicate in any way, she dies." Harper again pointed back to Jennifer. "Her blood will be solely on your hands. Now do you understand?"

"Yes, sir."

The lab was essential. Without the lab to guide her medical treatment, patients would die. He had allowed it. She would be very, very careful.

"And Doctor, you understand my priority about Montgomery?"

"Yes, sir."

Harper was clear. Of course Montgomery was his priority.

"Also," Paula said, continuing the same monotone, "we need to divide the patients among the registered nurses and allow the three nurse's aides to assist the RNs."

"No. One nurse per room."

"The nurse's aides aren't capable of this level of medical care."

"No. They'll have to do."

Paula looked up. "They're not actually nurses."

Harper was silent. She knew she was pushing.

"Give me your pager." Harper stretched out his hand.

"Pardon?"

"I said, give me your pager."

She reached into her pocket and handed him the pager.

Harper snatched it from her and scrolled through the messages. She was glad she had erased Matt's.

Paula cast her eyes back down. "What are you looking for?" she asked. She knew exactly what he was looking for.

"Nothing. I'll keep this." Harper slipped the pager in his pocket and left.

Sally smiled at Paula. "That worked pretty well."

"At least we have lab."

"It's a start."

"It's a crumb," Paula said. "That's all it is…just a crumb."

CHAPTER 26

Cara Beeson was escorted to the boardroom by two hospital security guards. She had insisted her producer and cameraman accompany her, but the guards' instructions were explicit, and her two associates were left in the lobby. She wasn't unhappy. Moments earlier, she had been waiting outside in the hundred-degree heat with forty or fifty other reporters from all over the country, including the four major networks and CNN. The hospital had given them virtually nothing about the crisis, and everyone was hungry for a story. Now she, a local reporter, had been chosen to talk to the police and FBI.

She knew why she had been chosen. They had watched her reports on TV. Her sources were as good as or better than theirs, and they wanted her sources. They couldn't have her sources. She'd go to jail first. If that's what they wanted, the meeting would be short. If not, maybe she'd pick up a tidbit or two. Anything at all. All she needed was a single new fact. Then she could go live, likely with a national feed, with a bunch of network anchors fresh off their airplanes standing around, watching her with their hands in their pockets, drooling. She needed one new fact. She might have to make one up.

$$\wedge$$

"We need your sources," Matt said.

"I won't reveal my sources."

Matt thought it best to be blunt. Forget the pleasantries. It'd be good to know who was feeding Cara Beeson information from the inside, but it wasn't essential. "We're not playing games, Ms. Beeson," Matt said. "This is a serious situation."

"If that's it, this will be a short meeting."

Cara Beeson was sitting in a gray metal chair in the corner of the boardroom. Matt sat across from her, with Reese to his right and Simmons to his left. The three of them essentially surrounded her, creating a perception that she was blocked. Matt didn't expect her to move, and she didn't. She was bluffing, at least about leaving. He'd see about her sources.

Reese pointed at her. "We'll throw your butt in jail," he said, "and get a court order."

"Whatever. You have time for that?"

Matt smiled. She was tough. "Ms. Beeson, let's be honest." He slid a fraction closer. "You want a story, and we want the bad guys. We were hoping we could work together on this."

"I see," she said, still serious. "And exactly how would that work?"

"It's not our usual practice," Matt said, "to allow exclusives…"

"I'm listening."

"But in this case, when it's over, you'll be the first to know."

"Hmm." She paused and then briefly smiled. "Seems to me that when it's over, everyone will know."

"Well, true," Matt said, "but you'll have access to the details that the others won't."

"I hate to be skeptical," she said, "but in criminal cases, that's usually not true."

"Ms. Beeson," Matt said, "you seem to have trust issues."

Beeson shook her head. "No comment."

"Okay," Matt said. "Fair enough. It's your loss. Actually, we don't need your sources, but we do need your help."

"I'm still listening."

"As you know, we have terrorists holding hostages in the intensive care unit, a militia group led by a so-called minister, Sam Harper. Harper apparently has been watching your TV reports."

"Oh, really?"

"He's ready to state his demands—we have no idea what they'll be. The only demand he's made so far is that he wants to go on live TV…to be interviewed…by you."

"I'd be willing to do that."

"Of course you would, but we can't let you do that."

Matt paused, and she waited.

"It'd be too risky," Matt continued. "If you became a hostage, we couldn't guarantee your safety."

"I understand what you're saying."

"Anyway, it's against our policy to allow maniacs to air their demands on live TV. He's threatening to kill people. His head is warped. Putting him on TV is a bad idea."

"The public has a right to know his demands. This is a human drama."

"No, they don't. The public has a right to be protected from this kind of violence."

"We don't create the violence. We just report it."

"We're not here to argue with you, Ms. Beeson. What we want is for you to tell him that it's against your station's policy to do live interviews. We don't want it to be an option."

"Our station is, of course, selective about these requests, but I can't see where airing his demands puts the hostages in danger any worse than they're in now. We all want the hostages to stay safe. In fact, appeasing him about the interview may make him more cooperative."

"It's not your place to make him cooperative. We're asking for your assistance in this matter. Many lives are at stake."

Beeson stood. "Gentlemen, thank you."

The three men stood.

"Frankly, I can't see the harm," she said. "It seems to me to be the right thing, and I'm willing to do it. Call me if you change your mind."

"We won't," Reese said. "Furthermore, for obvious security reasons we don't want this conversation repeated."

They moved aside as she stepped between them to leave.

"Off the record?" she said over her shoulder, smiling. "You should have said that before we started."

⋏

Gasping for each breath, Reverend Pettigrew appeared much worse than when Paula had seen him an hour earlier. He was cyanotic, his lips turning blue, and his breathing rapid, over forty times a minute. He needed a CT scan and possibly a thrombolytic, but because of Harper such things were now impossible. Pettigrew had refused intubation, and his decision would likely cost him his life. Only the blood thinner pumping through his peripheral IV might save him, if it affected the clot in time.

She knew the odds of that were unlikely. She was losing him.

"Toni, how's his pressure?" she asked.

"Sixty over forty and going down."

"Start him on a dopamine drip. He's not refusing dopamine. Is his O_2 on 100 percent?"

"Yes, Doctor. But his pulse oximeter is only 50 percent."

"That's the best we'll do without a ventilator."

A plastic oxygen mask had been strapped to his face with a rebreather bag connected below it. He had monitor leads attached to his chest and an IV in each arm. The monitor beeped a soft warning, signaling his dangerously low blood pressure.

Paula touched his forehead. His skin was cool, clammy, and he was sweating profusely. His color was ashen. He opened his eyes and turned them toward her.

"The situation is precarious, Reverend," she said softly.

"I know, child."

"It's made worse by this Harper person," she said, "but I promise he won't harm you."

"No harm will come to me, Dr. Barrett. Go protect your sheep. My shepherd is coming for me." He closed his eyes, resting back on the pillow.

Toni hung the dopamine drip and inserted the needle in his IV tubing. The clot in his lung was causing his blood pressure to plummet. Raising the blood pressure with the dopamine could help some. Paula wasn't optimistic.

Harper entered the room and moved to the side of Pettigrew's bed. Paula and Toni continued their duties, ignoring his presence. Harper watched in silence until Pettigrew opened his eyes and turned toward him.

"I hear you're a pastor," Harper said.

Pettigrew reached up and pulled off his mask. "Reverend Harper," he said, gasping. His voice was barely a whisper. "Violence is a sin against God."

"We are seeking a higher order. God condemns the God-haters and strikes down the unholy. We've come to bring justice to those who kill defenseless unborn children. Of all here, you should understand."

"I don't believe in abortions…" Pettigrew paused to gain his breath. "But what you are doing is crazy." He paused again. "The message of Christ is one of love…not hate."

"Murdering babies isn't violence?" Harper asked, raising his voice. "God has sent us to exact his punishment on the guilty."

"Are you the judge?" Pettigrew said weakly. "Jesus said…do not judge… or you too will be judged."

Paula saw that Pettigrew was exhausted. "Mr. Harper, please," Paula cried out, "Reverend Pettigrew needs his rest."

Toni reached to replace his oxygen mask. Pettigrew brushed it away.

Harper pointed his finger at him. "God's condemnation is upon those who do not rise up against the evil nation. God hates sin!"

Pettigrew sat straight up, using every ounce of his energy. "But not the sinner!" His voice was strong, but he fell back weakly in the bed when he was finished.

Paula jumped in front of Harper. "For God's sake, he's dying."

Harper reached over Paula's shoulder, waving his finger at Pettigrew. "You will receive your just reward."

Paula placed both of her hands on his chest and forcefully pushed him backward. "Bully me," she shouted. "Bully the staff. *But leave my patient alone!*"

Harper stared into her eyes, and she felt the cold hatred penetrating through her. He stood facing her for several seconds then abruptly turned and left.

Paula exhaled heavily. She couldn't believe she had touched him, pushing him hard out of the way. She had taken her own life in her hands. Her knees felt weak, and she reached for a chair next to the bed. Pettigrew was lying back in the bed, barely breathing. His eyes were closed.

"I'm sorry, Reverend."

He opened his eyes and looked up at her. His eyes were kind, comforting, unafraid.

"I'm not," he said softly. "Please remember…hate is not…of God. I *will* receive…my just reward…thanks be to God."

He closed his eyes.

"Doctor," Toni said, "we have to stand up to them. You did the right thing."

"I don't know," Paula said. "I just don't know."

What was happening? This whole situation was so overwhelming. She felt hopeless, confused. Patients were dying, and she was helpless to prevent it. What was Harper planning? Could they even predict? Could she and the nurses fight this monster? Or would he kill them all if they tried?

Matt, come save us. Please come save us.

Chapter 27

Matt took a deep breath and let it out slowly. He was prepared to radio Harper to inform him they were denying the interview, but Matt was reluctant. Harper had threatened to kill a federal agent within the hour. The hour was almost up. Matt was certain it was not an empty threat.

The boardroom was quiet. Matt had turned a chair to face the corner as he preferred no distractions, yet he could feel the eyes of those in the boardroom on him. A couple of voices at the far end carried on phone conversations, talking softly in whispers. The rest were waiting for Matt to begin.

Matt toyed with the radio. They couldn't allow the interview with Beeson. With a national audience, every nut case in the country would camp out in their local hospital, demanding equal TV time. And Beeson was no help. Her confirmation of station policy would have been useful, but more than he expected from a reporter.

No, the decision to deny the interview was a correct one. Yet within a few minutes of his conversation with Harper, either Jake's or Asher's body might be in the hallway, dead.

Please stay calm everyone, he thought, hoping they could sense his plea. *Stay calm, too, Paula. What will happen will happen.*

Matt clicked on the radio. "Sam Harper," Matt said. "Sam Harper, are you there? This is Matt Nicholson."

He waited.

"Sam Harper," he repeated, "come in, please."

The room was silent. Everyone was waiting. Matt's pulse quickened.

"Sam Harper, please come in."

Matt's radio crackled to life.

"This is Harper."

Matt exhaled in relief. "This is Matt Nicholson."

"I know who you are. Where is Cara Beeson? You only have a couple of minutes."

"Sam, we're working on that now. You have to trust us."

"That's not good enough, Mr. ATF man. If she's not here in ten minutes, someone dies."

"No one need die, Sam. Let me tell you what we've done for you. We've talked to Cara Beeson, but it's against her station's policy to do live interviews. She's trying to track down her station manager to get permission. The earliest she could do an interview is an hour…maybe two."

Matt waited. Several long seconds passed without Harper responding.

"Sam, are you there?"

After a tense pause, Harper's voice broke the silence.

"'And Satan stood up against Israel and provoked David to number Israel.'" Harper's voice was a flat monotone. "'Be not dismayed, for I am thy God, I will strengthen thee. Yea, I will uphold thee with the right hand of my righteousness.'" His volume was louder. "'Produce your cause, saith the Lord, bring forth your strong reasons, saith the King of Jacob.'" Harper was now almost shouting. "'Behold, ye are of *nothing*.' The unholy have chosen the fiery hell. The fiery furnace of Waco burns white hot, *consuming* the evil nation—"

"Sam," Matt cut in, "you're not making a lot of sense." Matt wanted Harper to stop and hear him. Matt needed a dialogue. "What are your demands? We're willing to listen."

"God forbid that we should *rebel* against the Lord and turn this day from following the Lord. He *demands* a holy sacrifice. The guilty *shall die* and be *swept* away."

"Sam, tell us what you want." Matt's voice grew louder. "No innocent people need be hurt. We can find a peaceful solution. Please, what are your demands?"

Matt paused, and it was quiet. Harper had stopped.

"Listen to me," Harper said finally. His voice was completely calm again. "You're not listening to me. Now someone must die. God's will must be done."

The radio went dead.

⋏

Paula shivered as she observed Harper. Seconds earlier he had been screaming into the radio, ranting at Matt like a lunatic. Now he was calm, emotionless. The transformation was scary. She had seen preachers on TV or in movies, yelling about hell and waving their Bibles one minute, then stone silent and frozen like a statue the next. An act for effect. Dramatics. Harper's antics were real. His mood swings were an unpredictable emotional roller coaster—convincing her of his instability, his unbalanced mental state. He was certifiably crazy.

Paula had been sitting at the nurses' station writing a progress note about Pettigrew on a note pad when Matt radioed Harper. She wished she hadn't heard their conversation. The staff heard, too. They hung their heads and said nothing. They were thinking the same thing: they all would die.

Paula thought about her parents and said a quick prayer. Would she ever see them again?

After Harper finished talking with Matt, Paula watched Harper cross over to the two agents on the floor and bend over Jake. That was five minutes ago, and Harper hadn't moved since. He was standing fifteen feet from the doorway—exposed and in the open. It was as though he was confident the federal agents wouldn't storm in after he talked to Matt.

He's defenseless, she thought. *Now's the moment. Come take him, Matt. Kill him now.*

Harper stayed in the same position hunched over the agents, staring down at them. Was he going to shoot one of them? Was he making good his threat? Behind Harper, Carl Joe was yelling, furious. Harper seemed oblivious.

Paula had never been more frightened in her life.

"We won't get the interview," Carl Joe shouted. "They're screwing with us, and they're gonna keep screwing with us. I told you that would happen. You can't trust them, none of them. We're on our own here, just like I said."

"We will get the interview," Harper said finally, without lifting his head.

"No, we won't," Carl Joe screamed louder, coming up close behind him. "We should demand a helicopter and fly Montgomery out of here."

"To where? Where would we go? We're better off here."

"Then we should cap these two sons of bitches right now—"

Harper turned angrily. "Watch your mouth, Carl Joe."

Carl Joe leaned forward toward Harper. "We should kill them both," he said, tapping his finger on Harper's chest. "Show them we mean business. Stop this bullshit."

Harper's reaction was swift. He seized the front of Carl Joe's shirt with both hands, effortlessly lifted him off the ground, and tossed him ten feet backward. Carl Joe landed flat on his back and slid several feet along the floor. Before he stopped moving, Harper was hovering over him.

Paula gasped at Harper's instant change. He was an animal, a wild beast losing control.

"You touch me again, Carl Joe," Harper screamed viciously, "and I'll kill you. Understood?"

"Yes…yes, Sam," he stuttered. His face betrayed true fear.

"What did you say, soldier?"

"Yes, sir. Understand, sir."

Harper stood upright and looked away in disgust. "Now back to your post, soldier," he said, dismissing him with the back of his hand.

Carl Joe scrambled to his feet. Before Carl Joe reached the doorway, Harper spun around toward the two agents, pulled out his weapon, and aimed it at Jake's head.

Paula held her breath.

Harper fully extended his arm and touched the tip of the gun to Jake's head. He pushed the gun into Jake's skull without emotion and stood frozen over him for what seemed like an eternity. Paula was certain Jake would die. She wanted to cry out and stop it. *Stop this madness!*

Suddenly, with an unsettling calmness, Harper slid the gun back into his shoulder holster, stepped over Jake, and casually walked into Montgomery's room.

Paula inhaled and realized she hadn't been breathing. She forced herself to breathe in and out as her heart pounded heavily in her chest. *Stay calm. Don't panic.* Maybe the violence was over. Maybe the murders would stop.

Carl Joe was leaning against the wall. She could see his anger. Tommy never moved from his position at the front. She must stay calm, finish her note on Pettigrew, start her rounds on the other patients. They needed her. Flo Pearce, an eighty-year-old woman, post-op appendectomy, was worsening rapidly from congestive heart failure. *Concentrate on the patients.* Arthur Hyatt, a fifty-three-year-old diabetic with a massive stroke, had a blood glucose over four hundred. Marcus Locke was a bleeding ulcer whose hemoglobin was eight and falling. *We're all going to die.*

"Dr. Barrett." She jumped at the voice. It was Toni behind her.

"Yes, Toni?"

Toni cast down her eyes, swollen and red.

Not now, Paula thought. *No more tragedies. Don't tell me, I don't want to know.*

"I thought you should know," she said softly. "We just lost Reverend Pettigrew. I'm sorry...but he's dead."

CHAPTER 28

"The situation is deteriorating," Reese said. "We must be prepared to lose some hostages."

It sounded harsh, but Matt knew he was right. They were running out of time.

Matt, Reese, and Simmons were huddled around the conference room table. Simmons was quiet, barely speaking. Though five local FBI agents had arrived, with twenty more on the way, Simmons had not repeated his demand to assume command. Not that it mattered much at the moment anyway. In the end, Washington would likely be calling the shots since the attorney general was involved. The ATF and FBI had an agreement or understanding that outlined procedures in overlapping investigations, and this situation was particularly complex. Generally, the ATF cases were the especially dangerous and more violent criminals. Harper typified their usual sort, and Harper was Matt's case. Furthermore, an undercover ATF agent was a hostage, and two other ATF agents were dead. Yet Harper was holding hostages at a hospital, so the FBI would claim jurisdiction as domestic terrorism, which it was. They, too, had one agent dead and one a hostage. Matt expected both agencies would claim jurisdiction, potentially causing confusion. He hoped Washington wouldn't delay a decision, suit-and-tie desk types calling back and forth on their cell phones, paralyzing the field agents from reacting swiftly when the time came. There was no room for error.

"We've reached his deadline," Matt said, "but we don't know his demands. This is unusual."

"Maybe he just wants on TV," Simmons offered. It was the first time Simmons had spoken in an hour.

"I don't think so," Matt said. "Harper has planned too well."

"Unless he doesn't have a bomb," Simmons said. "Without the bomb, he's nearly defenseless."

"That's a possibility," Matt agreed, "but I believe Harper. He has one."

"He had a bomb at Taft," Reese said. "It was trip-wired on a shed and killed two of our agents."

"Sorry," Simmons said sincerely.

"The site team just called," Reese said. "They are reporting the possibility of a third body."

"A third body?" Matt said. "Really?"

"Not far from the crater they found part of a sneaker with a charred toe inside. Must've been a body in the shed."

"Any idea who?" Matt asked.

"Not yet," Reese said. "But we'll find out."

Matt glanced up as Murphy walked into the boardroom. At six foot four and 250 pounds, solid as a rock, he was intimidating. They had worked together on numerous raids, and Matt found him reliable and level-headed, a dependable asset.

"Did you search the other floors?" Matt asked as Murphy approached.

Murphy nodded. "The dogs found nothing. The other bombs are a hoax."

"Are your men stationed?"

"Ten at the front hallway and eight each on the floors above and below at the back staircase, twenty-six total, thanks to the FBI and the Tulsa PD. We can go anytime."

"Good," Matt said.

"But we're not really ready."

"Why?"

"Because we're going in blind. And if he truly has a radio-controlled detonator…" He stopped.

"You'd be toast," Matt finished for him. *You and everyone in there.*

"This is a recent diagram of the area," Reese said, rolling out the map. "They just remodeled three months ago." He pointed to the hallway and staircase. "Are these the only two possible entrances?"

"We've considered several options," Matt said. "Through the ceiling here. Or scaling down the outside walls into these patient windows. Or going in either one or both of the two entrances. It boils down to the bomb. It only takes a second for him to push a button."

"If we could get a clean head shot on Harper," Murphy said, "we'd have a chance. But that's the problem."

"Can't send a solitary sniper down the stairs?" Reese asked.

"It may be our best option. Yet it'd be risky. If he's seen, it'd be over."

Murphy's statement hung heavy, and no one spoke. The odds against them were substantial. They couldn't allow an interview. They weren't yet ready to begin an assault. They didn't even have a solid plan. Matt knew Harper posed a greater danger if Harper believed he was in control—bolder and less prone to mistakes. But in fact, Harper *was* in control. As sick as it sounded, the death of a hostage might buy them more time. With more time, maybe they could save the others. It was a consequence, not a preference, but they'd need to be ready for whatever happened.

Matt's day was a jumble. Stan killed by a bomb. Harper terrorizing a hospital. Paula a hostage. Had it been just hours since this all started?

"So the plan, Mr. Nicholson?"

Simmons wasn't jabbing him. It was the question they were all asking themselves.

"So we're planning," Matt said, "to drop the fiberoptic video down from the fourth floor and see if we can take a look. We want to know for sure if Harper has his finger on the button. The equipment should be here within the hour."

"We have an hour?"

Simmons's statement was rhetorical, and no one answered. They all knew there was a good chance they didn't have an hour before they had another tragedy—a very good chance.

⁜

Reverend Pettigrew's eyes were fixed and dilated. Paula softly placed her fingertips on his eyelids and closed them for the final time. She laid her stethoscope against his chest. No heart beat or spontaneous respirations. He was gone.

She pronounced him dead at 1:23 p.m.—her last duty as his physician.

Paula gently stroked his forehead, sweeping his soft, gray hair from his brow—an act of intimacy she would not have allowed herself in life, so natural in death. His frail, fragile body, ravaged by his valiant fight, lay before her, empty of the kind wit and compassion she had known, lost to this world forever.

She couldn't shake the image of Reverend Pettigrew smiling as he faced death, confident of his final destination.

Could she have saved him under better circumstances? Did he want to be saved for this world?

Paula fought back the tears she felt well up in her eyes. No time for tears. Time instead to attend to the living who remained.

⁜

Paula informed Harper that Pettigrew had died, and he immediately ordered Carl Joe to throw Pettigrew's body in the hallway. At first, Paula was sick, ready to defy Harper. Then she realized Harper might be using Pettigrew as his dead hostage rather than one of the two agents. She was repulsed by the disrespect, but Pettigrew was already dead. The agents' lives might be spared.

Harrison's body was beginning to smell bad—the sweet, sickly odor of old blood and decaying brain tissue, the smell of death. The odor permeated the unit. Harrison was still propped in the chair, and she couldn't bear to look at him—his face bloated and black, his lifeless body mutilated, silently guarding the doorway. Why couldn't Harper throw him in the hallway? Why Pettigrew? Yet Paula knew Harper must throw out a fresh body, or Matt wouldn't believe him. He wouldn't be fooled by Harrison's body, not one in rigor mortis. Harper was too smart to try.

Harper didn't appear visibly upset about the interview's delay, but she suspected otherwise. With a dead hostage in the hallway, the interview might be expedited. Or killing one of them might prompt an action that would lead to their rescue. A rescue would be risky, it seemed to Paula, because no matter how fast Matt or the other agents stormed the unit, Harper could just explode the bomb, and it'd be over. Everyone would be dead. Harper was crazy enough.

As Paula reviewed her list of patients, she noticed Sally had entered each of the patient rooms. When Harper had agreed to the lab, Sally had drawn blood on every patient, ordering a complete battery of tests. It might be their only chance, she said. She was smart.

Paula watched as Carl Joe left his post on Harper's orders and strutted to the nurses' station, cocksure and arrogant, hands resting on the butts of two of his pistols.

"Okay," Carl Joe said to Harper, grinning. "Who's going to help me?"

"Take the orderly and the janitor," Harper said.

Carl Joe glanced briefly at Paula before aiming his weapon at John's head. "You heard the man. Get up and don't try anything stupid." He pointed at the orderly. "You, too."

With John holding the arms and the orderly holding the legs, they dragged Pettigrew's body out of his room. Carl Joe's gun was drawn as he escorted them to the front.

"Carry his body to the end of the hallway," Carl Joe said, waving his gun in their faces. "Tommy and I will be watching. If either of you try to run, we'll kill your sorry asses."

They lifted the body and started for the hallway. Paula felt helpless watching but knew she could do nothing.

"Wait," Carl Joe said. "Set him down there."

They gently lowered him to the floor. Carl Joe pointed his weapon at Pettigrew.

The shot rang out, and Paula jumped. She watched as Pettigrew's head recoiled at the impact, the bullet shattering his skull and the tile beneath it. She heard startled cries from the staff behind her. The two men jumped back, surprised and frightened. A pool of blood quickly formed at their feet.

Carl Joe turned to them. "Now," he said. "You take him."

They didn't move.

"Now!" Carl Joe yelled. "Take him now!"

The two men dragged Pettigrew's body to the end of the hallway, leaving a trail of blood on the floor, and returned to the nurses' station without incident. Two agents in raid gear recovered the body and then disappeared around the corner. For several minutes, Carl Joe waited with Tommy near the hallway, as if the feds might storm in. Then, almost disappointed, he returned to the rear stairwell.

Harper began pacing back and forth in front of Paula just outside the nurses' station. After two or three minutes, he lifted the radio and called Matt.

"Matt Nicholson," he said into the microphone, "are you there?"

He waited several seconds and then said it again.

The radio came alive with Matt's voice. Paula felt her heart jump in her chest. "This is Matt Nicholson," he said.

"One hostage has died, Mr. ATF agent."

"We are sorry to hear that, Sam."

"Do you want more? Are you listening?"

"We're listening, Sam," Matt said. "What do you need for us to do?"

"I want Cara Beeson here in thirty minutes, or a second hostage will die. This is your last warning."

"That'll be difficult, Sam. We can't—"

Harper clicked off the radio and dropped it in his pocket.

⅄

John had slipped in next to Jennifer when he returned from the hallway. His chest dropped, and he sighed heavily. Across from them, the orderly covered his face with his hands and sobbed. Harper paced back and forth several minutes after he hung up on Matt and then joined Carl Joe at the back. Tommy remained at the front. For a few minutes, the terrorists were out of their view.

"We're next," John whispered softly to Jennifer. His voice was barely audible.

Jennifer looked straight ahead and didn't respond.

Several seconds passed before John spoke again. "We can't let this happen," he said. "We need to figure out a way."

"Don't do anything stupid," Jennifer whispered back. "They're armed, and we're not. And they're crazy enough to do anything."

"That's my point. It's like Flight 93—if we don't do something, they'll kill us for sure. And everyone else here, too."

"Don't be a hero. You'll get us all killed."

Jennifer cast her head down. Harper walked by them to check on Tommy. He stayed at the front for ten minutes and returned to the back. He never even glanced in their direction as he walked by. Harper was out of sight, but as he paced by the back wall, his footsteps echoed over the nurses' station.

John spoke again, his voice as soft as he could. "I'm no hero," he said. "Besides, we can't do nothing, but maybe the doctor can."

"Dr. Barrett? Why her?"

"Access. Only she roams freely. Look around. He doesn't let anybody else out of his sight."

Jennifer shook her head. "No," she said. "We shouldn't even be thinking this."

"Yeah, maybe not." John leaned forward, his thin elbows resting on his knees. "It's too risky."

"That it is, but it's also a risk doing nothing."

"You're right. I agree."

Jennifer gave him a sour look. "Okay," she said, "I'll think about it."

"The doctor's the one to convince. She has the access."

"I'll think about that, too."

"Who's talking there?" Harper roared from around the corner.

John and Jennifer instantly looked down.

Harper burst into the nursing station. His face was red. "I said…who was talking?"

Harper walked around the inside of the nurses' station and paused in front of each of the staff. All kept their eyes down and no one spoke. He walked around twice before standing at one end.

"Nobody talking now, huh? In case you don't remember, the rule is *no talking*! You take us for idiots?" He paused briefly but obviously didn't expect them to respond. "You break this rule, and I'll be upset." He reached into his pocket and held up the bomb's detonator. "And I don't really think you want to upset me, right?"

Harper slipped the radio transmitter back into his pocket and abruptly walked out of the nurses' station.

John looked at Jennifer and nodded slightly. Jennifer's eyes caught his, and after a moment's hesitation, she nodded back.

It was time to begin a plan.

CHAPTER 29

Harper had been pacing for fifteen minutes waiting for Cara Beeson. Paula tried to ignore him. The conditions of the patients were becoming steadily worse, and he was distracting. *Concentrate on the patients.* Montgomery's condition was critical but stable, with nothing new, thank goodness. Flo Pearce looked terrible and might require a ventilator. Her congestive heart failure had decompensated since the appendectomy, and despite massive doses of diuretics, she wasn't improving. Sally had assigned Toni Perkins to Flo Pearce after Pettigrew died. Toni was capable. The other five patients in the unit were all listed as serious and required Paula's near-constant attention.

The laboratory was sending back the tests Sally had ordered through the vacuum system, and Paula was reviewing them for abnormal results. Harper had examined every report, as he'd said he would, obviously looking for hidden messages. The lab tests were helpful, and she'd order another set of tests in a couple of hours—if they had a couple of hours.

Paula glanced up as Sally exited Montgomery's room. Sally had not rested a moment since the unit's takeover, and neither she nor Paula had slept much the night before. Sally was the only nurse caring for Montgomery, and she was also coordinating the nursing care of the other patients. Her face was taut, her shoulders pulled back tightly, her eyes hinting at the stress they all were feeling. As Sally entered the nurses' station, she briefly turned toward Paula and winked, and then she crossed over to Harper. Harper stopped pacing as Sally approached.

"What is it?" he asked.

Sally cast her eyes downward and dropped her arms to her sides. "We can't go on like this," she said flatly.

"Like what?"

"We need more help."

Sally didn't look up. Her voice remained monotone. She was mimicking Paula's earlier conversation with Harper. Would it work again? Harper was preoccupied, and Paula thought Sally was risking an unnecessary confrontation.

"The nurses are exhausted," Sally said. "The patients are sicker. We can't continue."

"So?"

"We need help. If we don't get it, our patients could die."

Suddenly Harper reached out and grabbed her hair, pulling her to within an inch of his face. "No more concessions," Harper yelled at her. "You keep Montgomery alive. I could care less about the others. Do you hear me?"

She nodded and dropped her head. He released her, and she stumbled backward, falling sharply on the floor. Paula moved to her side and helped her to her feet.

"Too many demands," he mumbled to himself, ignoring them. Harper turned away and began pacing again. "Too many concessions."

⅄

"She seems to be resting better," Toni said, "but I'm still worried about her breathing."

"Her oxygen level looks pretty good," Paula said, gesturing toward the monitor.

"See how her breathing pattern is a little erratic? She may be getting weak."

Toni raised the IV pole after changing a bag of fluids. Each of the ICU rooms looked the same with identical beds, monitors, and equipment. Only the nameplate on the wall varied—a handwritten slip of paper in a clear plastic frame denoting a different patient. Paula looked at the patient sleeping. Flo Pearce had three monitor leads attached to her chest, an IV in her right arm, and an oxygen mask on her face. Her ancient, wrinkled body was covered to the neck by a white sheet. Her gray hair was cut short and was thinning on the top. She was as ill as Reverend Pettigrew had been. The whole scenario seemed oddly similar. Paula hoped for a better outcome.

"Let's keep going pretty much as we are," Paula said, "but let me know if her sats drop."

"I'll find you. I doubt you'll be going anywhere."

Paula smiled. The smile felt strange. Today was a day of little humor. "I'll be at the nurses' station, updating her chart."

Paula left Flo Pearce's room and crossed to the nurses' station. She plopped into the nearest chair to write a progress note. Leaning back, she closed her eyes. She was exhausted—tired of being trapped in the unit, tired of seeing people frightened for their lives, tired of people dying. She'd keep her eyes closed for only a moment. Her body sank heavily into the cushioned seat, weighted with fatigue, her mind drifting...

Harrison was whole, standing in the doorway. A young boy with blond hair and red cheeks ran to him, laughing and calling his name. Harrison tossed the boy high into the air and kissed him over and over. For a moment Harrison's face was bright, smiling. Then it quickly became distorted, the skin falling away from his skull, bloated and decaying. The boy, held in the air by his father's pale hands, began to scream, frightened, crying.

Paula awoke with a start.

The bright white of the fluorescent light that enveloped Paula accentuated the harsh reality of her surroundings. The muffled hum of equipment in a nearby room and the sharp alarm of an IV pump disrupted the mandatory silence. Harper and his two thugs stood at their positions as quiet as sentinels, ready for the inevitable assault. The helpless federal agents lay bound on the floor, caked with Harrison's dried blood and brains. The bomb, hidden in the IV boxes, was nearly close enough for Paula to touch, yet utterly unreachable.

Next to her in the nurses' station, the staff huddled together like frightened children. Paula was frightened, too, struggling to suppress the tears close to the surface.

The insanity persisted.

Jennifer's gaze attracted her attention, but when Paula noticed, Jennifer looked away. Paula was puzzled at her reaction until she saw Jennifer's finger cupped in her palm, pointing downward. Paula looked down and noticed the corner of a piece of paper underneath Jennifer's shoe. She was attempting to pass her a note.

Paula stood. She held a note pad in her hand, flipping through the pages and pretending to read the entries as she walked toward Jennifer. When she reached Jennifer, Paula peeked over the paper to check on Harper. He was standing at the front near Tommy. She lifted her foot slightly, and Jennifer slid the note beneath her heel. Reaching down as if to scratch her leg, she picked up the note and stuffed it into the note pad. She let out her breath slowly and looked around the unit. No one was watching. She closed the note pad and returned to the desk.

The message was on the back of a lab order sheet.

Dr. Barrett—

We must save ourselves before it's too late. We must have a plan. Only you have the access to make it work. You must lead us. Please help us.

Jennifer

Save ourselves? How can we save ourselves? Paula shook her head, not believing Jennifer would suggest such a thing. *We don't have guns...and they have a bomb.* She glanced toward Jennifer. Jennifer was looking away. *How can they ask me to do this?* Paula slid the note between the sheets of the note pad and set it on the desk. She was frowning. Could Jennifer be serious? Could she expect her to lead the staff to safety—without getting everyone killed? *Absolutely not! It'd be suicide!*

"You want a cup, Doc?"

Paula jumped. Harper was standing a few feet away, holding up the coffeepot.

"No," she said a bit too abruptly. "I've had enough coffee. Thanks anyway."

She turned her back to him and began scribbling a progress note, waiting for him to step up behind her, demanding what she had hidden in the note pad, demanding what he had seen. She dared not look at him.

Paula tried to slow her breathing, attempting to lessen her rapid heart, hoping not to betray her guilt. She stopped writing, unable to write without shaking.

Finally, after an endless moment, she heard Harper's footsteps. The footsteps were not coming toward her as she had feared but instead were walking away. He had not seen.

⋏

Harper glanced at his watch.

"Time is up!" he said to Carl Joe. "Now they'll know we're serious."

"Amen, Brother Harper!"

Harper leaned over Jake, grabbed him by his shirt collar, and dragged him out of the doorway. Jake groaned with the movement. Harper radioed Matt and waited for his response.

Matt answered promptly. "Sam," Matt said, "I'm glad you called. We've been working on your request."

"You're too late." Harper pressed the 9 mm to the back of Jake's head. "I want you to hear the sound of the weapon that kills your comrade."

"Wait, Sam. Tell us your demands. We want to help you."

"You'll hear my demands when I'm on the TV." Harper cocked his weapon and pushed it hard against Jake's head. "Mr. ATF man, say good-bye to this one."

"Wait, wait! We're working on getting Cara Beeson there, but Beeson told us it would take two hours to set it up. We need two hours."

"One hour…and not a minute more."

"That's impossible, Sam. If we could do it in one hour, we would. We can't. It has to be two hours. We're acting in good faith here, and we want you to do the same. In order for us to do our part, we want you to send out two patients first...as a trade. It's only fair."

"'Keep thy tongue from evil, and thy lips from speaking guile. Evil shall *slay* the wicked; and they that *hate* the righteous shall be desolate.' You're not listening."

"Sam, we're trying to do the right thing here."

"One hour. No trades. I'm going to count to three."

"Sam, don't kill anyone."

"One...two..."

"*Please.* If we could do it in an hour, we would."

"You're lying to me. I know it." There was a brief pause. He lifted the gun from Jake's head. "Two hours, then...but if I hear a rattle, if I hear a noise, the people in here are going to start dying. And if you're one minute late, then you'll be sorry you lied to me. Minute by minute. Hostage by hostage. Do you understand me?"

"Yes, Sam. We understand."

Matt wiped the sweat from his forehead. He turned to Reese and shrugged. "I didn't know what else to do."

"Tough choice," Reese said.

"He was going to kill Jake. I'm sure of it."

"I agree. You're fine."

Matt hated to beg. He hated that there was no exchange. He hated that he was failing.

"At least now," Reese said, "we have an absolute deadline."

Chapter 30

The nurse reached into the cabinet behind the rolls of tissue and grabbed the cell phone hidden there. She crouched behind the bed, holding the phone close to her, muffling the sound as she quickly dialed the number.

Cara Beeson answered.

"Cara," the nurse whispered to Beeson, "they're going to let you interview them in two hours."

"That's not what they told me. The ATF said it was against their policy."

"Against their policy? Harper just talked to the ATF. One of their agents, a Matt Nicholson, said they would."

"The ATF is probably setting them up. I doubt they'll allow an interview. They want to be in control."

"If they don't, it'll get pretty tense here."

"Be careful. They killed two agents near Muskogee. It's made the national news."

"They killed one FBI agent named Harrison when they first came in. The top of his head was blown off. The person they threw in the hallway was already dead. He was a Presbyterian minister named Pettigrew. He had died earlier of pneumonia."

"But they shot him."

"After he was dead...to make it look real."

"How's everyone holding up?"

"Not so good. We're all worried. It's really crazy."

"Hang in there, sis, and don't call me again if it could be dangerous."

"I'll be careful."

The nurse heard the sound of a man clearing his voice. Startled, she turned to see Carl Joe standing a few feet away. His large frame loomed over her, and he was frowning, his gun pointed directly at her. Toni's stomach turned, and she nearly vomited.

Arthur Hyatt's glucose was over four hundred on the lab test that Sally had ordered. Paula wasn't surprised the blood sugar was so high, because Harriet had been monitoring finger sticks hourly on a portable glucometer, and the results had been similar. Except for the poor control of his diabetes, Hyatt was the least serious patient in the unit and probably would have been transferred to the ward today. Paula had started an insulin drip, and his sugars were improving. Unfortunately, the real therapy for him was a transfer to a stroke rehabilitation facility, which obviously would be delayed.

"What's his blood sugar now?" Paula asked.

"Five minutes ago," Harriet said, "it was two hundred and seventy-five."

"That's better."

"Want me to increase the insulin drip?" Harriet asked.

"Yes, two units an hour." Paula pointed to the IV pump. "There...with that button."

"Thanks, Doctor."

"You're doing fine, Harriet."

"No, I'm in over my head." Harriet smiled and adjusted the drip. "Dr. Barrett, what are we going to do?"

"About the glucose?"

"No, about those creeps." She rolled her eyes out toward the nurses' station.

Paula shook her head. "I'm not sure."

"I was out there making coffee, and Sally said you'd think of something."

"Sally said that? I don't have any idea what we should do."

"Maybe we could all jump them at once."

"That'd be dangerous. We should wait until we're rescued."

Hyatt reached out his right arm and touched Paula's sleeve. "There won't be a rescue."

"Mr. Hyatt," Paula said, "I hope you're wrong."

"The threat of Harper's bomb will stop them. Don't wait until they kill us before you do something. I'm not smart like you, but I know you're way too smart to let that *preacher* outwit you."

"He's right," Harriet said. "Tell us what to do."

"I don't know what to do." Paula looked out toward Harper and watched him pacing. "I just don't know what to do."

⚔

The sound of footsteps echoed as Matt and Murphy walked down the long hallway. The fourth-floor surgical ICU was deserted, quietly evacuated. The patient rooms, a few hours earlier filled with hectic activity, were empty of beds and equipment. The lights were out. The computers turned off. Only the dim emergency lighting was still on, casting eerie shadows on the walls of the vacant unit.

Matt's pulse quickened. The awkward feeling he had experienced at Harper's compound stirred in his abdomen—the same dread he felt when the outcome was potentially disastrous. *Shake it off*, he told himself. *Follow procedure. Plan it right.*

Matt still smelled the smoke in his nostrils. The tiny cuts from the flying glass stung his arms and face. His shirt was stained and torn. His ears rang with a low-pitched sound, echoing the eruption that had engulfed him and Rice. Taft was too fresh in his mind.

He was fine, he had told Reese, but he wasn't—death of his partner, near death himself, victim and survivor. *If I had time to process it all*, he told himself, *think about it too much, maybe I'd be more upset. Maybe even a basket case.*

He needed to be here for sure. Revenge was powerful, motivating; he wouldn't deny it, but he was driven by more than revenge. Harper was a criminal. He was a madman. Matt was a professional, an officer of the law, here to serve and protect. He was here to do his job, no more and no less.

But when justified, when the time was right, he'd personally take the opportunity to blow Harper's head off.

The outline of the SWAT team at the end of the hallway formed against the faint light of the stairwell. Eight men in full raid gear with automatic weapons huddled in silence.

"Let's talk here," Murphy said, stopping halfway. "We don't want our voices to carry down the stairwell."

"Is your team ready?" Matt asked in a whisper.

"We have eight here, eight on the floor below the intensive care unit, and ten at the front. Just give us the signal."

"They're unloading the video equipment downstairs, so it'll be up here in a few minutes. Drop it down for a quick look. Then give me a report."

"Yes, sir."

"The situation is becoming more complicated. We told Harper we were working on getting the reporter. He's expecting us to produce her."

"That might provide the distraction to go."

"It might. But if we go, we'll have to protect her, and I'm not sure we can."

"She wouldn't be the first reporter to get hurt on a story."

"No, but an injury to a reporter would be almost as bad as an injury to Montgomery. The press would kill us. We can't screw this up."

"I'll see what we've got and call you."

"Good. You've secured the other floors?"

"Two men on each."

"That should do." Matt glanced at his watch. "We have exactly one hour and forty-five minutes. The deadline is fixed."

"We're ready on your order."

"I hope we get the opportunity."

CHAPTER 31

Paula had stepped out of Arthur Hyatt's room to talk with Sally when the commotion started.

Carl Joe dragged Toni by her hair out of one of the rooms, kicking and yelling, flailing her arms at Carl Joe. He threw her on the floor in front of Harper, but she was instantly on her feet, screaming at Carl Joe.

"Leave me alone!" she shouted at him.

Carl Joe grabbed the back of her head and shoved his gun in her face. "I'm going to waste her, Sam."

"Only on my order," Harper said sharply. "I'm still in charge here, soldier."

Paula and Sally moved quickly beside them.

"Let her go," Sally demanded. "Leave her alone!"

"What's this about?" Harper said loudly, raising his voice over the commotion.

Carl Joe hooked his elbow around her neck and tossed the cell phone on the table. "She was calling out on this. I think she's a federal agent undercover. I heard her say it was against ATF policy to interview you, and she told them I shot the minister after he was dead."

"I insist you let her go," Sally cut in, moving toward them.

"Let her go, Carl Joe," Harper said. He pointed his finger in Sally's face. "But *you* shut up."

Carl Joe pushed Toni to the floor, and Harper leaned over her.

"You weren't talking to the feds, were you?" Harper asked calmly. "You're the one who's been talking to the reporter."

Toni sat silent, her teeth clenched, her arms held tightly at her sides.

Harper picked up the cell phone and hit the redial. He listened for a moment, smiled, then hung up. "Cara Beeson just answered the phone. You've been calling Cara Beeson, haven't you?"

Toni looked away, refusing to answer.

Harper moved to the nurses' station. He grabbed Jennifer by her hair and pulled her upward, thrusting his gun under her chin. Harper turned to Toni. "Now, Toni. Tell me the truth. We wouldn't want things to get ugly, would we?"

There was silence.

"'Their land shall be soaked with blood, for it is the day of the Lord's vengeance. The angel of the Lord will exact his full measure. Today this evil will die.'"

Jennifer's eyes widened with fear.

"Toni," Harper said, "I'm not bluffing. You only have one second to decide."

"Stop, stop," Toni said, starting to cry. "I *did* call her. Cara Beeson is my sister. Don't hurt anyone. Please don't hurt anyone else."

Harper smiled. He released Jennifer, and she collapsed. Harper handed the phone to Toni. "Here, Toni," he said. "I want to talk to your sister."

⅄

Cara Beeson stood in the hot sun, sweating more than she liked. Her blouse was drenched and her hair soggy. Her makeup was streaking down her face, and she had used a box of tissues patting it dry. Yet the story was here, and there was no better place to go. She wasn't the only one waiting. Forty or fifty reporters from around the country were also waiting, complaining bitterly about the unbearable heat and humidity. As a native Tulsan, she thought she was accustomed to Oklahoma summers, but today would test anyone's tolerance—104 in the shade.

Beeson had a second reason for staying: Toni's call worried her. Toni seemed to have cut the conversation short, and then a few minutes later called back and hung up. The inside information was useful but not worth risking the life of her only sister. Toni, two years younger than she, was always the smart one. Straight As in high school. Scholarship to college. Top of her class in nursing school. She hoped Toni was smart enough to take care of herself.

Beeson's cell phone rang, and she reached to look at the incoming number. It was Toni's phone.

"Sis?"

"Cara, this is Toni."

Toni's voice was shaking. Beeson's worry increased. "I'm glad you called," she said. "Are you okay?"

"Pastor Sam Harper wants to talk with you."

"Is everything all right?"

Toni didn't answer. Harper's was the next voice she heard.

"This is Sam Harper."

His voice was coarse, husky, but she couldn't detect any emotion. She thought she must be the first reporter to actually talk to him.

"Is this Cara Beeson?" he asked.

"What have you done with Toni?"

"Your sister is safe."

"I want to talk to her."

"Maybe…when we have finished our business."

Beeson wasn't in a position to argue. "I know what you want," she said. "You want an interview…and they won't let you have one."

"That's true."

"I can interview you by phone, but on one condition."

"Are you in a position to make demands?"

"I want you to release my sister. Now!"

He didn't immediately respond, and she waited. She could hear him breathing.

"I'll release your sister," he said, "when I see the interview on TV."

Beeson didn't have many options. She could arrange the interview, but she had no guarantee he'd release her. "I can't promise a national feed, but I'm pretty sure we can get you on the local station…and probably live."

"If that's the best you can do."

"The networks may pick it up after it airs here. That way they avoid most of the criticism."

"When can I expect this to happen?"

"Give me thirty minutes. I'll call you back."

"I'll be waiting."

"Now, if we're through," Beeson said, "let me talk to Toni."

Toni came on the phone.

"I've arranged for an interview," Beeson said. "Harper said he'll release you when he sees the interview on TV."

"I'm not going."

"Why not? He said he'll let you go."

"I'm not leaving my patients. There's no one to care for them if I go."

"Toni, be reasonable—"

"Do your interview," Toni said firmly. "I'm not leaving. That's final."

"Okay, whatever you say." Beeson wouldn't argue. She'd learned years ago not to argue with her sister. She would arrange for the interview and then demand Toni's release. The deal was with Harper, not Toni, and she expected Harper to keep his word. She shook her head slowly. Trusting Harper with her sister's life might be foolhardy, but what choice did she have?

⅄

Tommy poured himself a fresh cup of coffee. "You've got to get Carl Joe under control," Tommy said to Harper. "I've known him a long time. He's not reliable under pressure."

Harper frowned. "I trust Carl Joe," he said firmly. "He's the one I trust under pressure."

"And shooting that patient in the head," he said, missing the sarcasm. "It's wrong to mutilate a dead body…especially a preacher."

Harper's eyes narrowed slightly. "You take up your position at the front, Tommy. I'll see to Carl Joe."

Tommy began shuffling his feet. He avoided Harper's eyes. "This operation isn't what I'd hoped for."

"Not what you'd hoped for? Not what Tommy wanted?" Harper jabbed his finger at Tommy. "This is a war...a holy battle. You take orders and do what you're told. You leave the decisions to your commander."

Tommy raised up his head and looked into Harper's eyes. "Carl Joe's going to crack if you don't watch him."

"You don't know when to shut up." Harper shoved his finger into Tommy's chest, pushing him backward. "Now resume your post, soldier."

CHAPTER 32

Harper gazed up at the TV monitor and smiled. He had bypassed the ATF's chief negotiator and succeeded in arranging the interview despite the ATF's refusal. Cara Beeson's image filled the screen. The outline of Saint Luke's Hospital was behind her.

"This is Cara Beeson, Alert Three News, with an exclusive report live from Saint Luke's Hospital in Tulsa, Oklahoma. As we reported to you earlier, a militia group calling themselves the Redeemed Believers and led by Sam Harper, a self-proclaimed pastor, are holding the attorney general of the United States, Ronald Montgomery, as a hostage, as well as two federal agents, seven patients, and fifteen hospital employees. The siege has been underway for seven hours, and Alert Three News has been providing continuous coverage. Inside sources tell us that one FBI agent has been killed and a patient shot. The militia group, some are speculating, is believed responsible for an explosion that killed two federal agents from the Bureau of Alcohol, Tobacco, and Firearms earlier this morning near Muskogee. We now bring you an exclusive live telephone interview with the leader of the militia group, Sam Harper." Beeson held out her phone. "Mr. Harper, you're live on Alert Three News. Tell us, Mr. Harper, why you have taken hostages at Saint Luke's Hospital."

Harper had decided to do the interview alone in one of the empty patient rooms. He stood in front of the TV holding Toni's cell phone. On the screen was a graphic of his full name superimposed on an image of Saint Luke's Hospital.

"We've not taken hostages," he said.

"You haven't?"

"No. We *are* the hostages. The federal government of the United States is holding *us* as hostages by usurping its God-given authority, conspiring with the United Nations for the New World Order and illegally stripping us and the American people of their constitutional right to bear arms and to preserve life and liberty. The liberalist agenda subverting—"

"Let me ask you this," Beeson interrupted. "Why Saint Luke's?"

"The criminal conspiracy of the health-care system, infiltrated by agents of the federal government, condemns itself. Saint Luke's Hospital is guilty of harboring an enemy of the people, Ronald Montgomery. Montgomery has been condemned by his actions. Instead of protecting the right to life, Montgomery promotes the murder of babies. Instead of protecting the right to bear arms, Montgomery instigates search and seizure. Instead of—"

"Have you made any demands?"

"Interrupt me again," Harper said angrily, "and this interview is over."

"Yes, I understand. Please continue."

"I quote Thomas Jefferson, 'All men are endowed by their Creator with certain inalienable rights, that among these are life, liberty, and the pursuit of happiness.' How can we have liberty if there is not life? Can we snuff out life and cherish our liberty? When we kill the innocent, we jeopardize the freedom of all the people. The federal government promotes the hollow lie that women deserve the choice to kill a fetus inside their own bodies. With the swipe of a pen, a few federal judges, bought and sold, altered the moral standard of millions of Americans. Right to choice? Where is it written? Where is the democracy of the people? The true motivation for the systematic elimination of unborn fetuses is the genocide of the white race. Abortion is the first step for the New World Order, which has as its highest priority the destruction of white dominance. But no nation in history has survived with absolute parity of opposing races. The genocide of the white race violates the natural order of mankind, replaced by the false, treacherous philosophy of equality as promoted by the United Nations.

God's will on abortion, this white genocide, is clear. God demands justice for the murderers."

Harper began pacing back and forth in front of the TV, the cell phone held tightly to his ear. "God's demand," he continued, "has been revealed to me. Beginning immediately, starting this very moment, every baby aborted anywhere in the United States will require that we kill one of the hostages. An eye for an eye. A tooth for a tooth. If one baby is murdered, we will kill one of the two federal agents. If more babies are murdered, we'll kill the other agent, the hospital staff one by one, the patients one by one, and finally the attorney general. If anyone tries to interfere, we'll detonate the explosives. This is our demand: *stop the murder of unborn babies.*"

"That seems impossible," Beeson said. "How can all the abortion clinics in the United States stop immediately?"

"The news media must assume the responsibility for informing the baby-killers of our demands."

"But how can—"

"Miss Beeson, a news blackout is prohibited. I trust that the pro-life groups and militia organizations of the people will help monitor violations. I thank you for your cooperation. Have a nice day."

The interview was over.

⋏

Matt was furious.

Every eye in the boardroom was fixed on the TV. Beeson was wrapping up her report with Harper.

"Get Beeson in here now, dammit!" Matt yelled at one of police officers near the door. He turned to the two FBI agents in front of the communications equipment. "Did someone forget," he asked loudly, "to monitor cellular transmissions?"

They shrugged in unison.

"I want immediate reports of all telephone calls, both wired and cellular. Can you handle that?"

Both nodded. Matt cursed himself for the oversight.

"He got to Beeson somehow," Reese said quietly, stepping up from behind Matt. "We're in trouble."

"Yes, I know. Our deadline is worthless."

"That's a problem. And Harper arranged for his own interview!"

"I wonder how? There has to be someone in the unit."

"It's the only thing that makes sense."

"But why Beeson?" Matt asked. "That's the part that I don't understand. If someone has information, why a reporter?"

"That'd be a good question to ask her."

"And I fully intend to do exactly that."

"Call Murphy. We need to be ready."

"Yes, sir," Matt agreed. He shook his head slowly. "We can't stop the abortions. One's done every few seconds. He'll kill everybody."

"I'll call the director," Reese said. "I think it's time to go."

⅄

Paula saw Harper gloating, proud of himself because of his performance, laughing and joking with Carl Joe near the stairwell doorway. The news would be national and probably international within seconds, just as Harper anticipated. Would Harper's ultimatum force him to act? His statement on national television wouldn't stop the abortions. The abortions would continue, and Harper would decide if he'd kill the hostages. Paula glanced at the two agents on the floor. They'd be first. Those in the nurses' station would likely be next. Jennifer first? John? The staff? The nurses? Then her?

Yes, without a doubt, they needed a plan.

Jennifer and John faced her, and from their look of determination, Paula knew they agreed. John began making a motion repeatedly with his right hand. He held two bent fingers against his thigh, and then plunged his thumb downward. Paula watched several times before she realized what he was doing.

A shot! John was demonstrating giving a shot. Paula mouthed the word, and John nodded.

Drug them! Why didn't I think of that?

They could drug them. But how? Oral? Intramuscular? What meds were on the unit? Who would give them? Her mind began to race with the details.

There was a chance this would work. It would be risky. Was it worth the risk? Could they possibly pull this off?

Did they have any choice?

⚓

Jane Harper turned the van's key in the ignition to start the engine and eased out of the parking space in the north lot. Her husband had expected them to watch together the result of their efforts from the portable TV in the van. Instead, she was alone as she had seen her husband triumphantly demand an end to the murder of millions of babies. Now his life was in danger. Once the truth was told, the feds would try to kill him. Every patriot would be silenced if the feds had their way. She would pray for her husband's safety and push away the fear of losing him. To worry about herself would be selfish. Sam was doing God's work.

The heat was sweltering. She had become soaked to the skin while waiting, but now the breeze caused by the van's movement created some comfort. *No sense staying at the hospital*, she thought. *I won't be any help if I'm caught.*

Sam Harper on national TV! He was a brave man. Jane's chest filled with pride. Of course Sam would explode the bomb if he needed to. He was a hero.

Jane followed the service road to the exit and turned north onto Sheridan Road. She lightly touched the envelope on the seat next to her. Besides the threat of additional bombs at Saint Luke's, he had foreseen several other possibilities in his contingency plan, and now she could help. The letter he left her contained the names and private phone numbers of over fifty militia leaders, connections her husband had all over the country. She was amazed he had the foresight to anticipate he might gain national media attention. Jane was instructed to call each leader, many of whom were likely following the story on TV, and enlist their help. She'd request that they would anonymously inform the largest hospital in their area that a bomb had been planted in the hospital's intensive care unit and would be detonated if the abortions continued. Then the leaders would notify the local news media.

She would change pay phones after making only three calls, just as he had instructed.

He was brilliant. Each hospital must consider the threat to be serious. As the reports became public, the news would drive the media to a frenzy, and law enforcement would be paralyzed. Her husband would gain even greater publicity. Their cause would be advanced. God would be glorified.

Her husband sounded relaxed on the TV, and she heard his confidence. His message was clear and unequivocal. His stand against the federal government and against the abortionists was courageous. He was truly a man of God, anointed and faithful.

She wiped the wetness from her eyes. *He's a hero*, she thought. *Will I ever see him again?*

Chapter 33

"**What are our** options?" Matt asked.

Reese, Murphy, and Simmons were gathered with Matt in the corner of the boardroom. Since the TV interview, the room had been bustling with activity. The four men ignored it, absorbed in their conversation.

"His demand is ridiculous." Simmons was the first to speak.

Reese nodded. "But I think he's dead serious."

"We're wasting time here," Murphy said, frowning. He pointed his finger upward. "We're in position upstairs. We should go."

"I want to call him again first," Matt said. "I want to see if he'll release some of the staff and patients. He's painted himself into a corner."

"We allow hostages out of there now," Simmons said, "and Harper will be able to stay closer to Montgomery."

"He'll stay right on top of Montgomery anyway," Matt said. "The more hostages we can remove, the easier on the teams."

"Then do it," Reese said. "Call the bastard."

Matt picked up the radio and called out. Harper answered immediately. He was waiting. Before Matt could speak, Harper was screaming into the radio.

"You lied to me," Harper yelled. "You never talked to Cara Beeson."

"Yes, we did," Matt responded, forcing calm into his voice. "And I can honestly tell you we consented to and were arranging an interview. You and I agreed to a time frame, and we were working on that schedule."

"Not one word you're telling me is true."

"It's absolutely true. We had agreed to a time frame, hadn't we?"

"Yes, but I didn't believe you."

"You should have. We're not playing games here."

Matt heard Harper pause. Maybe he did believe him. "Now that you've had your interview, we need to talk about moving some of the patients and staff out of the unit. They're a liability to you now. You only need the attorney general."

"Not one single hostage will be released."

"Let's be practical. You've made your point. Killing some of the hospital patients won't promote your cause. It just complicates the situation. Let's move them out so you don't have to worry about them."

"Either you're not listening, or you're just plain stupid. We're not releasing a single hostage."

"I have concerns about the possibility of meeting your demand. Give us something we can work on. We can arrange for air transportation and allow you to leave. You can walk away. End this now."

"You heard my demand. What I want is for all abortion clinics to close their doors and every abortion to stop. I want to stop the killing."

"We want the killing to stop, too, Sam."

"Then stop killing babies, or it will end quickly...instantly!"

"You've made the news, Sam. Don't limit your options now."

"My option is to stop listening to your lies. 'With their tongues they have used deceit; the poison of asps is under their lips.'"

"Sam, we want to work with you. As a sign of good faith, can we agree to send out just one patient? Maybe the sickest of the patients. Just one, to show we are working together on this."

"Don't force us to kill someone. You'll have no one to blame but yourselves."

"So just one, Sam. Can we agree on a single critically ill patient?"

"'And they shall go forth, and look upon the carcasses of the men that have transgressed against me; for their worm shall not die, neither shall their fire be quenched; and they shall be an abhorring unto all flesh.'"

The radio went dead.

Paula was in Montgomery's room with Sally when she heard Harper smash the radio on the tile floor, shattering it into pieces. Hearing Matt's voice was reassuring, but from what she had heard of the conversation, she doubted Matt could negotiate an end to their dilemma. Harper seemed dead set on killing a few hostages. His demand was unachievable, and its failure would soon force him to a decision. Time was short.

"How's Mr. Montgomery?" Paula asked Sally.

Standing across the bed from Paula, Sally grasped the bed rail for support as if she might fall over from fatigue. She looked haggard, exhausted. She had spent most of the forty-eight hours prior to the terrorist takeover with Montgomery, and the lack of sleep was taking its toll.

"I've weaned the ventilator to flow-by," Sally said, "and his oxygen concentration is down to 40 percent. If the circumstances were different, I think he could be extubated. He's off the dopamine. The balloon pump is off. He probably would be up walking the halls if he could."

Montgomery opened one eye and winked and then quickly closed it again.

Paula glanced over her shoulder, looking out at Harper. "Sally, we need a plan."

Paula knew Sally was the only other person who could move freely throughout the unit. Her assistance was essential. If Paula were to do anything, Sally would have to help.

"I've come to the same conclusion."

"Good," Paula said. "I thought I'd have to convince you."

"I've been thinking about it for a while. What are your thoughts?"

Paula lowered her voice. "John suggested a shot," Paula said. "It's a great idea. Giving some drugs may be the best we've got."

"Sedatives?"

"That'd seem the most logical."

"He's carrying the detonator. Whatever we choose must work instantly, and they must all three fall asleep at the same time."

"They will…if we use massive doses."

"Enough to kill them?"

"I'd be uncomfortable with that. Enough to stun them."

"Like diazepam?"

"Diazepam would have to be IV. Oral or intramuscular diazepam would work too slowly."

"I seriously doubt they'll let us start an IV."

"Of course not," Paula said. "So what meds do we have on the unit that we can use?"

"Quite a selection, actually. I'll check the med cabinet and let you know."

Sally gave Paula a quick smile. She'd help; even exhausted, she'd help. God help them all.

⚓

Harper crossed over to Paula as she left Montgomery's room. Carl Joe trailed behind him.

"I want an update on his condition," Harper said to Paula.

Harper's eyes narrowed as he looked directly at her. Carl Joe stood behind him, his eyes wandering around the room, unfocused, distracted.

"His condition is about the same," she said. She didn't lie.

"What are you doing in there?" Harper asked. "He hasn't improved at all since we got here."

"He's had a myocardial infarction and congestive heart failure. He's lucky to be alive."

Harper leaned forward. "You're keeping him sick on purpose, aren't you?"

"Why would I do that?"

"I want him off the ventilator."

"That's impossible. He'll die. He can't breathe on his own."

"I want him up and talking. He can't talk with that tube in his throat. I'm going to put him on live TV."

"You heard him," Carl Joe said, jabbing his finger at her over Harper's shoulder. "He wants him well."

"You'll do whatever you want," she said firmly, ignoring Carl Joe and gazing straight at Harper. "That's plenty obvious. But I won't stop any treatments until it's medically indicated. If I stop the ventilator, he won't be on live TV because he'll be dead."

Harper paused a moment at Paula's comment. "Then when will we see improvement?"

"It could be weeks…sometimes months."

"That's not quick enough. You're spending way too much time on the other patients. I want you to concentrate on Montgomery. I want him talking by this evening."

Harper's request was ridiculous. "Why did you choose here?" Paula asked. "This is a Catholic hospital. Many of us here don't believe in abortions. What about us?"

"You think you deserve mercy?" Harper said. "You all sinned when you decided to treat Montgomery."

"So what? He was having a heart attack and came to our emergency department. We took him in. It was the Christian thing to do." She knew she was pushing. Harper couldn't care less. He had his agenda.

The phone rang in Harper's pocket. Harper pointed his finger at her as he checked the incoming number. "You just do exactly as I say. And about Montgomery, if you're stalling…"

He looked back up at her and their eyes met. She looked away.

The threat was clear.

⚔

Cara Beeson could see the police officer scanning the crowd of reporters. She knew who he was looking for. The cell phone was ringing. *Hurry up and answer, Harper.* Standing in front of the Alert Three News truck, she wouldn't be hard to find. She expected them to be unhappy with her for explicitly defying their order. She had no choice. Her sister's life was at stake. In addition, it was a sensational story. Her interview was picked up by every national news organization, and for the next several hours her face would be plastered on millions of TV sets around the world. The officer was coming in her direction. *Answer the phone, Harper!*

The phone rang twice more before Harper finally answered. Beeson went straight to the point. "I'm calling about my sister," she said. "You said you'd release Toni when you saw your interview on TV."

"You did your part, Cara Beeson. I said I'd release her, and I will."

"It needs to be now. And even if she's unwilling to go, you have to force her."

"Yes, yes, I'll release her now, but I have another favor."

"What is that?"

"I'd still like to do a live interview. I want to put Montgomery on the TV."

That's impossible, she thought. *There's no way I can pull that off.* "I'll see what I can do," she said, "but you have to release my sister first."

"Okay," Harper said. "I'll do it."

"Then I trust you'll—"

"Ms. Beeson," a man's voice interrupted her. She turned to see a police officer standing next to her. "You need to come with me, and I mean *now!*"

⅄

Paula pretended to scribble a note on Montgomery's chart at the doctors' desk as she discreetly surveyed the unit. Harper was hunched over the cell phone, talking quietly. Carl Joe had returned to his position at the back. Paula occasionally glanced up at Sally as she casually rummaged through the medicine cabinet, writing notes on a piece of paper beside her. If Harper or Carl Joe noticed anything unusual, Paula would distract them. She would speak up loudly if they approached, asking Sally a question about one of the patients, a signal that one of the men was nearby.

At least they were starting. Sally would list all of the medications, and they'd choose one—a medication that was easy and fast, one that could incapacitate their aggressors quickly. They must decide carefully. The choice could save their lives.

From across the unit, a shrill alarm sounded from Flo Pearce's room. Paula and Sally instantly turned to the noise and saw Toni standing in the doorway.

"I need some help here," she yelled, waving them toward the room.

Toni was animated, excited. Paula heard her urgency. Flo Pearce must be coding.

As Paula entered the room, she noticed that Flo Pearce's face was mottled blue. Her eyes were rolled back, and her mouth hung loosely open. She was not breathing. She was nearly dead.

"What happened?" Paula asked Toni.

"She seemed to be fine," Toni said. "I just turned away for a second, and the next thing I knew she had quit breathing. I looked up on the monitor, and she was in atrial fib. I don't know which came first."

"Did you check her airway?" Paula asked.

"Of course." Toni attached oxygen tubing to an Ambu bag, preparing to manually breathe for her. She slipped the device over Pearce's face and began squeezing the plastic bag to force air into her lungs. "The airway is open."

Sally stepped up next to Paula and placed two fingers on Pearce's femoral artery in the groin. "She has a pulse, but it is weak."

"And a rhythm," Paula said and pointed to the monitor screen. "Let's intubate her and see if we can improve her ventilation."

Harriet wheeled the crash cart into the room. "I've come from *my* room to help," she said with a wry smile, "if they don't shoot me first."

Paula reached out her hand. "Pass me that laryngoscope."

Toni and Sally tugged the bed out from the wall, and Paula positioned herself at the head of the bed. She checked the light of the laryngoscope first, holding the handle with her left hand, and then pushed the blade gently into Pearce's mouth, displacing the tongue to one side. She lifted upward and forward, and the larynx fell open, exposing the pair of firm gray vocal cords. With her right hand she threaded the endotracheal tube through the center of the vocal cords, slipping it perfectly into place.

"We're in," Paula said and removed the guide wire.

"Good job, Doctor," Toni said.

Sally connected the ventilator tubing to the endotracheal tube and then taped the tube to the side of Flo Pearce's face. Toni switched on the ventilator.

The ventilator rhythmically clunked as it breathed for the patient, and within a few breaths, her oxygen saturation level began to climb.

"Her color's already better," Toni said, pointing to her face as she listened to her breath sounds.

"And I feel a pulse," Sally added as she again checked the femoral artery.

Pearce wasn't clearing mentally. Paula had hoped the increased oxygen would help her wake up, but at her age even a short period of poor oxygen to her brain cells was detrimental. "She's still out of it," Paula said. "We may be in trouble."

"You don't need that breathing machine for her." The voice came from behind.

They turned to see Carl Joe standing in the doorway.

"What are you talking about?" Paula said.

"The breathing machine isn't necessary."

"For God's sakes, she's coding. We *had* to put her on the ventilator."

"Well, stop it. Harper wants you to spend your efforts on the attorney general. You're wasting your time with her."

"We can't stop it," Paula insisted. "She'd stop breathing."

Carl Joe pointed to Toni. "Turn off the ventilator."

Toni shook her head defiantly.

"That's an order," he said.

"Not on yours or anyone else's order."

Carl Joe pushed past Paula. "Then I'm pulling the plug myself." He reached down and yanked the power cord from the wall. The ventilator stopped its motion.

"Stop!" Toni cried out. "Don't do that!" She reached to the ground and pushed the plug back into the wall outlet.

The ventilator instantly restarted, resuming its clunking sound.

"Stupid bitch!" he yelled. He reached up to the top of the control panel and flipped the power switch to off. "Don't touch this. I'm warning you!"

Toni stood tall, defiant, her eyes staring straight at Carl Joe. She leaned across the ventilator and flipped it on.

"Leave her alone," Paula shouted at him. "You can't kill this patient! This is murder!"

Slowly Carl Joe slid his gun out of his belt. "You touch the machine again," he said, aiming the gun directly at Toni's face, "and I'll blow your head off." He flipped the switch off. The machine went dead.

Toni never flinched. Her eyes never left Carl Joe even for a second as she reached over and turned the ventilator back on.

The discharge from Carl Joe's weapon snapped her head backward and slammed her body against the wall. Blood instantly showered Pearce's bed and the equipment around her. Toni's face quickly drained of color as her body stood propped against the wall. For the briefest moment her eyes met Paula's. Pleading. Begging.

Then she collapsed.

Chapter 34

The president of the United States personally called and discussed the crisis situation with Reese. Grounds for blame were laid. *If success*, Matt thought, *the credit will go elsewhere; if failure, the ones to blame will be obvious.* The president said to "expedite a situational solution," but the experts in Washington couldn't decide how to proceed. Some wanted the SWAT teams in now. Others wanted them to stand around for as long as it took until Harper was ready to give up. These weren't a bunch of Branch Davidians holed up at their own fortified compound, Matt knew for sure. These were terrorists in a hospital, and they were holding innocent victims hostage. Washington would give the signal to go. Matt was certain of that.

Matt watched as a TV reporter summarized the latest developments. She was an attractive black woman flown in from Atlanta for one of the major networks. She was live, broadcasting worldwide. Saint Luke's Hospital loomed large behind her. *The media has created an incredible circus*, Matt was thinking, as interviews from around the country were flashed on the screen. A spokesman for the Catholic diocese, Bishop So-and-so, decried the violence at one of their Catholic-affiliated hospitals and pleaded for a complete ban on abortions by all clinics in the United States until the crisis was over. The Coalition for Life, a national pro-life organization, issued a press release supporting Harper's demand, though calling for a release of the hospital hostages. They also vowed to set up monitoring stations at every abortion clinic in the country and report violations on their Internet site. The reporter flashed to another interview, where a spokeswoman for the Women's Choice Council, a women's group supporting abortion rights, promised a protest at the White House with a hundred thousand women within a few hours to force the president to end the siege using federal forces. Matt marveled at how the media could stir up controversy.

"The director's on a plane," Reese said. "He'll be here in about ninety minutes. He wants constant updates. He said the decision to go is ours."

"I'm not surprised. Murphy is setting up the video equipment now. We'll see what we've got."

Matt turned and saw Cara Beeson entering the boardroom. She was escorted by two huge police officers, one on each side. Even Matt would have been intimidated. Beeson walked erect, her shoulders pushed back, but her sheepish grin and furrowed brow betrayed her failing confidence. Reese was furious and was ready to chew up some inept local reporter who had disregarded his order and foolishly arranged for the interview.

"What the hell were you doing?" Reese barked as she approached them.

"I can explain," she offered.

"I'd call it aiding and abetting during the commission of a known felony and obstructing a federal agent from performing the official duties of his office." Reese pointed his finger in her face. "You're going to jail, sweetie." Reese waved Simmons over.

"Please, let me explain." Her bravado had left. Her shoulders were slumped, and her face had lost its color. "My sister, Toni Perkins, is one of the nurses. She's the one who's been giving me information. Harper caught her with her phone and said if I did the interview, he would release her. If not, I feared for her life."

"Write down her phone number," Reese said, handing her a piece of paper.

She scribbled down the number.

"Despite your sister," Reese said, taking the paper from her, "your actions are unacceptable. You've committed crimes, and worse than that, you've endangered the lives of everyone in the unit."

"I didn't know what else to do."

Reese waved his hand at her comment. "You could have involved us in the decision."

"My phone rang. I thought it was my sister. It was him."

"The damage you did is inestimable."

Beeson dropped her eyes and didn't respond.

"You've put the lives of federal agents in danger," Reese said. "We don't accept that."

Reese wasn't about to let up on her, but Matt could tell Beeson was done. She had focused on the story. Harper's interview was too good to pass on. Her sister just added fuel. She'd act remorseful, but he wondered if she would have done anything differently. She'd be famous, and they were left with the consequences.

"You've made every abortion clinic a target," Matt said. "Because of Harper's demand, every nut in the country will want to bomb an abortion clinic. It's great to be on live TV."

"I want her cuffed," Reese said to Simmons, "and escorted by these two uniformed officers to a car out front. I want her arrest visible. Maybe it'll make the evening news."

Simmons signaled to one of the FBI agents, who proceeded to cuff her.

"I want her taken downtown," Reese added, "printed, body searched, and booked."

The agent nodded.

"Wait," Matt said. "I'm confiscating her telephone."

The agent removed her phone and handed it to Matt. The two officers escorted Beeson out of the boardroom.

"She's really screwed things up," Reese said as they watched her leave.

"The confrontation with Harper was inevitable," Matt said, "with or without the interview. One good thing—the incoming numbers on her phone just might come in handy."

⋏

Paula gently cradled Toni's head in her hands, and with every fifth compression, she pinched her nose and breathed a short firm breath into her mouth.

Toni's blood was splattered all around her body and was quickly forming a pool around her head. The blood was warm, sticky—the quantity alarming. The entry wound was small and in the center of Toni's forehead, but much of the back of her skull was missing. Paula knew that though they were frantically trying to save her life, their efforts were useless. Saving Toni's life was beyond their weak, mortal power.

Sally was straddling Toni, compressing her chest with outstretched arms, rhythmically pushing downward on her sternum. Tears streamed down Sally's face. Paula was thinking there was little use in continuing, but Sally needed to. Until Sally was finished, they wouldn't stop.

"You're wasting your time with her." Carl Joe was standing over them, his gun still drawn. "Just like the old woman."

Paula realized that Flo Pearce's ventilator wasn't on. It was silent. Carl Joe had turned it off.

"Leave us alone," Sally snapped.

Carl Joe pointed his gun at her. "It's time to stop this. Don't you think I'm serious?"

"What are you going to do?" Paula asked. "Kill us, too?"

Carl Joe swung his gun toward Paula. "I will if I have to."

Harper's voice boomed from the doorway. "No one kills anyone without my direct order."

"Apparently *he* does," Paula barked at Harper as she looked up to meet his eyes. "Aren't you in control of your men here?" She turned back to Toni to give her another breath.

"Lower your weapon, Carl Joe," Harper said sharply.

Carl Joe didn't move, his gun still aimed at Paula's head.

"Soldier, you heard me." Harper pulled his weapon from his shoulder holster and pressed it against Carl Joe's temple. "Soldier, lower your weapon. That's a direct order!"

"Sally," Paula said, "it's no use. She's gone. We should stop."

Sally stopped her compressions, gently lifting her hands off Toni's chest. She covered her face and rocked forward, and then immediately sat upright and cried out. Her cry was a guttural groan deep inside her, growing slowly to an agonizing, piercing scream, heartbreaking, devastating. Finally, she covered her face again and started sobbing deeply. As Paula reached out to touch her shoulder, Sally suddenly rose to her feet and turned toward Harper, her face contorted with anger.

"You murdered her!" she yelled. "You murdered Toni!"

Before Paula could stop her, Sally rushed Harper, screaming and cursing as she repeatedly pounded her fists against his chest. Harper lifted his arms, attempting to deflect the blows, but Sally continued her assault, backing Harper into the corner.

Paula was on her feet in an instant. "Stop, Sally," she begged. "Please stop."

Carl Joe calmly took a step to position himself behind Sally and raised his gun in the air above her head. Sensing his intent, Paula leaped forward and grabbed his arm. With little effort, Carl Joe jerked his arm from Paula's grasp and then pushed his hand hard against her face. Paula stumbled backward, tripping and falling over Toni's body. She looked up as Carl Joe's gun came down sharply, clubbing the back of Sally's head. The force of the blow brought Sally to her knees. Her body went limp, and she fell unconscious to the ground.

⚓

The orange plastic ribbon of the police barricade stretched the length of the service road on the north side of the hospital, about a quarter of a mile away from the specialty wing. The mobile vans and semitrailer trucks of every major network, including all the local stations, abutted the barricade, pushing as close as allowed. Reese was specific in his instructions to arrest Beeson in front of the news media, and a police car was waiting.

One of the uniformed officers escorting her had a tight grasp on her arm as they walked, the other officer positioned a few paces behind. Beeson looked completely dejected. A police car with its lights flashing was at the dead center of the media, and a crowd of reporters were already beginning to gather around the car. They could smell a story developing. Of course, they would recognize her and see her in the cuffs, immediately suspecting something hot.

When Beeson and the officer were within forty feet of the police car, the reporters rushed them, cameras and microphones jabbing the air around them, reporters screaming questions over one another. Beeson looked down and didn't respond. The officer gripped her arm tightly and attempted to look serious. He'd make the evening news.

The reporters shoved closely against them, and the officer extended his arm, pushing through the crowd. As they neared the car, a redheaded woman elbowed her way through the media and stood in front of Beeson and the officer, blocking their way.

"You need to move," the officer said.

"You bitch!" the woman yelled as she pointed at Beeson. "You risked my husband's life."

Beeson lifted her head. "What do you mean?"

"My husband's a hostage, and you risked his life with the interview."

"Ma'am," the officer said firmly, "you *have* to move now."

"The public had a right to know," Beeson snapped.

"You cocky bitch! Here's the public's right!"

The blow was lightning fast as Laura Hyatt's right fist slammed into Beeson's chin, sending her sprawling backward. A dozen video cameras whirled around to catch the action. The officer took a step to one side as she fell, and he smiled briefly. Beeson lay crumpled on the ground, her wrists cuffed behind her, tears forming, defeated.

Laura Hyatt, her arms on her waist, stood defiantly over Beeson. "Your viewing public has just spoken."

Laura lifted her middle finger in disgust and then quickly turned, disappearing in the crowd.

⋏

Paula and Harriet carried Sally to the nurses' station, leaving the bodies of Toni and Flo Pearce in the room. Sally was awake, with a small gash on her scalp, and Paula was applying pressure to control the bleeding. *If the bleeding doesn't stop soon*, Paula thought, *I'll have to suture her.* Sally had been unconscious for several minutes and still was a bit groggy. As Paula assessed her, she noticed her pupils appeared normal, equal in size, and reacting to light. There was no blood or spinal fluid draining from her ear canals. Paula did not feel crepitation or a depression in the skull bones that might indicate a fracture.

Paula would keep Sally quiet and watch her neurologic status for a few minutes. If she had a brain hemorrhage, it would be obvious soon enough.

Harper, Carl Joe, and Tommy were near the back, arguing. The situation was deteriorating badly, and everyone knew it. Though Paula was worried about what would happen next, the view of Toni's face wouldn't leave her— Toni's eyes looking at her the moment she died, questioning Paula, begging Paula to save her. Paula couldn't save her. Paula wanted to pick up Toni's body in her arms and carry her down the hallway, carry her away from here, away to safety. But that wouldn't help, wouldn't bring her back to life...and Harper would never allow it.

Paula held the washcloth tightly against Sally's scalp. "It's a good thing you have a hard head," she whispered.

Sally managed a brief smile and looked up at Paula. "Haloperidol," she said softly.

"What?"

"Haloperidol," Sally repeated. "We have plenty."

Paula glanced nervously up at Harper and saw he was preoccupied. "For the plan?"

"Yes, for the plan. We had a patient who was schizophrenic, and we gave it to her through her nasogastric tube. We have the liquid, and we also have the injectable. I can run through the list of the other medications we have, but this is it. This is the one we should use. Let's start this thing."

Haloperidol, Paula thought. She tried to remember her pharmacology. An odorless and colorless liquid. An antipsychotic that was highly sedative. Dosage? Onset of action? The usual dose was 5–10 milligrams. They could give them 50 milligrams...or 100. The onset would be rapid.

"The injectable works quicker," Sally whispered.

"Won't work. As soon as we injected them, they'd shoot us or detonate the bomb."

John was listening and leaned over to speak. "How about in their coffee?" John asked quietly. "Have you noticed how much they drink?"

John was right. They were drinking coffee continuously. From the beginning Harper had allowed Harriet to make the coffee with no oversight whatsoever, so that would help. Harriet could pour 600–700 milligrams in the pot so each cup would get 100 milligrams. Harper and his men would drink a cup of coffee, and within a few minutes they'd be out cold. The staff could then take their weapons, tie them up, and call Matt. If the plan worked.

Paula lowered her voice even further. Harper and the other two were still at the back. "They need to drink their coffee at the same time," she said. "How can we ensure that will happen?"

"We can't," Sally said. "But even if all three drank at exactly the same time, since every person's metabolism is different, it'll take effect at different rates. If one of them falls asleep first, the others might get suspicious. And if it works too slowly on Harper, he might realize he's been drugged."

"Do we have any other choice?" Paula asked.

They all shook their heads.

They're right, Paula told herself. *We don't have any other choice.*

⅄

"I had to shoot her," Carl Joe said. "*You* said they were spending too much time with the other patients." He pointed at Harper. "Besides," he added quickly, "the old lady had already died. That nurse defied me twice, and I had to put her in her place."

"You had to kill her?" Tommy questioned sharply. "That's ridiculous. Just for switching on a breathing machine?"

"That's enough from both of you," Harper said. "I'm commanding this unit. Is that understood?"

They both nodded.

"You've complicated our situation," Harper said. "This is a mess."

"We've had nothing but bad luck," Tommy said. "It's been since Carl Joe shot that dead preacher. Mutilating dead bodies is bad luck."

"Shut up, Tommy," Carl Joe snapped.

"Both of you shut up," Harper said. "I told that woman reporter that I'd release her sister, and now you've killed her, Carl Joe. This is a problem. I was hoping she'd interview Montgomery live. Think she'll do that now?"

Carl Joe knew better than to answer.

Tommy raised his arms in disgust. "I'm ready to turn myself in," Tommy said.

Carl Joe stubbed his finger in Tommy's chest. "You try to turn yourself in, and I'll kill you myself."

"You're not killing anybody else," Harper said, "unless I say so."

"I told you he was out of control," Tommy muttered. "If only you had listened to me—"

"Both of you, back to your positions," Harper snarled, "and keep your eyes open. This is the last time we can meet like this. They're going to storm in the unit any second. If they do, you can kill as many people as you want."

"What about those dead bodies?" Carl Joe asked, pointing back toward Flo Pearce's room. "The nurse and the old lady? We can say we killed two hostages because we knew two abortions occurred. Saw it on the TV."

Harper shook his head in disgust. "You think we can just throw the reporter's sister in the hallway? How smart would that be?"

Carl Joe hung his head. "Yeah, I see that."

"But putting the old lady out there is okay."

"Yes, sir."

Harper pointed at Carl Joe. "I agree with Tommy, though. No more mutilations. Is that understood, Carl Joe?"

Carl Joe nodded.

"Have the janitor and the orderly throw the old lady's body in the hallway like they did the last time. I'll watch the position in the back until you get that done. Are we all in agreement now?"

Tommy and Carl Joe both nodded.

"Good. Then take care of it and get back to your positions."

⚑

Paula sat in the floor of the nurses' station and held Sally's head. The bleeding had nearly stopped. She offered Sally some pain medication, but she refused. She wanted to stay alert.

Paula watched as Carl Joe forced John and the orderly to drag the body of Flo Pearce down the hallway. It made her sick. She felt the anger rise inside of her, and she wanted revenge as strong as any emotion she had ever felt. Harper must be stopped. It was time to gain control.

After John and the orderly returned to their places in the nurses' station, Carl Joe took up his position at the rear. Tommy remained at the front. Harper stood close to Carl Joe. Paula watched Harper listen in the stairwell for several minutes. Apparently satisfied, he crossed over to the nurses' station, rolled up a chair from the doctors' desk, and sat down in front of them.

"Killing your nurse was unfortunate," he said. "I'm sorry that happened."

Paula turned away. He was sorry that it had occurred, *not* apologizing for the action. Harper's eyes were cold and hard despite his mild, controlled voice. His words were condescending. They were the hostages, Paula thought he was saying, and his tone relayed the message.

"We all need to work together," he continued. "You need to follow orders. It's just that simple. Follow orders, and you won't get hurt."

No one responded. Most of the staff had their faces hidden in their hands or against their knees. Harper was intimidating, and they were afraid to look at him.

"It'll all be over soon," he said.

A brief shudder ran up Paula's spine. She looked up at him. "Don't order us to kill patients," Paula said, attempting to sound confident, "like Carl Joe did with Toni. We won't do it."

"I don't expect you to kill patients." He turned to Sally. "Are you all right?"

"Just peachy," she said.

"Good." Harper pointed over his shoulder. "Then go take care of Montgomery."

Of course no sympathy, Paula thought. *It's his agenda.*

"For the rest of you," he said, "I want you all to get back to work. Get back to work and follow our orders. Does that sound so hard?"

Without waiting for an answer, Harper stood and walked away.

Chapter 35

"**M**urphy," Matt said, "what did you see?" Matt spoke into the hands-free headset. Murphy had dropped the video cable, and Matt wanted a report.

"It's a mess," Murphy said. "They've stacked beds in the stairwell and barricaded the back door. You've seen the layout of the unit, right?"

"I've got the map in front of me." Matt rolled it out on the table.

"We're looking through a foot-square window in the door, so our view is limited, but we can see all three of the perpetrators. The one whose description matches Harper's is standing in the middle of the nurses' station, and that's where most of the staff are. We see one man at the front. Another's at the back. Harrison's body is next to the back door, propped on a chair."

"Harper must think we're idiots."

"The patient rooms are on the outside. It's hard to tell which ones are occupied. Two men are on the floor near the back doorway on their abdomens. Their arms and legs are bound, and they aren't moving. They could be dead or injured. They're covered with blood."

"Jake and Asher, I bet. I hope they're alive. How much of a problem is the barricade?"

"A big problem. We can drag the obstructions out of the way, throw them down the stairs, and then push through the doorway, but that'll require twenty or thirty seconds. If we don't get a quick head shot on Harper, none of this works. Our only hope is to slip down to the landing and shoot through the window. We watch on the video until Harper's in the open and then take a clean shot through the barricade at him. If we can take out Harper, we'll come in simultaneously from both entrances. The front's not barricaded, but it's a long hallway and easy for them to defend. If Harper hears us, or we don't have a clean shot, we'll fail the objectives."

"Despite those challenges," Matt said, "the directors of both the ATF and FBI have agreed with the SWAT approach."

"That's good news," Murphy said.

"We're expecting our director on site within the next forty-five minutes, but we've been given clearance to go."

"Then give us the order."

"I'm coming with you."

"I hoped you would."

Matt looked across the table at Simmons. "You want to come?"

Simmons nodded.

"And Simmons, too."

"We'll need all the help we can get," Murphy said.

"I'll get back to you." Matt switched off the headset.

We'd be fools to wait much longer, Matt thought. Harper had murdered five already. That counted the female patient carried out into the hallway but not the John Doe toe at the bomb site or Jake and Asher who, Matt hoped, were still alive. Fortunately, Baskins had survived surgery and was in the recovery room. Though Paula didn't know it yet, her courage saved the guard's life.

Matt hoped he could save hers.

Abortion clinics around the country were responding in various ways to Harper's abortion demand. Some clinics declared they would stop until the crisis was over. Others flatly refused and vowed to conduct business as usual. Regardless of a clinic's stance, large crowds of pro-life and pro-choice demonstrators had gathered outside the doors of nearly every abortion clinic in the country. A few clashes had already occurred from both sides. No serious violence reported...so far. Harper's demand had captured the attention of the world, and millions of viewers were tuning in. Harper's ploy was succeeding. The sooner they shut him down, the better.

Those around the boardroom were quiet. The assault would begin soon.

"Murphy's anxious to go, isn't he?" Reese asked.

Matt nodded.

"We have received the go-ahead order from Washington," Reese said, "but I want you to review our options one more time. Let's hear it."

Matt had considered only three options viable, and he summarized each one—with Reese criticizing them, as Matt had expected. "We rejected," Matt said, "cutting a hole in the ceiling or entering through an outside window."

Reese nodded. "Won't work. He'll blow the place."

"That's what we think," Matt said. Matt saved his preferred choice for last. "We believe the stairwell is our best option." Matt hesitated a moment. "Though not without serious risk."

"It never is," Reese said.

Matt suspected Reese had decided before Matt had started but wanted him to run through it all to confirm his choice. If the plan went to hell, it was Reese's ultimate and final responsibility.

"Are *you* ready?" Reese asked.

"Yes. Murphy and I have worked out the details. We'll only have two or three seconds of surprise. As soon as we see all three in the open, we'll take out Harper first. Then we'll rush in front and back with flash bombs, loud blasts, and maybe tear gas. We have to take out Harper instantly, or it is all for nothing."

"Let's call Harper one more time," Reese said. "Make sure we've made every attempt."

"Whatever you think."

"He'll think we are still negotiating. We'll try only once. If no response, we'll go."

Matt would make the call. Reese was right about trying, but Matt wasn't optimistic. In Matt's view, this situation was past talking. Time for force. But he'd be patient if Reese wanted patience. He only hoped their patience wouldn't risk the lives of any more hostages.

⅄

Paula searched in the drug cabinet looking for the liquid haloperidol, acting as nonchalant as she could, checking on a medication for a patient, nothing suspicious or out of the ordinary. Haloperidol was the best they had—an antipsychotic that caused serious sedation that worked quickly. The onset was often within minutes, but the dosage varied from person to person. She recalled one patient on her psychiatric rotation in medical school who was wildly psychotic and required four burly orderlies to restrain him for over thirty minutes even after receiving a 100 milligram dose. Yet an elderly female in a nursing home might sleep twenty-four hours on 2 milligrams. For the three terrorists, 100 milligrams each seemed like the right dose. Harriet could brew a fresh pot of eight cups, drop in 800 milligrams, and each cup would be a dose of 100 milligrams. More than enough to knock them out for a few hours.

Sally had wanted to help find the medication, but she had felt dizzy when she stood, so she sat back down. She was holding an ice bag on her head with her eyes closed, and Paula thought she might have dozed off. The head injury had stunned her, and though Harper had insisted Sally go to Montgomery's room, she was too weak. Paula hoped she could be helpful when the time came.

She glanced at Jake and Asher on the floor. One person could untie them when the haloperidol began working on the terrorists. The agents would know what to do. If they could get guns to the agents, the situation would be over.

Paula found an amber medicine bottle with the patient's name on the label. She held it up to the light—almost full. The bottle held 400 milligrams total, and in a full pot of coffee, that was 50 milligrams per cup. Why would Harriet make a partial pot? She would have preferred 100 milligrams per cup, but this should be enough…she hoped.

She also found the injectable and loaded up three syringes. She'd carry two and pass one to Sally. They were the only ones mobile enough to give injections. Once the men fell asleep from the haloperidol in their coffee, she and Sally could inject them—if Sally was able to help.

Harriet was in Arthur Hyatt's room, peeking out of the curtain. Paula screwed open the bottle and poured the contents into a white mug. *Less noticeable*, she thought, *than a medicine bottle sitting next to the coffee maker.* Paula set the mug on the counter where Harriet could easily reach it. Harriet nodded and closed the curtain.

All that was left now was for Harriet to pick up the mug and make a new pot of coffee.

⋏

Matt slipped out of his trousers and tossed them in the corner as he changed into raid gear in one of the empty rooms on the fourth floor. He unbuttoned his white shirt, covered with the stains of black soot and ripped in several places by the flying glass. Eight hours ago he had been riding with Stan, discussing Stan's kids, his dogs, and his pitiful golf game. Now Stan was dead. This was his chance to set things right. Harper had turned his life upside down. He had killed Stan, and now he could kill Paula. Matt had felt anxious before, but now he felt calm, determined, his brain sharp. He slipped on the bulletproof vest and fastened it behind him. The vest would help in a firefight, but wasn't much help in an explosion. If a bomb exploded, he'd be dead before he felt it. Just like Stan. Instant. Painless.

Matt checked the ammo in his .40-caliber Glock and slipped it into his belt. Washington was putting the pressure on them. Would he be one of the scapegoats if they failed? Maybe, but that didn't change his mind. Harper wouldn't budge. He heard it in his voice. Harper was on a suicide mission, and there was no sense negotiating any further. Matt's patience was gone. Time to convince Reese. Time to act.

Act fast and be deadly.

⋏

Harriet strolled nonchalantly into the nurses' station and poured water into the two-quart plastic tub. Paula sat across from her, bent over a note pad, fumbling through the pages, purposely ignoring her. Harriet reached into a drawer beneath the coffee maker for a packet of coffee and dumped its contents into the filter. They had decided to pour the medicine directly into the coffeepot after it was brewed. Paula wasn't certain if the haloperidol was heat stable. The brewing could inactivate it, but the heat of the coffee in the pot could as well. She had no way of knowing. Harriet flipped the switch on and then leaned against the counter to wait.

Adding the medication to the coffeepot without being observed was crucial. Paula was certain Harper would notice any activity out of the ordinary. A misstep here could be fatal. The white mug with the haloperidol sat innocently next to the coffee maker. Harriet would pour herself a cup into the white mug, decide not to drink it, and return it to the pot. Then they'd be ready.

The coffee had just finished brewing when Paula saw Tommy stand and look toward Harriet.

"Harriet," Paula said, swinging around in her chair, "what was Mr. Hyatt's last blood sugar?"

Harriet saw Tommy approaching. "The last one I did was a couple of minutes ago, and it was two hundred twenty, Dr. Barrett." Harriet quickly poured coffee into the clear liquid inside the mug.

"Good," Paula said. "His blood sugar's improved."

Tommy entered the nurses' station. "How about a fresh cup?" he asked.

"Sure," Harriet answered, reaching for a cup on the shelf above her.

"I'll just take that mug there," he said, pointing, "if that's okay."

"No," Harriet said and glanced at Paula. "I poured that for the doctor." She stepped across the nurses' station and set the mug next to Paula. She turned back to him. "Styrofoam would be easier for you, wouldn't it?" She poured him a cup.

Tommy lingered for a couple of minutes by the coffee maker. He stood four feet behind Paula, and she breathed in and out slowly, fighting the anxiety she felt building. What was he waiting for? Had he noticed something? She bent over her note pad and continued writing a progress note as though he weren't there. Finally, he started whistling and headed for the front, occasionally stopping to sip his coffee.

Tommy's cup contained no drug. All the haloperidol was in the mug beside Paula. Now Tommy would have to drink a second cup.

"I don't want this coffee, Harriet," Paula spoke out so her voice could be heard. "I've had too much coffee already today."

"Then I'll just put it back." Harriet poured it into the pot and rinsed out the mug, setting it upside down in the sink.

Pouring coffee back into the pot was certainly out of the ordinary. Would Harper notice? Paula glanced at him, and his attention seemed elsewhere. Lucky for them. They deserved a break.

Paula closed her eyes and let out a slow breath. All that was left was the waiting.

⚔

"Now he won't answer the radio," Matt said. "This is bad."

Reese, Simmons, and Matt were in the hallway on the fourth floor. Murphy and his men were at the end of the hallway, prepared to go. *It's time to make a decision*, Matt thought. It was Reese's call, but Simmons, as acting head of the FBI, must agree. The ATF and FBI would have to be together on this one. Good or bad.

"What do you think?" Reese asked.

Matt waited for Simmons's opinion.

"I don't know," Simmons said. "I've considered all the options. We certainly can't wait two or three weeks in a standoff situation. We are on a time limit. The patients put us there. I hate to say it, but if it was just the hospital staff, it wouldn't be as complicated." He shrugged. "We could wait until Harper falls asleep. It'd be fewer targets."

Reese shook his head. "I doubt that would help. He could be awake another forty-eight hours."

"I'm sure you're right. We've got about ten or twelve special ops coming in, but they won't be here for another six or eight hours."

"Only so many team members fit in the stairwell," Matt said.

"I agree," Reese said. "That shouldn't delay us." He turned to Matt. "What do you think?"

"The sooner the better."

"Why is that?"

"The longer we wait, the more likely Harper will think we'll strike, especially if he's cut off communications. The media has created a circus outside the hospital, and we know he's watching the TV. We should choose a time and go."

"I think you're right. We should go." Reese turned to Simmons. "What's your decision?"

Simmons was quiet for a moment and then nodded his head slowly. "Let's do it."

"Okay, Matt," Reese said. "Drop the cable and see what you've got. The signal is yours to give."

Matt nodded. "Then let's go!"

人

"Fresh coffee," Harriet announced to the unit, as she had each time she brewed a new pot. She poured herself a small amount as if to drink it as she returned to Arthur Hyatt's room.

Paula pretended to write on the note pad and watched. Tommy was drinking his first cup at the front. His first cup wouldn't help them. He'd need a second one. Neither Harper nor Carl Joe had come to the nurses' station for a cup, so they had none. But even if Tommy drank a second cup and no one else did, he would pass out in a drugged stupor. Harper would obviously notice. That would not be pretty.

I just need to be patient, Paula told herself, but it wasn't easy. She felt her adrenaline rushing and her heart racing. She tried to calm herself by slowing her breathing down. It wasn't helping. But at least her thoughts were clear. They had a plan, and it could work.

Drink some coffee!

Carl Joe stood and said something to Harper that she couldn't hear. Harper moved to the back wall to cover as Carl Joe crossed to the nurses' station. He reached the counter and poured himself a cup. Paula tried not to watch, despite her uneasiness.

"Hey, Tommy," she heard Carl Joe say behind her. "You want another cup?"

She saw Tommy nodding. Carl Joe poured Tommy a second cup and carried it to him. They talked a few minutes before Carl Joe returned to the nurses' station.

Carl Joe held up the pot. "Sam?"

Harper shook his head, declining.

This is a major problem, Paula thought. The haloperidol might only take a few minutes to work. If Harper didn't drink any coffee, and Carl Joe and Tommy fell asleep, the consequences would be serious. Harper would be furious.

Carl Joe returned to the back. He set his coffee on the floor and sat down in a chair against the rear wall, near Harrison's body. Carl Joe seemed oblivious to the dead man near him. Harper leaned over and began talking in a low voice. Paula strained but couldn't make out the conversation. *Harper needs a cup too*, she thought. *He needs it the most.*

Carl Joe reached back for the coffee and bumped the cup. The slight tap of the Styrofoam cup sent it flying, showering the floor with the steaming brown liquid. Carl Joe jumped up, cursing.

Paula gasped. She found herself standing...and Harper was looking directly at her.

CHAPTER 36

Carl Joe had cussed loudly after spilling the coffee, and Harper had screamed at him for five minutes for his foul mouth, an especially bizarre reaction, Paula thought, to Carl Joe's transgression. Now Carl Joe was sulking in the corner while Harper guarded the back door. The tension in the unit was thick. Carl Joe had actually taken the verbal beating better than Paula had expected, yet she thought he was on the edge, likely to be pushed over by even the most insignificant event. A confrontation like Harper's reaction to his cursing definitely could do it.

The staff was frightened. Jennifer was gazing straight ahead, absorbed in her thoughts. John was looking down, avoiding eye contact with anyone. The two respiratory techs and the orderly had their faces buried in their hands.

Sally had bled through two washcloths before the bleeding had finally stopped. Paula had attended to her wound, tying strands of hair together rather than suturing, quick and easy, and it seemed to be holding. With Sally improved, Harper had insisted she return to Montgomery's room, and Paula could see her through the sliding glass door, recording vital signs. She was facing away, and Paula worried she wasn't paying attention. Sally had one of the three syringes, and Paula might need her immediately. If she was preoccupied, she wouldn't be much help.

Maybe she didn't need Sally. Maybe this was all a mistake.

Tommy was drinking his haloperidol, but neither Harper nor Carl Joe had any at all. The plan would be exposed as soon as Tommy fell asleep. What would Harper do then? There was no antidote for Tommy. Once he drank it, it would begin working. Tommy would fall over, and Harper would know they had tried to drug him. He'd know it was her idea. She was sure of that.

Carl Joe walked away from the corner, his back to Harper, and entered the nurses' station. He stood in front of the coffee maker quietly for a moment and poured two cups. He stuffed his weapon in his belt, picked up a cup in each hand, and then crossed the unit back to Harper.

Paula saw Carl Joe extend the cup to Harper. Harper took it, smiling. Was Carl Joe appeasing Harper with this gesture? Was Harper back in control?

In any case, she thought, *all three men are holding a cup of coffee with haloperidol. The plan is working.*

⅄

Matt huddled around the video monitor with Murphy, Simmons, and the SWAT members. The stairwell was dark, and only the faint glow of the monitor cast its soft light on the serious faces of the team of agents and officers.

No one spoke. Murphy motioned to one of the agents, using hand signals to lower the video camera, and the man started silently forward to position himself near the railing.

Eleven men in full gear, faces blackened and covered, automatic weapons held cocked and loaded, stood along the wall or crouched at the end of the dark hallway, prepared for the strike. Ten others were at the front, and eight more were two floors directly below them, waiting for the signal. Matt could hear the men's breathing and suspected they could hear his. He felt his heart pounding and the sweat moistening his forehead, but the sensation was adrenaline, and he welcomed it. His excitement mingled with apprehension and concern. He was ready.

Matt glanced up and caught Rick Rice's eyes. Rice nodded slightly. Matt nodded back. Matt's thoughts flashed to Stan Gill and Rod Baker. Rice's thoughts were likely the same.

The plan was simple. It usually was. They'd drop the camera by its cable through the railing to assess the situation in the ICU. All parties possible would be identified, with Harper the most crucial. When it appeared safe, Matt would signal Murphy's best marksman, who would inch partway down the staircase and wait. As soon as Harper came into view through the window, Matt would use Beeson's cell phone to ring Toni's, hopefully providing a moment's distraction—enough time for a single clean head shot on Harper.

Matt had considered every contingency earlier but now dismissed them from his thoughts. Once the strike began, contingencies were distractions. Single-minded concentration on their goal was essential to success. And they would be successful. Innocent lives, including Paula's, depended on it.

Paula watched as Carl Joe and Tommy drank their coffee. Harper hadn't touched his. Harper carried his coffee in his left hand and the detonator in his right. Within minutes Carl Joe and Tommy would be sleeping, medicated to unconsciousness, yet Harper would be completely awake.

She had to do something.

Paula slipped her hand into her lab jacket and fingered the two syringes. Could they hold Harper and inject him when both of his men fell asleep? Could four or five of them overpower him if she gave the signal? Would the haloperidol work before he killed them?

He was in control as long as he held the detonator.

Why wasn't Harper drinking? Did he suspect? Was he too paranoid? Surely not. How could he know?

Sally stayed in Montgomery's room and hadn't left once since her head injury. Paula saw her still facing away from the doorway, busy with Montgomery's care. Only Sally could help Paula. Harper would be immediately suspicious if any of the other staff approached. She needed Sally. Paula couldn't do it by herself.

Paula counted the seconds, thumbing through the note pads, writing a note here and there, pretending to check labs, wasting time.

How much longer should they wait? Should she signal Sally that she was ready? Their only hope was to move within an arm's length at the moment

Harper noticed Carl Joe and Tommy sleeping, somehow grab the detonator, and inject him quickly.

Paula's mind was racing. If Tommy or Carl Joe fell asleep, they'd miss their only chance.

Inject Harper quick…then pray they all wouldn't die.

⋏

The agent inched the cable over the edge of the stairwell landing as Matt watched intently on the monitor. The first view of the floor below showed the tangled furniture and equipment, creating a barricade at the doorway. The jumble of beds, chairs, and IV poles appeared formidable. Matt understood why Murphy was nervous. Matt signaled the agent to freeze the position of the cable while Matt and Murphy studied the monitor. They needed to choose the location for the sniper wisely, but Harper's position inside the unit was critical to that choice. After a few seconds, Murphy pointed at the screen, indicating his preference. His marksman nodded.

Matt signaled for the cable to be lowered several inches until it dropped just below the top of the window. For the first time Matt could see the unit. It was an open space, larger than he expected, and the lights were bright, which would be to their advantage. The agent slowly swept the camera from left to right. The unit itself was not in particular disarray. No overturned beds or other barricades. No broken glass or scattered trash. No hostages with shotguns tied around the necks. The unit appeared almost tranquil.

As the camera swept from the left, Matt saw the patients' rooms, including where Montgomery must be. The nurses' station came into view next. Several people were on the floor at the center. Paula was sitting at the desk bent over, apparently writing. His heart jumped. Paula appeared unharmed, without any guards or guns near her. The scene looked deceptively peaceful. The calm before the storm.

She was in the greatest danger. Would he be able to protect her?

The sweep finished on the right with another set of patient rooms and then returned to center. Matt could see Tommy at the front. Carl Joe was at the back. Harper, the person he most wanted to see, was standing in the center of the field of vision, facing away from the camera.

A perfect head shot on Harper!

They were ready to move into position, and Harper was standing in the open. Now was the time for Murphy's marksman to slip down the stairs to take his shot. Matt raised his hand to signal.

Suddenly, Harper turned and faced the doorway. He was looking straight at them, staring.

Matt held his breath. Did he see the camera? Did he know they were there?

Harper stood frozen, fixated, staring toward the doorway for several seconds. Then as suddenly as he turned toward them, he turned away. Matt quickly reached down, grabbed the cable, and jerked it out of view. If Harper had seen the cable, they would have missed their chance. Matt looked up at Murphy. His face revealed his worry, too. Should they back off and try later, or go now? Matt's pulse quickened. He wiped the sweat off his forehead. Matt surveyed the men around him and observed their resolve and determination. They were ready. His eyes met Murphy's. Murphy gave a quick nod.

It's time to go, Matt thought. He signaled the agent to drop the cable.

⋏

Paula bent over the desk and tried to breathe normally. The unit was too quiet, and she knew why. She stole a glance at Tommy, and he was sitting in a chair leaning against the wall, unconscious. They were lucky he was out of Harper's view and hadn't fallen on the floor.

They wouldn't be as lucky with Carl Joe. His eyes were heavy, and they occasionally closed. Unfortunately, Carl Joe was holding his cup of coffee in his hand, and as soon as he fell asleep, Harper would instantly know.

Though Harper was behind her, she felt him looking at her, and she was afraid to move. He was holding his cup but not drinking the coffee. Of the three men, it was their luck that he wouldn't be drugged. Paula tried to concentrate, deciding what she should do next. *This was all a mistake.*

"Carl Joe!" Harper's shout pierced the unit.

Paula turned to see Carl Joe's arm dropped at his side, his coffee cup on the ground beside him, the coffee splattered on the floor. His eyes were closed, his body motionless. Carl Joe's body, as if in slow motion, slid feet first out of the chair onto the tile floor, the back of his head landing with a loud thud.

Harper tossed down his coffee and reached Carl Joe instantly. He knelt beside him, shaking him vigorously.

"Carl Joe," Harper screamed, "what's wrong?" Harper turned to the front. "Tommy. I need your help now!"

Paula was on her feet, watching the scene unfolding. She felt a shudder down her spine. *Harper will kill us all!*

λ

Reese's voice crackled in Matt's headset. Matt raised his hand to his ear to signal Murphy he was receiving.

"Matt," Reese repeated.

Reese didn't expect Matt to respond since Matt couldn't talk—his voice would be heard down the stairs.

"The director wants to be on property when you go," Reese said, his voice loud over the earphone. "His ETA's fifteen minutes."

Matt wasn't waiting for the director. It was time to move. Waiting was risky.

"Hold up for now," Reese continued. "We'll be there in a few minutes."

Murphy lifted his hands, wanting an explanation. Matt tapped his earpiece as though it malfunctioned and shrugged. Murphy shrugged back.

If they delayed another minute, people would die.

Matt pointed to the agent holding the cable and signaled him to drop it. Go! Go! Go!

λ

Paula took a step toward Harper. "Is he okay?" Paula asked, wanting him to hear her concern.

Harper pointed his finger at her over his shoulder. "You stay right there," he snapped.

Paula didn't move. Harper bent over Carl Joe, examining the back of his skull for injuries. He reached down and laid the detonator on the floor beside him.

Paula saw her opportunity.

She slipped the syringe out of her coat pocket and pulled off the plastic cover. She held the syringe with its open needle in one hand behind her back and inched toward Harper. He was bent over Carl Joe, facing away from her. His leather holster hung loosely from his left shoulder with the handle of the gun toward her.

He won't stay in this position long, she thought. *Just a few seconds.*

She crept silently forward, staring at his bulky arms flexing as he lifted Carl Joe. The gun was in the holster. The detonator remained at his side. If she could kick the detonator away...

Paula's arms were shaking. Her body trembled. She was barely breathing. *Steady. Be calm. Do it now. Do it now!*

She slid in behind him and lifted her arm high, the syringe in her fist poised in the air, her thumb on the plunger, ready to strike deep into his arm.

Kick the detonator! Push in the plunger!

Harper shook Carl Joe. "Wake up!" Harper yelled, unable to rouse him. "What the hell's going on here?"

All of a sudden, as though he could sense Paula behind him, Harper swung around to face her. For a moment his eyes were wide with surprise.

Do it now! Do it now! Paula kicked away the detonator swiftly with her foot, watching it spin away from them, and shoved the syringe down toward Harper with all of her strength.

Harper reacted instantly. He ducked to one side, missing her strike, and then swung his massive arm toward her, knocking Paula backward. She fell hard into the wall, the syringe flying from her hand, and she cried out as the air rushed from her lungs.

"You drugged the coffee," Harper bellowed. "You stupid bitch!" He reached out to retrieve the detonator from a few feet away and then turned back to face her. "And you thought you could drug me, too!"

Harper's face was contorted with anger as he moved toward her. Paula slid herself backward until her body was pressing hard against the tile wall behind her. She shoved her arms into the floor, pushing herself away from him, away from his crazed eyes. The panic rose inside her. *My God, my God, he's going to kill me!*

"God smites the disobedient," he screamed at her, holding the detonator for her to see. "He destroys the wicked."

Harper was close to her face, his skin red with anger.

"The angel of God is merciful. His justice is measured." Harper paused the briefest moment before adding coldly, "Now you're going to die."

Paula felt his thick, powerful right hand surround her throat, his grasp squeezing the air from her, crushing her. She pushed away at him, fighting for her life, but his grip wouldn't weaken. The strength of his massive hand held her neck like a vise. Her chest fought for breath. Her arms flailed at his muscular shoulders in vain. The blackness began to overwhelm her. It would soon be over. She had failed.

"Hey, you bastard!" Sally's voice came from behind him. "Leave her alone!"

Harper released Paula and turned on Sally, enraged at the interruption. Sally backed away as Harper stood.

Paula gasped and coughed, drawing in a deep breath. She pushed herself up, forcing herself to her knees.

"Now all of you will die!" Harper screamed, moving toward Sally.

Sally took another step backward, avoiding Harper, and at the same time tossed her syringe to Paula. Harper swung around as the syringe flew by him, his eyes wild with anger. He saw the syringe land in Paula's hand, and he lunged for it. The weight of Harper's body fell on her, pushing her against the wall, forcing the air from her lungs. She stabbed the needle blindly with all her strength and felt it hit flesh, the soft pressure of human tissue. She shoved in the plunger and let it loose.

Harper pushed away from Paula and fell backward. The syringe, its plunger showing the full dose delivered, was protruding from his right thigh.

CHAPTER 37

Matt was panicking. The agent had dropped the cable, and the view was good, but no Harper. Matt had signaled the sniper to move into position, and he was cautiously inching down the steps. Hopefully he would see Harper better from his vantage point. If no view of Harper, no head shot. The entire operation depended on it.

"Matt, this is Reese."

Reese's voice was again crackling into Matt's headset. Matt wanted to turn it off. He had decided the course. Nothing Reese could say would change his mind.

"The director's ETA is twelve minutes. He wants to be on site. I want you to mic click twice. I want a confirmation."

Murphy was looking at Matt, his eyes questioning. He seemed to see Matt's distraction. Matt shook his head. Murphy was better off not knowing. Matt would take full responsibility. He was convinced it'd be a serious mistake to wait. Screw Reese. Screw the director. It was his call.

They just needed a head shot.

⅄

Harper propped himself up on his elbows and stared at the syringe in his leg. Reaching down, he pulled it out and tossed it to the side.

"What was in it?" he asked, looking up at Paula, his eyes narrowed.

"Haloperidol," she responded, meeting his gaze.

"Will it kill me?"

"No, just sedate you," Paula said, forcing calm into her voice. She eyed the detonator in his hand. *Keep him talking*, she thought. *The medicine will work.*

"How much time?"

"It'll make you sleepy, but it won't hurt you."

"You gave it to Carl Joe and Tommy, too?"

She nodded.

He tried to raise up on his elbows and slipped. The medicine was already taking effect.

"I still have the detonator," he said and glanced toward his hand. "And I can still use it."

"Reverend Harper," Paula said, "don't kill anyone else. Too many people have already died."

"Montgomery deserves to die."

"But the patients here don't. They've done nothing wrong."

"Innocent people die every day. Are they so innocent?"

Paula noticed the subtle slurring of his speech, and his pupils were dilating. She saw that his finger was resting on the button. If he pushed down with the slightest pressure...

"These innocent lives," she said, "are in your hands. Please don't hurt them."

Harper stared blankly toward the ceiling. "God's will must be done," he mumbled. "The God-haters must die." He closed his eyes and was still.

Paula leaned forward and cautiously reached for the detonator. Her hand was shaking badly as she inched toward him. Harper's finger was touching the button. Was he asleep? Could she take the detonator from him?

Suddenly, Harper's eyes flew open. His face was red, consumed by the ugly fury of his hatred. Paula was shocked by his viciousness.

"Behold Armageddon!" Harper screamed, lifting up the detonator.

Paula held her breath as he thrust the detonator high above his head.

The shrill ring of a cell phone erupted from Harper's pocket, startling him.

Paula watched in horror as the left side of Harper's head exploded, its contents showering outward in a rush of red. The blast shoved Harper's body sideways, yet for a moment his arm remained lifted upward. Paula saw Harper's hand contracting around the detonator as his arm began its lifeless fall to the floor. She reacted instantly, kicking out swiftly and striking hard against Harper's forearm. The detonator shot from his hand and flew into the air. Paula lunged forward with her arms reaching out, sliding hard against the floor. Her body came to a stop, and she looked up. The detonator fell into her out-stretched hands.

Paula lay motionless for several seconds, gently holding the detonator. She felt the object's lightness. It was a toy. Their lives were held hostage by a toy.

She had caught it. She had caught the detonator, and the bomb had not exploded.

As Paula's hands began to shake, she placed the detonator carefully in a clear area on the floor, not trusting that she could hold it. She moved next to Harper to examine his wounds. The bleeding was profuse, and his body was lifeless. He was dead.

Paula sighed deeply. It was over.

人

A loud crack was followed instantly by a blinding flash of light.

"Get down! Get down! Get down!" yelled the SWAT team as they burst in the rear doorway.

Ten men dressed in black, with hooded ski masks and automatic weapons, converged on Harper. Other teams from the front and rear converged on Carl Joe and Tommy. Within seconds, all three terrorists were surrounded.

Paula watched and felt relieved. The rescuers had arrived. As the tension released from her body, she started trembling. Her hands began shaking, and she couldn't stop. Sally and John stood over her. She looked up at them, and they nodded. They had done it. They were safe.

The SWAT team quickly searched Harper and secured his weapons. They searched Carl Joe and Tommy, rolled them over, and roughly handcuffed them.

One agent picked up the detonator, removed its batteries, and placed it in a plastic bag. After stuffing the bag in his pocket, the agent moved close to Paula. "Ma'am," he said, leaning over, "it looks like we're a bit late."

Matt pulled off his mask and reached out his hands. Paula jumped to her feet and threw her arms around him.

"No, not really, Matt," she said as the tears began flowing. "Your timing is absolutely perfect."

Chapter 38

The intensive care unit swarmed with activity. The bomb squad had dismantled the bomb and moved the components to a special armored vehicle. Initially the authorities had wanted to evacuate the unit of patients and staff, but Jake was certain the bomb wasn't trip-wired. Carl Joe and Tommy remained in their drugged stupor as they were loaded onto gurneys and carted off to the emergency room, where they would be medically monitored under heavy guard until they woke up. Matt insisted Jake, despite his strong objections, be immediately evaluated by the physicians in the emergency room, and he was escorted away by a couple of stern-faced nurses.

The unit was jammed with FBI and ATF agents, photographing the crime scene, fingerprinting every surface, gathering evidence. Matt stayed near Paula the entire time, and his presence comforted her. She said he could help the others. He said he had done his part.

When the unit was secured, the agents allowed the usual hospital staff to return. Two or three physicians were assigned to each patient, and the patients' conditions were thoroughly evaluated. Lab tests were drawn. X-rays were taken. Dr. England extubated Montgomery, and he was breathing well with the tube out of his trachea. Dr. England also removed the aortic balloon, and Paula wasn't surprised that Montgomery was maintaining his blood pressure without the balloon pump. It had been turned off for hours.

Paula and Sally made sure Toni's body was treated with respect. Sally had personally washed her, bandaged her head, and changed her into a clean gown. The staff had gently lifted her onto a gurney and covered her with a sheet. One of the agents had initially objected, saying it was a crime scene, but Matt intervened, making sure it wasn't an issue. *It's a good thing,* Paula thought, *because neither Sally nor I would have complied. We're done following orders.*

A few minutes later, the patients' families were permitted in to visit their loved ones. Laura Hyatt was the first to enter, and she loudly insisted she wouldn't leave again until hell itself froze over. No one doubted her.

Paula felt compelled to check out each of the patients to their attending physicians and specialists, updating the doctors on the patients' medical conditions throughout the ordeal. One of her own partners would follow her asthmatic patient. All the doctors insisted she rest, but the checkout was good medicine for the patients...and for her.

Matt suggested they move off to one side, and they watched the commotion from a quiet corner. She was glad to be alone next to him. She needed to talk, and he must have sensed it.

"It's odd," she said softly to Matt. "Just a few minutes ago, I was preparing to die." Her voice quivered a bit, and her knees still seemed like they might buckle at any time beneath her. Her hands were still shaking.

"We waited too long," Matt said matter-of-factly. "I'm sorry you were frightened."

She leaned against him and felt his strength. Her mind drifted to Reverend Pettigrew, struggling for hours with his disease, and dying with such great courage. In contrast, her near moment of death came too quickly for thought. In an instant she was ready; but instead of dying, she had lived. Somehow, strangely, the moment seemed to confirm what she had already known to be true, and she felt a peace at the knowledge.

Matt squeezed her hand gently, and she turned, meeting his blue eyes. His face was strong, but soft. His eyes were penetrating, as if able to see deep inside her. Though vulnerable, she didn't feel exposed. Rather, she felt a fulfillment, a completion. She pulled Matt closer to her.

"I was doing everything in my power to save you from harm," he said, his eyes growing moist.

"I know," she said, and she leaned to him, kissing him. The kiss was deep and long, with a passion she had longed for and dreamed of, but had never allowed herself to feel.

He had saved her from harm, and at that moment, she knew he always would.

Montgomery asked Paula and Matt to come to his room. Matt introduced Paula to Reese, and Reese introduced James Bentley, the ATF director. Paula shook hands. Jake and Sally, cleaned up, heads bandaged, were present and standing at the bedside. Jennifer was in a chair near Montgomery.

Paula was completely exhausted after spending two hours in interviews with federal agents. She was ready to go home, but Montgomery had personally requested her company. How could she refuse?

Montgomery pointed to Paula. "She's quite the woman," he said.

"Person!" Jennifer corrected him.

"Okay," he conceded. "Person."

Paula noticed Montgomery was holding Jennifer's hand. Paula winked at Jennifer, and she winked back.

"In any case, Dr. Barrett," he continued, "you're a hero." Montgomery turned to Sally. "And so are you, Ms. Carpenter."

They both blushed. Matt pulled Paula tight to him. She felt his strength.

"Dr. Barrett defied Harper and saved Baskins's life," Jake said seriously, "devised a plan, overpowered the terrorists, and rescued us all." Jake smiled. "Sounds like she should be an ATF agent!"

They all laughed.

"I'll stick to medicine," she said softly. "And Jennifer saved your life, Mr. Montgomery."

"I know," he said and squeezed Jennifer's hand. "She's quite a *person*, too!"

The ATF director, Bentley, spoke for the first time. "The reporters are clamoring for your story, Dr. Barrett. It'd be nice if you could make a statement to the press."

"Sorry, but I'm busy. I have an invitation to dinner...I think." She smiled at Matt and hugged his waist.

Matt laughed. "She's absolutely right. Anywhere she wants to go."

Murphy held out Paula's pager. "I found this on Harper. I believe it may be yours."

"Nope," Paula said quickly. "Not mine. My calls are covered, and I'm taking a few days off."

Matt slipped his pager off his belt and tossed it to Murphy. "Actually," Matt said, "that goes for me, too."

Reese took Matt's pager from Murphy. "Why don't you make it a week, Matt?" he said, smiling. "Your calls are covered, too."

"In that case," Matt said, "*I'm* hoping to spend the week with someone special."

"And who might that be?" Paula asked, smiling at him.

Matt grinned. "You should definitely know the answer to that question by now."

Paula reached out and took his hand. "I know the answer," she said softly as they started for the door, "and I've never been so sure of anything in my whole life."

The End

ACKNOWLEDGMENTS

I am deeply grateful for all the encouragement by friends and family to continue my writing. I am blessed and humbled. I would like to thank the many readers who helped by adding criticisms and ideas that improved the book, but especially Angie Jackson, Donna Williams, Rosemary Holderman, and Ellen Booth who were kind enough to read the manuscript twice.

I am the most grateful for my beautiful wife, Karen, who loves me and supports me in everything I do. There is no greater feeling in all the world. Lastly, I dedicated this book to my three children, Amy, Rachael, and Daniel. I am incredibly proud of each of you. I love you all so very much.

About the Author

Dr. Reinking received his doctor of medicine degree from the University of Oklahoma and is a Fellow of the American Academy of Family Physicians. He is currently practicing medicine in Tulsa, Oklahoma as a member of the Warren Clinic and at Saint Francis Hospital, where he serves as a medical director. Among his many honors and privileges, Dr. Reinking has served as president of the Oklahoma Academy of Family Physicians, taught medical students and residents, given lectures on a variety of clinical and medical administrative topics at local, state, and national forums, and has been a contributing author for several national publications of the American Academy of Family Physicians. Dr. Reinking was named the 2011 Oklahoma Family Physician of the Year.

In the community, Dr. Reinking has provided medical care at free clinics in the Tulsa area; coached his son's baseball teams; mentored youth on mission trips to assist the poor of rural Kentucky, inner-city Houston, Reynosa, Mexico, and Jamaica; and traveled to Africa on multiple occasions to provide medical care in rural Tanzania. He is currently serving as chair of the board of Literacy & Evangelism International, with the mission of improving literacy among the world's poorest nonreaders, particularly in Africa, South America, and Asia.

Dr. Reinking and his wife, Karen, live in Tulsa, Oklahoma. They have three children, Amy, Rachael, and Daniel, and one granddaughter, McCartney.